The Pillagers' Guide to Arctic Pianos

The Pillagers' Guide to Arctic Pianos

Kendra Langford Shaw

PANTHEON BOOKS
New York

FIRST HARDCOVER EDITION PUBLISHED
BY PANTHEON BOOKS 2026

Published by Pantheon Books, a division of Penguin Random House LLC,
1745 Broadway, New York, NY 10019.

Maps by David Lindroth Inc.

Library of Congress Cataloging-in-Publication Data
Names: Langford Shaw, Kendra, author
Title: The pillagers' guide to arctic pianos / Kendra Langford Shaw.
Description: First hardcover edition. | New York : Pantheon Books, 2026.
Identifiers: LCCN 2025023624 | ISBN 9780593702437 (hardcover) |
ISBN 9780593702451 (ebook)
Subjects: LCGFT: Epic fiction. | Novels. | Fiction.
Classification: LCC PS3612.A5824 P55 2026
LC record available at https://lccn.loc.gov/2025023624

penguinrandomhouse.com | pantheonbooks.com

Printed in the United States of America
1st Printing

The authorized representative in the EU for product safety and compliance is Penguin Random House Ireland, Morrison Chambers, 32 Nassau Street, Dublin D02 YH68, Ireland, https://eu-contact.penguin.ie.

For

Johnathan, Freya & Violet

A fifty-five-gallon steel drum is sometimes called the Alaska State Flower. Hundreds of them lie around wherever people have settled. I once considered them ugly. They seemed disappointing, somehow, and I wished they would go away. Gradually, they become tolerable, and then more and more attractive. Eventually, they almost bloom. Fifty-five-gallon drums are used as rain barrels, roof jacks, bathtubs, fish smokers, dog pots, doghouses. They are testing basins for outboard motors. They are the honeypots of biffies, the floats of rafts. A threat has been made to use one as a bomb. Fifty-five-gallon drums make heat stoves, cookstoves, flower planters, bearproof caches, wood boxes, well casings, watering troughs, culverts, runway markers, water tanks, solar showers. They are used as rollers for moving cabins, rollers to smooth snow or dirt. Sliced on the diagonal, they are the bodies of wheelbarrows. Scavenged everywhere, they are looked upon as gold.

JOHN McPHEE, *Coming into the Country*

GLACIAL FRONT
RESURRECTION MOUNTAINS
Arctic City
Kamikaze River
SINGING SPRUCE FOREST
Disillusionment Bay
WILD BEARD FJORDS
Panhandle Island
Archipelago of Lost Saints
0 MILES 400
0 KM 400

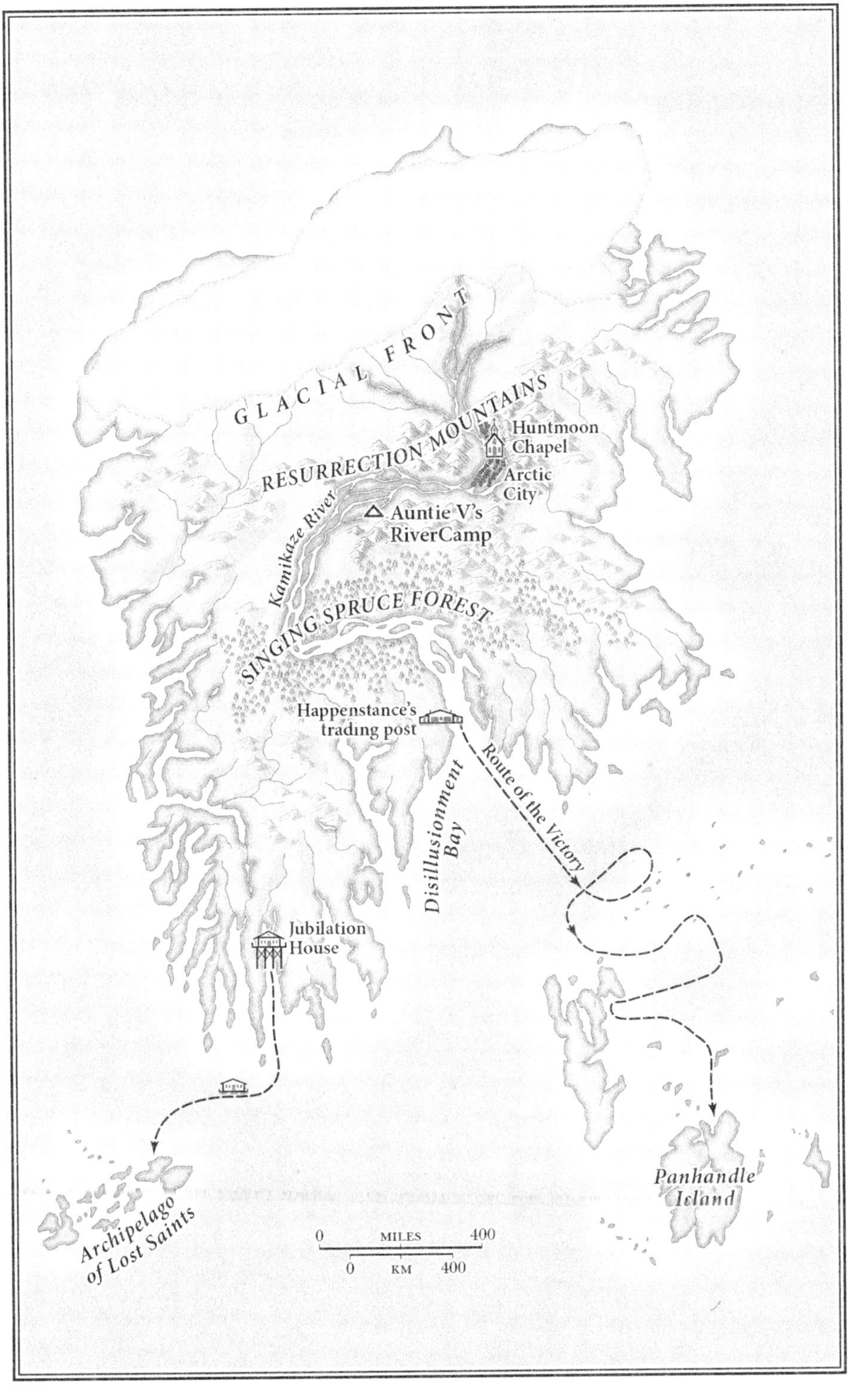

GLACIAL FRONT
RESURRECTION MOUNTAINS
Huntmoon Chapel
Arctic City
Kamikaze River
Auntie V's RiverCamp
SINGING SPRUCE FOREST
Happenstance's trading post
Route of the Victory
Disillusionment Bay
Jubilation House
Archipelago of Lost Saints
Panhandle Island
0 MILES 400
0 KM 400

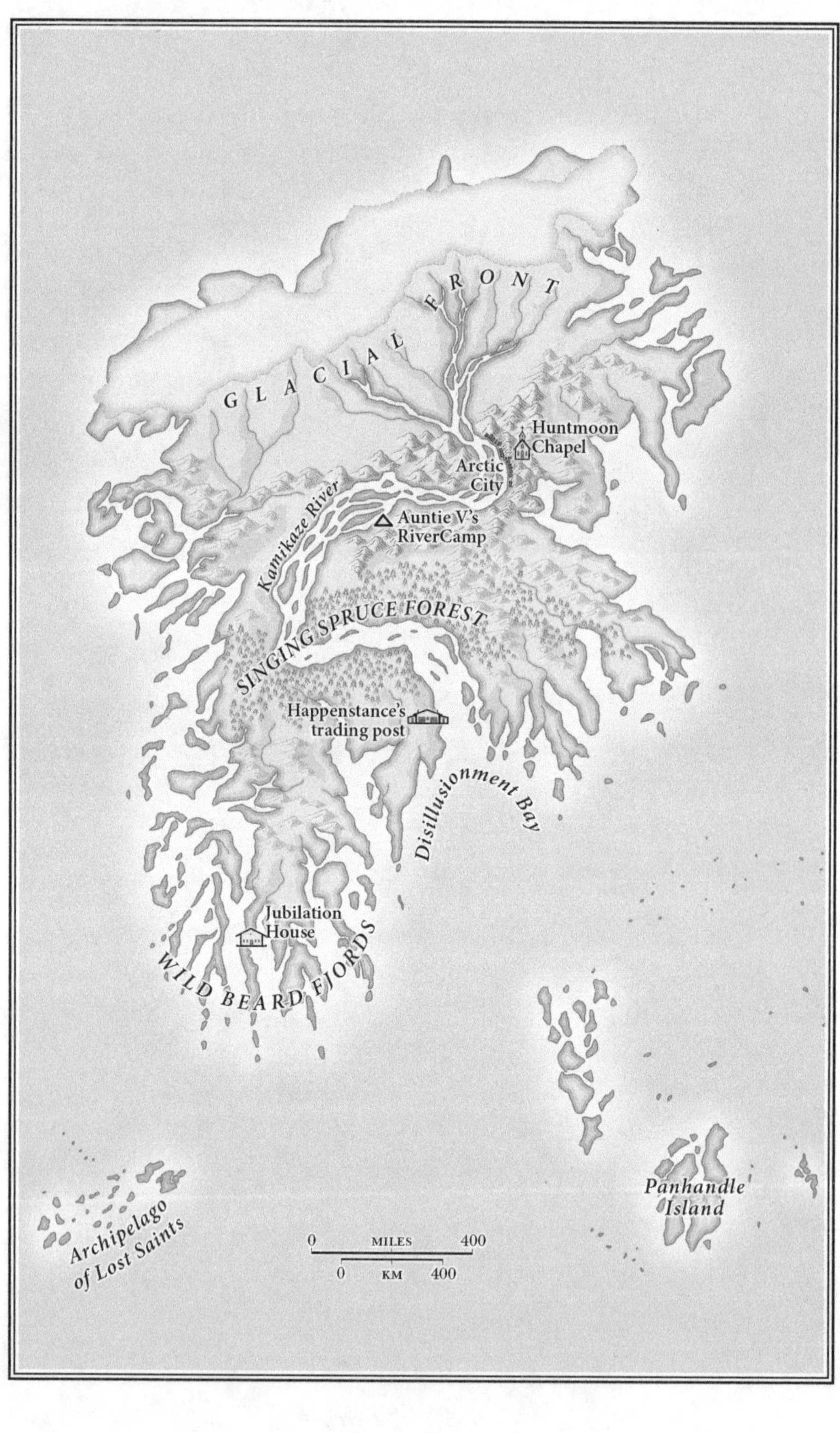
GLACIAL FRONT
Huntmoon Chapel
Arctic City
Kamikaze River
Auntie V's RiverCamp
SINGING SPRUCE FOREST
Happenstance's trading post
Disillusionment Bay
Jubilation House
WILD BEARD FJORDS
Archipelago of Lost Saints
0 MILES 400
0 KM 400
Panhandle Island

Part I

Jubilation House

Milda

Disillusionment Bay
Late October

My little brother, Finley, drowned the first time wrestling the Napoleon pianoforte under the galactic starlight of an Arctic sunset; the way he later told the story, the piano had it coming. Our family had spent the day knee-deep in Disillusionment Bay, gigging beach frogs and slugging fireweed tea. Our parents were up the sand, loose and recumbent, snacking on octopus jerky and reading aloud journal entries my great-great-great-great-grandfather kept as his family traversed the territory to homestead a new life. Beside them on the blanket my little sister, Temperance, sang as she patted black sand into fritters and called to me: "Here's your pancake, Milda!" It had been a long, dreamy day, I remember: honey in the air and the sharp crick of apples crisping on the trees. Down the beach Madam LeFleur stood on the porch of her boardinghouse beating slugs off a yak wool rug. Floatplanes droned overhead. Deep in the Singing Spruce Forest bear hunters unsnapped their rifles and began the long lope home.

I was sticky with salt and Finley was out too far. He was a strong swimmer for a nine-year-old, but no more than seventy pounds at full stomach. That was nothing against the rip curl. At first I didn't pay too much attention to him—Finley was always diving after oddities. Always before, he'd resurface within a breath or two, brandishing a tuning fork or an urchin shell. A brand-new trophy to add to his collection in our attic eaves. Earlier that summer he'd spent weeks gathering bones from a dead sea lion, then wired the skeleton together and mounted it in the attic rafters so that it hung over our hammocks. Not long after, we'd rocked to sleep one night while Finley guessed what the lion might've eaten for a last meal and if he'd mated for life. *Bones don't tell you that kind of stuff,* I said. Ever since then we'd swung to sleep in silence.

Finley's knobby elbows finned the surface as he swam out past the break. The moment before I lost sight of him he turned back and called, "Do you see it, Milda?"

I looked beyond him: nothing but breakwater, the ocean a lace of algae blooms.

Then my little brother was gone.

Before I registered what was happening—what *might* have happened, that dark yaw of despair threatening to swallow our family whole—my mother was up and high-kicking against the tide. We, the Spahrs of Jubilation House, were a family of bravado and rosin, heart tattoos along our collarbones, moles tucked into nooks and crannies. My mother, Viola Bloomer—pinochle enthusiast and pilot—drew a great breath and dove after her son, legs butterflying up into a neat pike. A terrible minute passed. Two, then three. Temperance let loose a banshee wail. I felt my father's hand on my shoulder.

When they resurfaced I could see right away that something was wrong. Our mother had Finley hooked by the armpits and frog-kicked the pair of them toward shore. Finley's legs were limp, his head lolled to one side, and our mother's forehead furrowed to the task as she gulped oxygen and beat the waves with her free arm. All at once they were on the sand, Finley splayed at awkward angles, chest pale and delicate, rib cage like a stack of wishbones. Squatting beside him, our mother beat her fists against his sternum. Tick-tock went Finley's feet to the rhythm, tick-tock.

"Is that breathing?" my father asked.

Then all at once I found myself braced over my brother, knees and palms grinding into sand, my lips pressed to his—Finley's dark as huckleberries, mine thin and sun-scabbed. Our buckteeth clinked painfully. A breath and two and three and four and five. Then all at once Finley was up and pushing against my chest, spluttering between us what looked like a gallon of sea bilge. Proteins and lipids and organic clots of fish scales. I suspected that a silverback whale must've gotten him. Chomp-chomp. I held out a hand to help lever him to his feet but Finley brushed it aside, slicked back his hair, and looked at me. Irises the color of spruce.

"I was winning," he said.

WE KAYAKED HOME. It took forty-five minutes for our family to glide from Disillusionment Bay to Jubilation House. As we drew close Finley whistled for Abraham Lincoln, the fourteen-hundred-pound sea lion we considered our family mascot. Abraham splashed up and led us through the mouth of our fjord. We'd lived in this same abode my whole life, a salmon-colored fisherman's shack built on stilts deep in the Wild Beard Fjords. Not really stilts—our parents had recovered a quad of decorative poles originally installed along the homesteading trail up north near the territory's capital, Arctic City. They'd driven these stilts into the fjord's volcanic bedrock and suspended Jubilation House's foundation between them. Raven. Grizzly. Sea Lion. Kelp. *The four pillars of the Apocalypse,* our mother called them.

A veranda swept around three sides of our home, the boards so knotty that high tide geysered up through the holes. We roped our kayaks along the western side. I cleat-hitched the double-hatch Finley and I shared to the dock and removed the spray skirts. "Catch me if you can," our mother said, dancing between knotholes as we unloaded the hatches. I carried the basket with the remains of our lunch across the veranda and into the house, set it on the kitchen counter, and struck a match to light the stove underneath the pot of Black Futsu soup that Viola had prepared earlier for dinner.

Inside, our living quarters were cramped: a spartan kitchen with a butcher's sink, knife-sharpening station, and indoor eating table. That morning it had been my job to scrape squash pulp for the soup, and leftover rinds still littered every available surface; once dried we'd store them on the veranda as treats for Abraham Lincoln's good behavior. As I set out soup bowls, the rest of my family clattered around the living room clipping wet clothes to the fishing wire suspended as a drying rack above panoramic windows facing the fjord's mouth. Jubilation House's view was expansive—all day we watched floatplanes land and ski off toward Disillusionment Bay.

Temperance wandered into the kitchen and hugged my thigh while I ladled the soup. "I'm cold," she said. At four years old my little sister couldn't take off her own wet suit. "Hold still," I said, and unzipped it down the back. She wriggled her arms free and I wrapped a tea towel around her shoulders to keep her warm. We all wore the same home-cut suits, patterned each year from mail-order neoprene. Temperance's suit, like mine, had frayed at the seams from wear and tear. We looked forward to the spring, when our mother would sew us new ones.

The family's sewing machine lived most of the year beneath my parents' bed in Jubilation House's only bedroom: tiny and plank-walled, with a backup generator in the closet. We kids slept in the attic. Finley and I in our sailor hammocks, Temperance in a toddler bed propped up on caribou antlers. Each morning we clattered down the ladder to brush our teeth together in the family's shared bathroom: walls the color of arsenic, our pipes squealing while suctioning fresh water from the cistern bolted beneath the house.

After we'd all changed into dry clothes, we carried our bowls to the table on the veranda. Our mother relayed the full story of the rescue as we slurped our soup: Finley had been backstroking, ebbing with the current, when his heel struck something immobile. He put his head under the water and there, marooned just below the surface: the Bloomer Napoleon pianoforte.

"And you thought to yourself, *Aha,*" our mother said, blowing on her spoon.

"—and I thought to myself, *Aha,*" said my brother.

The Napoleon was a musical treasure heirloomed to our family's ancestors and lost on the original homesteading trail many generations earlier. A barmy, sepia-tinted photo of the pianoforte hung in our living room alongside a nine-foot grizzly bear skin from the same expedition. In the photo, our great-great-great-great-grandfather Moose Bloomer—just a young boy then—draped a protective arm around the Napoleon's music stand. Behind Moose the pianoforte's lid was propped open to showcase solid gold hammers molded into the shape of tulips. To the modern viewer the Napoleon was, clearly, already the star of the shot—hickory-smoked, flutes sweeping up to mirror the family's hopes for a better life on their new parcel of deeded Arctic land.

That hope had never bled out. Though stability remained one of the scarcest resources the Territory of the Arctic had to offer, it hadn't stopped Finley from turning his eyes back two hundred years to the original pianofortes in the hopes that they might once again save us. He'd dove below the waves and embraced the forte's body. A piano nobody had seen in centuries yet I could picture the scene as clearly as if I'd seen it myself: the forte blackened with mold, my brother's miserable pluck.

Our mother swept the air with her arms as she pantomimed swimming to rescue him. Sharp-finned strokes. She spoke fast, almost out of breath, telling the story: "I had to get to him." I could see that her hand was shaking, just slightly; the rescue had shaken her. She mimed putting her head under the water. "There he was, I could see him," she said, and described spotting Finley wrapped around the the piano's body, the pair of them barrel-rolling toward the drop of the continental shelf.

Finley pushed away his bowl. "You know I only needed like one more minute to bring her up," he said. "It was a premature evacuation."

"One more minute and we would've been mourning your funeral. You were sucking sea water," I said.

"You don't know, you weren't down there."

I watched Temperance fetch the sack of marbles she'd gotten for her fourth birthday and shoot them down the veranda. She cheered when they reached a hole and plopped into the sea. "I know what drowning looks like. You keep diving like that and that's where you're headed," I said.

"I don't need a chaperone," said Finley, crossing his arms.

I grabbed his bowl and stacked it atop my own; *clatter clatter,* too loud.

"Kids," said our father. "Can't we all just enjoy being alive together for one minute? Relish that? For thirty seconds?"

Nearby, Jubilation House's generator thrummed, a grinding mash of cogs that drowned out our voices. High on the roofline, solar panels powered down. Seas sloshed underfoot. The farm's seaweed braids stretched from the veranda's railing all the way to the roof's peak—this was where we clipped up our farm's catches as they dried: octopus fry, mussels for pickling, hops, kelp ribboned like lasagna. All flapped overhead like prayer flags.

The sale of these crops was a small part of how we afforded our family farm's existence; the rest came from our mother flying charters. We ate what grew in the earth beds that circled the veranda and harvested crops from the fjord's floor. Salt berries, brineweed, cucumbers julienned for salads. In our free time we dove for artifacts that could be traded at Disillusionment Trade Post for soy sauce and panels to recharge batteries.

After dinner, we went inside for bedtime tea. My mother lit a burner for hot water and got down the samovar. I opened the tea jar and scooped out a family serving. Home-grown, the herbs irritated my gums. We sipped from our cups, brushed our teeth, and then we kids climbed the ladder to the attic. As soon as the hatch had closed behind us Finley flicked on a flashlight and pulled *The Big Book of Homesteader Crests* out from underneath his quilt. The book was the closest thing the territory had to an encyclopedia of pianofortes. It would be years before copies circulated across the territory, and beyond to the continent—by then our sleepy, off-grid fish town of Disillusionment Bay would be barely recognizable. That future was still to come, though looking back, it seems clear that my family's impending misfortune had its genesis that October night.

I pulled my quilt up to my chin as light from the attic's windows refracted through the sea lion's bones. When we were little, our parents made us wear bells around our ankles, secured with locks, so they could hear where we were in case we fell off the veranda when no one was looking. A whimsical security, but a security nonetheless. Only when the bells stopped chiming did they have to worry. Now that Finley and I were old enough to swim on our own, I realized, we did so without a bell choir chorus; either of us could dive and never resurface.

"It could have been some other family's Napoleon," I said.

Finley clicked off his flashlight. "It wasn't."

WHEN I AWOKE the next morning, Finley was gone from his hammock. This wasn't unusual—my brother often went for a sunrise swim with Abraham Lincoln. I descended the ladder expecting to find the rest of our family at breakfast. Typically my parents fried herring roe with the eggs they scooped, warm, from the chickens we kept cooped on the western side of the veranda. The door to the veranda stood open, and I could see the rest of my family had gathered around the outside eating table. Stretched across it was the Banana, the bright yellow double-hatch kayak that Finley and I shared.

Immediately I spotted a deep crack snaking the length of the Banana's hull. The worst breach I'd ever seen. Though our family had other kayaks, the Banana was the only double-hatch, and the only one Finley and I were allowed to paddle outside the fjord by ourselves. A deep crack meant it would be out of the water for weeks. Now we'd both be stuck at home until it was repaired.

I ran a hand lightly along the cut. The damage was not clean and fiberglass slivered my fingers. "What happened?" I said.

"How am I supposed to magically see an underwater boulder?" Finley said, all huff and bluster. "Up it comes—*whoosh*—from nowhere."

"So you did this," I said.

"It's called an accident, Mills."

If I'd been in the anchor hatch, where I typically sat, I would've kept us from fishtailing across a boulder. I knew this. Instead, Finley had, as usual, behaved with no regard for the physics of his own life—how much air he needed, what his sister wanted, the pivot a double-hatch needed to change direction. "How are we supposed to get around now?" I said.

"I had to see if it was still there," Finley said. "The Napoleon."

"So you went back all by yourself in the middle of the night?"

"Everyone was sleeping."

"There's a thing called waking people up," I said.

Our father went into the house to fetch a tube of caulk. Unlike the rest of us, Fry T. Spahr had not grown up in the Territory of the Arctic. He was a transplant from the continent, where his family still operated a paleontological dig. "You couldn't walk to the barn without stepping on a triceratops jaw," he said of his boyhood. His sister and extended family still lived down south, though Fry hadn't seen them in years. As a young man he'd left home to fish his way north along the two-thousand-mile island crescent arching from the continent up to the Panhandle Islands. He'd intended to make his way farther north to work an oil rig dredging cash off underwater wells near Mount Resurrection. Instead, he'd met our mother.

Viola Bloomer had hocked her family's famous octopus rosettes outside Disillusionment Trade Post every summer since she was a little girl. Our father first spotted her standing behind an elaborate display of twisted octopus arms salted in vinegar. Spectators pressed on all sides of the Bloomer stall jawing about weather and angling for the best sight line. Viola, she knew how to put on a show: her performance included a pair of iridescent puffin beaks she strapped to each hand and used to pinch up rosettes and toss them into the crowd. My father always said that until that exact juncture in his life, he'd considered himself sure of heart and immune to bedevilment. "I did not come to the Arctic to be bedeviled by love," he said, "but bedeviled I certainly was."

Our mother was eighteen and tall, spackled with the same pattern of freckles that now tattooed my own collarbone, her hair dyed an impossibly brilliant forget-me-not blue. "And then *poof,* love," my father said. "No coming back from that." According to Fry, three weeks later, on their honeymoon, our mother had said, *Hey, so I've got my eye on this sea farm,* and he'd said, *Okay.* That was how decisions were made in the Spahr family from that point on: our father making little effort to tether Viola to earth as she aimed her floats toward the sky.

Now he squeezed caulk from the tube and, using his thumbs, massaged it slowly into the Banana's cut hull. "You could've gotten stuck, or lost. We wouldn't have known where to look. Anyway, it's a double kayak. It's made for two people."

"I left a note, thank you very much," Finley said.

Our mother picked up the farm's logbook from the table and opened to the most recent entry. "You mean this note? The one that says 'Dear Mom, gone hunting.' "

"That's right."

"I thought you meant abalone. Not looking for that piano in the dark."

"If we don't get it soon, it'll drift away. You know that," Finley said, voice muffled as he pulled a sweater over his wet suit. Blush-shelled sea slugs marched up the chest and down each arm—my mother's iconic knitting.

"I can't imagine it's in any shape, being in the water all this time," our father said. "You almost drowned yesterday. And that was daylight."

Our mother slowly closed the logbook. "If the gold hammers are still there—"

"Someone's probably taken them already," our father said, cutting her off.

"Gold doesn't float, Dad. The forte was heavy. It's there," said Finley "If Mom fires up the plane we can swing over, pick it up, *badda-badda-badda,* we're rich."

It was an unmistakable fact that my brother and I had each grasped, and grasped early—our family was poor, at least relatively speaking. Although our parents had always made enough between charters and farm crops for the five of us to subsist, there was never anything left over. Jubilation House's electricity, plumbing, stilts, and flood insurance hadn't been updated in years. Our mother was the last of those with the Bloomer surname and our family's primary breadwinner. A precarious responsibility. She had taught our father—and later, us kids—to catch, breed, and salt octopus arms, but she flew charters all summer to make up the lion's share of our income. Viola flew bear hunters hundreds of miles north and skimmed tourists over Arctic City's stone chapel so they could witness it slowly sinking into the Kamikaze River. Each summer, she logged thousands of flight hours in our family's rickety plane, then returned home for winter.

In all seasons Jubilation House stood gridless; our fjords were accessible only via kayak or floatplane, and our mother was the family's only certified pilot. Although everyone in our family was adept with a paddle, it took at least forty-five minutes for Finley and me to reach Disillusionment Bay on our own. That was township proper, though our tiny community only had a few services: a boardinghouse, ranger station, cemetery, and plane dock. We ordered what groceries we couldn't grow ourselves from the trade post. Finley particularly loved these visits because they gave him a chance to haggle.

Though our mother had always made clear that any of her children could one day take over the farm, even as a young girl I knew this to be a fictive generosity. It had always been clear to me that our family's lifestyle fell most naturally to Finley. He had the habituation, the right temperament for pressurized, deep-sea work. Each morning after breakfast he strapped a tank of oxygen between his shoulder blades and backflipped off the veranda. Clicking on a dive light, he spent hours scoping our fjord's floor. On good days he resurfaced with sacks of apple-gilled mussels or cucumbers he'd found writhing blind in sediment, easy plucking for the day's lunch. But often as not he returned empty-handed. A quick rinse under the rain cistern on the veranda, then chores and education. The following morning he'd dive again.

I both admired his persistence and gritted my teeth in jealousy. As isolated as we lived, my brother was also by nature an isolationist. I, meanwhile, had long hoped to find a way to shrug off that side of the family birthright. I wanted to forge my own path—move south to the continent for university; raise a family within spitting distance of a library. I intended to partake in the community my childhood had lacked: music, museums, festivals. I believed these things essential to my ultimate happiness, my home thus far having been made in what most would consider a remote, wild territory. I'd never had a best friend outside my siblings, and though we lived in a beautiful place, I wanted to see more of the world than the narrow sliver of it that we glimpsed from our veranda.

But entry into this new life was a costly endeavor. Ferry tickets, rent, the expense of food on the open market—like most kids in the fjords, I had never left the territory and had no frame of reference for life on the other side of the Arctic Reef. I knew only that it would cost a great deal more than living on the sea farm that I had been raised to run. "At least here you'll always sleep for free," my mother liked to say.

What passed for our schooling was conducted via correspondence, with our parents each supplementing the subjects that came naturally to them. My father provided lessons on paleontology, homemaking, and climate change, while my mother taught aviation, geography, and history. The grammar of the English language I mostly cobbled together myself. Once a month the mail plane dropped off a trunk of schooling equipment: microscopes and geology tools; dehydrated shrooms and propagation kits. Reference materials were available upon request from Panhandle Library, and over the years I accumulated a small book collection of my own.

I got the idea to husband a goat from one of the guidebooks I requested, and soon after I adopted a russet-bearded nanny named Parsley, who now slept under my hammock. I was learning to make cheese with Parsley's milk and hoped to sell it the following summer at the trade post. Most mornings I milked her while listening to Temperance sound out practice words from a homesteader cookbook, a green leather pocket primer from which I too had first learned to read. The recipes included Napoleon butter horns—doughy crescents now famous in the territory for their longevity; they were so named thanks to my ancestors who'd hauled north the first Napoleon.

"If we leave now we can be back in time for lunch," my mother said.

"What about today's charters?" my father said, capping the caulk. "They're already booked."

My mother waved a hand to dismiss his concern, saying, "We can handle losing a couple flights."

"Season's winding down—there aren't that many chances for fares left."

"A big score will make up for it," my mother said. This was technically true, though like my father I worried about our family losing charter income in the meantime. What would this mean for the big order of supplies we needed to get us through the winter? I was just a kid and didn't read our family's account books, but as the oldest I'd heard my parents worry about money for years.

"And what if you don't find it?" my father said.

"*Dad,*" said Finley.

"It happens, people go looking for things all the time and never find them."

Viola put her hand on his arm. "But who would we be if we didn't at least try," she said.

A few minutes later I watched as my mother and Finley climbed into the family's floatplane, the ChickenCrusher 3000, a float-jacked quad-seater with red leather seats, a hatch big enough to load a bear, and a dancing hula figurine on the dashboard whose hips always aimed north. Double props flipped horizontal so that the plane could hover straight up and out of the fjord. The furious lap of water against the stilts as the plane lifted, this was the playground in which my siblings and I had first learned to dive, to hunt. Aside from the severest of winter days, aside from my own ambition to explore the grander world, when I was growing up, it had felt as if there was no force alive great enough to extricate me from these waters. As the Crusher took off hot and low, I caught a glimpse of Finley in the passenger seat, a cross of zinc oxide swiped across his forehead. Then our family's plane broke east toward Disillusionment and disappeared.

FROM THE TIME I was little, I'd been in charge of feeding our octopus herd each morning. We kept them penned in a pair of old submarines just inside the mouth of our fjord. That day, once Temperance finished breakfast, I zipped her into my old life jacket, a seafarers' orange stamped KAMIKAZE FARMS, and retrieved the compost buckets from the kitchen. The panniers snapped on either side of our mother's single-hatch kayak, plastic saddlebags reeking of coffee and moldy fruit. I slid my arms into my own life jacket and climbed down onto the narrow seat before helping Temperance squeeze beside me. Wedged together in the hatch, spray skirt cinched, Temperance chatted happily to the animals hunting breakfast all around us while I paddled toward the breeding tanks. Chittering seagulls, otters clapping abalone shells like castanets.

The fjords of my girlhood were a festival of bounty. As part of my schooling I kept meticulous notes on the local flora and fauna and ever-shifting geography. I marked my maps with every neighbor I knew and some I only suspected. Drowned sled ruts, hot springs, and other landmarks gleaned from textbooks were there one year and gone the next. I didn't know how long even my own reports would be useful, as just beyond the mouth of our fjord the ocean was a maze of disappearing landmasses. Tourists who visited each summer found the territory, year after year, severely altered. But still I recorded my observations—for my own posterity, if for no other reason.

Even as the fjords surrounding us grew increasingly unpredictable, Jubilation House remained a miraculous, secure constant. And as Finley and I grew up and took up the privilege of paddling beyond the fjord's mouth on our own, we developed a set of unique precautions against the unknown: my brother strapped a harpoon to the front of the Banana while I embroidered the local geography onto maps and quilts again and again, tracking both where we'd been and the best path back home.

It took five minutes for me to paddle the kayak to the octopus pens. By age eleven I'd spent an incalculable number of hours loitering on the wooden platform attached to the submarines we used to corral the herd while my mother dove down to tighten bolts and scrub away stars of rust. She was their leader, never clearer to me than when watching the octopuses as they rose to greet her—pebbled skin sparking red, limbs bartering trinkets for Viola's love. When she finally climbed out of the water she'd bring several juveniles with her; cradling one like a newborn, stroking its beak, she'd call, "Ready, set, go!" as I raced the others across the platform. Sometimes she'd pop an umbrella and open a box of puzzles and we'd eat oysters, tossing the shells into the sea, as the juveniles clacked blue circles and red squares into their slots. "That's right, little one. Well done," she'd whisper as she plopped them back into their tank. Then, to me, "Third porthole's getting loose. Remind me to bring the wrench tomorrow." And we'd paddle home.

Now I cranked open the lid and Temp and I peered together into the water. Everything a murk of lava grit and flatulated ink. A hen called Queenie threw three arms over the lip and Temperance leaned down to scratch her nape. While I dumped in the buckets—a fizzle of dried clam tongues and squash rinds—Temperance began to sing. She picked an old prospector melody about reindeer and hot springs that could melt the fascia from your muscles. Even at four my sister had a wide, operatic voice that sonographed through water. The animals floated up to her in a mingle of limbs and geysering funnels.

I knew we only had a few days, a week at most, before winter set upon the territory, hard. From then until spring breakup we would live in isolation. Hibernation season. What local neighbors we knew in the fjords kept their own privacy. This was as much a matter of practicality as of civility considering that we all needed our winter stockpiles and, like our family's, most subsistence farms in the region were well into their failing years. Between the havoc homesteaders had wreaked upon the territory two hundred years earlier and the ocean's progressively cooked-up temperatures, wild halibut had basically become an endangered species. It was still possible to catch trout if a person brokered a deal with local river camps, but wild salmon were increasingly not worth the trouble: many flaccid and gummy, with the filthy afterbite of gasoline.

Each winter our family lived off the preserves we jarred during the summer. We kept our pantry stocked with smoked sea meats, pickled kelp, and shelf-stable pasteurized goat milk. Owing to the fact that the ice pack shifted every year, Finley and I were permitted to ice-skate to the mouth of our fjord, but no farther. This resulted in a brooding season for our entire family, one that further chafed Finley and me against each other. Finley because he preferred to spend his leisure in the water; me because we were wholly cut off from the greater world and all I hoped to achieve in it.

I knew our parents would never make enough money to send me to the continent for university, there was no question of that. If I wished to leave I would have to purchase a path out myself. The payout on the Napoleon—those decadent gold hammers the real prize—well, if it ever came, it would likely be larger than anything I could ever raise alone. But I knew too that this funding would belong to our whole family first, and their priorities differed from mine. Both my mother and Finley would want to purchase an additional fjord, rehab the plane. Our father insisted we needed to update the house's plumbing. The family drinking water was stored under the veranda in a cistern that hooked up to the house through a series of pipes that froze, moaning, when it got cold. They had to be strapped with defoggers each winter to stop them from splitting out the walls.

At four years old Temperance couldn't express much in the way of external desires, but if she was anything like me, I knew that one day my little sister would conjure a list of luxuries she'd only previously read about: factory lotion and mangoes and underwear that hadn't been spun by hand. I believed that these conveniences would make our home life significantly more habitable, and I believed too that if my family lived in comfort, it would be easier for me eventually to leave. When I returned to visit, it would be to a cozy, electric nest festooned in solar bulbs and aquaponic fountains. My parents standing on the veranda, sun-toasted and convivial, welcoming me home.

I was only eleven that October, young enough that I thought I had plenty of time to save. My optimism was high with the goat cheese. The summer before, Finley had taken the relics he'd found on his dive trips and spread them on a blanket on the beach near the entrance to the plane dock. Tourists had been eager to shower him in coins. If, selling my cheese, I could make even half of what Finley had raked in, I felt I'd be doing quite well. With any luck, one day I might expand my repertoire—creams and curds, herbs wrapped in velvet ribbons.

After the octopuses finished nibbling the compost, I picked up a long pole. Dipped it into the water and unlocked a porthole. The herd would soon figure out they were free to leave, at least temporarily—one by one, they'd squeeze out of the frame. At sunset they'd return clutching new prizes. Decapitated anchovies and mussels piled into middens all across the tank floor. These remains were brushed out several times a month, sometimes by me, strapped into my mother's vintage oxygen tank and wet suit. I had an attachment to the herd, to all the farm's animals, though I tried not to get too friendly. I knew that eventually they would be harvested, dried, salted, and bagged. One of us kids was typically responsible for stringing up the hatchlings, which we called "pips" in honor of the first hen, Pippi, our mother ever domesticated. We spiked them between the eyes and clipped them to the veranda ropes. In fair weather we jerkied our produce in the air. *Salted by the elements,* read the farm's tagline.

Our herd was made up of wild-caught hens naturally acclimated to living in large, peaceful communities. They were well trained. As part of my evening chores I'd paddle back, close the porthole, and seal them in for the night. Their loyalty to our fjord and their tank—it amazed me how they returned again and again when their whole lives seemed the worst form of captivity. I imagined that if I were in their position I would swim out one day and never return. Some of the herd might struggle at first—they'd grown up domesticated, after all—but eventually they'd adapt. The intertidal zone around our fjord was fertile with anemones and crustaceans. But they returned at exactly the same time every evening. Squeezed back through the porthole and took up nesting among their loot. Eager to resume the pleasures of familiar rituals.

Like our octopus herd, the Crusher returned home later that night. The plane docked alongside the veranda and both Finley and our mother climbed out through the passenger door. I could tell from my brother's posture as he swung a leg over the veranda railing that they had not been successful. They were both sandy-bottomed and fractious. How many times had we returned empty-handed and sour after oyster diving or hunting hens? Squabbling over the first hot shower? I knew that people cold and in low spirits did not often have the kindest words for one another.

I put down the seed catalog. My father and I had been taking turns reading aloud entries while Temperance hounded lightning bugs that thrived around the garden beds. Of everyone in the family, my father and I were most alike in temperament. It was my father who purchased wool rugs for the living room and hung boughs of spruce around the windowpanes for Christmas. Without him our home would almost certainly have been festooned only with our mother's neglect: stoic, salt-weathered wood everywhere. Though Viola had once put energy into fixing up Jubilation House, for her it now functioned primarily as a landing hub. For six months of the year it was no more than a pit stop between charters. The busywork of existing in our day-to-day life—making sure we had clean water to drink, dental hygiene, that the animals that depended on us for food had enough to eat—fell to the rest of us.

Like my father's, my life was governed by the melody of routine. Already I had picked out several new crops to plant in the spring. Salt beets and tomatoes-of-the-sea engineered to be sown directly into the shallow ledges of the continental shelf. Our entire family was expected to take part in spring planting. A week of breathing through an oxygen tube while troweling up the seafloor surrounding the house's stilts. The crops were essential not only to our own family but also to our neighbors, who would likewise turn over portions of their own yields in trade. The community in the fjords was made up mostly of peaceable, salty-earth types content to tend earth beds and trade wheels of cheese. They candled their own candles and brewed their own brew. I knew, for this was how I was raised too. It took a great deal of care to sustain our lives. Once or twice a year the community came together for larger celebrations: weddings, births, funerals—but these occasions were fleeting. It wasn't unusual for us to go weeks—even months during hibernation season—without laying eyes on anyone outside our immediate family.

Now Finley and our mother sat down at the veranda eating table. They went to work flaking the plates of barbecue anchovies that my father and I had prepared for them. My father tipped the samovar of tea into cups and passed them around. Bone china, imported, each featured a painted vignette of early homesteader life. Pianos roped to sleds. Bales of wire hauled to restring the instruments tatted into elaborate drying racks for salting fish. I watched my father take a flask from his hip, lean across the table, and dribble a shot into our mother's cup. He distilled a home brew potent enough to disinfect wounds.

Our mother scooped up anchovy meat with the fingers of one hand and with the other grasped her teacup and tipped the contents back. Then she leaned forward and rested her elbows on the table. Viola, like most Bloomer women, was tall and long necked; serious; a lover of floatplanes and homesteader romances: "They're not just fish guts and cabin framing. They were real people, they had souls," she often mused about the teacup characters. Now she undid the chinstrap to her pilot's cap. "It wasn't there," she said. "It wasn't anywhere."

Finley hunched over his plate and scooped meat into his mouth with both hands. "Problem number one was the tide," he said. "Problem number two was it's dark down there. Mom had to keep shouting coordinates, it was ridiculous."

"Excuse me, but I thought you knew exactly where you were going," I said.

"There's such a thing as currents, you know," he said, wiping his mouth with the back of his hand. "I'm no trident."

The men and women of the first expeditions shared a desire to construct a "northern outpost of mannerly society," our history books reported. *They hoped to create a cultured, musical civilization, a desire that sprang up in response to the prevalence of wild, parched towns across the American West.*

The instruments that officials on the continent had arm-twisted homesteaders into bringing as proof of their civilizing efforts were fortified beasts built by enterprising carpenters at the last ports of call. Moneymakers. People still talked of the originals from the earliest expeditions. The Ahab. The Mayflower Bluefin. A Psalmist that belonged to the territory's first reverend. A handful of Ravenwoods with *Ho for the Homesteading Act!* wood-burned around the family crests. These pianofortes—the fleet that would become the territory's lost instruments—had been waxed against the salt air. They'd been fitted with what turned out to be the last of elephantine ivory: full cut, aged, and priceless in a modern market. Many of these lost instruments—the Napoleon among them—were one of a kind, unwieldy models no longer built in the modern day. "Built for tumble," Viola liked to say. "Built for adversity."

Built for adversity, it turned out, meant that the fortes were so heavy that few made it all the way to the Glacial Front. In the span of a single generation, an estimated ten thousand pianos and their accompanying paraphernalia—millions of spare keys, hammers made of every metal—were abandoned, too burdensome to carry along the eleven-hundred-mile sled route snaking through the Singing Spruce Forest, the Resurrection Mountains, and the territory's now-drowning capital, Arctic City. Before I was born it had been possible to walk many of these ancient sled grooves. Our parents had honeymooned in these ruts, Viola and Fry sharing a sleeping bag at the bottom of a six-foot sled groove, orange tent spread overhead. "Deep as a grave yet half as reverent," our father joked.

Now this old sled route was almost entirely underwater. In the years before I was born, off-gasses and fossil fuels had cranked up the Earth's temperature, melting the northernmost glaciers and swamping most of the territory's old-growth forest. Most pianos had lived their lives on land and were only now underwater, but the luckiest had drowned long ago: washed downriver with spring melt, sunk to the bottoms of lakes. Even with rising temperatures, the territory's frigid waters were too cold to propagate many of the phyto-organisms and toothy bioluminescents that broke down hardwood. The real enemy of decay was oxygen—sink a piano deep enough in Arctic waters, no air, no light, no warmth, and it could hibernate intact for centuries. I had seen evidence of this preservative phenomenon many times. The hull-wrecked remains of a homesteader ship in a nearby fjord hauled up and sold to a continental museum. A wooden mask with ivory fangs that Finley had found on a dive. Even the stilts that vaulted our house above the waves. They all lasted much longer than they should have. It would take another century, more, before the wood on the best-sunk pianos degraded beyond repair.

Though this had long been true, the economic possibilities of this phenomenon had never been fully explored. Gold hammers held their value, that was well understood, but the value of the lost instruments themselves had never been broadly considered. That was soon to change.

SIX MONTHS LATER. Late April. Plum trees blossoming in electric florals. Madam LeFleur's grandson Jude went diving for abalone in the Panhandle Islands and practically swam into the Ahab Grand; like the Napoleon, it had been on the first expedition north. The forte was handcrafted out of blond oak. Three-legged, it had earned its name because one leg resembled the stubby, bare wood of a whale captain's false limb. The piano was more than a dozen feet wide with three keyboards overset like shark teeth. Any kid who'd grown up in the territory had seen drawings of the mythic Ahab their whole life.

Jude was a proficient diver who favored an underwater camera. As a high schooler he dove to document creatures he spotted on the shelf floor. He sold his photos and glyphs in Madam LeFleur's boardinghouse, the trade post, and eventually through brokers on the continent. After he discovered the Ahab, the LeFleur family paid to haul the relic ashore and restring the boards. Then they advertised across the continent and sent proposal letters to major museums. Not a week later the Smithsonian issued a smug press release welcoming the Ahab as the centerpiece of their *Cultural Artifacts from the Territory of the Arctic* exhibit.

By the time summer hit in earnest, classifieds in the *Disillusionment Tribune* were chock-full of ads for future recoveries. The paper was our only all-weather source of communication. Telecom broadcast towers throughout the territory sunk every year, cutting off phone lines and internet service until they could be repaired—sometimes years later. Many families chose not to bother with anything more than a satellite cell for emergencies.

WANTED: PSALMIST KEYS. 88 PLUS FLATS. FULL-CUT IVORY ONLY. BUYER NOT GULLIBLE.

WANTED: ORIGINAL FLUTESKY. WILL CONSIDER INSTRUMENT MISSING ONE LEG BUT NOT TWO. PAYMENT IN TRADE.

WANTED: MOTIVATED COLLECTOR SEEKS MAYFLOWER BLUEFIN FOR FUN & PROFIT. MONEY AS THEY SAY IS NO OBJECT.

When our mother wasn't flying paying charters, she and Finley spent most of their time hunting for the Napoleon. This left me to paddle alone twice a week to Disillusionment for groceries, while back home my father packaged the farm's wares. I picked up the family's supplies at the trade post, then spent my afternoons legs dangling off the dock, watching new MiniGalaxies and quad-skied Wigwams lift and land. In every direction the world was lighting up, visitors flashing GPS coordinates and ripping strips from the *Disillusionment Tribune*. It unnerved me, seeing all these strangers flock to my hometown.

Disillusionment Trade Post quickly became a regional hub of activity. During one of my visits I watched an auction for a Rose-Player dating from the seventeenth expedition. It had been scavenged from the Kamikaze River by a Native tribe that held rights to the banks.

FOR SALE BY OWNER: COZY ROSEPLAYER SEEKING FOREVER HOME. ORIGINAL HARDWOOD. MOVE-IN CONDITION. PEDIGREE UNKNOWN.

A factory-issue forte missing half its keys, the RosePlayer was a mass-produced model that would never come close to fetching the price of the Ahab. But that didn't stop museums on the continent from ferrying up waves of research teams who cleaned out the trade post before embarking on their own hunting expeditions. "Not even a cup of beans left? A cup of magic beans?" I joked, running a hand along the bare shelves. Happenstance didn't even look up from his ledger to reply, "It's not magic, it's called an economy. Check back Friday."

For long-term families like ours, the fragility of this new industry was both exhilarating and terrifying. Exhilarating because our lives were suddenly peppered with a new crop of outsiders, outsiders who brought with them news of a culture from which I had always been relatively cut off. Literature and citrus fruits, fashion and marshmallows. To me, by then twelve years old and curious, this new generation of foreigners appeared effortlessly cool in their "Leaf Off" fair-trade T-shirts and recycled rubber sandals. "They're not even half practical," our mother said. "Tell me how they're going to protect you when you step on a fishhook."

Still, I found plenty to idolize about these outsiders as they descended upon us en masse. They took pictures of seaweed and ravens and showed them to one another as though they were treasures. On the hottest days entire families unfurled technicolor quilts across every square inch of Disillusionment sand. I unfurled my towel right alongside them. Packed together so densely that none of us could stretch flat, we all baked crab-backed in the heat. It was the largest community I had ever seen in one place and there I was in the midst of it. But inevitably the visitors retreated to the boardinghouse for dinner, and I kayaked home alone.

I studied the flood of tourists more closely than anyone else in my family. I was fascinated by how flummoxed they seemed in my world, how confused the newcomers were by the staples of the life I took for granted. Hitch knots and spray skirts, saline converters; sea meats cubed and sold by the tin. Watching them, I wondered what might similarly perplex me when I finally arrived down south: Would I too wander jaw-gaped through their trade post? Would I sniff my lunch and shove it aside, repulsed? Was it possible that I might find the foreign quality of their life as alienating as they seemed to find mine?

Historians typically cast "boom times" as golden opportunities—everyone knowing there was zinc in the hills and oranges by the wagonload to pulp. But in truth, I began to realize, it was terrifying to see your life suddenly tied to a product that would inevitably disappear. I had no idea how many total fortes had been lost or how long it would take to bring them all up. I knew only that they couldn't replicate themselves. Once they'd all been found, the world would move on.

As I entered my teenage years, the spike in the township's population started to lose its luster. It began to feel to me like living in the static of a radio tuned to the wrong frequency. White noise and arguments. Every surface, from the trade post's baskets to LeFleur's port-a-johns in the woods, seemed to be greased with sun balm. The beach was always littered with sour pickle wrappers. Children wreaked mayhem through the tidal pools. Kazoos screeching, they pulled washed-up forte pedals from the surf and jousted with them up and down the sand. It was a level of chaos many in the territory had moved north to escape.

I spent most of my free time then sunbathing and dreaming about leaving. Finley, meanwhile, spent all of his trying to make our current home a better place to live. When he wasn't fishing for keys and other loose parts, he and our mother flew religiously over the territory's waters, still looking for the Napoleon. Viola at the wheel, throwing back espresso beans as she dipped the Crusher in and out of fjords, way too fast for the stomach of any copilot save Finley. My brother returned home boasting about their only catches worth remembering: one cache of ebony flats, and a music stand twelve feet tall. Taken as a whole, they were not what anyone would have considered a successful team.

The last summer they hunted together, Finley was fifteen, and, on his birthday, our father made a great show of querying him about the passing of childhood. Why not put these adult matters out of his mind? Enjoy what remained of his childhood freedom?

Finley nodded, ate his cobbler, then climbed into the cockpit to wait for our mother. They flew together only a few months more—a long time considering it was their last season—until Viola could no longer suffer the pitches in altitude. Viola at the wheel, coiffured and disciplined, Finley hanging a rigged-up brass detector out the window, watching the dials for a ping that would indicate a sunken forte. Pop banjo music blasted out of the speakers, both of them singing their voices hoarse to our mother's favorite band. Not once worrying about scaring away prey. Pianos of course couldn't hear them coming.

THE WINTER I TURNED seventeen, we, the Spahrs of Jubilation House, were struck by the first tragedy that we could not claw our way back from: a genetic skin cancer crisis left to run amok. When I thought about the years leading up to our mother's illness, I often imagined that if our circumstances had been more lush, if Finley had recovered the Napoleon as he'd long promised to do, or if our mother had not spent two decades drying marine animals under a thinning layer of ozone—perhaps the whole family would still be together, sipping jellyfish sours on the veranda on muggy summer nights.

The most probable of those fantasies—the exhumation of the Napoleon—did not happen that first year, nor in the years to follow, so our family was unable to auction the relic, and therefore had no money to rehab Jubilation House. The dream of what that alternate life might have been sometimes slipped in and out of my somnolent hours. Upgraded solar panels and a barnacle-sloughing cistern. Stilts jacked much, much higher above the tide line.

My parents too clearly dreamed of such a life for their family. Late one night I descended the ladder to hear them whisper-arguing through their bedroom door. "We have to do something." My father cleared his throat. "We could always—"

"Don't say move."

"The kids could go to school, you could stop flying all those busted-ass charters."

"So I'm suddenly supposed to be a completely different person who wants completely different things?" my mother said. "This is our home—we're not just going to abandon it because it needs some work. I'm not going to be one of those cowards who flees when things get tough—you think it's not rough everywhere? Here or there doesn't matter, we just have to figure out what we're willing to live through. I pick this. Obviously."

"You've never lived anywhere else," my father said. "It's not called running away if you just want a better life for your family."

Cough-cough. My mother rustled the quilt. "You don't know it's better, you just know it's different. You haven't lived on the continent for years. What if we get there and it's the same? How would we explain that? To the kids?"

"Flora says—"

"Your sister just wants you home to run the dig," my mother said testily. "That's all she cares about. She'd tell you the horses were crapping rainbows if it made you buy a ferry ticket."

"Waterline's up another couple inches this year," my father said. "Fact."

The groan of bedsprings. "Tell me something I can't see for myself," my mother said.

I stepped back from the door. My mother had founded our family life on what some would consider trivialities, but I knew them to be Viola's linchpins. Harvesting octopuses. Taking tea on the veranda. Pods of otters weaving through the stilts. Even though she couldn't keep up with these regular routines while sick, I knew she loved the fjord, our beast of a floatplane, the slug and pull of hauling in a loaded net. And I knew too that neither my father nor I could beat the hope of resuming these simple pleasures out of her. The threat of rising tides was just another in a long list of inconveniences, like the cost of fuel, or the fact that our vegetable garden had to be pollinated by hand. For Viola these were always going to be necessary expenditures—the only question was where to find the money.

I climbed back up the attic ladder and stretched out in my hammock. My mother was a long-range descendant of homesteaders in the territory and subscribed to the notion that all good families, certainly we Spahrs among them, were dynasties unto ourselves, each generation saddled with a new iteration of the same old passions, flaws, pursuits. Pilots begot more pilots, homesteaders more homesteaders, sea farmers more sea farmers. From a young age Viola had taught me to tenderize our newly harvested pips by spanking them against the veranda railing—octopus meat needed to be beat up to taste right. The bruising rattled the entire house frame. It was my mother's nature in action, one I recognized that she'd passed on to Finley—a brutal force of will, the belief that any adversity could be overcome as long as one wielded enough leverage. For myself, I saw our house as one that no amount of hard work could save; eventually nature would force us all to higher ground. The tide line rose a couple of inches every year. The stilts could keep us from drowning in our beds for only so long.

As Viola grew sicker, our father frequently shut himself up in the bathroom, the record player looping through recordings of old cowboy ballads. Finley shot down a flock of ravens, forbidden according to tribal law, and braided the feathers into a crown. The skulls he spiked on the veranda's railing. I continued filling orders from what remained of the farm's stock, attempting in what small ways I could to keep everything running.

From that perspective, the last years of my childhood—I must call them that, for losing a parent means becoming an adult in one fell swoop—were a blur of familial necessity and the unbearable humidity of impending disaster: burnt corn muffins, typhoon fundraisers, combing Temp's tangles. For over a year our mother hooked into drips of cotton-candy-colored IV bags. We fed her pureed kelp. Our father special-ordered boxes of vitamins, and she grew weaker by the day. She couldn't leave the bedroom, so her food and medications were brought to her on a tray. I sponged her limbs nightly and washed her wispy hair in a ceramic bowl. The only other time I had seen something wither before my eyes was after the naturalized octopus hens gave birth. They barricaded themselves in deep, dank corners of the breeding tank, twirling ribbons of eggs, until their pips were ready to survive on their own. Then the mother hens crawled out and died. This knowledge of natural rhythms, undisruptable life cycles, rankled in all of us—the whole family. And our grief broke us apart along lines of old division.

It seemed to hit Temperance hardest of all, and the long winter nights were no help. I often awoke in the dark to find my little sister gone from her bed. This was Temperance's habit at the time—eleven years old that winter, she often climbed into bed with our parents. Our father at least was a hard sleeper, a good sleeper compared to the rest of us, all malingered with Viola's insomnia. "Midnight fever time," our mother would say when we descended the ladder at three in the morning, eyes like superheated moons. Probably I would have made room for Temperance in my hammock had my little sister ever come to me, but at the time we were not close. Growing up so far apart in age, we had never seriously considered the thought that we might be of comfort to each other as sisters.

How quickly all neglected things begin to rot—that was something I'd learned living stilted over the ocean. Ice groaned where it joisted up against our house's stilts. The Crusher floats thrummed against the dock—the plane basically fuelless but ready. Our pantry was more bare than I could remember. As the winter wore on, it wasn't clear how long our family would be able to go on like this, struggling to bear up under the weight of our own life.

. . .

EARLY THAT SPRING, Viola—the last of the so-named Bloomers—did not wake up for breakfast. Finley and I paddled the Banana to Disillusionment Bay to alert Ranger Starr, the only certified backwoods guide in the fjord, who our mother often had flown to distant rescue sites. We stopped first at the trade post, where Happenstance said, "I saved this for you kids," and rolled a dragon fruit across the counter. We took the fruit to the front steps of Madam LeFleur's boardinghouse and I split it open with a knife stored in my boot. The pulp tasted sour; I tossed the magenta rinds to the gulls. Afterward I knocked on the door of the ranger station, and when Ranger Starr answered he cleared his throat twice before saying, "I'm sorry to hear about your mother."

"Me too," I said.

As we were leaving the ranger's station, Finley peeled off for the trade post just as I spotted Jude LeFleur. The young man who'd recovered the Ahab years ago walked up the beach and dropped a sack of abalone at my feet. He wore a wet suit rolled to the elbows that exposed the brilliant blue veins on his forearms. The ocean tried its best to turn every living creature cold-blooded in the spring months. He sat down on the boardinghouse step. He was older than me by several years and attended school down south on the continent. Each summer he returned to help his grandmother run the boardinghouse. "You'll want to soak those first," Jude said, gesturing toward the abalone.

"You didn't have to do that," I said.

"If you stay, I'll fry them up for you."

"We should get back to the farm," Finley said loudly, walking over, carrying a sack of groceries from the trade post; he was eager to get home.

Jude shrugged and kicked the sand with his bare foot. "Another time," he said.

"Thanks for dinner," I said.

"Come on, Mills." Finley hoisted the abalone over his shoulder. "Let's go."

The ice in our family's fjord broke not long after, and this was perhaps the only thing that saved us. Finley quickly went back to his old habit of strapping on his metal detector to swim laps around the house. From the eating table on the veranda I had a full view of the fjord—my brother in a winter wet suit keeping time with Abraham Lincoln. He resurfaced every day for lunch with goggle marks welting the skin around his eyes. One afternoon I was in the kitchen when the veranda door slid open and there he stood, wet suit zipped down to his waist. Flippers slapping, he crossed the kitchen and broke a hunk off the bread I'd just pulled from the oven.

"This tastes way past its prime, Mills."

"It's bulgur," I said.

"I mean, but still."

"We don't have anything else."

"Mail plane just dropped, that's what I was coming to say," Finley said.

"Food?"

"Yeah, but come on, it's a big raft."

I knew as soon as we got the order into the kitchen that it had been placed by our mother last fall. It included all of our favorites: toasted sesame oil and canned starfruit. Chops of caribou for our father to grill; peanut butter and a mermaid doll with a flossy pink updo for Temperance; arrows Finley could fletch with feathers from our chickens; and for me, colored pencils to illustrate my maps. An envelope taped to the bottom of the crate contained individual packets of seed: the spring crops. Planting would begin soon; it would have to if our family was going to make enough off the summer harvest to live another season, let alone afford to send me to school on the continent the following year. I had saved a good portion of what I'd need for a ferry ticket but was anxious that at any moment something might come up that would defund my plans.

I worried even more now that we all seemed to wake up every day freshly crusted in some new dust of our mother's responsibilities: food, mail, the octopus herd. During the day I practiced perpetual motion, fulfilling the tasks expected of me, the tasks that kept our life afloat, and at night I sunk low in my hammock, dreaming of arid skies, of one day falling asleep to any sound other than the persistent lap of water.

The grocery delivery came with a stack of old newspapers. Finley spread them across the kitchen counter. Most of the news was routine. Madam LeFleur planned to build an extension to the boardinghouse to host weddings. Ranger Starr had gotten himself ordained via a correspondence course. But it was the classifieds that caught my attention.

FOR SALE: PANHANDLE ACADEMY TO AUCTION PINK FLUTESKY. PROCEEDS TO BENEFIT WALRUS RESCUE IN THE ARCHIPELAGO OF LOST SAINTS. COLLECT A RELIC AND SAVE THE WORLD! SUBMIT BID IN WRITING TO RANGER STARR.

FOR SALE BY OWNER: RAVENWOOD AS IS. MARKS ON HOOD. IN NEED OF A NEW SOUNDBOARD—PERFECT STARTER PIANO FOR NEW FAMILY. MARKET PRICE OBO.

WANTED: THAT BLOOMER NAPOLEON LIKE I ALREADY TOLD YOU PEOPLE I NEED IT. I AM A RICH MAN WHICH MEANS I HAVE MONEY. THIS IS YOUR TICKET TO A NEW LIFE, ALL ABOARD, YOU KNOW WHAT TO DO.

The last ad galled me—the proprietary insistence of someone, anyone, laying claim to what we all considered our mother's birthright. Our own birthright, really. Though I hadn't been out there with Finley and our mother looking for the Napoleon, I'd cooked dinners and made beds for six years while they flew. So far we had nothing to show for any of it.

I thought of all the new-age prospectors who'd migrated into our homeland over the last six years and all of their planes: that huge flock of mechanical birds scanning our waters for value, vulturing up our antiquities. Climate refugees and contract pilots and freelance internet providers no longer interested in stringing telecom wires across the territory. Discount riggers selling the equipment needed to dive for pianos out past the break of the bay. Fortune seekers, all. I had no idea, really, what they'd already taken: chippy consoles in full spats, buckets of keys, even the skeleton of someone just trying to find a little peace in the aquatic twilight. They weren't going to stop until the territory's bones were picked clean.

"Looks like strangers poaching into our personal territory," Finley said. He eyed me—my brother had our mother's eyes: *popeyes*, our father called them, for they were the bulbous eyes of fish. "The Banana won't take me for distance on the open ocean and there's nothing left around here I haven't already scoped a thousand times." For a minute he chewed his sandwich, thoughtful. He looked out toward the fjord's mouth when he said, "I need to get farther, like a couple days out. Camp. You know, deep-dive the Lost Saints, see what's actually down there. I need to get back in the air."

No one had touched the Crusher since Viola's death. I'd figured our father would want to sell the plane soon. "There's barely any fuel left," I said. "And you don't have a license."

"You started piloting at my age."

"Because my feet could reach the pedals. All I know is enough to fly in case of an emergency. I'm not a pilot."

"This is an emergency. I was planning our summer route at the post the other day and Happy said these people advertising"—he pushed the newspaper across the counter—"most of them don't even live up here. If they want the Napoleon that much, it's really got to be worth something—like, buy-the-fjords rich."

"Or there's nothing out there and this is all a waste of time," I said. "We have actual crops to plant and you're supposed to help me."

"Who cares about some measly kelp vines?" Finley said. "I know you're my sister, but you're seriously deluded if you think the farm's going to make it without Mom's flight income, and neither of us is old enough to take over her charter license. We need a Big Catch."

This was the one sentiment we'd all taken care not to discuss.

How much longer we could go on I didn't know, none of us knew, and I wished at least to have a choice in our family's future. If Finley couldn't find the Napoleon, he wanted one of the other top payouts. While I didn't know exactly how many there were, I did know that, at that point, there were still plenty left to find. And Finley wasn't picky.

"You want me to fly you," I said. "You want me to be your pilot."

"What I need is a tank of fuel."

"You don't have any money."

"You do," he said. At once heat flashed through me and my throat constricted. I took a sip of water and coughed it right back up, liquid dripping from my chin. I struggled to catch my breath. Seeing my panic, Finley picked his teeth a moment, then added, "You'll get it all back when we find something. It's a win-win."

"You taking my money for a private project is supposed to be a win for me?"

"It's called an investment." There was a smear of sauce at the corner of his mouth. "Look, if you don't want to make any more cash for yourself, I can just go by myself."

I thought through the implications of this proposition as I picked at the remains of my lunch in silence. In front of me was a plated rosemary pork sandwich topped with tomatoes. I took a bite. Somehow, and I didn't understand the black magic of it, that sandwich was the best thing I'd tasted in weeks. Finley held up his own version—same bulgur bread, sweet-and-sour sauce smeared across a pork chop; we saluted with our lunch meats and ate while listening to the pluck and sorrow of cowboy funeral ballads leaking out the bathroom door. Bleached with the grief of losing our mother, I could not shake the feeling that my brother and I were regarding each other as a pair of bears recently surfaced from hibernation. Wary, unsure whether we should ultimately embrace or turn tail and each run our own way.

Watching Finley eat, I saw too how his bones had started to grow too big for his skin. At fifteen his shoulders were just about to breach into prominence. He had our father's wholesome nature and the curled muttonchops of an eighteenth-century cabin boy. Temperance and I, on the other hand, had both inherited our mother's scaling height and cowlicking hairline. I knew that Finley would fly himself if I turned down his offer, and I tried to imagine him up there, straining over the dash. Dogged and unimpeachable. Perfectly unwilling to recognize his own limitations. I thought back to the afternoon on the beach when he'd nearly drowned going after the Napoleon the first time, both of us just kids. How at least I'd been there to breathe air back into his lungs.

My brother had our mother's mercurial, off-key temperament—the one that had lured all our ancestors to a northern, wild territory. Viola had passed it down to him, and now that we were both half orphaned, there didn't seem to be anyone else on the planet who had the wherewithal to temper his impulses. *Somebody has to take care of things when I'm not here.*

"Okay, I'll fly you," I said. "One run."

"Seriously?" Finley said; such exuberance.

I stood. "Get my atlas."

Today when I fly again over the fjord where I grew up, I think about how vulnerable and lonely we were that spring, how rough the waves seemed as they slicked up through the knotholes. At times I wondered if deep down I lacked my own ambition, if I *had* to latch on to my brother's. But I don't think that was it. I wasn't a natural-born pillager, true, but I knew the territory and where, exactly, it was breaking apart. I was tall. Finley and I had a camaraderie born out of loss—not as unusual as you might think—and everything up there was changing so fast. At the very least I was someone who could eventually graph, *This was here, this was there, this is where we are now.*

The Crusher's cockpit smelled of tea leaves and burnt sugar. Our mother's flight goggles, right lens busted out, lay strewn across the dash. I snapped them on and cranked the engine. The song "The Queen of Cabbage Laces" blared through the speakers, knocking both of us back in our seats. Finley leaned out the passenger window to help me navigate around the house and out of the fjord. My mappings, the casual atlas I'd amassed during our childhood adventures, lay propped open between us. Looking at them, I realized that until that moment I had perhaps mistakenly conceived of my life as a mere extension of that two-dimensional expanse. A map that scrolled on and on into the future. I was following along in the only snowshoe tracks I could see, completely forgetting to look up at the birds diving and swooping, unmoored by gravity, the inversion of the moon and stars as commonplace to them as the fjords were to me.

Preservation, even just the preservation of a family, was never as easy as people imagined. It took work, a real commitment of spirit. Somebody had to decide what to petrify, what to slice free, what to transmit to the next generation. One day we would all degrade; freezing that process, halting time—that was the work of science, or religion.

The skies over the fjord were florid and empty. My hands shook as the Crusher skied, full throttle, past the veranda, past the breeding tanks, out to where the water was black and teeming with the secret lives of fish. For a moment we were caught in a wild yaw, and spray splattered the windows. The waves attempted to kick us back to the house. Failed. One of the floats hit something underwater and only our life belts kept us from smacking our skulls on the Crusher's ceiling. Just as I started wondering if I'd made a huge mistake I remembered something, flicked the elevator, and suddenly we lifted off, pitching, up, up, up, into the clouds.

And then we were flying.

Part II

Piano Hunters

Moose

Disillusionment Bay
Early May, first homestead expedition

HO FOR THE ARCTIC TERRITORY!
Brethren, Friends, & Fellow Countrymen:
THE GREAT HOMESTEAD LAND GRANT
of the Territory of the Arctic is now open for settlement.
MILLIONS OF ACRES.
Claim your parcel today!
The Territory of the Arctic has never had a crop failure!
Has never had any frozen grain!!
Has the greatest produce yield per acre!!!

The ship dropped anchor on the shelf of Disillusionment Bay and the homesteaders spent their first evening in the Territory of the Arctic off-loading the pianos. "Haul those asses, men!" hollered Rocket, the guide who met the ship, as the five Mayflower brothers muscled their family's Bluefin forte to the top of the gangway.

Humpbacked and shored up on cast-iron legs, the Bluefin was a girthy instrument, and the precarity of the whole situation caused the assemblage of prospective homesteaders fanned out along the beach to break into worried ruminations. The late spring tide, which had been whomping out since they'd disembarked early that morning, was now rolling back in. The clot of men hunkered at the base of the gangway stood among a stubble of seal skulls and kelp pretzels.

Moose Bloomer appraised the sky: a swirl of ultraviolet and salt-colored stars. At twelve and one-quarter years he was no expert in the field of sun calculations for the month of May, but it didn't take a forecaster to see that nightfall was foundering fast. His family hadn't off-loaded their Napoleon yet, and darkness wasn't going to ameliorate the situation one iota.

Earlier in the day, Moose had strategically positioned himself back from the fray. He stood now atop a hymnal box, which afforded him a superior view of the action. Nearby, Thornton Huntmoon—the closest approximation he had to a friend—mucked around digging up clams. On the ship Thornton had exhibited some weak-gutted tendencies Moose did not primarily care for, but there were no other fellows their age worth knowing, so they'd struck up a friendship in spite of their differences of opinion.

"Where's your uncle?" Moose asked.

Thornton continued jabbing his spade into the sand around the hymnal box, seemingly oblivious to the fresh clam dimples blinking along the tide line a few feet away. Early May was the end of shellfish season, Moose's homesteading books had concurred; all the gummy clots of meat so proliferative on the beach right now wouldn't be safe to eat the rest of the summer. By the time a new crop washed ashore that fall, their families would be snug hundreds of miles north on new homesteads. Thornton waved dismissively at the tree line. "He went off with Auntie to say a prayer."

"He'd better get back soon if you're going to get your Psalmist before dark. I never heard of scripture making anybody's muscles stronger."

Thornton sat down on the hymnal box and braced the spade across his legs. He wore short pants, and the spade looked gigantic balanced across his bony, hairless knees. He brushed sand off the handle and said quietly, "He's got me to help him."

"At least you guys can lift your instrument," Moose said.

"I saw you help load the Napoleon," said Thornton.

Moose stomped his new boots, rattling the hymnal box; already sand had itched its way under his socks. Such a distraction could not be tolerated. "Yeah," he said. "I helped."

Along the tree line preparations were already under way for supper: the yeasty whiff of soda bread crusting in Dutch ovens, kettles whistling. Families who'd already off-loaded their instruments now knelt around rings of stones, blazing up fires. Moose's own mother strode about their campsite with purpose—snapping dust off their mattresses and whipping together a skillet of sweet potatoes and maple butter. Unamelia Bloomer was an apple-cheeked woman with stalwart hips, and even from this distance Moose could see how her belly was gourding up with his new little brother. Una slit a sockeye, slipped one hand inside, and hinged the fish open in a fluid motion. On either side of her women trussed their own game: boiled beachfrogs stripped of their legs and white-pimpled hens hastily plucked and set to roast. The air burned with charcoal. Was this the land of bounty they'd been promised? Why yes, to Moose's eyes it certainly appeared as such.

Right then all he wanted was a full dinner on dry land. Five weeks on the boat up from the continent had wreaked havoc on his guts and he needed a plate of sustenance, the leisure to evacuate himself in private, and the cushion of a few hours' sleep before he was expected to surmount the physical expectations of his new life. But his family's Napoleon was still roped in the ship's bilge of a hull, and if they needed a boarding pass to their new life, that was it. In Moose's opinion it was truly a swindle the way everything had been arrayed. Issuing each family a map and an orange flag, the deed to their land hinging upon their ability to "civilize." They were required to bring salt pork, botanical texts, and pianos—music, music being what would elevate the territory from raw, unbroken land into a homeland worth having. There was no way Moose's new stepfather, Arthur, would delay retrieval of the Napoleon until morning.

Though Moose had drawn the misfortune of coming into his life under the shadow of dubious paternity, he and his mother were both now Bloomers in name and deed—equal participants in their family's upcoming settlement. They'd been roped into this dream right alongside the piano. It was a bewitching promise of security, a life where they weren't required to depend on the charity of others. All they had to do was mount their sled and follow their guide, Rocket, through the Singing Spruce Forest to their new deeded plot of land.

The whole voyage everyone had been whispering, Wasn't it such a blessing that the journey wouldn't be all rain and tents and broken legs. Why, they'd have music to carry them along! Moose had to hand it to everyone for cottoning on to the bright side of their paltry situation. Because if anyone had asked him, he would have put forth that hauling huge instruments into uncharted territory was a dangerous prospect. Even working in perfect togetherness, he and Arthur could barely lift the Napoleon.

The Mayflower brothers scuttled from one side of the ramp to the other as the Bluefin, that gluttonous duchess, shifted her weight. Their forte was a family heirloom, wagoned to the edge of the continent before being loaded onto the ship north. It was eighteen hands tall at the apex, the boards stained a rich cobalt. Moose had witnessed the playing of this feat of nature only once, the night before the ship had left, when the Mayflowers conducted a family choir. Mama Mayflower rapped metronomic time against her hip to guide her brood. The Bluefin's keyboard sat low: it could be played from a standard piano stool, but the body served as an eighteen-foot sound tunnel. The music blew out of vents hatched into each side, slits in the wood that reminded Moose of gills. When the vents were propped wide open, it could be heard for miles.

The five Mayflower brothers grappled now to hold the instrument level on the swaying gangplank. Dropping it would entail a forty-foot fall into the water if they were lucky, onto shoals if they were not. The fellows might dive free, but the Bluefin would hit the rim of the continental shelf and bust open like a festival pumpkin. Nothing would wreak disaster for their family's future more quickly.

As Moose watched, the youngest Mayflower brother skidded. Cried out. A fine glitter of shell dust drifted off the edge of the ramp. Another boot skidded. Then suddenly everything went careening.

The brothers were out of control and terrified as nine hundred pounds of oak and ivory swung the full bore of its weight toward shore.

"Get her on the left!" hollered Rocket.

Before anyone on the beach had the chance to reckon how to help, Papa Mayflower came bursting out of the crowd. A large man wired through the biceps, he sprinted up the ramp. He dropped a shoulder and impaled himself along the Bluefin's broad side. This stopped the piano's rickety descent, but the force strained him, that was clear. The brothers jockeyed for better holds. When they regained a semblance of balance, Papa dropped back and they resumed their descent, more carefully this time. Moose sensed a wave of relief issuing from those spectating on the beach, though he himself felt sick at the sight. It was a fine feat of strength that only proved what might be demanded of him going forward. A great deal more than his body and spirit presently seemed capable of giving.

A couple of months earlier he had just barely unified his senses around the idea that his mother had remarried during what any decent human would consider his pivotal years. Before Arthur they'd lived in a single-room apartment with a communal bathroom; everyone from babies to the elderly crammed against the sink each evening to brush teeth and gossip. When Moose wasn't at school, he and his mother picked caterpillars off the tomato crops they grew in the community garden behind their church or hiked deep into the nearby hills foraging mushrooms and salmonberries. He'd tap Morse code messages to the boy in the apartment next door through the thin walls, and he and Una ate their supper off an ironing board that folded down from the wall beside the stove. It jarred Moose's sensibilities when they moved with Arthur into their own free-standing house on the outskirts of town. He'd still been waffling on whether Arthur was truly an improvement to their existence when his new stepfather came charging home waving a flyer about free land—all they had to do was claim it. Most of the paper was taken up by the headline: HOMESTEAD ACT: TERRITORY OF THE ARCTIC. Underneath this headline was a crude black-and-white sketch of a mountain range. The following paragraph, in text almost too small to read, described the available plots as "ripe" and "uncultivated." That was supposed to be the plus side. What was there to think about? Arthur said. They'd better hop to, pack their bags!

Stretched on his belly in front of the fireplace, Moose had been working all afternoon on a ledger of long division, daydreaming about the coil of pride that'd warm his stomach when he turned it in and his teacher said, *Now, that's another good job there.* "What about school?" he asked.

"School of the real world's what we got here."

Moose believed he lived in the real world. Behind him the fire snapped, and suddenly it felt blisteringly hot; sweat dripped down his back. "But the year's not over."

"Well," Arthur said, shrugging. "I can't help that the ship leaves Thursday."

Moose's hometown in the Rocky Highlands was nobody's idea of a metropolis, but it had always seemed to him a fine place to root down and construct a life. Located a few miles from a trail clogged with Conestoga wagons, over time the town had managed to waylay enough western migrants to support a barbershop, clothier, two chapels, and a bank so secure it had only been robbed twice. For years there'd been a rumor circulating that the region was primed to get a sheriff, a job Moose wouldn't have minded having himself one day. That is, if people could ever get past the fact that he was the illegitimate offspring of Una Price, piano player and tomato canner.

But before any of his childhood dreams had a chance to spring into fruition, Arthur appeared in their lives. Moose's stepfather believed that they'd misperceived their hometown. There were too few laws, Arthur said. The streets were uncouth, with nothing in the way of real civilization to offer a young family. Arthur had heard that miners crazed by gold dust picked each other through the cranium. The trade post was stocked with buffalo rifles! And people said outlaws rode around kidnapping little boys the size of Moose to raise in whatever manner they pleased. He insisted that there was no point trying to civilize their hometown further, considering Moose and his mother had already suffered there for a number of years. When Arthur met them they were still in the thick of the kind of hardship people in the church referred to as "scratching around." As in: *Let's all chip in a few coins to keep fellow parishioner Una Price from scratching around again this winter.*

As far as Moose knew, the Price family's only living passel of relatives was back East in a peeling Victorian. He had long been under the impression that even if he and his mother had managed to scrape together the coin to go back, an impossibility in and of itself, their kinsmen were not the sorts of people who would have welcomed them home with apricot pies and feather mattresses. What help they'd received over the years had come at the hands of church ladies who took payment by smoothing Moose's cowlick and promising his life to celestial glory. It was through these church ladies that Arthur had been introduced into their lives, he being strategically seated next to Una and Moose at Sunday service one week.

The day that Arthur came home with the flyer, Moose watched his mother's reaction. Una was rocking in a corner, making progress on one of her cross-stitches: a portrait of a hoary-haired pirate holding an elephant tusk. She stuck her needle in the man's ear. "None of us knows how to build a cabin," she said without looking up. "We could all freeze to death."

"You've got me and you've got Moose."

"You've never built a whole house before."

"I know how to read a blueprint. I know how to follow directions," said Arthur.

"It's a long way to go. Who says we'd even make it?"

"That's why we've got to start now, Una-bird. Get there in the summer so we have time to make it great before the snow sets."

"What about food?" Moose said. "What are we going to eat?"

"It's not like we'll be living in some random sod attic. You're both going to have beds, you're going to have pillows and rules. This is a genuine"—Arthur read from the flyer—"*Northern Outpost of Mannerly Society.*"

Moose's mother bit off the end of her thread. "That sounds like a racket to get a bunch of people to move to the middle of nowhere and starve."

Arthur unscrolled the flyer and held it up. "You don't get it. This is for educated folks, traders, musicians—it's the type of place we could raise our grandchildren." Underneath the grainy mountain was an even-smaller-print paragraph, which he read aloud:

> In addition to satisfying each of the aforementioned criteria (abode construction and various improvements as yet to be determined), each household to be awarded a Certificate of Homesteadization must be outfitted with at least one pianoforte. In the eyes of this committee, an instrument of this caliber, and one member's reasonable initiative toward playing, will be proof of the homesteaders' good faith in the establishment of a Habitable Civilization.

"But that's absurd," Una said. "We're supposed to cart an actual piano across the permafrost? On what?"

"A sled. Well, a ship first, then a sled."

"You can't run a sled in the summer."

"Guide says if we load it right, we can run it over mountains," Arthur said.

Moose gestured for Arthur to pass him the flyer. He scanned the page and looked up: "I don't play the piano and neither do you."

"Your mother does," said Arthur.

"Barely," said Una.

"You know the basics, that's enough."

Moose's mother was no virtuoso, but he knew she could hack out "Shine, Shine, Little Comet" and the like, which was more than Moose could say for either Arthur or himself. Una was right—there was something ridiculous about this whole proposition if half their train wouldn't even know how to play the instruments they were required to haul.

"I don't know why we can't just do all this right here," Una said.

"You know why we can't," Arthur said gently. "Look, all they're asking is a reasonable initiative. That's it! I mean, nobody's going to get one hundred and sixty acres free and clear for nothing. They're giving away land and they want to make sure we're going to stick around when the going gets tough."

"How tough?"

"Oh, sure, we'll get to that. First we've got to click our thinking into motion, Una-bird. Perseverance. Steely mouthed subsistence survival. Aren't these the lessons we want to impart to Moose"—he dropped his gaze—"and any future youngsters?"

And *wallah*, just like that Moose knew that Arthur had her. Una was always keening on about how she wasn't primed for the task of imparting to her son all the life skills he should have been gleaning at the knee of a father. And now here was just such a father figure, right in front of her, volunteering to begin that very imparting process. As a single mother she'd navigated the world with kindness and swishing skirts, but these were not the tools Moose would need to grow into an independent and fiscally prosperous man—especially not if he wanted a family of his own one day. Arthur's model was key to the optimization of Moose's future. "What do you think, Moose?" she said.

What Moose thought was that earlier that afternoon a neighbor had invited him to watch a sow whelp her first batch of piglets and he wished like hell now he'd gone. If he was being honest, the journey sounded like it would promise a significant level of arduousness. He wasn't sure he would be able to surmount the challenges of cabin building and piano hauling considering his current weight (poor) and abilities (uncultivated). Not to mention, Arthur was no great survivalist; he had nothing for credentials when it came to bear country. The way Moose saw it, it wasn't hard to imagine that they might end up exactly where they were now, selling tomatoes to passersby, only next time in a place even more rural, where everyone thought the fruits overpriced.

"Would I get my own bed?" Moose asked tentatively, picking at fibers on the rug. He wasn't keen to move again, but perhaps he could find solace in the freedoms this new life promised.

Arthur grinned. "Son, you can have your own room."

Una stabbed a thread into the pirate's temple. A few more follicles and the picture would be ready to hang in the collection mounted above the fireplace. A raggle-rough ensemble that included an eye-patched bird trader, a buffalo hunter with a hot pink rifle slung across his shoulders, and a bull rider flung halfway to the moon. Though Moose had never applied much pressure to his mother on the subject of his biological father, if her taste in art was anything to go by, he'd been sired by a man with a love for adventure. That same taste for adventure must reside somewhere within himself, he decided, even if it was just hibernating quietly. Maybe all he needed were the right circumstances for it to spring to life.

In the end it wasn't really so much to ask of either him or his mother—the two of them having spent the bulk of his childhood being kicked from one drafty domicile to the next by an endless stream of landlords. Hog-bellied men leaning in the doorjamb: "Miss Price, Miss Price, what are we going to do with you?" Following Arthur up the trail at least meant the hope of land, the chance to scratch together their own livelihood. As his mother knotted the thread, her new ring caught the lamplight. A knuckle-size black pearl cut in the current fashion. Moose watched her fiddle with the ring, and in that moment it occurred to him that any protestations he might have mounted weren't going to sway her decision. There was nothing for him to do but believe that, when push came to shove, he'd be useful and strong. The deal between all of them, it was clear, had already been struck.

MOOSE COULD SCARCELY make out the outline of Thornton and his uncle at the top of the ramp, their Psalmist balanced between them. A light-boned instrument, the Psalmist was about the size of a harpsichord, and they had no trouble lifting her. Moose watched them descend a few steps before he heard Arthur calling for him. They were scheduled next. His stepfather had already strapped up for action: rope looped around his chest, sun goggles pushed back into his wild brown-and-pepper mane. Both he and Rocket gestured up the gangway with intent, making plans for the dismount. Moose hopped off the hymnal box and mucked over.

"People have a right to haul what they want to haul," Arthur was saying.

Rocket spit in the sand. "If you can't lift it yourself, you shouldn't be bringing it."

"A tad unreasonable, don't you think?"

"I've been living here my whole life and I don't need any of these trappings to keep food in my belly, a roof over my head," Rocket said, gesturing at the detritus of trunks scattered about the beach. Their guide wore a simple leather tunic and pants, with cords around his neck from which dangled a knife pouch and various tins and feathers Moose didn't recognize. He didn't look like someone who'd be strapping a china tea set to his own sled, but he was also not the first person to try to talk them out of hauling their lives' goods.

Arthur crossed his arms. "It's about more than that."

"No, it ain't. You want to live a good life, then stop believing what everybody else says you need to make it good. You could squat down right here, save us all the trouble—it's no worse than where you're going, believe me."

"You don't sound like someone who wants to be a guide." Arthur pulled down his sun goggles and snapped them into place. He kicked his boots against the gangplank, then took a handkerchief from his pocket and wiped away the last grains of sand.

Rocket watched him, bemused, before turning his attention back up the ramp. "You bring this prepossessing mess into those trees and not everyone's going to make it out alive, that's all I'm saying," he said.

The Psalmist's four legs were planted on the sand. Thornton and his uncle lifted it up, one side at a time, and wedged planks under the feet so it would slide. They pushed the instrument up the beach to their campsite. Moose looked at the sky. The stars were winking up pretty good. Fist-size knots of celestial cartilage imbued with a meaning he hadn't yet learned to read.

Arthur clamped a hand on his shoulder and said, "Let's go."

By the time they'd mounted the Napoleon on deck, the captain was hollering for the crew to drop sail. The waves were really kicking up a racket. Owing to vertigo, Arthur and Moose barely managed to angle the Napoleon to the top of the ramp. "Lower it down for a minute," Arthur said. "Can you see?"

Below, sea urchins winked in the starlight. They'd have liked nothing better than to pincushion Moose's fat cells from one end of his body to the other. It seemed to Moose he could quite clearly see the dangers in all directions. "Yeah," he said.

"We only get one try."

"I've got a grip."

"On my count. One, two, three."

This was muscle-bending work, man's work, maneuvering a forte down the ramp. Arthur tried to lighten the mood with promises of midnight badminton, but it was all Moose could do to keep his attention on the task at hand. When they reached the halfway mark, his fears began to ease. Perhaps he could achieve more than he thought after all—"Easy now, slow down," Rocket was calling—perhaps Moose actually had more physical capabilities than anyone had suspected.

"Hold firm," Arthur said. "Steady."

Moose was relishing the thought of some wink-eye when out of nowhere a wave knocked up against the ship, tossing about bits of foam and shell. The ramp bucked. Moose's grip slid. The Napoleon was slick with spray. The ramp swung toward Arthur and the forte rammed into his stepfather, pushing him—*one, two, three, four*—backwards. Moose lost purchase and fell, kicking, in the opposing direction. His tailbone struck something sharp, and as he tried to scramble to his feet he heard Arthur call: "Look out."

The Napoleon had shifted momentum and was railroading straight across the ramp toward him. Arthur applied himself to the back legs, issuing grunts of exertion. He must have been having some effect because the forte's legs cleaved the veneer off the ramp in three neat strips. Then the only thing between the Napoleon and the edge of the ramp was Moose's own body. Holy stars. He braced his feet against the front leg to hold the piano back. The instrument issued a creak of annoyance. Moose was jackknifed across the ramp, eyes roaming the sky as the forte pushed him toward the edge. He could hear Arthur's boots scrambling for traction. The force of the piano's weight buckled his knees, and the next thing he knew his head and neck had slid free of the ramp and dangled out, midair.

Moose was five feet tall, flat, that summer. He'd been raised on a diet of legumes and apples. Arthur was forty-four and already wolfishly gray at the temples. They were neither of them equipped to handle a situation of that caliber. Not alone, certainly, but clearly not together, either. The Napoleon weighed roughly 550 pounds. Moose didn't have to fully understand the mathematical equivalents of force projection to know that in the battle of humankind versus the physics of a falling piano he'd aligned himself with the losing team.

Suddenly there issued a tremendous crack as the leg against which Moose was braced gave way, folding up underneath the piano's body. The full weight of the Napoleon came crashing down atop his thighs. He couldn't move. Up flared a sunrise of pain. Moose was in a true writhe of discomfort, hollering curse words, and it became impossible to deduce the full mechanics of what happened next. For there was Moose, flailed, helpless, and there was Arthur, dropped to a squat, a shoulder pushed under one of the Napoleon's remaining legs. In one smooth motion his stepfather stood up, swinging the instrument up and onto his back. Arthur jostled to shift the weight, then proceeded down the ramp easy as a hermit crab carting a shell.

Moose clambered up as best he was able and went hobbling down after him, yelling for the crowd to break ranks. There was an impossible catch in his left hip, but he didn't let it slow him. Arthur hit the beach and kept on toward camp. Moose trailed behind him and couldn't help thinking that this must be just the sort of thing a man does in terms of familial devotion and life betterment. At the time, he knew nothing of the Arctic aubade, how it incited Vikings and fishermen and soldiers to pillage, trawl, and slaughter. The way it rejigged the blood. He only knew that families on the beach were cheering. His stepfather had fortitude, Moose had to give him that, and he felt his spirit buoy at the thought that perhaps Arthur might be able to shepherd them all safely to their new home after all.

THEY PASSED A hasty night on the beach. Around four in the morning, the sun rocketed up from her sleeping place, balming the tents in light. Moose peeled back the tent flaps and peered around. On either side of him families were already zipping into their overalls. Down the beach rose the spires of music stands. Somewhere a pianist significantly more adept than Una plucked out a sonata. Though the instrument was in tune now, the melody likely wouldn't hold long on the trail. Families had been warned and many had chosen to unstring their fortes preemptively. Moose watched Thornton walk toward the waves. His aunt chased after him, handkerchief flapping. She caught him by the shoulder. In one quick motion she dabbed the cloth in the waves then swabbed Thornton's face. Moose looked away, embarrassed by the naked display of motherly affection.

Strapped against Auntie Huntmoon's back was a baby called Pumpkin. In a few months Moose expected to have his own tyke to transport in just such a fashion. His first sibling. He'd longed for a brother from as far back as he could recall and had already fostered an augury of the two of them sledding the territory as free men. Tipping their hats to ladies and lodging in the haylofts of obliging strangers. Moose would have to wait for his brother to grow out of his milk years, sure, but at least he wouldn't be homesteading alone for the rest of his life. His mother and Arthur would eventually pass away, that was just the locomotion of things, and after that he'd need help digging wells and birthing reindeer. The two brothers could even husband their own wives when the time came, everyone living within hollering distance, drying lines perpetually strung with yak-skin diapers.

"Let's get these mothers loaded!" Rocket bullhorned. "We've got land to cover."

There was a jovial attitude toward the work of packing up camp that first morning. Arthur was still riding high from his glorious feat of strength the night before. As they all breakfasted, Moose's stepfather kept mentioning how itchy he was to sally forth. *No holds barred! Loose the dogs!* And such and so forth. After finishing his eggs, Arthur pulled on his boots and went to work hitching the dog team. Moose was so distracted undertaking his mother's instructions—snapping bugs off the tent, prekindling the night's firewood—that he almost didn't register the moment their ship left for good.

The horizon was a thin orange wire of sunrise. Moose sat on the sand and watched as the ship's sails angled out of the bay. Over the next few weeks, whenever he found himself suffering a malcontented stomach, or roving with a fit of insomnia, he harkened back to the image of their ship sailing off the edge of the Earth in its hurry back down south to the continent. For it was only as he watched everyone who'd gathered around him on the beach wave goodbye that Moose had his first inkling, a painful spasm of reality, that now they were really on their own.

Who knew when the next ship would arrive, or if one ever would. As far as Moose knew, the territory didn't have a grocery store, chapel, or textile mill. He could not simply tap wall messages to the neighbor boy—*hey, ask your mom if we can borrow an egg*—when they ran out of something. No matter how well they stewarded their supplies on the journey over the next four months, eventually they'd have to forage, make, or grow what they needed to survive.

A fellow like himself might have fidelity to a cause for any number of reasons. Love. Loyalty. Fear. He personally hoped the journey would grow him into the man he'd always destined himself to be. As swiftly as possible, considering they were embarking on the last and most difficult leg of their journey north. From the moment the ship's mast disappeared on the horizon, it was clear—there was no possibility of retreat.

Temperance

The ship Victory
Four months after Viola's death

For thirty-three days and nights Temperance Spahr had been swashbuckling aboard the good ship *Victory*, otter-knotting the sail lines alongside Captain Crockett's motley crew of juvenile mourners. A dozen girls, sunstroked and lost; ears pierced with trout hooks, hair braided into challah Mohawks. They hailed from every faith and creed in the territory—one who worried a rosary, one toe-webbed like a duck, one with veins branching across her hand in a birthmark shaped like a singing spruce. Temperance brought her father's dry humor and her mother's moles in the shape of an ammonite on the side of her neck. Each one of the girls had been indentured for a different loss, but their mission remained the same: they'd all been conscripted to learn how to swab their lives back together. Mourn and swab, swab and mourn, that was the Crockett protocol. Salt would scour the grief from their souls.

It was two in the morning and Temperance had drawn night watch in the nest. She rubbed sunscreen across the back of her neck and started up the ladder. After her mother had died that spring, Temperance's father fell into a depressive fallow and her siblings took up hunting the Napoleon; they were gone for such long stretches, everyone had agreed it'd be better if Temperance had her own adventure to keep her occupied. Now they were deep into the skunk days of July and even the stars beat down hot.

The ocean had been pitching all night and the matcha cakes Crockett had forced upon Temperance during their morning communion were a gluttonous helix in her guts. Rung by rung, she climbed. Temperance loved the view of the world from the nest. The ocean dark and magnificent, crashing against barnacled shoals. As she neared the top of the ladder the ship suddenly veered.

The ladder went into a spin and the world lost its fulcrum.

Around and around she twirled. The motion was too great for Temperance's stomach. Her guts burbled up and she vomited a slipstream of bile and cottage cheese down the front of her overalls. By the time she reached the platform she reeked. Goldie reached down to help her clear the railing.

"Yo-ho," Goldie said.

Temperance's one true friend on the ship, Goldie Mayflower, had a strip of blood-clotted sailcloth wound around her head to protect the nub where her earlobe had been torn free during their latest diving expedition. The wound was fresh. Temperance knew because she'd watched Crockett sew it together with a sanitized fishhook. Temperance had herself lost three of the nails on her right hand, a molar, and half of an eyebrow. None of the girls had gotten through the journey unscathed.

"How's the world looking?" she asked.

"Still nothing," said Goldie. "Are we even sure the whales are coming?"

"Crockett says yes."

"Nobody said it was supposed to take this long."

For weeks the *Victory* had knifed south through the Panhandle Islands, reversing the route of the earliest homesteaders. They'd stopped at historic ports, including bush communities where children ran shirtless down the beach. Then on to a kelp-ale brewery run by the Huckle family, where a farmer spent all day in the smoke shack with Crockett. The pair emerged at sunset wink-eyed, tucking in wrinkled shirts. The goal was to immerse the girls in the territory's heritage. "Best way to get rid of grief is to drown it," Crockett said. Back on board the ship each night, the crew ran through chores. Desalinating water. Rigging. Swabbing, of course, plenty of that. At sunrise they single-filed down the ladder to their compartments belowdecks—twelve obedient owlets finished hooting down the moon.

This was when the girls cried, as they went to sleep. Memories came wailing out of them, they couldn't help it. Plum Happenstance, who'd lost her cousins to a fever. Goldie Mayflower, whose twin brother had fallen from a three-hundred-foot spruce and snapped his neck. She described the strangle of her brother's cry, the way he'd landed on the ground in a gigantic bruise. Temperance's mother, Viola, had wanted to be buried at sea, but in early April the family was afraid that the sluggish winter current would instead settle her on the fjord's floor. So her father augered a hole in the ice, wrapped Viola tight as a mummy, and the family stuffed her into a crab cage to await breakup. Viola bobbed off the back of the veranda until the ice fully broke a few weeks later. Temperance could imagine how someone might see this as morbid, but mostly what she remembered from those early weeks was how they'd all bumbled through life, sleeping late and smashing teacups. Milda. Finley. Her father. They'd all barely kept their own wounds from blistering up through their skin.

After Temperance's siblings took up flying, Fry had spent most of his time shuffling around the house in a bedraggled blue bathrobe. He scissored stacks of coupons for products the family would never use. He began and stopped over a dozen letters to his sister, Flora, and when Temperance found these she secreted them away. Eventually he began to finish the letters and send them off. Flora wrote back in a terse, blocky script: We need help down here too. Dad's trying to invent a new dinosaur from all the leftover bones. Laughter. Write back.

Goldie passed Temperance the telescope. "Good luck," her friend said, and started down the ladder. Usually the girls were scheduled double Dutch in the nest, but tonight Temperance had drawn the last straw. Perfect-pitch, shy Temperance, a sack of ivory molars in her pocket. Fallen from the mouths of dead homesteaders, the molars had become top currency on the ship. Temperance had found hers panning a creek.

She peered over the railing to the deck below, where the rest of the crew crouched around a dice circle. Hattie Pope called the prevailing percentage and everyone slapped down bets. Ivory molars. Half a kiwi. A sack of raw shrimp. For over a week their ship had been doldrumming in the lower half of the Panhandle Islands waiting for the pod of silverback whales that would propel them home. The ship had no engine; wind-powered, it had drifted south with the currents. At the same pace, the return journey to Disillusionment Bay would've taken over a month. But once a year, always in July, silverbacks migrated up through the Panhandle Islands and any ships lucky enough to catch their wake sped north to Disillusionment Bay in a few hours. By now the girls had been gone from their families so long they'd grown reckless. A drum started up and Temperance could smell shrimp broiling in their shells.

After the shrimp were eaten and the shells pitched overboard, the older girls—Hattie Pope, Meriweather Starr, Plum Happenstance—challenged each other to feats of astronomy. Telescopes snapped open as the crew reclined on the deck, their hair washed in moonlight. A hundred feet up, Temperance reclined in the nest, glassing the cosmos through her own scope. That night the sky was all Aries and Cassiopeia, a slew of Ursa Majors pawing west. Temperance studied the stars for so long that when she unsuctioned her eye she felt dizzy. She pulled a tea flask from her hip and took a drink. As part of grief therapy Temperance was required to break tea with Crockett twice a week—the captain had an ear for imparting sympathy and it didn't take a psychiatrist to fathom why.

Behind Crockett's desk hung a portrait of a young girl with blunt-chopped bangs: the original Victory. Crockett's daughter had drowned in the Panhandle Islands over a decade earlier. Like Temperance's mother's, Victory's soul now drifted somewhere in the troubled waters the ship floated. Captain Crockett spent each therapy session nudging a plate of matcha cakes across her desk, wimpling her hands. *Any new epiphanies, Temperance?* she'd ask. *If you had a nightmare, what would it be?*

Temperance rattled off the answers she suspected the captain wanted to hear. For nightmares she feared the ocean sloshing into her family's living room. For epiphanies she'd learned that no matter how far she traveled, she still looked like her mother, she still missed her family. What she didn't share with anyone was that no matter how well she expended her energy during the day, when she tried to fall asleep at night, she plunged into the same recurring dream. A ghost-washed reel of Viola resurrecting, only to die again the moment Temperance jerked awake. Every night, she'd try to stay awake as long as possible, but it wasn't easy. She didn't have enough seniority for a porthole, so for entertainment she strobed a stethoscope across the ship wall hoping to pick up the *bawk* of seagulls.

That night Temperance swept her telescope across the horizon. According to Crockett's charts the silverback whale pod that the *Victory* was waiting for was officially overdue. Temperance was an excellent scout, but even she couldn't spot plumes where none existed. Their ship was a red-sailed replica of the one that their ancestors had sailed north in over two hundred years earlier, and it had taken weeks to drift this far south. If they had to wait for prevailing winds, they might not get home for months. Temperance wanted nothing more than to return as swiftly as possible to what remained of her family: the bristle of her father's mustache, her sister's sourdough, Finley lapping the house in an old dive suit. When Temperance closed her eyes, the first thing she saw was the view of Jubilation House from the mouth of their fjord: solar panels rising like the tips of a fossilized mountain range. From sea level into clouds.

Before boarding the ship, Temperance had pulled out one of Milda's old atlases to study the geography between the Spahr family and the greater land of the southern continent. Jubilation House was two thousand miles north by sea and Temperance had never in her life been south of the library on flagship Panhandle Island. Her whole childhood her father had told her stories of the world he'd left behind when he came north—the western half of the continent a knuckle fight over water. Drought, drought, everywhere. A luckless life, or at least that's how he described it. As a young man he was romanced by the idea of subsisting in a place where the whole world was water, the ocean lapping greedily at any remaining crusts of land.

Mist drifted across the waves now. At first there was nothing to see beyond the ship's bow. Then a great mass of baleen rose from the water. A whale head. Temperance stood up. She glanced at the sky to memorize landmarks for mapping celestial navigation. Back home Milda would want to know everything so that she could add detail to the navigational star charts their mother had insisted they memorize.

Elusive and maternal, silverback whales roamed the territory in huge pods. Extended, cross-bred families of half and stepparents, brothers, surrogates, and aunts who would spend the next few weeks in the Mount Resurrection coves birthing new calves. From there the pod would swim north as a legion, filling the sea with silver.

The crew had been practicing the protocol for this moment since day one. Temperance was half blinded by the luster of the stars, but on the ship she had a clear responsibility. It was her job to hit the pitch that would send the rest of the crew into action. None of the other girls could reach the upper register: a series of high Es and higher still. But Temperance had a voice. As she began to sing, the deck below sprang into motion. The girls pocketed their spare marbles. They swept up the cards. Providence began scaling the rigging to cut down the mizzens.

Twinkle, twinkle, chanted the stars.

Sails dropped. *Whump, whump, whump.*

Up the whales rose, twisting in the air.

One minute Temperance was still singing the alarm and the next her skull whacked the railing hard enough to flare firelight. She went sliding. Her knees hit the balusters, and through the slats she could see the girls below grabbing for holds. Water came sloshing over the deck as the ship abruptly changed direction. The entire nest keeled sideways. Temperance hooked an elbow around a baluster as the *Victory* tucked into its hairpin turn. Directly below, Crockett twisted the wheel. In one smooth motion the mizzens took the air and the ship spun ninety degrees to face north. The pod of silverbacks was now behind them. The North Star, that friendly ball so familiar to Temperance's childhood, blazed bright. If she had suffered disequilibrium on the ship, discomfort even, now everything in her life seemed to align along an old, familiar meridian.

Up went the flukes.

Down the whales dove.

Nature's propellers, the whales created their own current. Crockett helmed the ship hard into this new energy stream, and suddenly the *Victory* was clipping fast, maybe too fast, future star charts sparking through Temperance's memory at supersonic speed. Crockett whooped. For a captain, she was fearless; for a woman, she had stature—six foot two with shoulders that could plow a field. The *Victory* tilted slightly prow up, and the oyster shells colonizing the hull rainbowed in the starlight. At the base of the ladder, Providence bird-hooted to let Temperance know that she was coming up to relieve her. Shift finished.

Temperance went to join her shipmates for breakfast. There was a certain kinetic energy among them as they ate—they were in cahoots somehow, in a way they'd never been before. Headed back to Disillusionment and their respective homes. After eating, those off duty went belowdecks to curl up in their compartments for their last sleep on the ship. Deep below them, the whales were flipping flukes, the current they generated serving as a gigantic set of oars. Temperance pinched closed her eyes and pulled out her stethoscope. Over and over she roved the wall of her bunk, trying to catch what she'd been waiting for more than a month to hear—a Hansel and Gretel map home beaten to the rhythm of the whales' heartbeats.

BACK IN THE FJORDS, Jubilation House looked as though it had been poxed. The windows were aquarium-scummed. Temperance's siblings had stacked the remains recovered from their recent hunts on the veranda and covered the piles in tarps. Temperance didn't spot any large enough to be whole pianos, but there were certainly more piles than Finley and her mother had ever brought back. She saw that a thick ring of mussels had begun growing where the waterline sloshed against the house's stilts. Clearly her father had not been keeping up with the house's maintenance in Temperance's absence.

It began to rain as the ship slanted into the fjord, first sliding past the breeding tanks. The Crusher was usually roped against the veranda but had clearly been moved to the back side of the house for the ship's visit. The *Victory* docked. Fry slid open Jubilation House's door and stepped onto the veranda, and Temperance tossed him a rope to secure the ship. Then she vaulted the railing. Two steps and she was in his arms. Her father smelled of banana pomade and salt. As she hugged him, she heard him invite the crew inside for tea to wait out an incoming storm.

Muffle-muffle, came Crockett's reply.

Fry chuckled. "Good one," he said.

Temperance's shipmates came to stand in her living room like lost grasshoppers, cold, wind-whipped from sailing all night. Like her, they all just wanted to go home to their families. The silverback pod had by now left them. The whales would continue up north to the sea coves, but none of the girls lived that far. From Disillusionment it would take a day or two in fair weather to deliver the rest of them back to their families. In a storm it would take even longer. Fry filled the kettle and lit the stove. He opened the kitchen cupboards, seemingly to look for something to eat, but all Temperance could see were utilitarian staples. Flour. Sugar. Coffee. Jars of raw octopus arms marinating in the family's special sauce. Someone had placed a vase of sea vegetables on the table next to the record player. She walked over and dropped the needle, and the air filled with a bluesy harmony.

There was a clatter overhead as Temperance's siblings came crashing down the ladder in time to the music. Milda first, looking so much like their mother that Temperance's throat cramped. Milda was wearing Viola's fawn-skin pants and flight cap. She had their mother's collarbone, stiff as a copper pipe. But it was Finley whose presence changed the chemistry in the room. Temperance could feel the girls around her preen as he swung off the ladder. Her brother wasn't much for height, but he'd always been rich in charisma. Wavy brown hair, a scar dividing one eyebrow in half. He squatted in front of Temperance so they were eye level and with that crooked smile said, "Welcome home, sister."

Temperance hadn't had more than a few saltwater rinses the whole time she'd been away, and she knew she smelled grisly. Crockett had frequently admonished the girls to take better care of their personal hygiene. *You're getting to a certain time in your life,* she'd said, raising her eyebrows as though transmitting a whistle the girls were supposed to hear.

Despite her smell, Temperance leapt into Finley's arms, and he swung her around the room. Temperance had always been told that of all her mother's children, she was the one who'd wanted to shell up inside of her forever. Viola'd had a long, dry November labor with Temperance. *We just couldn't coax you out,* Fry explained. *You were uncoaxable.* After many agonizing hours Temperance probed a foot down the canal—a genteel lady testing bathwater. Recognizing her chance, the midwife seized Temperance by the ankle and yanked her prune bottomed and yowling into the world. Everyone in Temperance's family fixated on the tale of her birth, that single moment at the dawn of life when she was leg-dangled from her mother—as though that was the most formative part of her life story. What nobody talked about was how an event like that caused such a cataclysmic rift that the moment itself no longer really mattered—your whole life just became aftermath, aftermath. Everything trying to fit back together. Muscles stitched, cord knifed, contractions shrinking down a spongy, uterine shell. *No more babies,* the midwife had said, her hands between Viola's legs as she tried to fold together her mother's ragged ruins. It was a tenuous business, ugly, repairing the damage done by tearing apart people so fundamentally enwombed in love as a family and a daughter such as she.

Temperance moved into the kitchen and set out teacups. She spooned fresh herbs into the samovar and poured hot water from the kettle. Outside, the storm picked up. Rain beat against the windows. Lightning flared near the mouth of the fjord. At the rate the winds were blowing it would likely be hours before the sea calmed enough for the ship to set sail. "At ease, crew," Crockett said. The girls took their teacups and sat on the living room's couch, which had been positioned to overlook the veranda. They took off their boots and unbuttoned the top collars of their uniforms. Temperance regretted this turn of events; she'd spent thirty-three days longing to be home with her family—and only her family. Now because of a rainstorm the crew would be stuck at Jubilation House for hours, if not longer.

Over by the sink, Milda began whipping sourdough batter for pancakes. At seventeen her knuckles had already ossified to the size of pearls. They clinked against the bread bowl. You couldn't hide a single muffle in this house. The walls were mostly newspaper and hand-me-down insulation. Temperance sat on the couch beside Goldie. They watched wind snap the kelp vines stretched from the veranda railing to the roof.

Goldie wrapped a blanket from the couch around her shoulders; it was a cozy knit that still smelled like Viola's spruce-needle soap. "So this is your house," she said.

"So it is," said Temperance.

Off to the side, Plum Happenstance leaned against the counter where Finley was packing a basket. As soon as the storm lifted, he and Milda planned to take off on another hunting trip. "So, what was it like growing up with sisters?" Plum said. "Did you learn how to be sensitive and all that?"

Finley snapped open the picnic basket and in went a jar of marinated octopus pips and dried huckleberries. In went salt ham and powdered eggs and sauerkraut. "Hand me those oranges," said Finley. Her brother had ended his commitment to the conversation there, Temperance could tell by his tone, but Plum didn't catch the nuance. "Because it seems like it would be a good thing," she said. "Learning about the female condition and whatnot."

Just then the music picked up a familiar riff—three notes, that was all it took to recognize their mother's favorite song: "The Last Stand of a Chicken Named Republic." With the ceremony of siblings, Temperance looked at Milda and Milda looked at Finley and

Finley looked at Temperance. A telepathic triangle. Temperance walked over and lifted the needle.

"I'd probably go with you, if you asked," Plum said. "Where're you going anyway?"

"We can't take any extra weight," Finley said.

Here, for the first time since Temperance had known Plum, she felt something resembling sympathy for the girl. This was the narrative Temperance had also been fed her whole life: how the Earth was formulated in teams of two. Gulliver and his travels. God and Abraham. Milda and Finley. It didn't take more than elementary arithmetic to figure out that in the Spahr family Temperance was the third wheel: the one always left behind. As she set another record to play, the chimes under the veranda began to tinkle. The chimes were Viola's invention—her mother had eviscerated a dozen cuckoo clocks and knit the innards into something resembling a tide predictor. Outside, water began to geyser up through the knotted boards surrounding the eating table—if Temperance could compose a symphony of her life it would start with a moment like this: the storm breaking wide open.

"Hatches," Fry said. "Now."

When it came to storm protocol, everyone in the family had a job. Finley went monkeying up the attic ladder. The ceiling shook as he sprinted across the boards. Latches popped. Solar panels whined as they folded flat against the roof. Temperance pushed into the bathroom, climbed in the tub, and creaked open the window. Crawled through. On the other side she dropped into the chicken coop they kept mortared to the side of the house. The birds were already frantic. Although Temperance could usually see to the bottom of the seabed—seventy-five feet of the clearest water imaginable—today the whole fjord had turned opaque. A bad sign.

The family's kayaks were moored just beyond the coop. They whipped at the ends of their ropes but held. If Milda was doing her job inside, she'd be pulling down pots and anchoring anything that might brain someone if the wind spun through the house. Their father's job was to crank the manual backup generator in his closet.

Click, whirl—through the bathroom wall Temperance heard the motor sputter to life. The chickens flocked at her feet. She picked one up and tossed it through the window into the bathtub. Another, and soon the whole flock was chirping inside. It was her duty to seal the birds in the bathroom, to fetch Parsley and bring her to join them. Without their animals, life on the farm would be impossible to maintain.

Before climbing back inside with the birds, she looked toward the mouth of the fjord to gauge the severity of the storm. That's when she saw Finley gripping the *Victory*'s lead line. He was fighting the ship, and Temperance quickly realized that no one had dropped anchor. They hadn't expected to be docked long. Behind her brother, the ocean had turned the color of gasoline: oily plums. The *Victory* bucked sideways and Finley lurched with it. He wouldn't be able to hold the rope much longer. Cold and barely plastered together, Temperance used the railing to pull herself against the wind toward her brother. Maybe together the two of them could hold the ship until the storm broke. Wind whistled in one ear and out the other. The chimes under the veranda took on a frantic quality, and Temperance felt a strange force gathering under them. The bully-jockeying of tectonic plates, subterranean galaxies duking it out for power.

Finley braced a boot on the railing for leverage. Temperance grabbed the tail of the rope behind him. But it was only in her hands for a moment before the water around the *Victory* dropped, bellying Finley into the railing, bellying Temperance into him. They peered together over the drop. In a rush, water receded halfway down the stilts, exposing anemones and the remains of last season's kelp vines. The *Victory* sunk so far that the crow's nest came level with the house's roof, and for the first time in Temperance's life, Jubilation House felt perched eerily too high—a crow's nest to the rest of the world. But this was merely a passing thought, for in the next second Finley threw her over his shoulder and sprinted back to the house. The door slid open, then closed, but not before the moon laid down a winning hand and the tide reclaimed its rights to the fjord. A fury of a current swept back toward them, and suddenly it was clear that Temperance was wrong, dead wrong—the house was actually perched much too low.

For the first time in Jubilation House's history waves came rushing up over the veranda and into the house. Into the living room, where records flotsamed up; the kitchen, where Milda jumped onto a counter, upending her carefully pounded ball of dough; their father's bedroom, where it seeped into the wardrobe drawers under his bed. Every fisherman sweater their mother and Milda had knitted him would soon proof up with mold. In the span of only a few seconds it seemed Jubilation House had dropped a foot below sea level. Negative one.

Milda's dough ball rafted into the bathroom, and Temperance sloshed after it. Parsley the goat bleated at her from under the table, and she picked the animal up and slung her over her shoulders. Parsley's legs quaked, and she released a hot stream of urine down Temperance's chest—cursing, Temperance waded on to check the birds in the bathroom. She dropped the goat in the tub with the chickens. Through the wall she could hear pandemonium breaking loose in the kitchen, but only for a moment. Then a great force struck the house.

Temperance didn't see it, but she learned later that the *Victory* had crashed into the veranda. She went down, they all went down. Parsley's hoof chipped Temperance's tooth and she started bleeding. A jellyfish floated up into the toilet bowl. Some dark shape shadowed past the bathroom window, and when Temperance slid open the glass, she saw that the chicken coop was gone. The entire veranda had been torn loose. It was being dragged off toward the deep end of the fjord, where it was currently strangling the shipwrecking *Victory*. Both were sinking.

Potential salvage floated all around the house. Kayaks, crab catches, earth beds, whatever had been under the tarps strapped to the veranda. Spare parts? Keys? Loose bales of piano wire? Temperance's siblings would need all of those to repair the wrecks they hoped to find. Now all of their supplies, everything they'd already found that summer—it had all been swept away. Eventually it would settle on the fjord's floor and they'd have to dive to recover what they could.

Just then Milda's dough bobbed out from behind the bathtub—if there was one thing Temperance could do, she could catch it.

The bathroom door creaked open. "Everyone okay in here?" Milda said.

Temperance had been five weeks at sea. Her pockets were full of ivory molars, her hair nested. The bathtub was filled with chickens, and both Temperance and the goat were rank with urine. Milda stepped into the room and Temperance held out the ball of dough.

"You're welcome," she said.

AS SOON AS the storm quieted down, Milda and Finley flew to Disillusionment to report the now-stranded girls. Everyone else went up to the attic to wait for the water to slack out of the first floor. They strung their wet clothes from the rafters, and the room quickly took on the look of a neglected alley—girls squatting in corners eating cans of cold beans. Fry jacked open a skylight and climbed out on the roof to reset the solar panels. The attic was a single room running the full length of the house. Diamond-shaped windows cut into the eaves every few feet provided a 360-degree view of the fjord. Temperance watched Captain Crockett staring out one of these windows as the *Victory* slowly sunk.

The ship was the captain's livelihood. Temperance felt sorry about it—clearly the captain was forlorn, and Temperance had felt a similar loss. Viola had been the family's fulcrum, and with her gone, they faced the same reality as Crockett. A vision, a livelihood, slowly sinking before their eyes. Kamikaze Farms had enough stock to fulfill orders for a few more months before they would need to harvest another crop of octopus pips. Those sales would buy them electricity, fuel, and trade goods, but the farm's crops had never paid the full measure of their bills; for that they'd relied upon Viola's charter income. To make matters worse, without their veranda they had no drying lines—the front door now dropped straight down to the ocean.

By sunset the water had calmed enough for the crew to dive to the shipwreck. They lined up in pairs to use the Spahr family's scuba tanks and took turns mermaiding down. When it was her turn, Temperance tried to find her bunk. Through some of the portholes she could see clothes hanging in closets, garb wafting. The ship was still unstable, so Crockett had forbidden them to swim inside. But that didn't stop the girls from reaching for whatever they could grab. Arms and arms. In her rush to greet her family, Temperance hadn't bothered to bring her supplies off the ship with her; her compartment didn't have a window, so whatever was left in there would now be archived for all time. Instead, she made off with an iron pig used as a paperweight on Crockett's desk. Nothing she'd ever really wanted until it was the only thing left to take.

The Crusher returned with eggplants, beet sodas, and a telegraph from Crockett's insurance company with news of a custom ferry that would pick up the girls tomorrow and take them home. Temperance's shipmates took the flurry of this news in stride. The older girls assumed the project of demarcating the attic for the night—they winched extra hammocks and assigned quilts. Plum commandeered the spot closest to Finley, where Temperance usually slept, but Temperance didn't put up a fuss. She was vulnerable to loneliness just like anybody, and she knew that as soon as the clouds cleared, every single person in the house would take off for the hinterlands to which she was not invited. The girls back to their families. Her siblings gone for days at a time, sometimes weeks, leaving her alone with a father who slept all day and wore magnifying goggles to adjust the generator.

When Temperance was little she thought that her siblings were her closest friends, but in the last few months their relationship had taken on a cadence entirely apart from her. They pored over Milda's maps; they gave each other hand slaps. When Temperance tried to see what they were doing they fended her off. *Go play, go play,* they said, and she knew to take her nuisance elsewhere. Temperance had always thought that the natural inclination in most families was to draw close in tragedy, but the opposite seemed to be true of hers—after her mother died, everyone but her seemed to want to get as far away from Jubilation House as possible.

Sometimes Temperance wondered what might have happened if the world had allotted her family a different hand. If her siblings weren't required to shoulder the weight of their family's future, maybe Finley would have romanced Plum, or someone like her, into marriage. Settled his lots and had a family. But if there ever was a turning point for the Spahrs, it was Viola's passing, and after that it no longer seemed like any of them had much choice in their trajectory. Maybe at one time Finley could've had this life or that. Maybe he could've sung tender ballads on the continent or filed for a patent on his brass detector. Instead, he had seemingly doubled down on his peculiar view of the world—he needed a fortune to sustain their life, as had always been true, but now the mantle had settled firmly across his shoulders. And he could see no further.

IN THE MORNING Temperance woke first. The girls were still snoozing logs, so she made her way downstairs. Her father was getting ready to rappel out the kitchen door to survey the trauma done to the stilts. He was shirtless in a testicle-pinching harness. Webbed shoes. He walked backwards down the grizzly bear pole until the water hit his knees. Temperance had spent countless hours fishtailing between the stilts supporting her house, studying the animals' faces. The raven: wings like a collapsed umbrella. Kelp carved hard, all wild fronds. The grizzly bear almost bashful, peering out between claws. Her favorite was the sea lion—fat and happy, he clutched a pair of sockeyes cross-sliced to show veins and hearts, the fish eyes inset with ivory marbles.

Fry unclipped his harness and dropped into the water. Down he dove—as far as his breath would take him. The stilts were seventy-five feet tall, each carved from a single trunk. No one in the family could make it all the way to the fjord's floor in one breath. He bobbed up for air. Dove again. The Banana double-hatch, Milda and Finley's favorite kayak, floated now where the veranda had been only the day before. Temperance pulled the lead line, and when the kayak was close enough she jumped down into the captain's hatch. She paddled to the breeding tanks to check on their herd. When she got to the platform, she roped off the kayak and cranked the lid to the first tank. In the water the pod looked small, an optical illusion. But when they sprang into the light, she immediately saw that a new litter of pips had been born.

The pips were unexpected. Temperance washed her hand through the water as they rose. Limbs reached for the lip of the porthole. A person could search the world for a thousand years but wouldn't find another invertebrate as versatile as a cephalopod. Part dinosaur, part mollusk. Three-hearted and beaked, some of Viola's herd even understood basic math. Temperance's fingers brushed their slimy beaks. The herd's birthing cycles were unpredictable, but when they happened, they hatched ten thousand pips at a time. A tsunami of thumb-size baby octopuses now filled the tank. Feathery suckers braceleted her wrist, pulsing against her skin.

Their mothers, Temperance knew, would have already crawled back to their burrows and begun to decay. Temperance had named each of the hens, had planned to swim with them out to explore the wrecked *Victory*. She'd hoped they would be able to squish inside and fetch the lost trinkets from her bunk. But of course this would be impossible now; the mothers died not long after giving birth.

Without Viola, a tank full of pips would take weeks for the family to dry, salt, prepare. Temperance's mother was the one who spent long nights bruising the meat, thwacking speared pips against the veranda railing. Later Milda and Finley would bring out a ladder and take turns clipping the catches to the drying ropes that had once run from the veranda railing up to the roof's peak. Now all of that infrastructure was underwater.

In the distance, the engine of the ChickenCrusher spluttered. Temperance twisted around to watch the plane float out from where it had been roped against the back side of the house. She knew her siblings had climbed into the cockpit via their father's bedroom window.

Milda and Finley were garbed for flight as usual. Milda spun the wheel. The Crusher rounded the house; it had to float through the fjord's mouth to take off. Temperance didn't know where they were going or how long they'd be gone. Maybe they'd return with a catch, maybe not. She didn't relish their job. She knew her siblings and knew what it was to serve alongside crew members when companionship didn't come easy. Trapped together in a cockpit, they'd still need to do all the basic human activities, only without any privacy. And no matter how bad things got, neither could quit; they needed each other to get home.

Just as Temperance turned back to the tank, Queenie floated up. Queen of Kamikaze Farms mollusks, she was the oldest hen in the tank. Queenie rose out of the water grasping for Temperance, twisting one of her limbs up Temperance's arm, then around her neck. At first the squeeze was comforting; then suddenly Temperance felt desperation in the matriarch's pull. The hen's time was near. Queenie weighed several hundred pounds, and when she dropped her weight, Temperance lost her balance and slid into the water headfirst. She managed briefly to grasp on to the porthole lip to catch a breath. The family kept one of Finley's rudimentary harpoons mounted on the deck beside the porthole for emergencies such as this, and Temperance reached for it as Queenie again pulled. Then up went her legs. Temperance Unamelia Spahr disappeared into the breeding tank in a flash of galoshes.

In the tank everything was flowery and freezing. The herd of pips spun around her, nibbling, as stirred-up grit clouded her vision. Temperance knew somewhere deep below, among crushed-up trout skeletons, rested the graveyard of all their mothers. Soon Queenie would lie among them. Mature, reproduce, die—a short life cycle. Since Viola had died, Milda was the only one who cleared away the corpses, and she hadn't been in the tank in weeks. Now that Temperance was in the water, Queenie latched on to her back and tentacled up under her shirt. The matriarch secured herself around Temperance like an external rib cage. Temperance tried to buck free, but she couldn't, and when she tried to kick to the surface, she couldn't do that either.

The new pips pressured her from all sides, grabbing, sucking, arms corkscrewing. She'd managed to grab the harpoon and she jabbed it out in front of her now, but this didn't seem to do much good. She could feel a thousand mouths scouring arcs of dead epidermis from under her nails. The herd, this new herd, tasted her. Their beaks grated away her skin and within moments she was both flayed and without fear. Each new litter of pips had likely done this with her mother, Temperance realized—they had imprinted themselves on her. That was why their farm's herds had always been so loyal to her, so eager to return home as long as she was there. Her mother had been more than their caretaker; in their own way, they had loved her.

All at once Queenie released her. Temperance floated up toward the light. If she'd had skin that morning, it was gone now, replaced by a thousand nervy kisses that would eventually bruise into a fantastic nebula. Scars to last a lifetime.

Moose

Singing Spruce Forest
June, first homestead expedition

At first, life on the trail was all nut feasts and merriment, fortes trilling at odd hours. The dogs shook free their winter coats, plushing the ground underfoot with fur. Rocket had mapped the expedition's four-month journey north along an old-school trapper route, a trail that wound through the Singing Spruce Forest before reaching Arctic City. Just past the capital they'd ford the Kamikaze River, and from there the families would stake homesteads across the permafrost. The trail's ruts were well traversed, deep and crusty from years of trapper use. Spruce trees rose three, four hundred feet into the air on either side, branches so dense that they nearly blocked out the glory of the Lord.

Nearly, but never entirely. Sunlight came dappling through the boughs sixteen, twenty hours a day, and steadily increased in duration. As the weeks wore on it only grew worse. Moose and his mother spent a great deal of time taking preventative measures: creaming their foreheads with sunblock, tightening their hats. They were fair-complexioned, and this made them susceptible. Unlucky, Rocket said, because in the territory the summer sun was a devil none escaped.

According to Moose's best guess, their guide was in his early fifties. The only child of a trapper and a Native woman, Rocket had been raised among the tribes that owned most of the territory's land. The ruts their sleds followed cut through Native land on all sides. An easement, Rocket called it—otherwise they'd never have been able to access the homesteader plots along the Glacial Front. To Moose's eye, Rocket was enviably resourceful, always knowing which way to piss out of the wind. He wore his hair in a wild grease, braided along the sides, and carried the salty whiff of Arctic candy—dried knots of seaweed, a taste requiring a nuanced palate—which he tossed freely to the children. Moose fed his portion to the dogs, who licked his fingers clean for the salt. Rocket ran a fleet-footed balsam sled at the front of the train and from there did his best to motivate everyone else onward. In the mornings he was always snapping his whip and whistling for compliance. And every afternoon, he broke off-trail alone to scan the terrain ahead.

"Where do you think he goes?" Una asked, cracking eggs for soda bread, yolk dripping down her fist. "I thought we had a map."

"I'm sure he's just double-checking the route," Arthur said.

"Because if this trail doesn't work there's another one?"

"Better to know the problems before we get there, Una-bird."

Into the bowl: flour, handful of grain, buttermilk.

"Somebody has to check that we actually are where we think we are," Arthur said.

Una punched her fists into the dough. "Sounds a lot like being lost." Gently, Arthur took the bowl from her. He pulled off biscuit-size blobs and dropped them with a sizzle onto the grate over the fire. "It's a journey," he said. "There's a difference."

Their journey had a strict schedule. If they were still on the trail when the first snows fell in September, they wouldn't survive the winter. So when they started out each morning, Arthur captained their sled in a dead sprint, hupping the dog team and wiping sweat from his eyes. In the early days he was a figure of celebrity owing to the heroics of his descent with the Napoleon. Whenever the train broke for rest some new person was always calling out, "Look, there goes Muscles! Way to face the music, Bloomer!" To look at Arthur you wouldn't think him capable of such a display of physicality, and that only made the story spread faster. Moose's stepfather was tall, toothy; he wore jodhpurs and copper-rimmed glasses with a magnifying lens that could be lowered to examine miniature objects. Overnight Arthur had blazed so high in the train's esteem that he was readily taken in by the rest of the men, who spent their evenings together worrying about whether they'd brought enough supplies.

Each family on the expedition had received a Homesteaders' Survival Checklist, and they had all flurried to purchase their goods in bulk. Salted meats, tents, leather chaps, sleep blinders, buckets of sunblock. There was no telling what awaited them. No telling, except for the known dangers: bears, sunstroke, broken legs, river crossings. In addition to the reference tomes his own family had packed, Thornton Huntmoon had managed to smuggle along several issues of his favorite serial, *Old Testament Tykes*. Already Moose had gotten good use out of the borrowed books, having spent a great deal of time on the ship fighting seasickness. He found himself naturally attuned to the biblical children, wandering for years in the desert.

On the ship Moose's family—the three of them meeting the bare requirements for a unit—had been ushered to a plank-walled cabin. Una, hair sweated at the temples from the malaise of a fledgling pregnancy, had immediately dossed herself down on the mattress. She did not budge for the remainder of the journey. "Please, Moose," she would say, arm crooked over her eyes whenever he pestered her about eating. "I cannot, I just cannot."

Left to their own devices, Moose and Arthur had wandered the decks. They showed up to the mess at mealtime. When one of the sailors sky-fished a flock of pigeons, they ate their squab and grits along with the rest of the ship, no complaints. From what Moose could muster at these gatherings, he didn't possess much in common with his shipmates, or even the other families aboard—at least that was how it appeared at the outset. They were all of disparate creed, virtue, and ambition. Looking around the train now—gums bleeding, elbows patched—he had to admit that they did not present themselves as the most upstanding of citizenry.

Every family had packed ridiculous items out of sentimentality. Oak bureaus, sets of rose china. These luxuries weren't technically against the rules, but they were discouraged. Didn't they already have enough to worry about? Moose's mother had brought her sheaf of cross-stitches, stripped of their hoops and pressed flat between the pages of a family hymnal. But she'd also packed her wedding dress, a crystal decanter, and a squat stove known as a "RabbitBurner" that cost more than the Napoleon. "What if we get there and need something we don't have?" she had said. "Better to bring it and not need it than not to bring it and need it later." At the time this had seemed reasonable to Moose, but now that they were on the trail he was beginning to ascertain the complications of this plan.

When Arthur wasn't yucking it up with his new gentleman friends, he spent the evenings around their fire reading up on homestead economics. There was no cap to his ambitions. Would 160 acres really be enough? Or should they bid for two sections? What troubled Arthur was that nobody had a realistic concept of the topography—there were supposed to be lakes, and a river, but would they be close to a water source? Would the plots be fairly adjudicated? Arthur didn't want to be assigned a permadesert or a plot half billy-goated up a mountain.

Caretaking the pianos kept everyone busy. One hundred and fifty-seven pianos for 157 families. Seesawing their way through the Panhandle Islands, the homesteaders had tended these fortes, whispering promises about the leisure and honey they'd find once they were settled. Though the Napoleon had proven an all right choice, with the distance of time Moose could now admit that it had not been his first preference. In the carpenter's studio, he'd gravitated initially toward a green-oiled hopper. Knee-high, light, with a phonograph nailed to the lid.

"Very economical." The carpenter had watery gray eyes and a voice like a wasp. "The sound on this one is good for half a mile."

"Looks like it'd break down in about two days," said Arthur.

"I assure you the bones are very sturdy."

"We're looking for something with more heft."

The carpenter adjusted his tie and flourished a hand toward a shape tucked into a back corner. He pulled a cord and a drape rose up off a walnut-skinned instrument. The body of the piano domed skyward, and inside Moose spotted hammers made of gold smelted into the shape of tulips. This would be a pricey surcharge, Moose knew. Drawing a key from his pocket, the carpenter applied the tines to a string and there ensued a faint buzz they could all feel behind their tonsils. "Holds a tune year-round," he said. "Rain or shine."

"Dampers?" said Arthur.

"Hare."

"I expect those hammers are real gold. That must add to the cost."

"Well worth it considering where you're going. You'll always have the gold to sell if you get in a pinch."

Una nestled herself on the bench. She stroked the keys. When she began to play, Moose stepped back to get a full gander at the prospect. The Napoleon was three-legged, which would make it prone to falling out of balance. There was definitely an argument to be made for a more compact model, one that wasn't so damnably heavy, but it was tough to mount a strong opposition to a thing of beauty, which is what she was.

"How's it sound?" he asked his mother.

"Like a real peach," said Una.

The Napoleon was a bit of a bear, that was for sure, but in situations like that you had to rely on your gut, and it didn't take a scientist to see that Arthur was mulling, *Should we take this piano?* and his mother was already winking toward him, *Yes.* They had settled on this, their monstrous butterfly—a second later they'd purchased her, and just like that she was pinioned with all of the Bloomer family's hopes.

FOR THE NEXT several weeks their sleds cruised through the Singing Spruce Forest at a steady clip. They remained on schedule, even a little ahead of it, as the world buzzed with what everyone called the Big Slow Ones: mosquitoes as large as radishes, with probes that could bite through leather. At night they weighted the edges of the tents with rocks to sleep in peace. During the day their best defense was to heed Rocket's advice: "Run through the summer, sleep through the winter."

Like anything, this was easier said than accomplished. Moose's new boots were green-broke; blisters quickly flowered. And he was still recovering from the bright nebula of bruises splayed across his thighs where the Napoleon had landed on him, though he kept this injury to himself. By the end of each day his left hip ached something awful.

Because of his bruises Moose traveled at a slower pace than the adults. For cover he fell back to walk with the gang of little tykes. Eight- and nine-year-olds, they weren't good for much besides beating off a porcupine, but as a group they were keen for Moose's approval. Thornton typically chose to hang back with him, and this gave the tykes even more opportunities to pester the boys for attention. They covered more ground than just about anybody else, having been tasked with collecting the twigs that the trailbreakers—the able-bodied young adults who cleared debris off the tracks ahead of Rocket's sled—left behind. The twigs were bundled into sets of kindling. One for each sled. Moose preferred this work to his other chores, as the slow pace gave his hip a rest and it was in all ways superior to walking alongside Arthur, who stank like a poached skunk and was always quizzing him on boreal arithmetic. *What's the last day to plant beans? How many cuts does it take to gut a trout?*

Moose's mind had never pleasured itself with numbers. He understood the need for them and Arthur's trunk of reference books, but looking around at the land's evidence of bounty, he wasn't worried about production. Wild grasses swished against the sleds' bellies. A thin skein of ice covered the Kamikaze River, but as soon as it broke, the trout would come spawning. Rocket had already told Moose that he was headed to his family's trout camp after their expedition finished. Tribes held rights to the riverbanks, and each summer they built temporary smoke tents and gutting tables to catch a year's worth of fish.

Leftover trout from the camps got traded in Arctic City. "Right on the chapel floor," Rocket had explained. Moose could scarcely imagine the mayhem of a fish market in the Lord's tenement: pews stacked with salted fillets, the eye of God shining down through a window of stained glass. He wouldn't mind seeing such a consternation of humanity himself—it might even herald him fondly back to memories of hocking tomatoes with his mother. *Cherokee. Beefsteak. Red Sally.* He was quick about sacking up the fruits, his mother had always commented on that; he could gauge weight in the palm of his hand. Those numbers were the only ones that had ever come natural to him—the weight of value, what he'd been given and what he then owed.

AFTER THE SLEDS were firmly staked at the end of the day, Mama Mayflower gathered the little children unto her to impart lessons. She was currently chalking their way through the constellations and Moose enjoyed gaining knowledge that Arthur did not yet possess. *Orion,* he'd practice by the fire as his stepfather scrubbed char off the cooking grate. *Ursa Minor.* Mama Mayflower promised that one day there'd be an Arctic City schoolhouse, a proper schoolhouse, where they could all learn algebra and French. But the farther they got from Disillusionment Bay, the more ridiculous this vision began to sound to Moose's ears. The model of schooling they'd left behind on the continent would not serve them up here. What they needed now was practical knowledge. How to spade a garden. How to track a deer. How to sight a rifle. How to caulk a smokehouse. How to make yourself appear stronger than you were.

Before arriving in Disillusionment Bay, Moose had had a picture in his head—no doubt perpetuated by poets, those hoodwinkers—that spring in the Territory of the Arctic would be all lowing yaks and docility. But in reality spring was a violent opera storming across the landscape, everything itching off winter coats and tearing through skin. Blueberry bushes popped with white flowers. Wild beets flowered before producing fist-size tubers. The train created a great fracas of noise with their herd of chickens flocking through the forest, egged on by the tykes switching the birds' legs to keep them in motion. Many of the sleds were eighteen feet long, whalebone slats loaded to the hilt with casked molasses, peanuts, seeds, salt pork, flour, and cast iron. They glided through the forest in a raucous parade unseen since the aftermath of Noah's great flood: dogs pulling impatiently at the harness, everything loosing its guts wherever it wanted now that they were all on dry land.

"I thought this was supposed to be a civilized trail," Thornton said one night as he and Moose headed back to camp after hunting hares. They'd had no luck, though Rocket had told them that nests proliferated in this territory. It seemed that the animals were still too busy twitterpating one another to fall for the boys' snares. "But so far it's all just mud and babies crying. I didn't come all this way just to have the same life I had back home," he said.

Over the course of their voyage Thornton had slowly yarned out his life story. His natal family ran a sugar beet farm: "Sounds sweet but it's not." He'd been birthed the youngest of seven boys, which he contended was about the cruelest blow fate could have dealt him. To make matters worse, he was always getting bucked off a horse or snapping an ulna, costing his parents their sweat-earned money in doctor's fees. When his aunt and uncle rode into town with their plans of missionarying to the population up north, his mother had wagged a broom in his direction and said, "I guess you better take that one with you." Thornton was still pretty much agog with shock that he'd been excommunicated from his family so easily. He resented that his aunt and uncle furnished him with a list of chores every day and ultimately felt he was an abductee to their cause. Moose concurred with his own sympathy, both of them being victims in the same cogs of progress.

"It is civilized. There's tracks," said Moose.

"I mean *civilized* civilized. Aren't there supposed to be trade posts? Or people? We haven't seen anybody so far. Where are all the Natives, even?"

"Maybe they don't know we're here."

"Oh please," said Thornton. "Have you heard us?"

It did strike Moose as strange that the forest was so unpopulated. Who owned all this land and what was their motivation for letting it lie fallow? When Moose had put his premonition to what civilization in the territory might look like, he'd pictured parceled lots, log cabins. Clear-cut fields in which to grow beans; sheltered all these years, the forest floor would be rich in loam. Nothing about what they'd seen thus far had the reek of civilization.

Back at camp Moose found his mother dressing a hare that Rocket had caught for them. With one hand cupping the back of the skull, she used the other to whipstitch the ears together. Unamelia scrubbed a lard lather over the skin, sliding her fingers into the hare's armpits. Then she rested the body in a large cast-iron pot and levered it over the fire. Even flayed naked, the hare was the largest Moose had ever seen—their family could eat on it for days. He didn't know if Thornton would consider this civilized dining, knowing that once the hare was ready, the Bloomers would eat with their fingers, grease dripping down their arms. But it was certainly easy to see how one could partake of an abundant life in the territory, a life that in the end might even turn out to be superior to the one they'd left behind.

"I could get used to this," Arthur said.

And if you'd heard the way Moose's stepfather had waxed on about the properties of their new home that night, hat tipped back, you would have been enchanted by the future too. They'd have over an acre of squash tripods, and that was just for starters. An orchard with ground mulched in rose hips. Off to one side of the homestead there would be a duck wattle, a rack for clothes drying, a smoker big enough to sleep inside. In the foreground the cabin, of course. The foundation would be fashioned of river stones and there would be a mud chimney; a glass window at Una's insistence; a loft for Moose's privacy. At the rate they were going, Arthur estimated they'd have the homestead's deed in hand early—by the end of August! Their time line was crucial. When Moose's new sibling arrived in late September, they needed to be perfectly primed to burrow down for winter. A few months napping under quilts, munching preserved carrots, and they'd be ready to emerge in the spring—rejuvenated! A family forever welded together. The tulips a-blooming, the sheep a-lambing, all four of them gathered around the Napoleon to sing songs of merry glory.

Moose wiped his greasy hands on his pants. "But nobody's even using all of this land out here—it's just trees," he said. "There's lots of places we could settle right now."

"We didn't come all this way just to live on borrowed soil."

"We could make it ours."

Arthur picked his teeth. "I didn't set the laws."

Moose looked to his mother—she grew larger by the day. There was a looming sense to her presence. Many of the other women on the trail spent their days trapping chipmunks or digging tubers, but with a baby lodged between her hips, Una couldn't keep up. She walked the tracks behind the last sled with the gang of grandparents. The old people were gouty, with intestines that had to be tended like moody stoves, and Una was always brewing them digestive teas. Every day after lunch she spread quilts over the ground and they all sacked out for a short rest. All limbs and lambswool curls, they napped for about an hour while the train rustled onward. This rest—and their unnaturally slow pace—meant they arrived at camp after the last sled.

One night Una hadn't turned up by dinnertime. Arthur sent Moose to backtrack the trail in search of her while he bedded down the dogs. Moose found her half a mile from the last sled, leaned up against a tree. Her hair had come unwound and she had high spots of color on her cheeks. She was breathing fast, trachea full of wind.

He knelt beside her. "Are you okay?" he asked, putting a hand to her forehead; no fever. He started to reach for his hip flask of water to offer her a drink, but she caught his hand and held it atop her belly. Moose felt his little brother writhing. Was that normal? How would he know? "Should I get the sled?" he asked.

Una shook her head, hair falling loose from her braids. She did not reach up to brush it back. This was uncharacteristic—since Moose was a young boy she'd oiled his hair every night, as well as her own; they might've been poor, but they'd never been disheveled. "I'm fine," she said.

"You don't look fine."

"I just needed to rest a minute."

The train was scheduled to arrive at the Glacial Front shortly before Una's due date in September. In the meantime her belly would only grow larger, perhaps slowing her even more. Moose worried about their family being left behind. They couldn't survive the winter alone. Besides which, neither he nor Arthur had ever delivered a baby—it didn't seem like the middle of the forest, alone, was an ideal locale to try their luck. "Can you walk?" he asked.

Una squeezed his hand. "Of course I can walk."

Moose helped her to her feet. On the way back to camp he could tell she was in pain, but she tried to hide it by querying him about every bit of flora he'd spotted that day. As he talked, she concentrated on her breaths. Sometimes he caught her looking at him in a certain way and he suspected she was wondering how in the hell she'd ended up in this same situation again. Pregnant, again. Circumstances again precarious, though this time her pregnancy was the ballast rooting her to Arthur and his uncertain dreams.

"You should ride if you're getting tired, Una-bird," Arthur said back at camp, dishing her a plate. "You don't have to walk every single step."

Una waved off the dinner plate and instead sat on the sled runner, taking small sips of water. When her flask was empty she screwed on the lid, then pounded it with the flat of her palm so hard Moose knew it would be difficult to remove. "It's too much for the dogs," she said.

"A couple more pounds is nothing!"

Una rubbed her belly. "You know it's more than that."

As Moose forked up dinner he ruminated on his regrettable lack of midwifery skills. Did his mother need medicine, counsel, or rest? How could a boy such as himself tell? The train did have a midwife and a barber-surgeon who pulled teeth and cut hair, but obviously no hospital beds or nurses who could tend those who needed extra care. He'd seen, once, a horse give birth to a breech colt. The mare thrashed, beating her hooves against the barn door, tail slicked with bloody placenta. New lives did not always come easily into the world, he'd gleaned, and he feared that if he pressured his mother further, she might also ascertain his own need to ride the sled. Moose had spoken to no one of his injury, though in private he allowed himself a limp to take pressure off his hip. By the end of each day nerves shot pain down his leg, again and again, and he had to lean against trees for support. But he hoped that if both he and his mother continued to exercise properly and prioritize their nutrition, they would in time heal. All they could do now was muscle through.

TYPICALLY AT NIGHT, after Thornton's aunt and uncle had fallen asleep, Moose's friend would filch a bottle of communion wine, fetch him, and the pair would scale up into what they called the arboretum. They picked a branch and sat, legs kicking, deep into the hot, white nights. Cool and leafy, pure in atmosphere—everything loftier than life on the ground. As they shared swigs from the bottle, Thornton tied ribbons in the tree branches. Accented with velvet bows he'd stolen from Pumpkin's trunk. "Don't want to forget where we've been," he said.

From somewhere one of them would produce a clam-and-cheese sandwich, which they would halve, giving one unto the other. As they chewed the snack, Moose often had the sentiment that things weren't shaping together precisely as either of them had hoped. This festered in him as they took turns deducing the constellations using Thornton's telescope. His friend narrated the mythological stories behind the rotation of the planets—how they were smack in the hip of the aurora's boudoir, a milky swirl signposted by Lyre and Herculean characters. "Trouble on all sides," Thornton said, and Moose could see it. However, the stars gave no premonition of what came next, no celestial clues about the best route onward aside from the blinking fog lantern of the North Star. Moose didn't even find this particularly useful as he already had a pocket compass with the same ability. And it was a good thing too, because as the summer solstice neared, the constellations became distant memories. The moon grew fainter and fainter and then one night, as though a magician had swept a cape across the sky, it simply disappeared.

Finley

Archipelago of Lost Saints
The day after the Victory *sinks*

One of the most famous relics in the Territory of the Arctic was first captured by Finley Spahr, swimmer and brother, in the summer of his fifteenth year on the planet Earth. Here begins his story.

The day Finley and Milda flew to the trading post on Disillusionment Bay to report Crockett's crew of stranded girls, they heard news of a potential score half a day's flight south. Another hunter was complaining about how thousands of walruses had taken over the Archipelago of Lost Saints: "They got nowhere else to beach up. You won't believe what they're hauling out of the sea with them."

"Why don't you go down and get what they've got yourself?" Finley said.

"I'm not fighting a walrus," said the hunter.

The following morning, Milda and Finley flew the Crusher south to see for themselves. Finley tried to keep the vibe in the cockpit light; he chirped along to the radio. Two more months of clean weather, that was it, before the water'd be too cold to dive. He held tight to the sense that they were flying on the edge of the history books—they might not have found the Napoleon, but no other team had either. And at least they had the advantage of lineage, that zippy polyphony connecting them back to their own history.

Finley had never trawled the Archipelago of Lost Saints with his mother. The area was so remote, cut of witching black rock, it had long been marked on maps: *land, inhospitable.* The islands were edged in a narrow powder of sand; no soil for crops. It wasn't a place any decent person would settle their head if they could help it.

For most of Finley's life, herds of walruses in the territory had found respite on bergs in the open water between the archipelago and the Wild Beard Fjords. They beached out on the floes between diving trips. But as the ice alternately froze harder and melted faster each year they'd been forced to congregate on land. Thousands of animals now packed the narrow beaches. The conditions were cramped, indecent. The herd was not at all quiet about their distress. Finley could hear the cacophony of their barks long before the islands even came into view—males jockeying for position, new mothers a milk buffet for their calves. Though he'd never heard of a human speared by a tusk purely out of spite, the world was clearly operating in a strange new order: the walruses had lost their home and this had seemingly instilled in them a feral disposition. How could there possibly be enough food in the area to sustain all of these animals? Soon Finley would be out there diving alongside them, and he wished he could whistle for Abraham Lincoln to serve as his bodyguard.

At the sound of the Crusher skimming low over the beach, a troop of pups rose from the sand and bounded off into the break. "Are you sure we should be diving down there?" Milda said. "Looks like trouble."

"I know how to swim," said Finley.

"Maybe we should wait for the herd to leave."

"You want to camp here for a month?"

Taking one hand from the wheel, Milda unlidded their thermos of coffee and slugged a shot. "You really think anything's washed this far down?"

As the Crusher buzzed over the sand, more walruses rose and flippered toward the safety of the water. The plane U-turned and for a moment Finley's window framed a pair of pups surfacing in the break. They had something clamped in their jaws. "Bingo," he said, pulling out the binoculars. "They've got something."

"All I see are tusks."

Finley adjusted the binoculars. "Looks like Walden hammers."

"How can you tell?"

"They've got a shape."

"Are they worth anything?" she asked.

"Depends how many we get."

Walden hammers—copper, now aged chalky green—were long and hook-nosed. Finley had seen one in person only once before, when he and his mother had camped on a plateau in the Resurrection Mountains. There was a well-trodden campsite on a plateau with a switchbacking trail down to Arctic City. Teams flew in from all over to land planes, sprout tents, and brag around the campfire. "It was a terrible, black current, the kind that don't care if you've got any plans for the rest of your life," the hunters would say. Happy from Disillusionment Trade Post periodically flew supplies up there, which he sold out of the back of a plane at marked-up prices. Finley and his mother never bought anything, though his stomach grumbled to see the grill trotted out. The aroma of caribou kebabs seasoned and wafting. He knew better than to pester his mother for coins; every dollar they made selling lost artifacts went toward fueling the tank for their next mission. They could no more spring for hot kebabs than Finley could magic up the location of the Napoleon. As he ate his dinner cold from a jar, he distracted himself by chatting with Happy and helping the elderly trade post owner load the wares he'd accepted as barters. This was how Finley had come to see a Walden hammer packed in sawdust. Happy claimed it would fetch a high price from a restorationist.

The territory was replete with spare parts. Many homesteaders had hauled with them what would be considered an absurd quantity of replacement keys, hammers, spools of wire. They brought anything they believed might be needed to repair their instruments over the next several generations. Slowly, as train upon train wound through the Singing Spruce Forest, these spare parts had been abandoned in bulk. Now many of these parts were relatively easy to scavenge.

The Crusher landed and Finley spent the first day in the Archipelago of Lost Saints collecting as many specimens as he could. Diving the shelf for these fossils was brutal work. The surf had a mind to suck him all the way down to where the bones of whales rested on the seafloor. Meanwhile, walruses kept slinking into the water for food, so as he rode out the break, the huge creatures somersaulted all around, giant asteroids hunting for a place to crash. Milda kept watch sitting on the hood of the Crusher. The plane floated just offshore. She held Finley's harpoon gun braced across her knees. By dinnertime she was sun-scorched and Finley had recovered a bouquet of five hammers.

"It's too dark to fly," Milda said as they climbed back into the cockpit. "We'll have to sleep here tonight."

"We can't go home yet anyway. I've got another day of diving, maybe two."

"Is there really that much down there?"

The Walden hammers had been out in plain sight, resting atop the sand. No digging. Finley hadn't even needed his detector. It was possible, then, that the body to which they belonged might be below, slowly molting parts. "Could be."

That night they slept in the plane, always uncomfortable, even in their adolescence. They were both of them now too tall to stretch flat in the back. They ate a supper of dried squid and huckleberries and dozed off twisted in their life belts, so close to the dash that Finley's feet kept flicking on the radio. In the morning they were snappish and dehydrated, agreeing only on the fact that they needed to decamp to actual land. Again Milda floated the idea of packing it all in and flying home—Soup! Pillows! Temperance!—but Finley knew that if they left now, she'd never bring him back. He didn't know how many expeditions he could convince Milda to fly, nor how much fuel they'd be able to afford if they didn't find anything. Strike while the iron was hot, as the proverb went, and double that with a skeptical sister.

The second day yielded no new artifacts. Dejected, that night Finley chose for them a campsite as far up the rocks as possible. There was a large ledge blocked off by a fallen boulder. It would keep them safe from the barking scuffles below. Finley lit a smoking fire and broke a pair of eggs into the skillet. Warmed by the thought of a dry shirt and hot food, he was getting ready to flip the eggs when he heard the sound of flippers clapping against rock. He peered around the boulder and there, maybe ten feet away, a bull walrus rubbed his tusks against the rock with the relish of a chef sharpening knives. He gazed at Finley, no doubt appraising him into butcher cuts, then opened his jaw to the sky and roared. Finley backed away. Even by walrus standards, the bull was well girthed—he'd clearly endured the barbs of time. One of his flippers had the raw, meaty look of flesh run through a prop. The bull had them cornered—trapped on a rock ledge, they had nowhere to go but down.

Finley looked around for his harpoon gun. He cursed himself for leaving it in the plane even though he knew that killing a walrus was a sin that would rack up a hefty fine. A sin, but look at those tusks. Strong enough to chop ice, they'd slide neatly into a human's intercostal space. Finley drew the diving knife he kept in his belt. The bull butted its head against the boulder. What could he want? To scare them? Perhaps this fellow had laid claim to this strip of beach and needed to show dominance. Finley had trespassed into the bull's realm. He was still trying to ascertain the best way out of this mess when a mass came whizzing by his head. Finley turned around to find Milda in warrior stance, volcanic rubble clutched in each hand. She had transformed into a wild sight—their mother's flyboy silk shirt torn at the collar, her hair a crown of braids.

She cocked her arm. "Duck," she ordered.

The first rock struck the bull in the chest. He bellowed. The second welted him on the shoulder and he began to writhe, no doubt trying to figure out how to extricate himself from his predicament. Flippers beat against the boulder. Finley looked around for another implement with which to defend himself, but before he had a chance to get his hands on anything, his ears were pierced with such a reverberation that he had to clamp his hands over them. He swiveled around to see Milda whacking the skillet against the rock that constituted the back wall of their makeshift campsite. The resonance was like a church bell sounding all across the island. For a moment the noise seemed to befuddle the bull. Milda struck the skillet again and this time the herd on the beach looked up all at once, hundreds of wattled necks twisting in unison.

"Get down!" she said.

Finley dropped to his belly just in time for her to loose the frying pan. It went flying over his head, over the top of the boulder, piping hot and leaking eggs. And so went dinner. He peered around the rock in time to watch the pan hit the walrus on the skull. It bounced down the rocks—flip, turn, twist—before landing facedown in the sand. Shaking, the bull began maneuvering backwards to return to the beach. It had taken some enthusiastic gymnastics for him to climb this far up their makeshift trail and now there was no grace to his retreat.

Finley turned to face his sister. "What just happened?"

Milda didn't answer. She was busy digging through their supply sack in search of alternative food. After a minute she rocked back on her heels, holding up the tins of smoked oysters they'd been saving for a celebratory meal. Considering what they'd just gone through, Finley consented with a nod. She opened a tin, sniffed.

"How did you know he wouldn't charge up here?" he said.

"I didn't."

This gave Finley something to think over. While Milda fried the oysters he watched the herd settle down for sleep below on the beach. Unlike the octopuses they raised on the farm, walrus mothers did not die as soon as they gave birth. They nursed their pups. They guarded them. Finley could not help but see the contrast to his own life, for after the ice had broken that spring, the Spahr family had properly buried Viola at sea. They'd towed her in the crab cage out to the Arctic Reef. Fry, with Temperance in his lap, paddled his own kayak. On his back he'd strapped a basket of chrysanthemum buds and they tossed these out over the water as Fry said a prayer. It was Finley who finally loosed the knot holding the cage to the front of the Banana. He coiled the rope in his lap. "Let her go, son," Fry said gently. "It's time." Finley knew it was irrational, but in that moment he wasn't sure if he could watch the cage sink without jumping into the water to rescue her. It no longer seemed peaceful to think of his mother drifting through hypothermic waters, unmoored forever from her family; his grip tightened on the rope. Though Milda couldn't see his face from the back hatch, his sister must have sensed his reluctance because she unzipped her spray skirt and crawled over the deck between them. He felt her hand atop his, prying loose his fingers, hot breath in his ear. "Together, then," she said.

After that, Milda had begun cutting his sandwiches into appropriate quarters and folding his underpants, clearly presuming herself in the role of caretaker, capital C. Her charges seemed to be both himself and Temperance, maybe their father too. It was clear she took the post seriously. Their kitchen smelled anew of yeast and vinegar, and Milda's greatest concerns seemed to be: (1) Temperance forgetting all about their mother, and (2) Finley rowing off and disappearing. He wouldn't call either of those concerns unnecessary.

Same as every other year, Finley's work ethic had exploded as soon as the ice broke. All around him he saw a farm in decline and knew he had to get to work. The kids had a long list of chores—feeding chickens, milking the goat, securing the octopus herd in their pen every night. Keeping the farm running without their mother was challenging but not impossible, however paltry the income from selling their crops. Still, it would never be enough. So for weeks Finley rose with the sun to dive the nearby fjords, returning home with loose keys and strings of piano wire that he piled on the veranda and covered in tarps. Spare parts wouldn't make him a fortune, but he knew he'd need them to repair any wreck he might find. Plus, Finley had long subscribed to the belief that if he was young and able, there was no excuse for not hunting as much as he could of what the world currently valued.

In the days of his great-great-great-great-grandfather Moose, this had meant hauling a sled loaded with a pianoforte across the permafrost to a new home on deeded land. To Finley's eyes neither of his parents had ever seemed to manifest such deep ambition. His father was content to tend house; his mother had flown just enough charters to keep the family in fresh wet suits. Finley could not imagine raising his own family with such a paucity of resources. Although Milda had good intentions, she did not seem particularly suited to accumulating wealth either, certainly not the level the family would need even to hold on to their current lifestyle.

Finley estimated that for the family to be sustainable they'd need enough to purchase the farm's mortgage outright, upgrade the plane, and expand the breeding tanks. He had no plans to live an adult life knocked around in the same painful, austere way as his parents, and he knew the responsibility for lifting them out of their recession—the simple life grooved for the Spahr children—lay with him. Living comfortably in his chosen geography, that had long been his primary aim. He imagined his own family one day festooning Jubilation House with Christmas hops, his own little tyke learning to paddle the Banana. Greed had never been part of his nature, but still he hoped to afford what other families had long ago achieved in terms of the conveniences of modern life: sanitation and heating ducts, coffee, dental work, telescopes, beehives.

Jubilation House was too far from land for bees to venture, so all through his childhood it had fallen to Finley to hand-pollinate the crops sprouting up in the earth beds on the veranda. Little green shoots. Day or night he was out there with an old toothbrush crusting pollen from one bud to another. This had been just another item in a long list of examples of how life in the fjords required one more step of work than it did elsewhere. Finley didn't mind, but he had no desire to continue living an austere lifestyle forever. Himself scowling at the ledger, his future wife bartering for discounts at Disillusionment Trade Post.

Finley sat awake long after his sister curled up in her sleeping bag, taking the time to work everything over in his mind. What it came down to was that when he'd first convinced Milda to start flying he'd conceived of her primarily as a pilot, forgetting that she was a sister first, and that one state did not cancel out the other. Rather, the combination complicated the terms of their partnership so that she was at once the person responsible for keeping him safe and the person responsible for flying him toward potential danger. Finley couldn't imagine Milda had an easy feeling about this, but deduction solved, he went to sleep.

He awoke early. Left in the supply bag they had a tin of sardines and half a thermos of coffee, so he hiked down to a spit of sand on the far side of the island. Most of the herd sun-napped in the dawning heat. If you didn't know any better, you'd think them a pretty picture: a mass of overlapping limbs and incisors. Pups snuggled to their mothers' bosoms. Finley hit the beach, waded up to his ankles, and picked a bundle of sea beans. On the way back up he found a terrace cut into the rock with just enough soil to support a few radishes and half a dozen alpine strawberries. He picked them and back on the ledge cut everything into a salad. When Milda woke up he passed her a bowl. He could see his sister taking in all the pieces individually, thinking this was an odd combination. He waited for her to proclaim, *Yuck, gross, Finley, why would you ever put these strange things together?* But she just smiled, and as God was his witness, she ate her entire serving. When she finished she held out her bowl. "Is there more?"

And he was sad to say, "Nope, that's it."

For the rest of the day, whenever he thought of her holding out that bowl, he was warmed by the idea that he'd sort of leveled the score in terms of their usefulness on scouting trips. It wasn't until they were back in the plane, Walden hammers stowed safely in the hatch, that he realized this new warmth he felt toward his sister was actually the seed of true partnership taking root. They'd been siblings all their lives but had always behaved like a set of kinetic moons orbiting each other in a lax kind of synchronization. Ceremonially linked though wholly blind to their influence on each other's lunar landscape. But that trip, something began to shift between them. An imperceptible realignment invisible to all on the outside. If you have siblings perhaps you already know this: a moon working alone waxes and wanes and inflicts a mild amount of gravitational force. But a pair of moons with a singular vision—they can disrupt the planetary alignment. They can send the tides swirling in the opposite direction.

. . .

BACK IN THE Wild Beard Fjords, Finley and Milda returned from their hunting expedition to find a FOR SALE BY OWNER sign on Jubilation House's roof. The first thing Finley did was climb up and tear it down. He couldn't fathom who would want to buy the farm in its dilapidated state anyway: overplowed sea beds, plumbing running off hauled water. That was how any real estate agent would describe it, though to Finley the house where he'd grown up would always be charming.

There was the way the mail plane loosed their correspondence on an inflatable raft that he had to swim after and tow home. Or how in the winter Parsley hoofcocked across the ice and they'd skate after her, scarves flapping. And now he had the memory of all those evenings last spring facing the ocean while his mother bobbed off the dock, thinking, *Well, Mama, sure looks like another fine day for the human race.* He'd chipped a hole in the ice around Viola's crab cage, both so he could talk to her and so Abraham Lincoln could leap onto the dock beside him. As he scratched the lion's ears he said things like, *Yeah, buddy, I know, I miss her too.* He didn't know what he'd do now if his father sold the place out from under him.

When Finley came down the attic ladder he found his family seated around the inside table. Fry Spahr wore his best accounting spectacles. As Finley walked over, Fry tried to shield the ledger with his elbow, but Finley still noted a vast column stamped "out of stock." The farm's margins were razor-thin even in good years.

Fry wore a relic of a T-shirt, vintage Kamikaze Farms, one sleeve held on by a fishhook. It was from the year Milda was a baby, Finley no more than a twinkle at the bottom of an ale glass. Closing the ledger, Fry waved a letter marked with handwriting Finley did not recognize. Postmark the color of violets. "I need to talk to you kids about something," their father said.

What Fry needed to talk about was his sister, Flora, imploring their family to move south to the continent. She called them wayward. If Viola wasn't there to pilot, she wrote, how could they possibly make a living? Did they even have a plan for how to get by without the charters?

"Moving would be a fresh start for all of us," Fry said.

In the silence that followed, Finley could hear Parsley, locked in the bathroom, bleating for attention. "That's your family, not ours," he said.

"You'll get to know them." Fry got up and fetched the samovar of coffee. He lined up their mother's favorite teacups, poured, and set in front of Finley the one painted with a sea lion, ivory nubs for eyes. "You're related if I'm related," he said.

Finley picked at the ivory nubs. "We don't even know Aunt Flora."

"Don't be petulant. She visited once when you were little."

"Okay, fine. I didn't know we were counting that one time I was a baby and I saw an aunt I've never met." Finley tried to stand so abruptly that his knees knocked the table. Coffee spilled. His teacup would've rolled onto the floor, shattering, if Milda hadn't reached out and caught it.

"Finn," she said.

"I'm not going, Mills. You know I'm not going."

Fry took off his spectacles and rubbed his eyes. "A fifteen-year-old boy is not going to live up here all by himself. You'll go to school, you'll wear shoes. This will be, you know, a real life."

"What about the house?" Milda said. "We can't just leave it."

"Water's rising. We already lost the veranda," Fry said.

"Mills and I are on a hot streak. The season's not even over," said Finley. "Didn't you see the Walden hammers? We've already made a catch."

Fry thumped the ledger. "This isn't a democracy. You go where I go."

"There's a thing called running away," said Finley. "Sometimes children do that."

"You have ten days to finish the season, but you have to get packed up first."

Milda looked about to rebut—perhaps their success earlier had persuaded her that they had a real future in this business—but instead she nodded. Finley figured this was probably a pleasing development for his sister; now she had the excuse she'd always wanted to leave. His father would return to his own sister and family; Temperance would have friends she didn't share blood with. The constellations seemed to be aligning for everyone in the family but him.

Over the next few days the kitchen table seemed constantly to be littered with Aunt Flora's letters: Send reservations. And, What's taking you so long? Dad is ailing. Clearly their father and aunt had been communicating for some time. *I have loose ends,* Fry had begun his latest reply. *I have things to tie up.* The first sentence was underlined. *I have loose ends*, he'd emphasized.

Finley took these letters into his hammock at night and roved his eyes over the words in an attempt to memorize everything he didn't know about his own family. *The tomatoes won't germinate,* Fry wrote. *Tourist hoppers are coughing smogs of cancer over the sky and everyone's catching asthma.* His father wrote that one of the breeding tanks needed repair, which meant hiring a water crane, but where was the money? Fuel for the Crusher cost more money than Finley had ever heard of, and although he and Milda paid for their own fuel, it was a stretch to cover the debt. Flora had responded: Sell the plane. There's no water to land on down here you know that.

As Fry made plans for their departure, Finley drew up a route for a final scouting trip. Late one afternoon he paddled to Happenstance's trade post to exchange the Walden hammers for canisters of fuel. As soon as they'd restocked, he and Milda planned to leave for the lower Resurrection Mountains. This would likely be their last flight, Finley knew that, and he wanted to stay out as long as possible; he planned to bring as much fuel as they could afford.

As a town, Disillusionment had rarely seen more vibrant days. The dock was flush with candy apple planes, four- and six-seaters with room to haul game. If Finley had learned anything from living in the territory his whole life it was that prosperity was like pollen in the air—it got everyone's dander up. Standing on the porch of the trade post, he watched the whole world rotate. Ranger Starr gathering a crowd for day hikes. CAMP HERE! signs staked in the town's cemetery. Madam LeFleur's palms printed in the blood of the hares she slaughtered behind the boardinghouse each evening to make stew for travelers.

Their community was amalgamated; that was the word Finley had learned in fourth-grade geography. The territory's population was made up of Natives, survivalists, hermits, rangers, guides, farmers, and reverends who, like Finley's own family, sought a life of subsistence. Making a living off the land had been a necessity for generations. Only now the prevailing crop of the era was man-made. Pianofortes.

"Season's winding down," Happy said when Finley stacked the Walden hammers on the trade post's counter. "You'll make more if you can hold out for the spring auction."

"I need the cash now," Finley said.

"You know where you're headed?" Happy said.

"Always," said Finley.

Up north, the flooded valleys between the Resurrection Mountains formed narrow, deep-water breaks that fanned out like the spokes of a bike wheel. Decades ago, when Finley's father had been a young man, a battalion of cranes hummed on the overlooking bluffs, beaks constantly dipping in search of crude. You could still see the scars of industry on some of the rock—fossilized tire tracks and rusted carabiners strewn about. Over the following few decades the water table had risen, driving these cranes inland and widening the sea coves favored as the birthing ground for migrating silverback whales. Finley and Viola had scouted this territory before and had once or twice stayed overnight at Auntie V's RiverCamp—the largest tribal fish camp along the Kamikaze River—but they'd never pushed deep into the outskirts of the permafrost where early homesteaders had staked their land.

FINLEY SPENT THE FIRST fourteen hours kayaking the coves. The Crusher raked in low, concentric circles as Milda tracked Finley's kayak, her braid Rapunzeling out the window. Below him spread an unheralded world of parliament clams, black sea stars, the shallows sliced everywhere in brilliant columns of light. The shelves themselves ended in abrupt, clean cuts—straight drops into black water. Floating over these abysses, he could feel the magnetized weight of the ocean sucking him downward—so easy to drown here, hardly any effort at all.

By the end of the second day, Milda was hot at the wheel and beyond the point of patience. It was time to head home. It would take five hours of flight to get back and Finley was clearly dallying. Ferry tickets and packed trunks waited for them. Although Finley knew many parts of their lives would be simpler down south, he knew too that he'd be forced to learn the rules of a culture heretofore foreign to him. He'd never had a government-issued ID in his name, for one thing. He'd planned to get his pilot's license in a few years the way most kids in the territory did: a few seasons test-flying low in the outer fjords where Ranger Starr wasn't likely to patrol, then down to Panhandle Island for the adjudication. But not once had he driven a car. He'd never been to a movie theater. Even his concept of bread—a dietary staple that his mother or Milda had always baked by hand—would change when they no longer had to grow their own yeast. Finley had no experience with societal norms, not in any traditional sense, having grown up in a world largely absent of creations such as municipalities and politics. And he had no desire to acquaint himself with these trivialities, either, since he knew the continent was a world to which he would never really belong.

Once Milda got him out of the water he knew they'd have to fly no-holds-barred to the ferry terminal. The headlights flicked on, off, on, off. *Time's up.* He kept his eyes on the water and did not flash back a reply. Spahr Signals, their mother called them, the family's own Morse code. Milda was an excellent pilot, though they'd been midskirmish their whole trip, having argued the entire ride up—Milda trying to sway him to an amenable mind about their family's move, Finley the opposition:

"You can still come back to visit."

"Visiting's not the same as living," he said. "Who's going to take care of the herd?"

"They're octopuses, they'll be fine."

"And Abraham Lincoln?"

"He knows how to fish."

Now the full breadth of Finley's mind was occupied with scoping the detector along the narrow shelves. He kicked his fins through shadows to relish what he imagined to be the last true taste of his childhood home. Finley believed each of the Spahr children had been born with their own immutable characteristics. His little sister, Temperance, had taught herself to play the lute; she could whistle out her ears. Milda had the high, altered mind of a stratospheric bird, their mother's closet of neoprene, and devotion—she milked her goat, Parsley, every day like it was her religion. As for Finley, he'd inherited the Bloomers' protruding shoulder-blade wings and Viola's persistence. He had once read that scientists were driven by two poles: their interests and the interests of their time, and he believed this was also true of families. All three siblings were hybrid creatures of their time in the territory, uniquely suited to their aerial-aquatic life. How could lungs like his, that opened so easily in water, survive down south in all that dry continental air?

A battering wind swept off the mountains. He knew that in a few hours their father would rise, crank down the solar panels one last time, rustle Temperance from sleep, and discover Finley and Milda hadn't yet returned. If something happened to them out there, lives back home would be altered forever. He pictured Temperance climbing onto the roof in the rain, lute tucked under one arm, hopeful that the right pitch might call them home. *When can I go with you?* she liked to ask, cuddling up beside him. *Soon. When you're older.* She'd sigh. *I wish I was older right now.*

Finley suspected that a time was coming when all of their stories would split—he and his sisters sliding over and under each other like broken, bloodied teeth—but it didn't feel to him like this was the right season. He was in the middle of this thought when the Crusher came whoopwailing out of nowhere, trapeze bar dangling low enough for him to grab. He was supposed to seize it with one arm, the kayak's lead with the other, and let his sister reel them both up into the belly of the plane.

The bar swooped. A narrow passage opened to his right and he paddled into it. Milda couldn't make the turn, so she clipped west. He'd bought himself time. Finley clicked the brass detector up to high and wanded it through the water. Though his family gave him grief about the sound, it was no slight invention—the detector had the personality of a clock and the brain of a jellyfish: *whomp-whomp* went the sensor. *Whomp-whomp. Bleeeeeeeeeeet.* He could hear the Crusher change direction and come pummeling after him. He flicked on his flashlight to graph Milda a message.

There's something down here, he blinked.

The Crusher's headlights flickered. *Trees.*

What?

Look underneath yourself.

Finley popped on a dive mask and stuck his head in the water. At first, nothing. Cold seabraid whipped his face. He pulled up. Spit in both sides of the mask and flicked on his dive light. Still he couldn't see. He let himself drift over to where waves lapped against a seawall jutting out from one of the mountains. An organic and improbable wonder of sandstone rising six or seven feet above the waterline. From up top he would have a better view; he began to climb. The wall was slippery and Finley thought fondly back to the crampons he'd packed in the plane. Crampons and grip chalk. Grip chalk and belaying rope.

He reached the top of the bluff. Stood his full height and took a view of the world. From up here he could see that the seawall actually hooked back around the mountain to form a large, natural barricade. It was the rim of what had once been a small prehistoric lake. He walked along until he came to the place where the wall joisted up to a bluff—no sign of caulking or other man-made implements. In fact, the rock wasn't constructed at all—it was one continuous half ring, the kind of imperfect damage done when something heavy and material broke through the atmosphere. From his father Finley knew that ancient asteroid strikes had augured similar craters in the continent down south, their bottoms chalked in dinosaur bones. He'd never seen one, but he imagined that standing on the rim of such a crater was not so unlike the hope he felt now, finally seeing what his sister had been trying to tell him from the air.

Trees. Ringing out from the bluff spread an underwater petrified forest stretching as far as Finley could glimmer. The famed singing spruce. In the homesteading era the majority of the territory had been covered in this ancient forest: trunks to hold up time, boughs soughing in the breeze. Homestead sleds wound through groves just like the one now beneath him—perhaps even this very one. Finley would only know for sure if he found sled ruts on the ocean floor. He wanded his detector through the water and the metronomics buzzed off the charts. Something was down there.

We're going to miss the ferry, Milda signaled as the Crusher came winging toward him.

If Fry hadn't done so already, their father would soon be loading their trunks onto the boat. Checking his watch, marking the tide. The ferry from the territory to the continent ran once a week and Aunt Flora had arranged to pick them up once they disembarked. At fifteen years old, Finley had no real hope of returning to the fjords, or the territory—not anytime soon. He'd be trapped down south in an arid, rocky town sorting diplodocus ribs, swimming laps in the town's chlorinated swamp pool. No thank you.

Floats to water, the Crusher landed and skied over in a stiff spray.

"Get in," Milda yelled.

As final straws went, Finley guessed this was as good as any. Before being slammed against a moment like that, he'd thought his world was an oyster of choices. He could climb into the Crusher's seat and let his sister bank him home. Or he could find work at a local river camp gutting trout headed for the smoker. Each of these paths might once have sounded like a choice, but Finley knew they weren't really—not for him.

He tightened the strap on the detector and dove into the trees.

Using a spruce trunk to pull himself down, Finley reverse-climbed all the way to the seafloor. Beneath the canopy the spruce had all lost their needles—the acidic wash they called a curl left only what could not be easily swept away: scaffolded branches with bark sharp enough to scrub off fingerprints. Packs of otters swam all around, weaving through the trunks in psychedelic formations. Finley arm-muscled through them, deep enough that the pressure popped little red stars on his wrists and ankles. Exploded blood vessels, indelible as any tattoo. His teeth ached. The air in his lungs seemed to bubble levity up to his brain; early-stage narcosis, easy to recognize, and dangerous—without fresh oxygen he'd soon drift to sleep. *Actually that's called drowning,* Milda would say. *Whing-whing,* the detector sang. Down and down he climbed but everything was inverted; it felt like he was walking on the underside of water, hearing something like music.

Like the good book said, there was nothing, and then all at once, light. A wink of abalone shells and beyond, a blue piano the size of a rhinoceros levitating a dozen feet off the forest floor.

Finley pushed off the nearest trunk and kicked in the direction of the impossible. As he got closer he could see that the forte was actually nested in the boughs of a spruce, kelped into place. Eighteen feet tall, cobalt blue, fitted with copper flats. The Mayflower Bluefin. An unprecedented find. An oily daguerreotype featuring the instruments of the first expedition hung on the wall in Madam LeFleur's boardinghouse. Perched atop the Mayflower Bluefin, a dozen children clutched a bundle of sea beans. Though Finley had seen this rendering of the instrument many times, it was another thing entirely to witness the scale of the forte in person. The piano was as tall as a house. Layers of algae scummed the boards, but this would scrape clean if he was ever able to get it onto dry land. Finley didn't know how he was supposed to feel in that moment of awe-striking luck—probably more in tune with his inner spirit. But giddy terror, that's what he felt. He needed air, he was out of air—then out of nowhere his sister's teeth appeared. She pressed an oxygen mask to his face.

Milda took his hand and together they swam through the trees. Once arboreal, now the seafloor was all nautilus crush, the original sled ruts overgrown with fraggly, hot pink sea anemones. Finley had never witnessed a delight to the senses more potent than drifting through the forest that afternoon, high on oxygen, their dive lights shining into a canopy as they scoped for more relics. He thought about how there was no use pretending he'd ever had an endless bevy of paths available in his life. In the few seconds it took for them to cut the Bluefin's vines, he and Milda had secured for themselves a future. Siblings starfished and shoeless, knives flashing in a synchronization they'd never been able to achieve on dry land. Water moved through the soundboard, striking raw, starlit chords as Finley sawed his blade against the mesh of kelp. He could feel something similarly deep-knotted within himself begin to loosen and fray apart.

When the vines were severed, the Bluefin took off like a hot-air balloon—straight up to the surface. *Amazing,* people would say later when he told the story. *Sounds like a miracle.* "Sure," Finley said. "But also, physics." He didn't know if the reality of what happened would ever ring true for scientists, but it was the truth: Milda grabbed one of the Bluefin's legs, he grabbed another, and the piano buoyed them up to the surface. An effortless levity tinged with fear: as though there was nothing to keep them from rising forever, into the air, then the heavens, past the angels, and straight to space. Until they broke across the dome of the sky, sibling and sibling, looking down on the world from a height so renowned he could never have fathomed.

Part III

Kamikaze

Hullulla

Huntmoon Chapel
June, ten years after the Bluefin discovery

Nine hundred miles north of Jubilation House, Hullulla Huntmoon and her moose, Gussie, blazed into Arctic City stinking of fish roe. She was still in RiverCamp waders, lost flies snatched in the tangle of her hair. No breakfast. Late. *Today we winch, tomorrow we haul, Saturday we caulk.* That tempo was set forth by the Reverend for moving Arctic City's stone chapel up Mount Resurrection, where they would rebuild it exactly as it had been before, each of the original stones slotted into the same place. Loath were any congregants—least of all Hullulla, considering she was his daughter—to rebuke his authority.

High noon. Commotion was up in what remained of the Old Chapel. Hullulla's father, Reverend Huntmoon, stood atop his pulpit surveying the river as divers surfaced from the Kamikaze with chunks of the nave's foundation. Two hundred years earlier, the Old Chapel had been built by Hullulla's Huntmoon ancestors on a bend in the Kamikaze River: stone and stained glass, with pews framed from old homesteader sleds. The backyard held a chicken coop with a kokorikoo rooster and a dozen laying hens; the eggs tasted so wholesome, like wheat and prayers. Ever since Hullulla was a little girl, the spring ice melt had flooded the Kamikaze River through the Old Chapel's graveyard. The Reverend said the dead didn't mind suffocating under the wildest river ever to break land. It was the living who could no longer tolerate the rising water.

The Kamikaze River streamed through Arctic City cold and desperate, grabbing for land on both banks. Built on a peninsula jutting into the river, the Old Chapel had been taking on water for years—long before Hullulla's cousin Jude LeFleur had recovered and sold the Ahab Grand, long before she'd hitched Gussie and headed out to RiverCamp. The Huntmoon family had shored up the chapel's foundation again and again, but nothing held. *The foolish man built his house upon the sand,* the children sang. *The rains came down and the floods came up and the house on the sand washed away.*

"Load 'em up," the Reverend said as the congregation stacked the Old Chapel's stones onto carts. They still had to travel twelve hundred feet up a switchbacking trail to the plateau, where they would rebuild the chapel on high ground. The carts were old milk wagons with low-slung bellies already drooping under the weight of the chapel's stone. *Bray, bray,* called the hitched yaks, ears beating clouds of blackstrap flies. Hullulla's brother, Ezra, and cousin Jude unsuctioned their dive masks. They climbed out of the river. All morning the Reverend's congregation had been winching thousands of pounds of drowned chapel rock to haul to an altitude where starlings twitterpated and bread wouldn't rise.

"Hear that?" The Reverend rapped on the pulpit. "This is our Tabernacle."

"May the Lord bless you and keep you," said Mrs. Huntmoon.

Hullulla hitch-fasted Gussie to the yak post and looked down the line of carts. Her family's entire operation was held together by fishnets and prayers. "Glory be," said she.

In the line of succession for the chapel pulpit, Hullulla now tied with her older brother, Ezra, for third place, both of them ranking behind their father and God the savior. She was a Huntmoon by heritage and the Reverend's kid by birth, so she'd grown up fatted on the indoctrination of holy service. Earlier that spring when Ezra had volunteered to run point on the chapel's relocation, Hullulla, twenty-five years old, had left home on her annual summer expedition to the territory's fish camps. Auntie V's RiverCamp held land along the Kamikaze River a few miles south of Arctic City, and Hullulla was welcomed to stay in exchange for shifts at the gutting table.

In the early days of the territory, Native tribes had claimed rights to all historically ancestral land, including all of the Kamikaze River. They'd granted homesteaders an easement to travel through the interior up to the promised homestead plots along the Glacial Front. Not many made it that far. Over the next two hundred years, Arctic City ballooned as migrants opened businesses and built houses on land leased from the tribes. Like the Old Chapel, many of these early buildings were now sinking into the river, and consequently the Huntmoons' congregation of farmers, railroaders, and permafrost kids filthy around the eyeballs had thinned significantly over the last decade.

But the tribal community remained a constant presence. If anything, Auntie V's RiverCamp seemed to become the territory's new default capital as it swelled each summer to accommodate local kids out of the pity of everyone's hearts—white-bred homesteader descendants hoping to stock the family with trout for winter. Fishing rights to the Kamikaze ran with the land and access had to be brokered through tribal leaders. Families flew up from as far south as Disillusionment Bay on fish-away vacations and brought cargo holds of dried clams and neoprene that they swapped for a few nights on the banks of the river. For a bootstrapping reverend, Hullulla found the location ideal. All summer the river camps were stocked with new community members, and Hullulla had never been a slouch at the reel. By day she hooked trout alongside her would-be parishioners. And when the sun set, she took her shift alongside them at the gutting table. *Head, tail, belly.* Auntie V had been calling count for years—all knives beat to her rhythm.

At RiverCamp, Hullulla had quickly found her moral center preaching atop a Custer&Sons forte baked into the Kamikaze's bank. Each Sunday she stood on this makeshift pulpit, skirts fishhooked into pantaloons, reading aloud from the Huntmoon family's heirloom copy of *Old Testament Tykes*. Although Hullulla had mastered rolling her tongue in her father's oratorical style before she was five years old, in truth the water was where she made her reputation. She liked to wade the river in the mornings when her shadow didn't forewarn the trout and the banks weren't overgrown with other fishermen. "Story, story," children chanted, running after her. Hullulla kept a sack of worms holstered to her thigh, and she'd toss a few at the kids as she baited her hook. "In the beginning there was a river," she said.

For obvious reasons she relied heavily on the parables of fish. Jonah's whale rising open-jawed; trout bellies heavy with cursed drachmas. Casting her reel to the rhythm of chapter and verse, she recounted what she knew of Galilean politics, the recipe for John's locust crisps. Most stories only needed to be relayed cold—it was sobering enough to translate a book where women turned to pillars of salt. There was a wealth of material in the scriptures about taking care of one's neighbors if you knew where to look—everyone deserved grace, everyone had needs. "Remind them the savior was a fisher too," the Reverend told her. "And all are welcome at his table."

Many of the trout running the Kamikaze were monstrous; they had nine lives. They came up sporting catch-and-release scars and gouged eyes—marks of old battles. Hullulla was often bloody knuckled at the end of the day. But the fish looked worse. She said a prayer as she slit their bellies, because who knew what might be inside—a hook embedded in gill tissue, an engagement ring, copper coins, a wooden whistle shaped like a bird.

Ivory was a given, that was the whole point. But trout didn't care about the petty human dramas of which mineral was top of the market. If they saw something shiny, they went after it gape-mouthed; then it was down the throat. Hullulla couldn't believe the cornucopia of gut rot she'd pulled loose that summer alone: thimbles, a mitten, pipes. Saltshakers and forks, both tuning and regular. Glass eyes. Plenty of milk teeth rotted from the mouths of homesteader kids. She turned the fish inside out and shook them with biblical conviction, collecting whatever fell loose from her catches to take back to the chapel's coffers. Most of the time she got what she came for. Piano keys. The ivory spine of the Arctic.

Sundays after fishing she held her own service on the riverbank and any and all were welcome, so long as they were willing to sit in the sand while she preached. One bit, two bits, three bits at a time, she passed the offering basket and took what she got. On flush days the children dropped whole piano keys into the collection. Later Hullulla bundled these into sets of twelve and sent them downriver to the trader. Measure and weigh, he bought ivory by the ounce. The keys were either sold to local restorationists or postmarked for the continent—southern musicians paid a steep price for Arctic ivory. A certain amount circulated in the local economy. Five ounces for a basket of apples, half a bundle for bookbinding equipment to repair the hymnals. The chipped remainders she brokered to local women like Auntie V, who whittled crochet hooks and chess pieces for tourists. A living, at least for the moment. The mammoths were gone, elephants overbutchered, and walrus hunting embargoed—if you wanted ivory free and clear, the Kamikaze River was one of the last places on Earth to find it.

THE TRAIL UP Mount Resurrection was a true hack job, barely wide enough for the carts. One side dropped to nothing, the other rose in a sheer face impossible to scale. Single-file, *clip-clop,* up the mountain they went. Hullulla pulled the halter on Gussie, who was hitched to a cart carrying a stained-glass triptych of the savior blessing loaves and fishes. *Here's your fish, here's your bread,* the savior seemed to say. *Eat and be holy.* A hundred baptisms had been administered under this window, dozens of marriages—including her brother and sister-in-law.

Maple and Ezra were married in the Old Chapel a few years earlier, standing in the same spot where all Huntmoons had been married for two hundred years. The morning of the wedding Hullulla rapped on Maple's door, saying softly, "It's me." Their chickens had flocked to the Old Chapel's roof—birds were no fools, they understood the danger of flood times better than anyone. During the service they cackled so loudly, Maple had to strain to repeat the vows. Ezra might have been promising his new bride anything—Hullulla could hear only the snippets: *love, promise, faith, family.* All the right ingredients. The water had tried to bully the wedding party off their feet, but they'd held their ground.

Now the Reverend led their procession up the mountain, followed by Jude driving the crane, then Ezra. Her brother was in charge of a trio of yaks nicknamed the Holy Trinity: father, son, and albino the ghost. Most of their congregation was already up at the excavation site jigsawing the chapel's original foundation back together. The crane Jude drove would be used to lift the rafters. It was a mild day and everyone chewed blades of grass. They recited creeds.

Hullulla looked back at Maple, who trudged behind their cart. When she looked again, her friend was gone. Gussie was on the upper ground of a blind curve and Hullulla waited for Maple to come back into sight. She called her name. "Maple," she said. Finally she jerked the bit and forced Gussie to stop. The moose leaned her flank against the mountain and Hullulla couldn't control the cart from that angle. She climbed down and tried to direct Gussie backwards.

The moose took two steps and the cart's back wheels veered. Rocks tumbled. They were three hundred feet above the ground, not even halfway to the plateau. The triptych came uncovered and shot flecks of blinding color into the sky. Gussie looked at Hullulla with bloodshot in the eye and Hullulla rubbed the moose's ears, speaking words of comfort. She pulled Gussie forward and the cart straightened; then she slid a hand down the moose's leg and roped her ankle into a hobble. She edged between the moose and the mountain—no room, but she managed—around the bend, and there was Maple. An unconscious bluebell.

Dress torn at the shoulder from where she'd fainted into the rock. It wasn't even the height of summer, but Maple, pregnant, was bright with sweat. Hullulla knelt at her side. She pulled Gussie's salt cubes from her hip sack and rubbed them against Maple's tongue. She patted her friend's cheeks. Maple jolted awake and struggled to sit up; in her hands a bunched-up dress, rose fingerprints down both arms. Using Hullulla for balance, she stood. She lifted her skirt and stepped out of her underwear and there it was, biology's unfinished helix, a knot of embroidery made so early it was both in the image of God and no one's image at all.

Hullulla squeezed Maple's hand because there was nothing to say. They'd been here before and this just kept happening. Month after month added up to a lifetime. Maple folded her underwear and tucked it against the mountain. Hullulla gathered stones. After a few minutes she had a pile. It was a better grave marking than some got, though that wasn't saying much. Maple picked a brush of fireweed and placed it atop the stones. On the way back to the cart she was fighting emotion, stopping every few paces for a wave of cramps, but when Hullulla tried to give her an arm she brushed her off.

Six weeks. You could rebuild a chapel in that time. You could memorize Song of Songs. Six weeks was plenty of time for lots of things though nowhere near enough for others. "Give him your burdens and walk into the valley of peace," said the Reverend.

"To everything, a season," said Mrs. Huntmoon.

How many times did this make? More than the hairs on Hullulla's head?

"Feels like at least that many," Maple said.

Hullulla rejiggered pieces of glass to make room for Maple in the cart—blue and green, a twinkle. She folded blankets and laid them into the new space. Still there wasn't enough room for a person. Together the two friends edged past the cart and stripped Gussie of her panniers. Hullulla spread a blanket across the moose's back. Maple climbed up. She sat sidesaddle and cut a decent picture, staring up the trail like a bride riding into Bethlehem. Hullulla loosed the hobble. Gussie was a good moose—she knew her burden had shifted and she took the route slowly. "*Click-click,*" Hullulla said, and off they went.

As they climbed higher, a great view of the territory swept open below. The Kamikaze could barely be classified as a river anymore.

Swollen to a heretofore unimaginable girth, the river spread from the base of the Resurrection Mountains west across the diamond-shaped homesteads that had been claimed by many of their great-great-great-great-grandparents, including the first Huntmoons in the territory. The original Huntmoons and their daughter, Pumpkin, had sledded along the homestead trail all the way to Arctic City. Like many families, they'd lost the forte they brought up from the continent somewhere in the first nine hundred miles. Rather than buying another one and establishing their own homestead, they'd brokered a deal with local tribes and built the Old Chapel on the river; they passed off their pulpit to the next generation. On and on this went until Hullulla's father.

Unlike the Huntmoons, other homesteader families had since dispersed across the territory. Bloomer. Crockett. Starr. Mayflower. Pope. LeFleur. Each of them had eventually secured their own sections of land along the Glacial Front and outfitted them with one-room huts, roof gardens, acres of wintershrooms. Hardly anybody lived on these original homestead plots anymore, and Hullulla couldn't blame them—rising water flooded more and more every year. What remained of Arctic City stretched like a long, smooth muscle along the Kamikaze River, giving way to river camps staking the bank south.

As they crested the bluff the ghost of the New Chapel rose up ahead—the empty air it would steeple, glaciers rising behind in a grand sweep of ice. The Reverend had selected this plateau after months of prayerful starvation—the lee between Mount Resurrection and Paradise Lost, summits framing the new House of God. *The wise man built his house upon the stone,* the children sang, and for once in history the Huntmoons were going to be those wise men.

The excavation site was already surrounded by piles of rock: the congregation had spent three weeks hauling up the building supplies for the walls, mortar, and framing boards. The Reverend and Ezra were at work with the crowd laying the foundation, the pair of them back-lifting four-man rocks. Hullulla's brother was in his twenties and could take the weight, but if the Reverend wasn't careful he might cantilever a vertebra—there was some damage not even God could repair.

She helped Maple down from Gussie's back. When her friend's feet hit the ground Maple pulled her hand away. Ask Hullulla to preach the covenant of forgiveness, ask her to recite articles of doctrine—she was rarely at a loss for words. But watching her friend walk over to join the crew preframing the chapel's walls, no letters of any alphabet came to mind.

They were not born sisters, of course. At eight years old, Maple had wandered into town newly orphaned and confused. The journey to Arctic City had taken so long that her snowshoes had broken apart along the way, and for the last few miles she'd struggled over crusty winter drifts in nothing but wool stockings. More than once she'd sunk all the way to her waist. She'd struggled along, following the Kamikaze's trajectory as best as she could, believing that if she stuck to a familiar waterway someone would eventually appear and rescue her. It was sheer luck that she hadn't broken through the ice and drowned.

Hullulla had just turned eight herself when little Maple had shown up at the Old Chapel, lips frostbitten peacock green, and she clearly remembered the moment. Maple wore patchwork and gingham, a yak fur caped around her shoulders. Underneath her hat, her hair had been a disaster of lice and feathers. Whether she was born with blue eyes, no one could say, but from that winter on they remained the shot-through color of Kamikaze ice. Hullulla had left Maple alone in the Old Chapel's nave while she went to fetch the Reverend. While she was gone, Maple had eaten all the communion wafers and drank half a cup of wine. The Reverend found her asleep in the front pew. He picked her up and carried her home to thaw by their family's fire. Three days later Maple woke with a belly full of broth, Hullulla stretched beside her, reading aloud from *Old Testament Tykes*.

Hullulla and Maple quickly developed a close friendship. Together they picked berries, toasted communion wine, milked their first yaks. The girls wedged themselves so tight together that the family thought of them as one entity: HullullaMaple. When they were twelve, they ran away from home on the anniversary of Maple's "Arrival Day." Late February and frigid. The plan, so much as they'd had one, was to skate south to Maple's family's old homestead and camp under the aurora. Maple wanted to know if things were still as she'd left them all those years ago or if some new family had taken up care of the land. That first day Maple and Hullulla had skated down the Kamikaze River, tipsy on newfound freedom. At lunch they pinned dried nettles in each other's hair. They made camp six or seven miles downriver and after a dinner of pancakes they fell into a sweaty, exhausted sleep, whispering dreams about tomorrow.

In the morning they awoke to what turned out to be one of the worst blizzards in the territory's history. Snow fell in pillowy hills so deep that they couldn't see the riverbank. The temperature plummeted—to say that they'd made a huge mistake was an understatement. Winter was not done. The drifts were soon three feet deep, and at that rate the girls suspected they'd be eight feet deep by nightfall. Likely they would have frozen to death if they'd broken camp to trek home, but they knew enough to hunker down and spend the day building shelter.

They trudged away from the river far enough to find the remains of a legless Roosevelt. They went to work piling snow atop the pianoforte's foundation to make a quinzhee, an emergency winter shelter made from a hard-packed mound of snow they'd hollow out with their fists. Once the pile was as tall as they were, a little more, they beat the sides to form it into a solid mass. Up went more snow. When finally the mound atop the Roosevelt was densely packed, they began digging out the inside. By nightfall they'd made enough room to crawl inside the snow cave and sit up side by side. They shared a tin of sardines and agreed to sleep. Packed together, the girls intertwined their arms. "Good luck to both of us," Hullulla said.

They made it through the first night in the quinzhee, but the next day, and the night that followed, snow continued to fall. Hullulla began to worry. Until that particular storm, the winter weather had been mild and at the time Hullulla considered them both intrepid and snowsmart. In reality she could now see they'd been fatally arrogant.

Their twinned desires—hers to strike out, Maple's to cuddle back up, somehow, with her dead family—made a dangerous cocktail.

Breath froze in their sinuses. There was no use trying to get outside to light a fire; even if they could find dry kindling, the air was too wet. They could not light one inside because there was no room and also because it would melt a hole in the roof. For food they had nothing left but a jar of unseasoned nut butter, which they passed between them, dipping and licking fingers, before stuffing their hands back into their mittens. Both were tired, Hullulla remembered that, and when they tried to hold a conversation one of them would invariably chin-drop to sleep. Their oxygen levels were low.

They'd never mustered the energy to dig the quinzhee any bigger, so there was barely enough room for both of them to sit up, and no room at all to lie down. The Roosevelt's boards provided some insulation, but they creaked miserably. The girls were constantly jockeying for space, elbowing and huffing. By the third day Hullulla wasn't sure which she was more afraid of: freezing to death or going mad with the irritation of being trapped together.

Hullulla was the first to get the chills. She awoke in the dark, slicked in sweat. She could taste bile in the back of her throat. Her head felt wispy. Though she knew it was impossible, she swore she could see the aurora's mosaic playing across the roof of the quinzhee, a bright purpling leaking down the walls to envelop her. When Hullulla woke next, the girls were sharing a coat. Maple sat splay-legged behind her, their arms tucked through the same sleeves; they even shared mittens. Maple's head had nooked against Hullulla's neck, pressing against a fret of veins.

As a girl Hullulla did not have a gentle nature, and although this had often proven frustrating in regular life, in times of distress it gave her a deep well of energy. "Maple," she said, shaking her shoulders. Her friend remained a ballast against her back. Hullulla felt sick again, but wrapped together as they were, she could not move. It smelled like one, or both, of them had fouled themselves. Hullulla unzipped their coat. Arms shaking from cold and dehydration, she pulled herself free and crawled outside to survey the storm.

The snow had finally stopped. The moon hung high, a jackaly crescent grin surrounded by stars so tactile Hullulla believed she could've snipped them from the sky. She felt a little better in the fresh air and struggled to her feet. She took a few steps. Her legs were sore. She breathed. Even with the storm over it would take hours for the snow to melt enough for them to reach the river, let alone skate home. They would have to make it through at least one more night. In the meantime they were both drowsy and still much too cold. Growing weak.

She crawled back into the quinzhee and began to undress first herself, then Maple. Shirt, long johns, socks, underwear, everything. She set the clothing carefully atop her own coat to keep dry. She needed to make sure they had as much skin contact as possible to share their body heat. As she slipped the underwear from her friend she realized that they had never seen each other fully naked. Unlike Hullulla's small chest buds, Maple's breasts had fully developed, and she had a curly puff of pubic hair, while Hullulla was still slim through the waist.

Working quickly, Hullulla drew her friend against her and with her free arm began to re-dress them as one body. Long johns, socks, pants, shirt; one coat, then the other. Once she had them zipped together, Hullulla drew their arms together down the sleeves. She tucked their hands between her own thighs. This was by far the closest she had ever been to another human being, including every member of her family.

They awoke the following day surprised to be alive. "Mapes," Hullulla whispered, "Mapes, wake up." If Maple wondered why they were wrapped like a pair of inverted conjoined twins, she didn't say so. The top of Hullulla's head was wet and she looked up to find the ceiling dripping. The entire quinzhee was illuminated in buttermilk light. Together they struggled out of their shared clothes and into their own pants and coats, then outside. Though it would be days before the snow melted entirely, the sun meant they could at least strike out toward home.

They strung their skates around their necks and trudged toward the Kamikaze River. If they were lucky, people would already be out looking for them. They'd told no one what they'd gone searching for and in hindsight it was clear that this was unforgivably negligent—a mistake never to be repeated. It was too easy to disappear in the territory, especially sneaking off to hunt memories without any form of backup.

THE HUNTMOON CONGREGATION worked all morning to rebuild the New Chapel. The Reverend called a stop only for lunch and this was when Hullulla and Mrs. Huntmoon picked up their shift. They might not have had five thousand mouths to feed, but there were plenty—Maple sliced bread, Hullulla pulled sardines from jars. "How's life at RiverCamp?" Mrs. Huntmoon asked her daughter, then added hopefully: "Meet anyone interesting?"

Hullulla knifed the head off a sardine. Of everyone at camp, Auntie V commanded the most fascination. She was the chief diplomat on camp order, food distribution, and the strict schedule that kept the smoker working around the clock. Unlike the Huntmoons' chapel, the river camps had no fixed location; year after year Auntie V's tribe conjured sandy riverbanks into a neighborhood with garbage collection and fuel pumps for visiting planes. It was quite a feat. Then at the end of the season they dismantled everything and carried gear back to their permanent winter homes in the interior. "Everyone's pretty interesting if you hear them out," Hullulla said.

Mrs. Huntmoon pressed her lips together. "You know that's not what I mean."

In the years when her brother, Ezra, had been gone from home, Hullulla had planned to take over the Huntmoon pulpit—she was the peach of her father's eye, that was clear to the entire congregation. As a little girl she had memorized leagues of scriptures. When the time came for her to soapbox she wanted to be ready. It was Mrs. Huntmoon who had frequently reminded her daughter that chapel services were only one part of their church's work. Not everyone communed best with the Lord under a man-made roof. "See the world first, meet people. Trust me, you'll see it's for your own good."

"What if I already know what I'm good at?" Hullulla said.

"You can be good at more than one thing," her mother replied.

The daughter of a reverend, Hullulla had always known that the primary directive in her life was to spread the good news of love and acceptance as far as her voice could shout. The Reverend had taught her to welcome lost souls to the table, anoint their heads with oil. Ask: *Are you hungry, are you thirsty, are you resentful, are you alone?* From her work at RiverCamp she'd come to understand that it was no trick of the imagination that so many disciples were fishermen—it took a particular aptitude to look out across a great expanse of water, or a great crowd of people, and know in your gut there was something out there worth recovering.

When the sun set, the Huntmoons' congregation trickled back down the mountain for the night. They would return in the morning to build the New Chapel's walls and begin assembling the stained-glass triptych. Only a few Arctic City houses remained above the waterline down below, and these had all been repurposed into dormitories to take in those flooded from their homes. There wasn't a bed to spare. The Huntmoons had already given up the Old Chapel's parsonage to flood refugees. They planned to camp on the plateau until the New Chapel's reconstruction was finished. When the last of their congregants left, the family lit a fire. They ate. Ezra, Jude, and the Reverend then took their bedrolls into the chapel. Hullulla's mother strung a tarp over the cart. The women lifted out the stained glass. Underneath, the cart's bed was lined with straw and they spread a quilt. Mrs. Huntmoon curled up to sleep.

In the light of the campfire Hullulla could see bruised shadows of loss ringing Maple's eyes. The day had been too full of change—first leaving the parsonage, then losing a baby—and Hullulla didn't know how to soothe either. "Come on," she said, clapping her hands. "Let's go on an ice run before bed."

Maple sighed. "I'll get the climbing gear."

When God had created the Territory of the Arctic, He'd wrought a landscape almost completely intransitive—what was buried rarely decayed. Encased in water, encased in ice, everything preserved much longer than it should have been. The glaciers behind the New Chapel were full of the heaved-up remains of mammoth tusks and homesteader brains infected with pox. Ice calved from the glaciers daily, flooding the valleys surrounding the Resurrection Mountains. The Reverend maintained that this meant they were living in a time of revival, the land shucking itself to be born anew, though Auntie V saw the world with a different eye. The permafrost was melting too fast, she said—it wasn't natural to force whole communities to scramble inland.

Maple billy-goated up the glacial wall—crampons, picks, she knew what she was doing. Hullulla followed. There was a ledge chipped into the glacier thirty feet off the ground, and here they sat. Hullulla knew that even if the New Chapel was preserved on this plateau, the town below wouldn't last long on the Kamikaze's banks. Their long, smooth muscle of civilization—the territory's original capital—had surrendered to the shifting climate. Perched on the ledge, she and Maple ate apples. They spit seeds into the air and talked of how they were feeling: babies, warm beds, congregants needing medical attention; what they feared, who they loved.

Before climbing down, Hullulla chipped blocks of ice from the ledge and loaded them into the packs. She tried to seesaw more weight to her bag but Maple noticed and said, "I can carry that."

"It's heavy," Hullulla said.

"Well, of course it is."

Mid-descent, Hullulla's pick slipped. Twenty feet later she hit the ground with a groan. She rolled over. She knew what a bruised rib felt like and this was it. She'd have Auntie V look at it when she got back to RiverCamp. Maple yelled down asking if she was okay. "I'm alive," Hullulla said.

"What happened?" Maple said.

Hullulla had no idea. She reached for her pick. There was something on the end and it was blood. Or a paste that used to be blood. Hullulla was pretty sure her own wounds were internal, and it was not until Maple's feet hit ground that she had the strength to lift the pick. There, lying in the grass, was a ring. A huge black pearl set in a simple gold band. Hullulla looked up the glacier for an explanation—how did it get here? How long had it been trapped?—but the glacial face stood opaque. Nothing to see. "Is that what I think it is?" Maple said. She held out her hand and Hullulla placed the ring in her friend's palm. "Dear Christ in heaven," Maple said. "What in the world."

Later, Hullulla waited until Maple fell asleep, then banked the campfire. She'd hitched Gussie not far away and she spoke softly to the moose before leaping onto her back. Gussie had been yoked all day and was chafed at the neck. It was late, well after midnight, but on a summer evening the light still held. At RiverCamp the fishers would just be gathering around the gutting table. Hullulla clicked her tongue in Gussie's ear and they were off.

Before the Huntmoons had begun reconstructing the New Chapel, the plateau overlooking Arctic City had supported several dirt airstrips—for years it had been a popular campsite for traveling hunters. It was not uncommon for planes to land and hunters to switchback down to the Kamikaze before walking south until they reached a river camp willing to let them catch their dinner. Auntie V's camp was one of the largest and had a reputation for welcoming outsiders.

When Hullulla rode into camp that evening, Auntie V's niece Saura met her at the hitching post. "New people," she said. "Come, come." A bright red floatplane had landed on the river and pulled up onto the sand. A thick rope secured it to the gutting table. Little children sat on the floats washing trout from the day's catch in buckets of crisp river water. They passed the clean fish to adults at the gutting table, who chopped tails, slit bellies, and glittered scales everywhere. The organs were pulled out and apportioned into bowls. Everyone had a hand in preserving the day's haul. Young adults carried racks of fillets to the smoker. Those whose hands shook and those who couldn't see well enough to tweezer out the trouts' tiny, brittle bones told stories or held babies or made sure the guests who walked into camp each night had a bowl of something warm off the fire and a plot of sand to raise a tent.

Saura handed Hullulla a bowl of smoked trout chowder. Hullulla ate, watching a young woman she'd never seen before struggle to pop a tent. Faded, nearly fossilized nylon with a bleached factory tag. The chowder tasted of river dill and hickory, and Hullulla spooned up mouthfuls as she called out, "Need a hand?"

The woman wore a flight cap and shaded her eyes with one hand as she looked up. Oil-stained palms—clearly she was the plane's pilot. She continued unloading tent poles from the back of her plane, dumping them on the sand. As Hullulla got closer she realized the woman couldn't have been more than a few years older than herself—confident and brisk, she had an unusual pattern of moles on the side of her neck. "Is it just you?" Hullulla asked.

"I have a brother around here somewhere," the woman said, threading a pole in one sure pop. "I'm Milda."

"You won't need a tent tonight—doesn't look like rain."

"That'd make Finley happy. It's too small for both of us anyway," Milda said.

Hullulla picked up a second tent pole and pushed it through the fabric. The tent took shape. Each of them anchored her pole in the sand. The tent didn't look big enough for one adult, let alone two. Milda spread a stained sleeping bag across the tent's floor and set down a food basket, flipped the lid: the inside was packed with tins of pickled meats. Hullulla immediately recognized the label. KAMIKAZE FARMS: SALTED BY THE ELEMENTS. "It's been a long time since I've seen one of those," she said wistfully. "My grandmother used to ship us a crate every winter. Is that your farm?"

Milda rubbed her thumb across the logo, then handed a tin to Hullulla. "It's my mother's recipe."

After peeling back the lid, Hullulla pinched an octopus pip no bigger than her thumbnail, dripping with tomato juice. Popped it in her mouth. It tasted like the salad her grandmother Madam LeFleur used to make for boardinghouse guests, served in tulip-patterned bowls. One day the salad had suddenly been stricken from the menu and Hullulla hadn't tasted the sauce since; she licked it greedily off her fingers. "I know who you are," she said. "Kamikaze Farms. How come you don't have a better tent?"

"You mean this old thing?" Milda patted the domed roof and the tent shuddered. "Runs in the family. Plus we won't be here long. Just gotta check off this area of the map."

"Is that what your brother's doing, hunting some rare river octopus?"

Milda peeled the lid back on her own tin. With one flick of her wrist—clearly a practiced motion—she pitched the pips directly into her mouth. Impressive. "Nah, Finley's probably already found a forte he thinks will make us a fortune," Milda said dismissively, juice dribbling down her chin; she swiped it away.

"Wait, you're hunters?" Hullulla said, thinking of her Custer&Sons half protruding from the bank around a sharp twist in the river. The Custer&Sons was a popular model, one of hundreds, and Hullulla's forte had been left on dry land so long, she didn't expect that it'd be a good candidate for restoration. But it wasn't worth taking any chances with hunters in the vicinity. "Which way did he go?" she asked.

Hullulla raced down the beach. When she'd found the piano, the ivory had been stripped clean and the inside reduced to an empty wood cavity: no hammers, no strings, just enough room for her leather-bound book wrapped in plastic. *Old Testament Tykes.* Even if the forte had been worth saving, she wouldn't have cut it out of the bank herself. Aside from it being her favorite place to commune with heaven, that summer she'd been using it as her sleeping platform.

She found Milda's brother spreading his own sleeping roll across the forte's top. "That's not yours," she said. Hullulla's blue-black hair reached her waist and was tied in a series of braids. Auntie V had recently inked an ornate medieval cross tattoo down her bicep. She'd planned to sleep atop the Custer&Sons herself that night so she could preach early the following morning before heading back up the trail to rebuild the New Chapel. The congregation would need her to help put together the stained-glass window that she'd shepherded up the mountain.

"You must be the reverend. Auntie V told us about you," Finley said jovially, hopping up on the Custer&Sons. He raised an eyebrow as he flipped through her copy of *Old Testament Tykes*. The book was now practically loose-leaf; a sneeze would gust the pages into the river. Hullulla's spine tensed.

"Put that down," she said.

Finley brushed sand off the cover and held the book out to her. "My bad. Someone left it inside this piano. No place for a book."

"You shouldn't go rummaging around in other people's things," Hullulla said as Gussie plodded around the bend and headed straight for her. The moose followed her down the beach every evening, pausing only to snag a few mouthfuls of grass. Hullulla caught her by the bridle and led her up the beach toward the Custer&Sons. She itched Gussie behind the ears with one hand as she reached for the book with the other. "Your sister's looking for you. I had to help her with your tent," she said.

"Not *my* tent." Finley jumped down off the Custer&Sons as Gussie dipped her head to smell him. Velvety lips nipped at the buttons of his jacket. Unlike most people, Finley was clearly comfortable around large animals—he didn't back away. Instead he copied Hullulla and scratched Gussie behind the other ear. The moose brayed in pleasure. "Good girl," he said.

"It's past her bedtime," said Hullulla. She signaled Gussie, and the moose folded into the depression in the sand next to the forte where she slept every night. Quickly, Hullulla squatted and tied the moose's legs into a hobble, then unbuckled her bedroll from Gussie's back. She slept in a one woman swag tent of her own invention. A portable sleeping unit that consisted of a sleeping bag with a built-in mattress and wire hoops at each end to hold up a thin, waterproof tent: large enough only for her. She motioned at Finley's sleeping roll atop the Custer&Sons. "That's where I sleep," she said. "And you can't take this piano with you. It belongs to the camp."

Finley kept glancing at her as he folded up his sleeping roll. "No problem. Where there's one there's probably more." He tucked his sleeping roll under his arm and cocked his head as he looked at Hullulla. He had bright, chartreuse eyes. "Maybe you could show me some good spots to look tomorrow?"

Though Hullulla knew plenty of people who'd tried, she'd never hunted fortes. She didn't make a lot from the ivory she pulled off the river, but the supply was at least consistent—and it gave her time to preach. She unrolled her swag atop the Custer&Sons, popped the tent, and crawled inside. She slept encased in a quail-feather quilt embroidered by Maple's delicate hand. Before she zipped herself in for the night she said, "Service starts tomorrow morning after breakfast. See you then."

Hullulla knew others considered her intense—she preached even if no one listened, she preached in foul weather, her boots clip-clopping across the Custer&Sons. Her sermons were lengthy and delivered from memory. But the following morning Finley sat in the sand with the rest of her congregation. A dozen kids eager for a story from *Old Testament Tykes* and a few elderly women, including Auntie V. "Welcome back," she said, glad to see Finley.

Waving her hands over a chalice, Hullulla consecrated a cup of moonshine and passed it down the rows. She watched Finley take a sip, then smack his lips. He ate the square of trout skin fried in dough. "Let us sing," she said, and he sang. It was clear he had not grown up with religion, but she saw that he quickly recognized her call-and-response. When Hullulla said, "Open your hearts," he saluted her, smiling, before chanting with the rest of the congregation, "We open our hearts."

She'd hoped to speak to him after the service but by the time she was done greeting the elderly attendees, he'd disappeared. Such was the nature of hunters; who knew where piano scouting took people, or for how long? He could easily be another in a long line of congregants she saw once and never again. As Hullulla thought of him flying off with Milda, that bright red plane skiing down the river before taking off, she felt a glimmering understanding of why he'd rushed off, for she was something of a hunter too, in her own way. As someone who'd spent her life nurturing faith, she certainly understood impossible hunts for treasure most other people could not see.

Moose

Singing Spruce Forest
July, first homestead expedition

Gradually, so gradually that Moose Bloomer almost didn't notice, things began to rattle apart. Little ways at first. By the beginning of July, for instance, Moose had developed horrific mosquito welts on his neck and at least one sled had busted up crashing down a ravine. With nowhere to brood, half the chickens had stopped laying. More and more often, fallen trees blocked the trail and the whole train had to stop for hours while trailbreakers were sent ahead to cut the trunks into firewood. Time for some of these delays had been planned into the schedule—everyone had known that at least some things would go wrong—but it seemed no one had factored in the time required to set broken bones and soothe new, rotten stomach viruses to which they had no immunity. Arthur grumbled each time the train halted, complaining to Moose that they were on the brink of falling off schedule.

On top of everything else, between the fluctuations in atmospheric pressure and the jostle on the trail, the fortes began slipping out of tune. This seemed to take everyone by shock, though Moose couldn't understand why. The ruts were rough, and if the strings were not properly calibrated they could easily rip the hammers from their holsters. Many instruments had been unwired for the journey, but those fashioned with specialty hammers did not have that luxury. The

Bluefin, the Napoleon, the Ahab, even the Huntmoons' Psalmist—they all had strings that needed to be loosened and calibrated daily.

Their Napoleon held its tune better than most, a fact for which Arthur felt great pride—every morning he rose before the rooster to check its status. Moose typically woke up to the sound of his stepfather fumbling scales. The instruments were meant to be played, Arthur said, that was the whole point.

While Moose disrupted the chickens in search of breakfast eggs, his mother would settle on the bench and tap out "All Things Effervescent and Luminous" or "Run, Run from the Bear, Little Susie." Unamelia was no maestro, but while she played, Arthur pressed his ear to the Napoleon's belly, listening for anything slipping south.

"Do you even know what it's supposed to sound like?" Moose asked.

"I know spoiled meat when I smell it."

This was a poor analogy, even Moose knew that, for meat once spoiled could never be made right. The fortes on the other hand might fluctuate in and out of tune, but their sour notes could always—or almost always—be reconciled. And some, the lucky ones, showed no sign of hardship at all: the Bluefin was one such example. Somehow the instrument managed to sound sweeter as time went on. In the evenings the Mayflowers—eight children in all, plus a set of grandparents—buzzed around to sing. Mama Mayflower, a strawberry-shaped woman with a Quebecois accent, led the family in a chorale that put the rest of the train to shame. They were the Bloomers' neighbors directly to the north and the towering mass of the Bluefin blocked any view they might have had of the trail ahead. "We're going to go blind if we have to stare at that piano's ass for the next three months," Arthur said. "Those boards are a goddamned eyesore."

"I don't know, I think it's rather lovely to look at," Una said. The Bluefin was the harbinger of the train. Because of its ridiculous height, Rocket sometimes asked Thornton to ride atop the piano and call down reports about the trail ahead. Thornton was the lightest of those deemed responsible enough for this task—the littlest kids being in danger of falling eighteen feet to a broken neck. Like the rest of the children, Moose nursed a sense of jealousy over this arrangement. Not only because the posting would have allowed him to rest his hip but because his gallivanting in the trees had attuned him to the pleasures of air circulation. Those on the ground spent their days besoiled as pigs while Thornton rode cross-legged atop a Persian carpet, hair blown back, snacking on walnuts. To have Rocket reliant upon him, to see what was coming before anyone else could—this would have been in all ways superior to Moose's life, which day to day consisted of coughing dust while Thornton called down, "Haven't you noticed that you have bird crappers on your hat again?"

Sledding took on a level of monotony, the days a blur of thistles and dogs frothing in exertion. It was surprisingly lonely on the trail, even with families on all sides, and Moose found no company in the little tykes. With Thornton perched high on his throne, Moose took to ranging as far as his leg would allow, mostly in search of evidence that anyone lived nearby. If this was truly a civilized route, where were the chapels? The trade posts? They hadn't even seen a single Native population so far. When he brought this up to Rocket, the guide reminded him that it was fish season and most locals were river-camping along the Kamikaze River. They had to rack up a harvest for the winter before they returned to the territory's interior. Moose understood this necessity, for these were ambrosial days, the air scented with pollen, and although they couldn't always see them, Rocket assured him that creatures from every walk of life were hauling north alongside the train. Trout, mating and dropping eggs. Caribou. They were trailed by a full siege of birds: geese, hawks, ravens. Look how they had already pecked out most of the stars!

The first actual cabin they passed was abandoned, built into the side of a hill: a wall of river stones, roof bright with stalks of boreal chard. Inside Moose found the remnants of a home deserted in haste. A dirty plate on the sideboard; a rabbit hutch containing a petrified skeleton. What had happened to these people? Spoiled water and disease? Had they been too faint of heart and decided to return south?

"Are these supposed to be our closest neighbors?" Una said.

"They'd have to still be here for that," Arthur said.

"Do you think they died? Or just moved?"

"I'm sure they're fine, Una-bird."

"I don't know, kind of looks like something terrible happened."

At the next abandoned cabin Moose discovered a toy battalion of tin prospectors. Lined up on the mantel, two inches high, the men's pans sifted what looked like moon dust. Each held a sign reading BEWARE! or STAY BACK! MINE, ALL MINE! He scooped them into his pocket, unsure if he meant to keep them for himself or if they were a gift for his new sibling. There would be precious few presents for his new brother when he finally turtled out his newborn head.

At least the prospectors would be a souvenir of the journey, though Moose wasn't sure how much he'd endeavor to remember about it later on. They were trespassing into a territory full of growth he had never experienced and did not even remotely understand. By the time they passed the third abandoned cabin it began creeping up on him, the realization that past human beings had found this land difficult to survive. Not the tribes, of course—Rocket said that they'd lived in the territory for thousands of years—but those who'd come after. Trappers first, then the families who'd apparently tried to make homes in the middle of the forest. Now their train.

At the beginning of each day, Moose was tasked with inspecting the sled to note cracks, dents, or wobbles. Arthur wrapped the helm in strips of animal hide that cracked under the duress of sunlight. These strips had to be regularly rewound. After they swiped the piano keys with a polish that Una had developed, Moose would steal a few minutes of solitude settled on the far side of the runners. Eyebrow deep in the story of Noah's son catching bullfrogs to bring aboard the ark. "Come here, little froggie," the boy said. One morning Moose was so lost in the regaling prose of this tale, he was completely startled when Arthur came fuming around the tip of the sled.

"Loose runner," his stepfather said. "Get the pulley."

They had to string ropes up through the trees to leverage the sled, which weighed several tons, off the ground so that someone could slide underneath to repair the runner. Moose threw the ropes and took his stance on the line. When they got the sled raised, slightly, they tied the rope to a spruce and took a look. One of the buckles holding a runner in place had come unholstered. Part of it was rotten. Arthur popped the lid on the repair kit—hatchet, hammers—and set to work cutting the buckle free so he could attach a new one. This work was routine, but time-consuming.

All morning their neighbors sledded past—the Pope family followed by the Happenstances, then sled after sled of families Moose couldn't identify. It took him and Arthur several hours to work the rotted buckle free and slide on a new one. By the time they finished and were able to join up again with the train, the Bloomers had fallen from their original spot near the front. Moose untied the rope holding the sled aloft. Arthur whistled for the dogs' attention. "Hup, hup," he said. They nudged in just ahead of the Huntmoons, and together their two families made up the train's caboose.

LATER THAT DAY, after they'd staked their sleds, Moose went to fetch Thornton—the Kamikaze wasn't far off and he wanted to pull a few fish before bed. As Moose lit a fire for his mother he heard the Huntmoons sniping complaints at each other as they set up camp. When he rounded on their sled, he saw Auntie Huntmoon half swallowed by the Psalmist. She had on her wrench belt. Moose didn't know her well, but she was a brisk little woman, the kind of person who had some sort of internal stabilizing fortification around which her world pivoted. She wore her hair strapped behind her ears in an odd pair of buns, and she was the first woman Moose had known to smoke a pipe, a habit that thoroughly embarrassed Thornton. Moose had never given Auntie Huntmoon much credence for her motherly instincts and today was no exception. There was poor Pumpkin on a dirty quilt, drooling. Thornton sat at the Psalmist's keyboard, depressed, waiting to play. Every few minutes Auntie Huntmoon would yell, *muffle-muffle,* conduct her arm, and then Thornton would strike a flat with his knuckle. They were tuning the Psalmist.

The Huntmoons were religiously dedicated to maintaining the forte, Thornton had told him. The instrument had been gifted to them by Thornton's mother—Auntie Huntmoon's sister—and he expected that one day his mother would visit to find out how well they'd treated it. His commitment to the Psalmist was such that he wouldn't range with Moose at night until he'd helped put it back into tune.

"Ready to go?" Moose said, impatient, kicking a clod of dirt.

Thornton gently closed the lid on the keyboard. "Let me grab a pole," he said.

"Don't stay out too late," Auntie Huntmoon said. She picked up baby Pumpkin and put her on her hip. "And don't even think about breaking your leg."

"Don't fall in the river," said Uncle.

Sighing, Thornton slowly got off the piano stool and fetched his fishing pole from their sled. "Stop it, you guys," he said, so quiet only Moose could hear.

From what Moose could tell, Thornton's aunt and uncle were decent people in terms of treating him right. But founding the territory's first chapel wasn't Thornton's dream; he wasn't looking forward to building pews or a steeple, was afraid of ghosts, and dreaded living next to a graveyard. He still blindly stoked the hope that his mother would send for him to return home. He wrote her letters every day, stowing them in his trunk until he could buy postage in Arctic City.

Moose struggled to understand how Thornton could foster such empathy toward the family that had kicked him out. The way he saw it, Thornton had been conscripted to a life his own parents had not chosen for themselves. At least Moose could say that his parents wanted him with them; they would never have sledded off without him, or sledded him off without them. Despite the hardships of the trail, the hardships he was undergoing in his own body, there was a comfort in knowing that they were undergoing them together.

He and Thornton walked in silence. When the tree line broke at the bank of the river, Thornton stopped. "My mother would love this vista," he said wistfully. Moose said nothing. He knew better than to open his yamhole about anyone else's family; the last thing he wanted was Thornton prying into his own. Lately when Moose looked at Una's belly he felt a deep sense of unfairness. The new Bloomer stewing in his or her amniotic sea was totally unaware of the trials and tribulations of the trail, or the fact that they were about to be birthed into a life that Moose had always coveted. Two parents. An older brother. Nobody offering you pennies out of the pity of their heart, nobody cutting your hair on the chapel steps. When people eyed the new baby in his father's arms, nobody would wonder how much was biology and how much love, they'd only be thinking: yes, this was life exactly as it had always been meant to be lived.

It began to rain as they descended the bank. Moose snapped his fishing pole together and threw his line into the water. He took off his hat to let the precipitation wash the mats from his hair. He'd had a particularly trying day, his leg cramping, and his parents had gone immediately to bed. Usually after Arthur returned from talking with the other men, he and Moose sat together beside the fire. Sometimes Moose smoked a bit of Arthur's pipe. But tonight he'd been left alone. He couldn't say why exactly the situation put his heart in a muddle, only that this was one of the worst parts of the trail—how much time there was to get lost in your own melancholic contemplations.

The riverbank had a small hillock, slick with mud, and he wasn't paying attention to the placement of his boots. He slipped, stumbling, and his bad hip wrenched. In one motion he tumbled forward into the shallows, the fishing pole jerking from his grasp. The water was cold. He fell to his hands and knees in the river, a sight that bemused Thornton to no end.

"Are you going to help me or what?" Moose asked angrily.

"What's the matter with your leg?"

"Nothing. I lost my balance."

Thornton waded into the water. "It looked like you were limping before."

The river had been covered with ice only a few weeks earlier. Moose's arms shook from the cold as he grabbed Thornton's hand. His friend leveraged him up and Moose looked him in the eyes when he said, "You're mistaken."

"You can tell me if something's wrong."

"I said I'm fine."

By this time the storm was becoming more severe. A real deluge, it turned out. Moose gathered his fishing pole from where it had washed up on the bank and he and Thornton made for the trees. He tried to calculate how long it would take them to get back to camp with his limp. Too long. He wouldn't be able to pantomime health the entire way. Rocket issued daily warnings about the vagaries of the weather up here, but Moose had never fathomed the possibility that the sky could transform so dramatically in such a short time. Where once the world had been dappled gentility, birds tweeting happy mating calls, now the wind came scouring through the trees.

"We should run for it," Thornton said.

"It's all mud."

"Don't you want to get back to a tent?"

Moose pulled on his hat. Water streamed off the brim. "It'll pass. I'll wait it out."

"You aren't going to catch anything in weather like this."

"Go ahead," Moose said.

Thornton took off in the direction of camp. Moose looked up the spruce he was leaning against: low branches. He could climb into the canopy. The cover would protect him from the worst of the storm and give him a place to rest above the mud.

Needles scratched his arms on the way up and he had a taste like sap in the back of his throat. He found a notch where two branches met and curled into a ball between them. Now he was soaked through and embarrassed from having tumbled into the river. His hip ached. Whatever the Napoleon had done back at Disillusionment Bay was more than a mere bruising; it had weakened him, lessened him somehow. He loathed the thought of Arthur finding out—his stepfather expected kin sure of their own footing in the world. A son who could take after him, hefting the family's future onto his own young back.

Moose was failing miserably at living up to this example. What if Thornton had already told Arthur about his fall? What if they trekked out in the rain to rescue him? He'd never hear the end of it.

Thankfully the rain stopped just as suddenly as it had started. An apple green rainbow arced over the river, the color refracted back up into the trees. Trout, thousands of them, flashed just below the surface of the water, called up by the storm. They were so plentiful, Moose knew that if he stumbled into the river now he'd be able to snatch one from the water with nothing but his own teeth. Snout down, jaw open. He was thinking he might at least try when he heard someone below say, "Hey, there's a boy in that tree."

Another voice, deeper. "Horse shit."

"I'm serious. Look."

"There's nobody."

"I can see him with my own eyes. Right there."

Moose peered down. At the base of the trunk stood a man wearing coveralls, flame red braids sticking out the bottom of his cap. "Hey, little fellow, don't be scared. You can come down now."

"I'm fine up here. I don't need help."

"Boost me up, Abe," the man said to his companion, before turning back to Moose. "I'm coming to get you, kid."

Moose evaluated. The thought of this man plucking him from the tree soured his stomach. "No, wait," he said. "I'll come down."

Carefully, Moose made his descent. When he dropped to the ground, the men eyed him suspiciously and he realized that the storm had probably wreaked havoc on his appearance. He felt his collar: torn loose; hair cowlicking to all hell. The man with the deep voice seemed to be the leader of the two—he had a shock of white hair and a matching handlebar mustache. A double-headed ax was braced across his shoulders. "Abel Huckle, Minister of the Grand Boreal Railroad Company." The leader swung the ax to indicate the red-haired man: "That's my deputy, Jack-a-pole." The blade flashed behind him into the trees, where Moose could just make out the shadow of a third man hammering a spike into a log: "And that's Petey."

"Hey, kid," said Petey.

Clearly the youngest of the three, Petey looked to be just a few years older than Moose. A raw gold nugget dangled from a chain around his neck. When he saw Moose eyeing it he held it up. "Pretty sweet, right?"

Beyond Petey a ladder of parallel logs extended back into the trees. Thick iron rails ran between them, joined every few feet by dinner-size fish plates. The beginning of railroad tracks, though they hadn't yet been fully assembled. "What is all that?" Moose said.

"You ain't never seen a railroad before?" said Abel.

"That doesn't look like a railroad."

"Well, it's not finished yet, that's why. We're just the advance team."

Moose tried to imagine a train whipping through these environs double, maybe triple the speed that the dogs managed. Passengers cloaked in fancy furs, stewards portering coffee. Moose's family would never have been able to afford train fare. And nobody with that much coin would ever join a train like theirs, crapping in the woods, wearing bear bells around their ankles. Their journey was primitive, solitary, powered not by steam but by their own will.

Moose looked over to Petey, now lugging a log through the trees. "Am I ever getting any help?" he asked.

"Settle down, we're talking with a guest," said Abel.

"It's heavy."

"So stop carrying it."

Moose wasn't sure what compelled him, but he walked over and lifted up the other end of Petey's log. They only had a few more feet to go to put it in place. Watching them, Abel pulled tinder from his pocket. Rolled tobacco into what looked like a corn husk and lit the end. He passed the smoke to Jack-a-pole. Moose could sense the warmth of camaraderie between them—the loose elastic of chosen family; he felt it himself on the nights when he and Thornton passed a bottle back and forth in the trees. He relaxed a little in the recognition and sat down on the newest railroad tie. His teeth chattered as he asked, "So where're you from?"

Abel blew smoke out his nose. "Here," he said, waving up at the tree canopy.

Moose could see nothing resembling a home in the branches—no tent, no tree fort of any kind. Jack-a-pole passed back the smoke, flicking char from the end, and Moose watched enviously as Abel took another pull—smoke warming his lungs sounded pretty good right about then. "No, I mean, do you live around here? 'Cause we passed some cabins," he said.

"We live wherever our bedrolls take us," Abel said.

"But this is the middle of nowhere," he said.

Abel laughed, coughing up smoke. "Who told you this is the middle of nowhere?"

"Well, clearly no one lives here."

"You're here. I'm here. What does it take to constitute a home besides two people in the same place calling it that?" Abel dropped the smoke's end on the ground and stubbed it out with his boot. "You learned about transitive and intransitive properties yet, kid? Everything starts somewhere, but that doesn't mean it all ends up in the same place. Like these tracks here, we could go this way, we could go that. One way leads back the way we came, the other where we're going." From a pouch on his hip, Abel pulled a flask of water and used it to swish his mouth. He spit, then took a long swallow. Wiping his mouth with the back of his hand, he said, "I'll let you in on a little realization it took me a lifetime to procure: nobody's got a home anywhere but the place their two feet are standing. You get me?"

"Boss, he's just a kid. He's got no idea what you're talking about." Petey squatted next to Moose and began pounding spikes into one end of the new tie. It jostled so hard Moose leapt to his feet. When Petey finished he walked along the board like a balance beam. Lined up spikes on the other end. "Where you headed, kid?"

"The Glacial Front."

Petey's hammer paused, spikes sticking up from the railroad tie. "Jesus."

"I'll thank you to keep the Lord's name out of your mouth, Petey," said Abel, tucking away his flask.

"Sorry, Boss." *Whack, whack*. In went the spikes. "But it's colder than a witch's tit up there."

"Don't scare the poor kid." Jack-a-pole cut his eyes at Moose. "You got family, kid? Ma? Some brothers?"

"We're going to be farmers," Moose said. "Grow beans and corn and stuff."

An unpunctuated silence followed. The men all looked away, clearly uncomfortable; what did they know that he didn't? Moose knew their lives wouldn't be easy, but everyone on the train had such optimism—until that moment he'd never considered that homesteading the Glacial Front might be a delusion. What if corn and beans wouldn't actually grow on the permafrost? They'd have nothing to eat but jerkied caribou and boiled river frogs, huddled together around the fireplace trying to stave off hypothermia.

He was still shivering—he needed to get back to camp to change into dry clothes. And the train only stopped for a few hours at the end of each day—long enough for everyone to eat and nap—before trudging onward. They'd be breaking camp soon. Arthur needed his help to hitch the dogs and load supplies. He wouldn't take kindly to Moose skipping out on his daily tasks. "I better get going," he said.

"You come see me in a few years if you need work—I could use another strong lad," Abel said, clapping him on the shoulder. "You know how to get yourself back to your train?"

Moose nodded. By now he could feel exhaustion beginning to creep from his brain down through his nerves. His leg pained him something unearthly, but at least the rain had stopped. Back at camp there would be dry food and the comfort of a tent; he could almost taste his mother's breakfast pie. He was displeased that he hadn't caught any trout and would be turning up empty-handed, but at least that was better than being carted into camp in the care of a Minister of the Railroad.

"It's not far," Moose said. "It was nice to meet you."

As he turned to walk away he heard them fall to arguing. That must have been their standard cadence: three men alone in the woods. Still, it certainly seemed to him that they had a good deal going: how much easier to travel as a trio than as part of a train of hundreds of souls and sleds. Moose tried to envisage himself and Thornton joining up with a railroad crew in a few years, backtracking through the Singing Spruce Forest, laying ties under the trees where Thornton now tied Pumpkin's ribbons. But he couldn't easily fathom the circumstances that would allow him to quit their new homestead—his parents and new little brother would need him. Besides which, there was no telling if a railroad through the territory would ever be operational, or if the tribes would allow what the men had constructed thus far to remain.

Hobbling back to camp, Moose considered what Rocket had said, that there were so many other forms of life moving in parallel fashion alongside their train. And not just animals, but people too. Maybe the abandoned cabins they'd passed hadn't actually been vacated forever—maybe they were way stations, temporary homes for people like Abel and his crew. In which case the fact that they were empty now had no bearing on how habitable or inhabitable the territory would turn out to be. Talk about a relief! Moose couldn't wait to tell his mother.

A pang hit Moose then as he thought of the toy prospectors he'd swiped: what if some little tyke returned from a river camp to find his favorite toys gone? Moose was no thief; he thought about taking them back, but the train had already come too far for him to return. He wouldn't take anything else, he decided, not when he couldn't be sure if the artifact might belong to a live person—especially a kid not much younger than himself, one constantly being transported from one abode to another. Never would he forget the humiliating stomach-drop of a landlord tutting, *Mrs. Price, Mrs. Price, what are we going to do with you?*

Back at camp a great tumult awaited him. Nightfall. Birds ruckusing. Everyone shouting orders: *No, the green one! I said hold still! I can't fix this blasted thing without more light.* Moose had hoped to find everything as he'd left it—tent raised, a plate of dinner awaiting him—but the storm had caught the whole train unawares. Trunks were scattered around his sled like wreckage from a ship. Wire had been strung through the trees to make a clothesline. Moose's underwear was clipped up to dry. Una had her back to him, stoking a fire, and he walked around to stand opposite her. She seemed tired, more tired than he could ever remember seeing her—hair in a frizzy braid, the color gone from her cheeks. He looked up. Their tent had blown up into the trees and was snared in the branches. The world smelled like wet dog. There was nothing in the way of food.

"You missed one hell of an aftermath," Arthur said. He was standing inside the body of the Napoleon scooping out buckets of water. "Grab a bucket."

"I thought a Napoleon was supposed to be waterproof," Una said, beckoning Moose over to her. She wrapped her arms around him and stroked his wet hair. "Isn't that what the salesman promised—rain or shine?"

A bucket of water splashed on the ground. "Well, there's two feet of rain in here, Una-bird, so you tell me."

"He said it was an all-weather instrument. If it's not waterproof, he shouldn't say it's waterproof."

Arthur stopped bailing for a moment. "We're in the situation now regardless," he said, then set the bucket on the soundboard. He unclipped the hammer holstered to his belt and held it out toward Moose, handle first. "It's nothing a drainage hole or two can't fix. Moose, I'm going to need you to slide under and pow, pow, pow, help drain this water."

Though his mother's dress was wet, Moose felt her body heat warming his blood. He didn't want to let go of her, certainly not to slide under a piano that had already crushed the strength from one of his legs. "Isn't drilling holes in the belly going to ruin everything?"

Arthur wagged the hammer, impatient. "Come on. We can patch it up later."

"I would have picked a different instrument, that's what I would have done," Una muttered to herself as Moose walked over to the sled. She jabbed a stick at the coals in the fire and turned her back to the Napoleon, saying so quietly Moose almost couldn't hear, "If we'd known then what we know now, I would have picked something else."

Moose eyed the space between the forte and the sled's belly; Arthur wouldn't fit. After the disembarkation they'd rebraced the front leg, so Moose knew there was little chance it would splinter now and crush him again. Still, there was a vulnerability to sliding under any weight this large—he wasn't Thornton, he didn't have an inherent trust of physics.

"Can't you just make a hole from up top?" he said.

"I'm not busting through the soundboard," said Arthur. "And we don't have time for evaporation. Come on now, if the wood soaks any more it's never going to play right."

Moose grabbed a fistful of nails. He slid under and began pounding them into the belly. Then with the hammer claw he pulled them loose one by one. Out dripped gray rainwater. "That's it," he could hear Arthur say. "Should be dry by morning." Moose could see several problems with their scenario—water had already soaked the dampers, and Arthur had done God-knew-what damage stomping on the soundboard—but he said nothing.

His stepfather leapt down, and Moose slid out. They changed out of their wet clothes and sat beside the fire, eating cold beets from jars.

What Petey had implied about the inhospitable climate on the Glacial Front plagued Moose. Falling into the river, the severity of the storm—clearly this land cared little for his personal predicaments. The pain in his hip was now so great that his hands shook. But before he could rest, he had to fish down the tent. His mother spread a blanket by the fire, lay down, and closed her eyes. Arthur gathered up the empty beet jars, rinsed them, and loaded them back into the trunks. They would refill them with their summer harvest. Moose's fishing pole was still strapped to his back and he pulled it free. He cast the line up into the trees and jostled until the hook snagged canvas. A few pulls and the tent came jellyfishing down: a huge hole torn in one side. It would take hours to resew. He spread the canvas over his mother's sleeping form and went to work loading trunks onto the sled. Rocket would be coming by soon with the daily report.

Only it wasn't Rocket who showed up as the sun rose, it was nineteen-year-old Minnie Mayflower. Blue dress gone transparent at the shins. She went directly to Una and shook her awake. Moose watched his mother struggle up, one arm under her belly. She held Minnie's hand. The two of them stared into the fire. Eventually they got up and walked into the woods together. When they returned Moose could see that Minnie had been crying.

"Minnie's going to walk with me today," Una said.

"Everything all right?" said Arthur.

"Babies don't stop coming just because it's an inconvenient time to have them," Una said. "I'll see you for dinner."

As Arthur *hupped* the dogs into motion it dawned on Moose that there was only so much he could discern about his fellow humans from the outside, even those purporting to be his family. If Minnie really was pregnant, this would not be resolved in a matter of minutes, or even hours. Anyone who had seen them all sled past that day would think them standard travelers, having no knowledge of how preoccupied Moose was with his own hip, Una's convalescence, Thornton's grief over his mother—how they were all constantly tending to their own internal bruises. It made Moose grateful for how many things in the world did not obfuscate their troubles. For all their issues, at least the fortes followed a progression of logic: deduce the problem, apply elbow grease, drill a hole in the belly to drain water. *Hup! Hup! Onward!* Not all reparations in life were so simple.

Milda

Wild Beard Fjords
July, one month after meeting Hullulla

The ChickenCrusher's radio bleeped. *Where are you guys?*

From Milda's vantage as the pilot, the world below was nothing but water, a few poppy seed flecks of land. A Ravenwood with HO FOR THE HOMESTEADING ACT! burned into the lid rattled in the Crusher's hatch. It wasn't easy to navigate with the extra weight and sweat rolled down her face. Earlier that summer she'd shorn her hair pixie-close to the skull and Finley flew shirtless, but still they roasted. The ChickenCrusher's cockpit was a tin-can sauna. Milda said, "Is it just me—" and Finley said, "Goddamn, it's hot."

For over a decade the siblings had hunted together all summer, every summer. Like any team who had flown together for years they'd developed a shorthand: Finley said, "There," and Milda said, "Bingo." He said, "We can lift that Hammerstein," and she said, "How high?" They had done all right by themselves—that was their father's phrase—by which he meant that they had achieved minor celebrity among the scouting crews. Not only for their lineage and enthusiasm, but because they were the Kids Who'd Found the Bluefin.

A photo of them with their first major catch hung on the wall of Happenstance's trade post. Finley and Milda rat-soaked and beaming, holding between them a copy of the *Disillusionment Tribune* with the headline: LOCAL SIBLINGS DISCOVER MUSICAL TREASURE

IN BOTTOM OF PETRIFIED FOREST. When they came to town, people still wanted to know what it was like, being them: *What led them where they wanted to go? Did they know right away they'd discovered a record-breaking debut?*

They'd told their story many times—most people had seen them interviewed on the talk show circuit. Milda with her nasally voice and old-fashioned velvet suit. Finley rakish, with that half-crooked grin. He would say, "I never wanted to catch the ferry," and Milda would say, "Of course, I knew my brother." When they got to the part about the underwater forest, Finley would say, "I had an intuition." This was Milda's cue to pat his arm and say, "He'd already drowned once trying to rescue a piano." Finley would clear his throat. This built the dramatic pause. "I wasn't going to let that happen again," he would say.

Milda adjusted the radio dials as their plane zoomed past their neighbors' homes. Like Jubilation House, many abodes in the fjords had been jacked up on tractor tires to get more life out of the stilts. This wasn't a long-term solution to the rising tides, but it bought time. But within the next year or two all farms in the fjords would face a stark choice: they could either fully replace their stilts—an insurmountable expense for most—or watch their homes disappear forever under the waves. Which way Jubilation House would go depended entirely on their ability to secure and sell another Big Catch that season.

Temperance sparked the radio again. "Seriously, you guys, dinner's getting cold."

Finley hit the responder. "Simmer down, sis, we're almost there."

Jubilation House soon came into view and Milda spotted everyone outside. Temperance and Goldie Mayflower on the far end of the new veranda tossing a rubber starfish to Abraham Lincoln, who leapt in the air to catch it before falling back in the water barking with happiness. Jude LeFleur reclining on the roof snapping pictures of the sun. Jude was now an environmental photographer, but he still managed his grandmother's boardinghouse every summer. He'd been commissioned by the continental university where he taught to put together background shots that would travel with an exhibition of the Bluefin as it toured the continent that winter.

On Milda's days off she flew him all over the territory. For weeks he'd been snapping photos of key moments of their lives: Milda in jodhpurs, staring down a field of walrus bones. Temperance rubbing balm into the octopus sucker scars freckled across her neck and chest. Finley, cocky at the wheel of the Crusher moments before a flight lesson. They'd visited the site of the New Chapel to help his cousin Ezra shingle the roof, then flown south to the Archipelago of Lost Saints, where Milda and Finley had once found a clutch of Walden hammers. "The frame, the light," Jude said, slackening his life belt. He leaned out the passenger window, Finley's window, camera *shut-tut-tutting* at high speed. Jude processed his photos in bleak grays and creams: "A good photographer only needs one spectrum. If you're relying on color to tell your story, you're doing it wrong," he said.

Already Milda had been talked into flying down for the Bluefin's fall and winter tour. The recruiter had floated additional tour dates planned throughout the spring: "Would you be interested?" There was a tidy profit to be made appearing alongside the Bluefin; a career, even. But leaving Finley alone in Jubilation House for the foreseeable future gave Milda considerable pause. He'd never been left alone; he'd never lived alone at all. "I don't know how long I can be gone," she'd said.

After Finley and Milda had recovered the Mayflower Bluefin, the Spahr family had struck an agreement. It was a historic catch. Though Finley was still a minor, he and Milda would not follow their father and little sister south. They'd adapted into capable, waterwise people with their own spirits and eyeballs, Finley said, and no notarized document could consign him to a dryland farmhouse two thousand miles south. Their father must have known that too, or at least he knew enough not to stalk down a judge. Whatever their motivations, it all amounted to the same thing: at the ages of seventeen and fifteen, respectively, the weight of maintaining Jubilation

House had shifted entirely onto Milda's and Finley's shoulders. The relentless mechanics of their life consumed the ensuing decade, and as Milda hauled tanks of freshwater for the cistern or swept out the octopus hens' old middens she developed a deep appreciation for the way her mother'd somehow always managed to project a veneer of stability over what was by nature a rickety, unstable enterprise.

And now, with Milda planning to be gone all winter—on the one hand, the freedom for Finley as a young man would be unprecedented; on the other, even he would be susceptible to loneliness. With Milda gone he'd be completely isolated. Milda knew he'd been seeing Hullulla Huntmoon since they first landed at RiverCamp earlier that summer; he created new excuses for Milda to fly him north every weekend to attend her services. But between helping her family rebuild the New Chapel and her work at RiverCamp, Hullulla had her own life. There was a brotherly flavor to Finley's relationship with Abraham Lincoln, but their communication clearly had limits. And Finley had all but given up piloting a plane himself, though Milda had been trying to teach him how to for years. He'd watch her and ask all the right questions about what she felt, how she perceived oncoming weather systems—at the wheel he could keep them alive, or at least he had so far, but he was tenuous, anxious as the world below swept past at high speed. She couldn't pinpoint exactly why the skill seemed so difficult for him to catch.

Milda dropped the Crusher to land in the fjord. "You know what wouldn't be the worst thing in the world?" Milda said as the plane's skis touched down. They unloaded the Ravenwood onto the platform over the breeding tanks, and Finley cut the line. Spray geysered up, and for a moment they couldn't see anything. "You and I going south together for the tour. Think about it: an all-expenses-paid trip around the continent. We'd get to see our biggest catch again."

"I've got to keep things running here," Finley said without looking up from the map.

Milda cranked the wheel, and the Crusher floated toward the house. "It's not going to do you any good to be up here alone all winter," she said.

The two of them had greased their elbows alongside each other for so many years that they now shared the property deed on Kamikaze Farms. Life on the farm had always been fiscally tenuous, even with their mother flying charters, even after finding the Bluefin, and Milda knew it simply wasn't possible for Finley to maintain the crops and hunt for new fortes by himself. Things might've been different if lost pianos were still abundant, but they'd caught fewer and fewer with every passing season. Even more glaring, it took longer to find each catch; Milda did not see a world in which that trend would suddenly reverse itself.

"Someone has to strip the wrecks," Finley said. "And there's the pips, the crops. It's a lot of work."

Milda killed the engine. "It's too much for one person."

"Who needs sleep?" Finley said, unbuckling his life belt. "Seriously, Mills, I'll be fine."

"Only two catches so far this season—how're you going to afford groceries?"

"Yeah, *so far.*" Finley lowered his window and climbed out until he sat on the sill, with only his legs remaining in the cockpit. "Look, I know you're in love and all, but you don't have to do everything Jude says all the time."

The Crusher's floats rutted up against the dock. Their home was pretty much the same as when they were kids, save for the new solar panels, the antenna that picked up Russian satellites, and a new veranda braced over steel struts. Unlike many of their neighbors, they had the means to buy the creature comforts that made life in the fjords feel surprisingly habitable—they bought their cheese precottaged, their envelopes prestamped. They had their own apiary now, a row of hives to pollinate crops grown in the earth beds. When Finley desired a pint of gin, he told Happenstance to ring it up.

The ChickenCrusher still served them faithfully, though Milda had her eye on a SeaBird for short commutes. During the off-season Finley searched for spare parts, as he'd always done, and restored the wrecks that they'd found. Milda cultivated pearls and wrote op-eds for the *Tribune*. They kayaked to the trade post to collect bundles of keys that Hullulla Huntmoon and others postmarked downriver from Arctic City. At night Milda read aloud their father's letters—full of new hale and cheer, everything punctuated with exclamation marks. *Dear children! How are you!*

For the most part Milda and Finley were companionable. They had deep love—the kind that meant they spiked each other's tea and sought one another's well-being. Together they troweled sea stars off their catches, daubed the cuts, and sanded the legs until they were smooth. The restringing they saved for Temperance—she had perfect pitch and could lay a new soundboard faster than anybody. During the school year she lived with their father down south, where she played lute in the school orchestra. They traded letters: *Will you? Won't you? Have you? When?* and she wrote back: *Do you know? Have you heard? Did I tell you? What about?* Fry shipped her up in time for the territory's piano auction every June, and Temperance played her siblings' restoration handiwork for prospective buyers: happy, fruity Mozart, light on the flats. *Clap, clap, isn't she wonderful? And how much will it be? Is that all? What a bargain.*

Afterward, to commemorate their mother's death, the three siblings would fill the ChickenCrusher with chrysanthemums. Milda flew. When they were out over the Arctic Reef—the great sieve between the territory and the continent—she'd raise the hatch and Finley and Temperance would sweep bloom upon bloom upon bloom out over the water.

Temperance was twenty-two that summer and fashionable in the continental way—a pink heart tattooed on one temple and glasses made from old factory cogs. Every morning, she took meter readings of the fjord's water and spoiled Abraham Lincoln with nips of Finley's homemade goat bacon. One thing Milda insisted on was that everyone in the family lather on sun cream every morning. The sun was almost nuclear in intensity, the ozone as holey as their old veranda, and with their family history there was no excuse for sunburn. Because Finley and Milda were often away hunting, Temperance had invited her childhood sweetheart, Goldie, to stay, and the girls skied everywhere on the family's new Kraken water machine: a bubble dome attached to a Jet Ski. It was like zipping around in a snow globe.

The Crusher docked alongside the Kraken, and Milda unbuckled her life belt. "You know there's a whole world out there, right? Beyond just us. Everything doesn't always have to be about work all the time."

Finley reached back inside and unlatched his door. It swung open and he hopped from the window down onto the dock. "That's subjective," he said.

"You're subjective," Milda snapped back, opening her door. She climbed onto the Crusher's float. Shut the door and for a moment leaned her forehead against the side of the plane and closed her eyes. She heard Finley greeting Abraham Lincoln—"Who's my good boy?"—and Jude's boots clopping across the veranda. He'd been waiting for her all day. But when she opened her eyes and turned around, it wasn't Jude's hand waiting to help her step up onto the dock. "I've got you, partner," her brother said.

FOR DINNER Temperance had fried starfish patties. They cracked open a cask of house kelp ale, brewed with the farm's hops. The new veranda was larger than the house's original and ringed in earth beds growing chives, sunflowers, basil, and huckleberries. There were no knotholes for water to geyser up through, and they'd never replaced the chimes that Viola had put in place to warn of rising tides. A warning system didn't really matter anymore as even with the tractor tires they'd stacked atop the stilts to buy themselves a couple extra feet, the house now flooded a couple times a year, just as it had when the *Victory* sunk.

Milda kept her books on a shelf built as close as possible to the ceiling, alongside other prized possessions, like the family's record player. The shaggy, nine-foot grizzly hide that had been passed down in the Bloomer family hung behind the dining room table and served as a marker for how high the water crept. A decade ago only the claws had gotten wet, but that summer water had risen nearly to the bear's navel. At the current rate of increase, it'd only be a year or two before the bear was unable to keep its head above water.

Milda had never gotten used to living below sea level. They dealt with it as best they could. She and Finley had cut a drain in the floor of every room. Now when it flooded they'd wait for the tide to slack out, then lift the hatches. This worked fine for warm weather, but in the last few years the floods had begun happening year-round. Late last winter a foot of ice had frozen across the whole first floor; they'd skated around the living room and kitchen for weeks. Frozen bathroom pipes didn't work, and while Finley'd found the whole thing adventurous, Milda immediately knew she didn't want to spend another winter sponge-bathing and squatting over an ice hole chainsawed off the dock.

"You know what wouldn't be the worst thing in the world . . ." Temperance was saying as she dished plates around the outside eating table.

Finley cut into his starfish. Chewing on the end of an arm, he said, "I already had this conversation with my other sister."

"You've never even seen where I live," Temperance said wistfully, sitting down across from him. She forked herself a fritter. Using a knife, she sliced off a dainty bite and swirled it slowly through the sauce on her plate. "Aunt Flora would like to see you, you know. And Dad."

Finley looked at her as he took a long swallow of ale. "They're welcome up here anytime," he said.

"The Ravenwood doesn't even have a crest, Finn," Milda said as she diced the rubbery meat. Her knife squeaked against the ceramic of her plate and she dropped her utensils in frustration. *Clatter, clatter.* Under the table she felt Jude put his hand on her knee. "How much could it really be worth?"

"You're not an appraiser," Finley said.

"It won't take you all winter to fix up one forte."

"Two," Finley said, pointing his fork first at one sister, then the other. "Two so far."

Jude squeezed Milda's knee. He'd grown up lonely, the opposite of Milda and her siblings, packed tight in Jubilation House. The closest things he had to siblings were his Huntmoon cousins. For school, Jude had attended Panhandle University, and like most of the school's graduates he immediately went south for work. Though they'd known each other since childhood, he and Milda had just gotten together at the beginning of the summer, when Jude came north to run the boardinghouse. There was something bashful in the way Milda felt about him. He had sinuses so crooked they whistled in his sleep, and after he'd kissed her the first time, sitting on her roof among the solar panels, she'd stroked her thumbs across his curly eyebrows, wipers clearing a foggy windshield; how murky her world had been before; how little she'd realized.

Jude had another month before he had to leave to start September's new semester. Before they'd reconnected, Milda had believed that she'd found something like happiness in the fjords with her brother over the last ten years. Her alliance with Finley had developed a natural yoke as they'd aligned themselves to the same cause, and when Temperance visited, the three siblings played like old times. Blazing bonfires on the veranda, marshmallow toasts, sunlight for days. The solstice was still illustrious. The skies full of glory. They grilled porcupine steaks and whipped corncobs off the veranda for Abraham Lincoln and his lion family. They turned the memories of their family over and over, like roasting chestnuts, until they were wallowing in nostalgia. Viola, in what looked like a neoprene balaclava, saying, "Get finned up. We're going fishing." Viola scraping oysters from the shell with her teeth. Viola diving, pulling her one true son free.

After dinner Temperance rowed over to the platform with her siblings to feed the new pips and examine the Ravenwood's soundboard. She could plait fishline faster than anybody Milda had ever seen.

Since the day Queenie had pulled her into the tank as a kid Temperance had kept a pair of marine-grade agricultural shears holstered to her back when she worked on the platform. She'd also brought along a crate full of tools she'd pilfered from Finley's old dissection kits.

"You have to put all the strings back in the exact same place they were before," Finley said, flipping the lid.

Temperance attached a magnifying lens to her glasses and said, teasing: "Not if you want it to play."

"He means their rightful places," said Milda.

They watched Temp observe the tangled heartmass of strings. Then she unholstered her shears. Bent deep and made her cuts. Copper wire sprang up everywhere, the forte's lid was flung drunk and wide—eyewitness to its own autopsy. As she worked, Finley snapped a battery onto his saw and cut new boards for the lid. Milda patched places on the flanks where the wood had rotted through, then pulled ivory keys from one of the dozens of buckets of loose supplies on the platform and started fitting them into sockets. Without a crest to guide their restoration, it would be a hodgepodge repair.

When the sun finally set, shortly before midnight, they packed up their supplies and loaded the kayaks to row back to the house. As they paddled toward Jubilation House, Milda couldn't help but think that if there were an instrument more delicately strung than the human family she had yet to encounter it. Webbed together by a complicated series of levers and spools, they were each constantly exerting and releasing tension. Forever torquing against one another in both miserable and nonmiserable ways.

THEY FINISHED THE Ravenwood's restoration a few days later and Milda paddled straight to Disillusionment to put it up for sale. She'd known Happenstance, the owner of the trade post, her whole life. She'd spent many childhood hours sucking molasses pops as her parents bartered down the price of flour. She glanced around the shelves as she walked in now. There was little fresh produce, only food that could last for weeks: tins of Kamikaze Farms's chowed octopus, an antiscurvy tincture that smelled like pollen. Milda walked right up and slid the text for their classified ad across the counter:

> **FSBO: HAND-RESTORED RAVENWOOD OF UNKNOWN ORIGIN. RSVP WITH BEST OFFER TO KAMIKAZE FARMS.**

"It's fully restored, ready to go," she said.

Happy flipped over the ad, jotted something on the back, and slid the paper back across the counter. "I can take it from you in trade. That's store credit."

"I'll have to check with my partner."

"Tell Finley you don't have a crest, you don't have papers, you don't have lab tests," Happy said, ticking these off on his fingers.

"He says it's worth something."

"Worth something to Finley doesn't mean it's worth something to everyone. I'm taking a chance on this, remember. It's me doing you the favor here."

Customers were sparse in the aisles of the post—in fact, the whole store was empty save for a lone pilot next to Happy's counter studying a tacked-up map of the territory. Ten feet of canvas that had been shipped up from Panhandle Island. When Milda looked at that map she had an inkling of the promise this vast swath of land must've looked like to her great-great-great-great-grandfather Moose—how hopeful he would've felt settling this territory back when it was one raw, contiguous piece of land. Everything connected to everything else. Now it was a wholly divided landscape of discrete ecosystems. The Archipelago of Lost Saints, the Wild Beard Fjords. Disillusionment Bay. The Resurrection Mountains, where they'd met Hullulla Huntmoon. Ringing outward, the map scaled farther than any of Milda's drawings—deep into territory that had never been civilized: ten thousand winks of land known as One-Man-Standing Islands. The flooded outskirts of the Wild Beard Fjords.

Milda tried to picture what her mother would do in her shoes, how she would decide to proceed. Viola was always returning home to gripe about Happy's entitled sense of inflation: *Sometimes he's a good man and sometimes an outright swindler, you know he is.* Happy had mathematical tabulations, but he also relied on gut instinct and trust. Those were the same commodities that had gotten Milda into the air all those years ago. They had just lost Viola—the force that had stabilized her childhood—and no amount of money, no catch, was ever going to bring her back. Mathematics could never restore their world to its known order—it would take currency in another form. A series of gestures. Washing a dish. Laundry. Scrubbing barnacles off the Banana. More than any cash payout, what she wanted for Finley now was to recognize that they could not go on forever as they long had; fortes were a finite, endangered crop, increasingly difficult to find. Two catches that year would barely make enough to pay the electricity bill through the winter. But for Finley to move on from their hunting years, he'd first have to believe that they'd exhausted all potential search sites for the Napoleon. He was the one who'd lost it all those years ago, and she knew he believed if his nine-year-old arms had been just a little stronger, their lives would've turned out fundamentally different.

"I want that big map," Milda said, pointing at the canvas. "Throw that in and I'll drop the Ravenwood off this afternoon."

"Hold on now, I decide what's for sale and what's not in my shop."

Milda held out the slip of paper with the Ravenwood's ad text again, but when Happy tried to grab it she snatched it back and said, "If you want what I'm offering, you'll give me what you have."

Happy shook his head. "You kids don't need to be going all the way out there."

"Can I have the map or not?" she said irritably.

"You'll be off-radar," he said. "Nobody'll know where to look if you go down."

"We're not kids anymore," she said, and rapped her knuckles on the counter.

Milda accepted what remained of the trade in fuel. They had always paid their own way, that was stipulated from the beginning, and the Crusher hogged fuel. Happy disappeared into the back and came out wheeling a cart loaded with fuel canisters. He slapped a label on each lid. *Held in trust for: Milda Spahr.* With a few of those in the hatch they'd be able to power deep past any previous points of no return.

Back at home Milda tacked Happy's map to the living room ceiling and lay on the floor to memorize the geography. They'd flown the lower part of the Resurrection Mountains, but they'd only covered a fraction of the ground ringing out from the fjords. When Finley came down the ladder later, Milda was already packing hunting supplies. Food and a portable stove. The fuel canisters were lined up on the counter.

"You sold it?" he said, full of appreciation. "Nice. What's my cut?"

"Half that fuel is yours."

Finley picked up a canister and shook it. *Slosh-slosh*. "This is all you got?"

"There was only one deal so I made it," Milda said. "Be thankful."

"I thought we were going to make actual money this time," Finley said, carefully setting the canister back in line. He leaned against the counter, and she could see his disappointment—worry, even. "That was a good haul."

Every haul was a good haul to Finley, that was part of the problem. The paltry crop they'd caught so far that year told Milda it was unlikely they'd find another forte before she left in a month. She dropped the lid on her packing basket and snapped the lock. She hoisted it onto her shoulder and headed for the veranda. "Well, excuse me for getting us enough fuel to fly a little longer."

"It takes more than fuel to run this farm," said Finley, following her. "You better hope we find at least one more big score before you ditch me."

THEY FLEW TO the outskirts of Happy's map, then swung south to loop lazy circles over the pinkie end of the Wild Beard Fjords. Down below stretched yawning canyons of rose-colored stone, walls cut through with ledges where puffins stored their treasures and trained their adolescent pufflings to take their first flights. The fluffy, befuddled teenagers watched as their parents skittered unwanted debris off these ledges, unbraiding the braids and untwisting the twists that had held the birds' early childhood together.

Finley pressed the map to the windshield and shaded in the swath of coast. This page in Milda's atlas was in deplorable condition, pencil drawings faint from solar exposure. She'd embroidered the waterways, and the margins were covered in Finley's illegible scrawl. *Psalmist in the fjords! Fjords? Fjords!* The Crusher skimmed over a plateau, skis barely clearing the tops of spruce.

"Anything?" Milda asked.

Spruce, spruce, spruce. "Nothing," Finley said.

The engine sparked. Milda flicked a dial. She took a shot of coffee and poured one for Finley. The Crusher dropped into a narrow fjord, a straight fall of 150 feet to sea level.

"Really look this time," Milda said. The outskirts of the fjords were hundreds of miles from the original homesteading trail, not exactly the most fertile hunting ground. There was unlikely to be anything out here, but getting Finley to cross land off their search grid was never easy. "We're running low on daylight."

"I can't see what isn't there," Finley said.

Milda tapped the clock on the dash. "A couple more minutes of fuel, then we have to turn back."

"Tell me something I don't know."

Amplified by the stone walls, the chatter of puffins rose to a deafening fracas. Milda could barely hear herself conjugate basic thought. A narrow strip of beach bottlenecked the fjord's threshold, and she pointed at this, hoping Finley would spot something they could bring home. They'd been flying since early that morning and she was eager for meat grilled over a hot fire, ales with Jude on the veranda, and the chance to uncramp her legs. Below: a narrow strip of sand covered with huckleberry bushes and loose seaweed.

On the horizon: the first flares of sunset. Milda was about to shade this swath of the map, crossing it out, when something on the sand below glinted.

Snug against the base of the cliff: a forte. Midsize, top blown free, up to its hammers in sand. "Holy fish balls," Finley said.

"I don't believe it," Milda said, twisting the plane's wheel.

Finely pressed his binoculars to the window. "Looks like a Psalmist."

"You're the expert, not me," she said, and scanned the water for a landing site.

"Then get us on the ground."

The Crusher U-turned, landed on the sea, and floated back toward shore.

UP CLOSE, they could see that the instrument was in deplorable condition: salvageable, but barely. It had obviously been out of the water for decades. A restorationist's nightmare. The cedar boards had weathered gray and the strings were knitted into something resembling a mammoth knot. Squatting, Milda plunged her hands into the sand to feel for keys. Splinters, splinters, empty sockets. "Ivory's gone," she said.

Finley looked up from where he was digging with a spade. "All of it?"

"Treble for sure," she said. "We'll have to see about the rest."

"I'll check for a crest."

Many families had burned their initials, or their family insignia, into their instruments. It branded them against theft. Finley snapped open the supply bag and pulled loose *The Big Book of Homesteader Crests.* Hundreds of pages of brands. The LeFleur swirl atop their Walden. *H* for Happenstance on a Flutesky with silver keys. Mayflower. Pope. Bloomer. Milda admired the craftiness of the carpenters who'd executed the most decadent of these instruments—some had been outfitted in precious metals, others with copper wiring, all so that the families who owned them could rely long-term on their value. Nearly impossible to thieve on the trail, the largest fortes were the closest things most people in transit had to a bank. Vessels into which the families poured their energy, time, and resources before they were officially designated a plot of land. Milda could relate to the predicament of this situation. Born to a house that would likely one day disappear under the waves, she knew enough to take value where she could find it.

The forte they uncovered on the beach that night appeared to be an early edition Psalmist. Four-legged. It was clear that the music stand had once been painted with gold filigree. Though the leaf had long washed away, Milda could see where it had been applied to accent a prospector's pan of gold nuggets. As they uncovered the rest of the keyboard she said to Finley, squatting beside her, "It's in really bad shape."

"I can put it back together," he said confidently, laying out tools on the sand. Picks and brushes. He selected a set of long tweezers and jammed them into one of the empty key sockets. They rattled around, then clearly found something and pinched. Out came a thin spindle of ivory, glassed smooth, and Finley waved it in front of her face like a prize. "Would you look at that."

The forte had been out of the water a long time. It looked as though it would fall apart as soon as they tried to lift it. "You've never done a repair like this. Maybe we should just keep looking for one that doesn't need so much work. It's in a hundred different pieces," she said.

"We can't leave it here. We can do this," Finley said, moving along to the next socket. In went the tweezers. "Either help me or stop complaining."

As a girl, Milda had watched Finley and her mother dream of finding a haul, any haul—even one like this. They'd never gotten close—as a team they'd had little practical luck. Their most lucrative find had been a twelve-foot-tall music stand that Finley had recovered wholly by accident. But that hadn't stopped him from committing to memory the stages for this sort of excavation. Attack the sand with a shovel and you risked disrupting the tentative equilibrium holding everything in place. No, you had to come at the problem sideways. It was not unlike how Finley had finally convinced Milda to be his pilot—first by softening her with compliments about her yeast-making skills, next by appealing to her sense of caretaking. Milda believed he needed chaperoning, she always had, and Finley had played this to his advantage.

He began digging a moat a few feet out from the Psalmist's body. When the trench was large enough, he climbed in and used his trowel to work, slowly, toward the instrument. Milda joined him and together they made careful, tedious strokes. When the keyboard came uncovered Finley probed a set of lock-picking tools into the sockets to see what might pop loose. They'd both read that sometimes homesteaders stored trinkets in the secret pockets behind the keys: engagement rings or pearls; valuables brought to trade. The first few sockets held nothing, but light pressure in the bass clef brought out a letter wrapped in oilskin. Milda tucked it into her pocket to read later.

When it was too dark to see any longer they climbed out of the makeshift moat and set up camp. Parachute tent. Sleeping bags. Finley took a flask out of a hidden pocket, uncapped it, and passed it to his sister. "For celebration," he said. "It's going to be a Big Catch, I can feel it."

To Milda the forte was a mess. It would take weeks of work to repair, and even then they wouldn't make much without a detailed history. They lay side by side on the sand to enjoy the feeling of alcohol illuminating their eyeballs. Finley had sweat through his work clothes and Milda could smell a similar heat coming off herself. Soon they'd need to rise and light a fire for dinner. In the morning they could finish excavating, lift the Psalmist free, and head home. "What're you going to do with your cut, when we sell it?" Finley said. This was a popular game they played after each find: *Yuzu trees*, Milda might say. Then, *No, a crate of floss*. "There's gotta be something you want," he said.

"You really think we're going to get a decent price?"

"Seriously, Mills, that's the easy part."

"I thought this was supposed to be the easy part."

"This is the hard part. The part nobody wants to do is always the hard part," he said.

Milda was quiet. "What are you going to do with your cut?"

The flask was in his hand again. Sand had crusted the rim but he didn't seem to care. The liquor soothed Milda's nerves now, she could feel it lulling her into a collective consciousness that had her looking at this land in a whole new light. If she had money, what would she do? In terms of Jubilation House the answer was simple. A new set of stilts. An addition atop the attic so neither of them had to crouch in the eaves to pull on their wet suits. A plane that didn't rattle like death's holy ghost when they reached cumulus altitude. Crates of oranges.

"You want to know what I'd do with the money?" Finley flopped onto his back in the sand. He put an arm behind his head. "I guess just more of this."

"Making sand angels."

"No, like, *this*." Finley sat up and gestured toward the plane, bobbing. The ChickenCrusher was haloed in puffins. They dove over the plane into the depths of the fjord, where plenty of everything, he mused, was still waiting to be brought up.

But what would happen to their world once all of this was exhumed? Would the ferries quit for tropical waters? Would the tourists disappear, taking with them their farmers' market coins? If the hunters all left tomorrow, they'd struggle to make it with just their farm's wares for income. The fortune they'd made from the Bluefin had gone quickly, and the Napoleon was still only a dream. Their great-great-great-great-grandfather Moose, who'd first sledded the forte north, had fallen on the territory wanting the same things as Milda herself—security, adventure; a home that couldn't be taken away. She could feel the weight of all that rooting her to this particular geographical pinpoint atop the planet. How much of what still kept her in the territory was gravity and how much her own free will?

Finley had always loved dragging things ashore: shells, at first, as a child. Child-size dentures. Ship wheels. That hook set early and deep. Milda had never felt such an impulse, yet here she was camping alongside him because she could not bear to lose a brother and he could not bear to lose their home, and these were the guiding stars of their young adult lives. It was all so clear in that moment; all so crystal.

THE NEXT THING she remembered, she was waking up, hungover. Morning. Both of them eager for home. They finished digging out the remainder of the Psalmist. Finley hooked pulleys around the body. The ropes ran all the way from the forte across the water to where the Crusher floated in the surf. They tucked their belongings into packs and swam out to the plane. Climbed aboard.

The engine grated, then caught. Finley manned the pulley as Milda steered toward open water. When she clicked into second gear—*Get ready to lift*—she looked down to see the Psalmist dragging across the beach. The weight dredged a groove deep as any sled trough. Along both cliffs puffins tweeted their complaints at the disturbance. They beaked up debris and dropped it from the ledges in protest. Twigs and ribbons torn from the braids of homesteader girls. Irises that landed on the water and swished toward the deep end of the fjord. The prop flipped horizontal and the floats lifted free. The plane hovered.

"Crank it," Milda said.

Finley whaled on the pulley.

The Psalmist lifted off the beach. As the forte reeled up underneath the plane, the puffins scrambled from their burrows and down fell a confetti of the past—pumpkin seeds and lace collars and sheet music splotched with their guano. None were items Milda would have collected herself, but she couldn't fault the birds for their drive: the appealing comfort of velvet; shards of bone.

For historical entrepreneurs, everything was a clue to what bygone people had wanted, what they had feared. Take the Psalmist, for example: Milda could hazard a guess as to the character of the people who'd left her behind. A light, compact instrument such as this probably had belonged to an elderly couple. The legs were not original to the body, so at some point it had sustained damage. Perhaps the lid had been torn free in a storm; perhaps it now hung in some backwoods cabin as a souvenir of the freedom the family would never achieve. She unrolled the letter she'd found behind the piano key and passed it to Finley to read:

Dearest Mother,

Where I write to you from I do not know for I haven't had a map for days and consider myself lost. I've had nothing hot to eat since the last of the hare. The ocean water is too full of salt to drink. Do not worry. At night the Psalmist keeps me warm. At night the birds come. I sleep well. Tell my brothers it's a land of bounty here, like Auntie promised, and there is hope to be had. Tell my brothers I have lived and seen enough. Tell my brothers one day I will lead us all back here.

Your dearly departed son,
Thornton

On the flight home Finley paged through *The Big Book of Homesteader Crests* a second time to see if he could cobble the Psalmist any sort of heritage. There were over a hundred listed Psalmists, none registered to anyone named Thornton. But the forte had to have belonged to someone—everything came from somewhere, everything had an origin. Milda knew prospective buyers would be more inclined to loosen their purse strings if they could throw a weighty tale behind the product. Marilyn Monroe's wisdom teeth. You'd bid for those, right? Amelia Earhart's skull. You'd throw down everything you had?

Goddamned right you would.

The Crusher reached the top of the cliff and aimed its nose

toward home. *Hold on to your girdles, ladies and gentlemen,* Milda thought—from here toward home it would be nothing but blue skies and egg sandwiches, the sun yolking toward her zenith. Their latest catch dangling between the plane's floats like the pendulum in an old grandfather clock.

Hullulla

RiverCamp
August, one month after the Psalmist discovery

Trout ran year-round, but when the sockeye migrated up the Kamikaze to spawn Auntie V ran RiverCamp hard, no time for leeway. For several weeks at the end of the summer the fish swam the river's current, washing residual metals out of their gills on their way past. After supper fishers stood at the gutting table until all hours, and Saturday nights Hullulla stationed herself across the table from Finley Spahr. Ever since he'd first attended her Sunday service at the beginning of the summer, the ChickenCrusher 3000 had landed at RiverCamp most every weekend.

At first they'd simply sliced fish and debated celestial mythology, the fulcrum of a dark star, how day after day they each miraculously survived. For as long as Hullulla could remember she'd innately understood the rhythm of spiritual life, but it took weeks for her to recognize the same rhythms in Finley's stories of life as a hunter: dive, grab, save. One trout, two, a bushel of fish.

As they talked, Saura and her cousins took turns sneaking up to push fish eyeballs into Finley's pocket. He pulled these out and, to the shock of the children, popped them in his mouth. Sucked them theatrically. "Delicious," he said. Saura squealed in delight when he set down his knife and chased her up the beach, snapping a salmon jaw at her braids.

One night Hullulla slit the belly of the salmon in front of her and out spilled not ivory but a thousand gelatinous orange eggs. *Plink-plink*, onto the table; precious cargo. She scooped them up, trying to cram handfuls back into the torn cavity as Finley caught Saura and they tumbled, laughing, onto the sand. She didn't realize how distracted she'd become watching them until she felt Auntie V's hand on her arm. Gently, Auntie V took the fish and poured the roe into the communal bowl in the middle of the table. *Focus up,* Hullulla chided herself. She grabbed another fish from the bucket at her feet and slit the stomach, pulling loose a slick ivory key narrowed at one end to a sharp point. "Give him your burdens and walk into the valley of peace," she said, holding up the key. It must've caused incredible discomfort in the sockeye's stomach—fish or not, that wasn't the kind of trauma anyone soon forgot.

"What if people don't have burdens?" Finley said, returning to the table. He flipped his knife in the air and caught it by the handle. "What then?"

Hullulla pulled out the sockeye's intestines, heart, liver. "We've all got burdens," she said, tossing a kidney to one of the dogs. Her hands glittered with scales as she gestured down the table: flip, scrape, the dip of tweezers pulling loose tiny bones. "Or what about this one? 'Cast your net and reap the Lord's bounty'?"

A crooked grin. "Does it have to be a net?" Finley asked. He held up a piece of periwinkle river glass pulled from the fish in front of him. It winked ultraviolet specks in Hullulla's eyes until she had to look away. Finley slid the glass into his pocket and said, "'Cause I've caught plenty of bounty myself."

The following Saturday the Crusher arrived early enough for Finley to help carry the week's panniers downriver to the broker. The ivory trader was a burly man with a greasy salt-and-pepper crown. He mulled over the load, dropping each key onto the scale. The results were recorded in a rotten little notebook. "Well," Hullulla said. The man held up a finger, cocked his head. "We're not going to wait forever," Finley said. The authority in his voice surprised Hullulla, and when the broker slid a handful of coins across the table she didn't even count them before saying, "That's not enough." The broker made a dismissive noise, and Hullulla monkey-brawled her fists on the table, knuckles down. They eyed each other. Without looking away the broker opened a drawer. More silver rattled onto the table. "That's what I thought," Hullulla said.

On the walk back Finley told her about the trade post on Disillusionment Bay where he traded for yeast and yogurt; gin when the farm was flush. He'd seen bundles of Arctic City keys stacked into bricks of twelve: sold by the octave. Wouldn't Hullulla like to see that for herself? As they single-filed through river grass Finley snapped off heads of grain. "My sister's leaving for the continent soon. I won't be able to get up here as often," he said, chewing chaff. They walked in silence for a few minutes before he added, "You could come visit me."

Hullulla was walking barefoot along the rocks bordering the Kamikaze to collect river cabbage to bring back to camp; suddenly her feet felt cold, too cold. She stubbed her toe and cursed. "The chapel needs me," she said, though this wasn't entirely true; Maple needed her, her aging parents needed her. She squatted and with one hand roughly hacked at the root of a clump of cabbage; with the other she pulled the head, dripping, out of the water. Finley unbuckled the lid of the pannier strapped across his chest and she dropped it in so forcefully he caught her hand. "Hey," he said. "We'll work something out."

After the gutting table closed down, Hullulla and Finley spread their sleeping bags underneath the Custer&Sons. He whispered to her about finding the Psalmist, about the strange islands on the map tacked to the living room ceiling in Jubilation House. She whispered back that Gussie had found a mate and would likely have a new calf in the spring. When the sun rose they were holding hands across their divide. "Pardon me," he said, and started to pull away. "Pardon you," Hullulla said, pulling him back.

THE MORNING OF the fall equinox, Hullulla rode Gussie up the trail to visit her family at the New Chapel's construction site. She brought with her panniers of river glass reclaimed from trout bellies. She and Maple held the pieces up to the light asking, "What do you think this was once upon a time?" before slotting them into gaps in the chapel's stained-glass window. For three months they'd been trying to rebuild the iconic chapel window. The centerpiece triptych had arrived missing key pieces and thus hadn't yet been installed behind the New Chapel's pulpit as planned. After scouring the trail, the congregation conceded that the original glass was long gone, so they went to work collecting whatever washed in from the river. Once a week Ezra soldered the new pieces into the triptych's gaps. It was nearly complete.

Hullulla's brother, Ezra, had promised their congregation he'd install the window in time for everyone to watch the fall equinox's sunset seep across the glacier. A holy moment, he said. The original triptych featured a panorama of loaves and fishes—something of an irony now, as the plateau was too high to grow wheat, too dry to catch trout. Patches of mosaiced river glass had fundamentally altered the picture, though exactly how wouldn't be clear until the congregation hoisted it into place that evening.

All told, the remaining Huntmoon congregation numbered less than a hundred, but they remained a community—Happenstances and Starrs and Popes, families banded together to preserve the homes they'd made in Arctic City. Over the next year tidy cedar homes would ring out from the New Chapel. Already plots in a community garden had been staked and planted with boreal chard, beets, huckleberries, and basil. Rocco Pope sold moonshine bottled in old milk jars from his wagon while the schoolchildren assembled the apiary that had arrived last week, bees in boxes smoked dormant. Mrs. Huntmoon and Maple had already started up a sewing mill in the chapel during the weekdays. Their pupils skinned deer, porcupines, and rabbits, then tanned the hides. The leather was waxed, edges beveled smooth, and sewn into vests, pants, and slippers. Superior quality.

Hullulla didn't know yet how she fit in the family's new home; unlike in Arctic City, they'd all be sharing the new parsonage, and Hullulla hadn't lived with her brother in a long time. He'd left home when she was twelve to contract with a three-person telecommunications team parachuting onto newly formed islands. Ezra Huntmoon, Anker Starr, Minion Huckle. Being the son of a preacher didn't pay lucratively, so Ezra had run off to spend his teenage years building broadcast towers. Her brother was born with a bicep and could really whale a hammer. Using what resources were easily at hand, their three-person team repaired or constructed towers tall enough to bounce signals to the outskirts of the territory. But the thing that few had anticipated about water rising the world over, all at once, was that it didn't rise equally everywhere. Every year some old towers sunk, and at the same time, new islands needed fresh telecommunication networks. So they busted up old railroad lines and sleds and felled spruce for supplies, built towers as tall and robust as possible, then kayaked to the next island and did the same thing all over again.

One day Hullulla's prodigal brother had come rolling home from this work after over a decade away. Drunk. One eye sickly green from a punch to the face. Hullulla had barely recognized him. He wasn't going back, he said; he was home to make an honest life for himself. Their parents gave him a bed and tended to his care. They nourished him body and soul in the parsonage attached to the Old Chapel until he was strong enough to stand before the congregation and take a turn leading sermons. Preaching didn't come to him naturally, it never had—and by then he'd spent years with a hammer for a best friend. At least the Huntmoon congregants were tenderhearted pacifists. Marrying Maple lent him security in the Reverend's eyes; he'd been properly yoked, finally, and even Hullulla could see that helming the chapel's pulpit was naturally a team sport.

"Have you seen the parsonage?" Maple asked, meeting her at the hitching post. She held out an apple cube in her palm, flat, and Gussie nibbled it up.

Hullulla looped the reins over the post, pulled them tight into a manger tie. "Not yet."

"Your room's just about ready," Maple said, voice full of excitement. "Come on."

Attached to the New Chapel, the parsonage had three bedrooms outfitted with narrow, lumpy beds covered in Maple's brightly colored quilts. They shared a bathroom with the New Chapel—a giant trough sink, composting toilet, and shower run from rainwater collected in a cistern on the roof. Maple led her to the farthest bedroom—through the window Hullulla watched Ezra throw a saw over his shoulder and stalk toward a small sapling grove. "When are you going to move in?" Maple asked. "RiverCamp's gotta be getting cold."

After a summer sleeping in the open air, being inside the parsonage stuffed Hullulla's head. Looking around the bedroom, she tried to imagine sleeping under the low ceiling, no stars to be seen. The lavender yak wool rug would never hold up to the tread of her fishing boots. On the dresser someone—Hullulla suspected her mother—had arranged the combs and ribbons she'd used for her hair when she was a girl. Above the dresser hung a heart-shaped mirror. It was a room designed for childhood Hullulla; single, lonely Hullulla preserved in a diorama created to look exactly the same as the old parsonage. It was not comforting, as she'd expected, to wander through this museum of her youth—rather, it felt eerie, festooned with banana velvet ribbons she couldn't remember ever wearing. Her fists clenched. To hide the reaction from Maple she stuck her hands in her pockets, sweeping her fingers against what she now thought of as her good luck charm, the black pearl ring.

Calved off the glacier months before, it was a treasure, a secret. She still didn't know what to do with it. Discarding it now seemed heartless, not to mention foolish—keeping it, complicated. "Remember this?" she said, opening her hand to show Maple.

"Better not show your mother," said Maple, smiling conspiratorially. "She'll get ideas."

Hullulla closed her fingers. "No kidding."

If Hullulla's parents saw the ring they would make assumptions; they would believe the world had righted itself into the natural order of a girl, a wedding, perhaps one day a baby. Finley Spahr was not the prospect her parents would have chosen for her, she knew that. He lived in a house slowly sinking into the ocean and relied for his income on an industry even less predictable than fishing; he threw out line after line in search of the inanimate. He was not a person whose motivations they were equipped to understand. Given the choice, her mother would no doubt have selected someone like Maple, devoted and practical. Patient. Finley had many admirable qualities, but allowing the world to unfurl itself around him in its own sweet time was not one of them.

"What's that?" Mrs. Huntmoon asked, appearing in the doorway.

Hullulla's palm closed. "Nothing."

Mrs. Huntmoon looked at her, and Hullulla saw a film of confusion in her mother's eyes—though it had been Mrs. Huntmoon who had encouraged her to see more of the territory, ever since Hullulla had left home that summer they'd had a prickly relationship. At least once a week her mother wrote beseeching letters: *Hullulla, my darling, I pray you haven't wandered too far from the Good Lord's flock!* Mrs. Huntmoon had married the Reverend young, a few years younger than Hullulla was now, in an elopement that launched her into a life of piety. She hadn't quit the church since. She garlanded pews for Easter service, dispersed alms—but even as a girl Hullulla had known that her father had the superior job. Once a week he stood at the pulpit pulling scriptural references from thin air, always managing to wring life lessons on generosity and persistence from Old Testament parables scribed by what he referred to as the world's earliest homesteaders. Thousands of years later, as Hullulla breaststroked out of the Old Chapel after service, their obsession with lineage and parting flooded seas sounded not so much like ancient history as like the prediction of a strange supernatural world to come. One that would take a lifetime to explain to a congregation, one Sunday at a time.

The three women walked through the shared bathroom and into the New Chapel's nave, where the congregation was fitting the final pieces of river glass into the last gaps in the window. A couple winks. What looked like a fish eye. Hullulla tried to imagine what the new, half-baked triptych would look like when it was raised into place. While the congregation worked, she went out the front door to feed Gussie. The moose had been hitched for hours and was lathered behind the ears. Blackstrap flies nipped her eyelids and Hullulla swatted them away. She overheard Ezra say, "What do you want to do?"

She peered around the chapel's corner. Her father and brother stood in the narrow bar of shade cast by the New Chapel, shelling pumpkin seeds with their teeth. "What do *you* want to do?" the Reverend said testily. "I'm not going to be preaching here forever."

When Ezra had left home to join the broadcast crew, he and the Reverend had broken on hard terms. Even though he'd eventually returned, the Reverend had never quite forgiven Ezra for once shirking the mantle of the Lord. Ezra spit out shards of shell when he said, "We can still put it up, but it's not going to look the same. You should prepare yourself."

Hullulla's stomach, empty of the fried trout she'd eaten riding Gussie up the plateau, went sour. It had been her job to shepherd the window glass to the New Chapel's site. She still didn't know where the pieces had gotten lost—maybe when she'd stopped to help Maple, maybe the first night after she'd left for RiverCamp; or maybe they'd never even been loaded onto the wagon to begin with.

"I guess it's better we put up something than nothing," the Reverend said sadly, pulling back on his work gloves. "Better at least the mustard seed."

It had been Hullulla's initiative to hunt river glass all summer to finish the triptych. But glass from the Kamikaze resurfaced milk-hued; smooth as ghee, it rainbowed different colors depending on who was looking. She was not blind to the fact that fit into the original triptych, river glass clouded the crisp, heirloom delineations. Loaves, praying hands, basket after basket of blessed fish. Now it all swirled together, an impressionistic hurricane. Of course the window would never look the same, how could it? And therein lay the Reverend's disappointment.

Quietly, Hullulla unhitched Gussie. She hopped up and rode bareback around the New Chapel in time to see ladders stretched up the back wall. It was time. Several men, including Ezra, climbed up and hooked their safety harnesses to the New Chapel's rafters. They hung, trussed. Down below, the saplings Ezra had sawed earlier that day were roped, loosely, to the first panel of the triptych. They provided a stable framework so that the glass could be pulleyed up and into place. Inside the chapel the congregation lit lanterns and flicked on flashlights. Gussie snorted and Hullulla said, "Whoa now."

From her vantage, Hullulla saw nothing but color. Amethyst and umbilical teal. Spurs to flanks, she guided Gussie away from the chapel in the hope of gaining a better perspective. Though the New Chapel had been built from the Old Chapel's bones, each stone replaced in the exact same notch, it now somehow appeared to her smaller than it had on the Kamikaze River. In the distance she heard Ezra calling, "Come on, come on, we're nearly there." Gussie's neck smelled of clay and vinegar. A moose wasn't easy to break—it had taken Hullulla over a year to get Gussie to lead with a halter. Now she pawed across the plateau.

On the moose, Hullulla was higher than the world, eighteen hands high. When she turned around to face the chapel again the afternoon had officially dimmed. She watched the congregation lever the second piece of the triptych up and into place. As light streamed through the stained glass, the glacier beyond lit up in Technicolor. It was a beautiful transmutation to witness: auroral violets and emeralds dancing across hundreds of feet of ice. "Ready, set, go!" called Ezra as the third piece of the triptych rose into the frame.

At her first communion, years earlier, Hullulla had drunk consecrated huckleberry wine under this three-piece window. Maple had knelt beside her in a matching white gown, high lace rimming both their necks. *And thus, and so,* the Reverend had said, passing them wafers. He tapped the crowns of their heads. Hullulla raised her eyes. The old triptych, the perfect one that no longer existed, had watched over her since she was a baby.

Now the burgeoning fall sunset streamed through the new window to hit the glacier full force. All three pieces of the triptych glowed, but there was distortion in the light. Where river glass replaced the original window's panes, the color projected on the glacier seemed to seep deeper into the ice. From a distance it looked like there was something suspended in the illumination. Hullulla kicked Gussie closer, and the whole picture came into view.

Just under the ledge where she and Maple had sat months earlier, chipping ice, a woman was frozen several feet deep. The remains of a woman. Her arms encircled a pregnant belly. The madonna was a one-eyed skull with a braid of blond hair. Naked. Most of her skin had been grated clean deep enough to expose muscle. One shin was stripped to bone. How long had this woman been frozen up there? Suspended and unbreathing? Watching them live their little lives trekking up and down from the plateau, a jealous guard to the treasure she'd found in her own belly.

The light shifted and just as suddenly as the woman appeared, she was gone. A mirage. In Hullulla's experience, sermons, or at least the good ones, tended to knit themselves together in moments such as these. Subtle cues, part happenstance, part faith, if she was doing the work right she hardly noticed until she was almost done. She began concocting a message to preach back at RiverCamp, how contrary to popular belief, the foolish man's house, built on a bar of sand, didn't sink all at once—it eroded slowly over time. A century, two, generation after generation of a family believing sand could be something it couldn't. The daughter in the story a girl like herself, who prided herself on a few choice skills—such as how she'd never lost a match with a trout, not one.

Now Hullulla gave Gussie her lead and they went tearing across the plateau. Down the trail, and they made time. When she glanced back, she could no longer see the shadow of the madonna—just watercolored spectrals meant to represent God's divinity on Earth. On the plateau the New Chapel's construction was preordained, each stone mortared in exactly the same place as before, but at RiverCamp her own triptych was still largely unmapped. Her future, imaginary children, even faith—it was all about perspective. What she was riding from didn't matter as much as what she was riding toward, and when it all came down to it, a savior could look like just about anything. A natal family projected across ice, a girl riding a moose away from her birthplace. A bright red ChickenCrusher descending from the sky, KAMIKAZE FARMS scrawled along the side.

Hullulla rode toward RiverCamp, where the flood was coming up and there was familiarity. A new family, a new tune set to the slap of children's feet. "Have you heard?" she'd say, swinging down from Gussie's back. "Have you heard the good news?"

Her congregants would rush up to greet her.

"What? What is it?" Finley would say.

"I'm back," she'd reply.

Moose

Singing Spruce Forest
August, first homestead expedition

By August they'd fallen so far behind schedule that their nights were reduced to spare two-hour breaks, not even enough time to justify setting up a tent. With the accelerated pace they could still make the homestead plots before snowfall, but there'd be no time to build structures or plant even the shortest-blooming of crops; most likely they'd have to sleep in their tents all winter. Unwelcome news. Almost everyone lapsed into a state of anxious stomach cramps similar to what they'd undergone on the ship. It was not uncommon to see someone break off midconversation and sprint to the woods, emerging twenty minutes later, red-faced and relieved. Their tempers, which had had peaks and valleys the whole trip, flared up as soon as they exited the forest and realized they'd lost all cushion of time. And so they stormed through the valleys of the muskegs, breaking things with their minds.

"I don't understand why I'm not seeing the North Star," Uncle Huntmoon said, glancing between a constellation chart and the sky.

"You're looking at a piece of paper," said Thornton.

"I'm looking at the sky."

Rocket set their path, but many families tried to keep track of the route themselves; who knew when the knowledge might be useful. Thornton snatched the paper from his uncle's hands. "You can't look for two things at the same time. Pick what you want the most and look for that first."

The ruts grew fainter the farther they traveled beyond the Singing Spruce Forest and many began to lack the confidence that they were still being guided at all. When the route disappeared entirely, trail markings had to be manually sourced, and this slowed them considerably. Without preformed ruts to smooth the way, the sleds were forced to break raw ground. Some days the whole train moved only a dozen feet. To make matters worse, logs were always falling up ahead, and the bear bells that shingled Moose's ankles scared away local game. He had to venture farther and farther each day to procure even a small hare. When he returned to camp everyone was always picking fights with one another:

"It's not the noise, it's the stench."

"You can't expect a man not to sweat when he's hauling his brains out."

"Would it kill you to take a dunk in the river?"

"Who ate the last of the salt pork?"

"Oh really? Oh really?"

"Don't take that tone with me, Edythe."

Violent outbreaks became commonplace. At night Moose awoke to the *wha-pump, wha-pump* of trailbreakers' duking fists. One evening as he mucked back with a hare strung up in his belt he heard a noise coming from some bushes. He peeled back the branches to discover the gang of young tykes—those who'd prodded along the chicken herd beside him day after day—beating a porcupine. "Roll it over," a boy said, probing the creature with his club. The children kicked at the soft belly with their boots.

For weeks, Moose knew, Arthur hadn't been sleeping. He'd been making a real nuisance of himself, truth be told, groaning on the mattress in frustration as sleep eluded him. So it was a relief to Moose when his stepfather simply stopped trying and instead sat up all night by the fire, purportedly keeping watch for bears. "I don't think you can stay up all night and still stay alive," Una said.

"I'll sleep when I need to sleep," Arthur said, staring into the fire.

Una put her hand on his shoulder. "You're exhausted. We're all exhausted."

"What we need is a plan for meat," Arthur said.

Thus far Moose hadn't shot anything larger than a hare, and the thought of tracking and laying waste to the caribou they'd need to get through the winter terrified the hell out of him. With time speeding past so quickly now, they would need to hunt enough to keep them in meat until the ground thawed next spring. But they wouldn't have time to waste then, either. Arthur sketched all night by the fire, rendering their new homestead, cookout, dog keep, and cabin. In the morning he fanned out these drawings with the sanctity of a reverend laying sacrament. To Moose's eye the sketches were mathematically precise, including plans for a dog harness that would rig up the team to plow a field. "Instant farm," Arthur said.

"I've never heard of dogs plowing a field."

"That's why it's called an invention."

Moose eyed their team basking in the sunlight. The sled was pulled by nine brother-and-sister pairs. Just yesterday they'd whipped the whole sled off-trail to track a strange scent. It had taken hours to calm them down again. Moose had seen other teams careen down ravines, and worse. The forty-one animals it took to pull the Mayflower sled were always vomiting up their breakfast, so the rest of the train spent all day tracking through their bile. Heaping more responsibility onto the shoulders of these animals didn't seem like the height of common sense to Moose, but as the expedition dragged toward its conclusion he knew that without them—without help of some kind—they'd never be able to build up the homestead in the way they'd envisioned. Plowed garden rows and jerkied salmon strung by the gills. A roof to keep off inclement weather.

Beyond the Singing Spruce Forest, the trees naturally thinned of their own accord, giving way to open valleys of scrub. These valleys were barricaded on either side by the rising peaks of the Resurrection Mountains. Although the stone engendered a sense of security in their location, the ground sponged underfoot. Moose's boots sank up to four inches with each step. Miles of muskeg-soaked fields stretched before them. Creeks cut everywhere. The world was all dwarf plants and alpine strawberries creeping their runners. It was difficult to acclimate to the sudden sparsity of vegetation, especially after spending months shrouded by the spruce.

With no forest left to log, the trailbreakers fell back to walk with the rest of the train. These fellows were in sad spirits and Moose couldn't blame them—for the last few months they'd lived in their own biosphere, chopping logs and calculating preliminary cartography. Back with everyone else, their duties were reduced to the drudgeries that Moose had been performing this whole time: hauling buckets of water, foraging meals for the dogs, aiding grandparents as they relieved themselves. Work with no glamour.

It was a welcome surprise when word filtered down the train that there would be a wedding when they reached Grizzly Bear Hot Springs. Minnie Mayflower and Marty Crockett, one of the trailbreakers. Most everyone had an inkling why, though even Una was careful to talk around the practicalities. "When it's love, it's love," she said. Moose couldn't believe the good fortune of this timing—a whole day at the hot springs would be ideal for soaking both his cares and his hip. He might even foster a brief sense of enjoyment. Reclaim a sense of his boyhood freedom. Looking forward to this respite lightened the spirits of everyone but Rocket. Their guide cautioned them against losing even one single day. "A wedding's not an emergency. I'll tell you what's an emergency and that's winter," he said.

Though everyone worried about it, the threat of snow was still impossible to conjure; it felt far away, unlike the daily realities of the trail. Of everyone, it was the youngest who took the hardest brunt of trail life. They slept as poorly as everyone else, which was to say almost not at all. Each afternoon the piano lids were bolted open so that anyone under the age of ten could bed down for a nap on the road. The largest instruments were flush with room, but with a mattress crammed against the soundboard of the Psalmist, Pumpkin could barely squeeze her meager shape inside. When Moose looked down the train it was to a disconcerting sight. Lids of pianos undulating like a line of wooden sails. All those skinny limbs flowering out of the tops of the fortes, the *whump-whump* of baby anklebones striking ivory. A drumbeat impossible to escape.

GRIZZLY BEAR HOT SPRINGS was made up of a trio of naturalized pools. Up close the water smelled of sulfur, but still managed to appeal. Dead trees scaffolded the rim, and all around the ground was covered in caribou skulls. Parched bone. The little kids went after these, kicking. Skulls flew through the air, coating everything and everyone in diatomaceous dust. By the time the Bloomers' sled pulled into view, the rest of the train had already staked out ground for the night. The train hadn't stopped this early in weeks, and there was a festive feeling to the whole atmosphere. They spread blankets around the rim of the largest pool. Neighbors brought out preserves. Sour pickles and honey. Gourds with warty turbans, beet syrup, wilted dinosaur kale picked wild. The LeFleurs had wheels of blue goat cheese to trade, and the kids were sent to gather up as many eggs as the hens could lay. Rocket walked around with a tapestry of caribou jerky, tearing off pieces for the children.

Everyone was in such a keen mood that it took little persuasion to get some of the best players congregated around their instruments. There was no pattern or logic among people in terms of who played and who didn't. Thornton, Grandpa Happenstance, Minnie Mayflower, a seven-year-old prodigy named William, and Moose's own mother. The smallest tykes were boosted atop the Bluefin so they could see. The instrument vented music not through its hood, like most of the others, but through a delicate series of gills along each side. The kids cheered and waved strings of bunting as Papa Mayflower lined up to walk Minnie around the pool to where Marty stood waiting.

It was a brief service, performed in a few lines by Rocket. Afterward, the young couple was gifted a basket of food and the Mayflowers' spare tent and sent off to a nearby ravine for a few hours of privacy. There was no confusion in Moose's mind about what they'd be doing. Enjoying for themselves the pleasures of adulthood, the pleasures of bodies grown into their natural state.

Around the pools, the rest of the train started to cut loose. The fellows turned their backs while some of the ladies denuded and went floating in the water. It wasn't a full show of indecency, but it wasn't entirely proper, either. Nipples, a handful of ballooned underskirts, slender legs kicking across the surface. Sunset rainbowed against the Resurrection Mountains and then Rocket sounded the whistle for the bathing parties to switch. Women out, men in.

Moose disrobed. At first he kept to the shallows, sponge-bathing his undercarriage. It had been some time since his last cleaning. Then he swam to the center of the pool and assumed the dead man's float. Music started up. Moose had heard the pianos played one at a time, but almost immediately his mother and Thornton took up a duet. They threw stanzas back and forth. The rhythm reminded Moose of learning to cast a reel. Back, back, release. Building on each other's progressions, the melody was lighthearted, everything major key. The sound of the Psalmist did not boom out over the water with the same gusto as the Napoleon's, but together they created a good ambience. Una freed her left hand from the harmony and clapped a beat against her leg. Other pianists started up. Grandpa Happenstance, Mama Mayflower, and later Minnie herself. The kids gathered around took up the rhythm, and soon everyone had joined in.

They played in concert, each person taking a turn with the melody before surrendering it to the next. The combination of music and hot water rendered Moose dizzy with relaxation. He watched the little tykes on the lid of the Bluefin stand up and one by one leap into the water. Over the top of all this merry noise, somehow he heard Thornton begin to sing.

Particular melodies had a way of haunting, underscoring nightmares, breaking the heart anew with old sentiment. Music could rend Moose deeper than any memory, even one turned over and over in his mind like a river stone. Long into adulthood, this song still remained one:

Oh, the tinkling of the Tronstein in the honey pine trees
Lures settlers to the off-key springs
Where the black spruce sings
Deep in the Glacial Front's lullaby ravines

The tune was jaunty. Before they knew it, they were all singing. Arms clapping around neighbors' shoulders. Moose's mother clutched her belly, laughing. "He's kicking, come feel this." Moose stroked over. He climbed out of the water and put his ear to his mother's belly. The little brother Moose desperately wanted swirled around, showing that he too could swim, and Moose felt a flicker of pride. He used his mind to telegraph back the message *See you soon, little guy.*

Nearby a young boy surfaced and tossed a rabbit skull to his sister. She set it atop her head and swanned about the water until it fell off and sunk. Bottles of wine were uncorked and bandied about, and after that everything went loose and lambent. The liquor was of a caliber Moose had not tasted before—spicy and mentholated, it singed the lining of his esophagus. People began to dance. Fathers and mothers crushed together in moist embraces. Braids whipped. His mother unfurled her hair into a gold cloud and the sun arched down between the curves of the Resurrection Mountains. Moose didn't know how long they blazed that night, certainly some longer than others—at some point he climbed inside the Napoleon for warmth, curled up, and fell asleep.

When he awoke, bodies were draped over every available surface. Fires smoldered. Empty pickle jars floated in the pools. Moose struggled up, his head protesting. He'd drunk too much and had an ache in his shoulder from sleeping twisted against the soundboard. It was dawn, but barely. Rocket was still conked out underneath his own sled, only his feet protruding. Moose was thirsty and didn't see Arthur or his mother anywhere. He climbed down out of the piano. He was kicking around the dirt for a canteen when from the far side of the pool came the *pop, pop, pop* of gunshot. A curse, then another series: *pop, pop*. He looked across the water and here's what he witnessed:

A grizzly bear paced twenty feet from Minnie and Marty's matrimonial sled, pawing the ground. The bear glanced sidelong, gauging his foes. They'd been flaying a caribou atop their Lockwood Console—its ribs cracked open, they were up to their elbows in blood and ligaments. The crux of the situation was clear right away: the bear wanted the carcass, but Minnie and Marty were trapped—if they ran, the bear would chase. If they stayed, the bear would eat them too. All told, the grizzly was grander than any illustration Moose had seen in Arthur's resource books, and in the years to come he never saw one to match that bear. All musculature and grit, the grizzly took one of Marty's bullets in the shoulder, rose on hind legs, and bellowed in their direction.

Moose had always thought that mammals were knit from the same materials as humans, but until he saw a bear in the wild he couldn't fully comprehend the animal's natural stature—the swagger, the meat in the shoulders. Moose couldn't help feeling that its bones were fashioned of a material significantly heartier than his own. Already the bear had been shot several times, but the rifle was for small game and the wounds barely seemed to faze him.

From the outset Rocket had lectured everyone on precautions for trekking through bear country. In addition to wearing bells, at night they sacked leftover food and pulleyed it into the air. The little tykes were only allowed into the berry patches if someone was tasked to stand sentinel. "The best we can do is alert the bears to our presence," Rocket said. "The rest is up to them." Moose knew that they couldn't prevent a bear from smelling them, from tracking them back to camp, but it was their job to do their best. Now it was obvious why. Marty and Minnie had enticed the hell out of the creature with their kill in plain view. Now there was nothing to do but see that they didn't pay for this stupidity with their lives.

Typically in the morning Moose allotted himself seven minutes to dignify himself for the day, during which time he swished water around his gums, unkinked sleep cowlicks. That morning one of his eyes was still crusted closed and his nightshirt was misbuttoned. He searched for where he'd shucked his pants the night before and scrambled into them. The bear's roar had woken the camp. All around him people were rising, scrambling for cover. Moose looked for Arthur. Most of the men were gone, he guessed either hunting or fornicating, so aside from Rocket and himself, the only available help looked to be a pair of too-young brothers flipping checkers in the dirt.

Moose grabbed his boots. His hair was matted in the back with sunflower suckers and instead of taking time to comb them free he swept his mane into a low ponytail. Arthur's popper—a snub-nosed instrument with a double-cock—had been discarded by one of the runners. Moose slid it into a holster and strapped the whole thing to his back. All of this happened in a flurry, and a good thing too, for in the next instant Rocket came tearing through camp. Their guide was wearing a pair of fish-patterned long johns with a leather flap at the rump. He was unshod and unkempt: one of his braids loose, the other completely undone. In his arms he cradled a gun with a four-foot-long barrel and a telescope strapped to the top. Seeing Moose, he yelled, "Let's go, Bloomer!" Rocket leapt over a fire and rounded the curve of the pool.

By the time they got within shooting distance of Minnie's sled, everything was mounting together. Marty continued to pop off shots, passing his spent rifle to Minnie on the other side of the sled and grabbing her freshly loaded gun. She reloaded while he shot, and in this way they kept the air a smog of smoke and whistles. The bear towered on his hindquarters, slavering profusely. Moose could see pocks in his fur where shots had landed, but nothing seemed to stall his menace. Moose's own rifle, a mere peashooter, would do nothing against a creature of this mass. The bear roared again, and Moose could see he'd reached the last of his patience—in another moment he would charge. If they had piqued him sufficiently, and Moose would wager they had, he could maul any of them.

"Get behind the sled," Rocket said as Moose slid into position. Minnie scooted over to make room for him beside the caribou's vacant head. The animal's mouth hung open: a set of crooked molars coated with caramelized plaque, pink tongue lolling to one side. Antlers sprouted from the head in a bloom of bone, growing upward in a tangled thicket. There was something unnerving about being crammed so close to a creature that could easily have outrun him even in his most superior conditioning. Moose shifted, turning his gaze away.

Minnie crouched on her heels, and Moose could see the rotunda of her belly just starting to protrude. Her gestation was months behind his mother's, but obvious to the eye. For a second he flickered with fear that the bear could incite a precipitous labor, with Moose as her only aide. In one hand Minnie gripped a hatchet, and with the other she pulled a heart-shaped locket from the neck of her dress. Holding it, she crossed herself and whispered a prayer. She extended the locket in his direction and intimated that he should kiss it. "Please," she said.

Moose did as he was told.

There was a scuffle and Rocket appeared by his side. He had never been this close to an industrial bear popper—rigged like a portable cannon, it had a wicked black fuse. Rocket produced a leaden ball, which he passed to Moose, and the damn thing nearly took his shoulder from its home. Working quickly, Rocket pushed the caribou's head around until the antlers served as a makeshift mount. He braced the popper atop them. Loaded it and took a view. The first angle was all wrong: even from his vantage, Moose could see the sight aimed at a spot in the trees several feet over the bear's head. Rocket cursed and drew the barrel loose. Jerked the antlers again and clicked the popper back into place. He knelt in the dirt but couldn't fit his eye to the scope. "Moose, I can brace it, but you've got to make the sight," he said.

"Dear Jesus," said Minnie.

Moose squeezed shut an eye and peered through the lens. The fright of seeing the bear at such a magnitude made him pull away, but he forced himself to look again. The scope swung wildly and there was a blur of activity to his left, the flash of metal as Marty braced a rifle against the Lockwood. He fired and ejected the casing. Rocket struck the popper's flint. Moose didn't know how long it took to make his final calculations, only that all at once the fuse hit the powder and there was a deafening roar. A force lifted him into the air and threw him back to the ground in a sharp burst of momentum.

The shot capped the bear in the belly. Spilling from the wound came several links of viscous pink intestine. As Moose struggled to his feet, more guts slipped out and the bear dropped to all fours. "Good," the guide said, and went to collect the popper from where it had been thrown, beaten, into the weeds. Moose tried to get up, but there was a sharp pain in his hip and his head went light. The creature was lamenting his situation, growling and losing blood, and in Moose's heart he felt a brief stab of guilt that he hadn't murdered the bear with a single shot. There's a particular misery to watching an animal whimper through his last rites.

The bear was no saint, but Moose could see it agitated his spirit to give up his life; he wouldn't go down easy. A great roil of energy came off him as he paced. The bear tried to spot them out of a bloodied cornea. You've got to watch a creature like this really carefully in his final moments, Moose knew. One minute he's bested and you're issuing puffs of relief, and the next he's broken into a run and everyone's scattering away from the sled in a wholly undignified manner: one dragging toward the water, one hopping backwards over boreal cacti, one throwing a hatchet, one firing aimlessly toward the sun.

The bear leapt into the air. For a moment he hung there, guts flapping like a funeral garland. Then the full weight of him landed atop the caribou, which is to say he landed atop the Lockwood, and everything went splintering out from under him in a great fission. A collapsing mess of animal and cellulose and ivory. The caribou's rack impaled the bear through the chest, and in this contortion, together, they broke through the forte's slats and came to rest on the ground. Though the bear was clearly dead, Minnie came running forward to beat the animal's head with her fists.

Marty set aside his rifle. "He had to take the piano with him, goddamnit."

"It's just an instrument," Rocket said.

"It was a wedding gift."

"The more important thing is your lives."

"Depends on how you define life," said Marty. "What happened to the kid who made the shot?"

Moose had been launched backwards into the reeds alongside the pool. Damp. Hungry. He tried to rise but there was no remaining power in his hip. Maybe he could live here now, soaking in sulfur waters only a few miles from Arctic City. Surely he could persuade his parents that they didn't need to go any farther. Here was good enough, here was more than good enough, he'd say blinking up from the mud.

"I'm stuck" is what he really said.

Rocket helped him stand, but there was no hope for walking. Moose picked up a loose Lockwood board from the ground and used this as a makeshift crutch. Limp, limp. Thornton would perceive now that his fall into the river had been no accident. Soon everyone would realize how this journey had already weakened spots in Moose's character. What would Arthur think when he saw how Moose had been rendered out of commission? Would his stepfather immediately ascertain the whole story? Moose was desperate to throw up an obfuscation. Instead of heading back to his own camp, he undid the knife from his belt and joined the ring of men preparing to skin the bear.

"Better get that leg looked at," Rocket said.

"It's not going to get worse if I'm just standing here."

"You took a pretty hard hit."

"I'm tough," said Moose.

How much pain had they already endured on the trail? They'd said goodbye to everyone Moose had ever known or loved. He'd eaten what may very well have been the last cherries of his lifetime sitting on the chapel steps, spitting pits at cockroaches. For the last few months he'd been sleeping on a mattress that stank of human sweat. He shifted weight to his damaged leg. Winced. He was no stranger to ignoring pain—like the bear, he'd been pocked in places, but the ligaments of his new home were still splayed out in his imagination. It was a fresh, bloody, primal enticement that served as enough incentive to continue on.

They skinned the bear. Rocket taught Moose how to work his knife so it didn't cut the hide, and as they neared the end, Marty said, "Fur's yours if you want it, kid."

"Mine?" said Moose.

"I'm sure as shit not hauling something that tried to kill me."

"You could trade it at the post," Rocket said. "Get a few more supplies."

"It's not a memory I want to hang on to," said Marty.

What remained of the Lockwood was collected and pieced out in a field. For hours Minnie wandered the wreckage, trying to figure out what could be salvaged. A few spare parts. Keys and half a dozen hammers. Minnie pocketed these as the rest of the adults emerged sheepishly from the brambles, buckling belts and tucking shirts. Arthur and Una turned up back at camp at the same time as the midwife, Patrice LeFleur—a moon-haired lady with a leather necktie. She was the closest approximation the train had to a doctor. She palpated Moose's hip, then rocked back on her heels and said matter-of-factly: "Your leg's been bothering you for some time."

"It was a hard fall."

She shook her head. "This is an old injury."

"It's been getting better," Moose said.

"Has it." The midwife walked over and picked a few fallen branches: skinny, each three feet long. Twisting Moose like a roasted pullet, she managed to trap his leg between the branches and lashed them together. "You can't just keep working it over and over, you've got to give it a chance to heal."

"I can't wear a brace, I've got jobs to do."

"You need to keep off it for a couple days."

Over the next few hours Moose was forced to submit to Una's ministrations. She mopped his brow. Spoon-fed him yogurt. Eventually he fell asleep and she fluttered off to her regular tasks. They were meant to strike camp by early afternoon and sled on toward Arctic City. When Moose awoke he realized either the midwife or his own mother must have dosed him with something. He was groggy and the sled was in motion. Cushioned on all sides by quilts, he'd been tucked inside the Napoleon like one of the napping tykes. When he tried to shift position, to lift himself up, he nearly yelled—whatever part of his hip had been decalibrated initially was now fully off-kilter: a nauseating grind of bone on bone.

Late in the afternoon Thornton showed up to walk by the sled as Moose rode, offering his friend a pear pudding. "So you can't walk," Thornton said.

"It's just a couple days."

"You could've told me you were hurt, I would've helped."

"Everyone says it's worse than it is," Moose said.

For the rest of the day Thornton walked beside the sled in his companionable way, neither of them vocalizing the fact that Moose's injury ruined what plans they had for their last weeks together. Of course in hindsight it was clear that this was the moment when their paths took their divergence. There was no guarantee that Moose would ever perform again as a proper companion, a proper friend, and soon they'd be settled on homesteads miles apart. Moose was not keen to admit any of this, especially to himself—back then he was still young enough to believe that there was no infirmity that couldn't be cured by sunlight and fresh air. When he finished the pudding, Thornton took the cup and gave Moose a handkerchief to wipe his face. The palliative nature of these gestures annoyed Moose—Thornton made an awkward nursemaid, and Moose had no desire to trumpet his needs as an invalid. He snapped at his friend, declaring that he just wanted to be left alone, for the sake of God, could he have a single moment of peace?

Given what happened next, Moose eventually came to understand that his initial good health must have served some purpose in Thornton's ability to keep up a good pretense. The following morning when they discovered that Minnie and Marty had taken off, Moose learned that his friend had slipped away with them. Not only had he stolen his own body and soul from his auntie and uncle, but he'd taken the Psalmist too.

"And that's why you don't pick an instrument a single person can lift," Auntie Huntmoon said, angrily scraping soot off the fire grate. She threw down her brush and put her head in her hands. "Makes it too easy to strike out on your own and now look at us."

"He might come back," Una said softly.

Moose feigned optimism alongside his mother, but in the pit of his heart he knew the truth. Thornton had performed some calculation and come out in favor of heading south before the trail became impassable with snow. He'd taken the only thing he knew he could trade, and if he was lucky he might get enough for the Psalmist to hitch a ride back to the bay. From there Moose guessed he'd board himself in a crate, slap on enough postage to get loaded onto a ship, and sail home. That's what he hoped for his friend's future, though the image of Thornton running through the woods with a forte strapped to his back while Moose lingered here, broken, filled him with a sense of injustice—knowing that even if he'd wanted to go with his friend, he wouldn't have been able to keep up.

Finley

Jubilation House
September, a week after Milda leaves

Finley hailed the boardinghouse's Kraken as it came whizzing through the mouth of the fjord. *Chai!* a bullhorn trumpeted. *Hot chai!* He'd been nervously waiting at the veranda table all morning, reading old *Tribune* articles and sucking down coffee, watching Abraham Lincoln play hide-and-seek with his pups for distraction as he no longer had sisters in the house smacking around, making a ruckus. This was his first time alone in Jubilation House. When he'd dropped them all off at the ferry dock, Temperance had teased: *You'll wail yourself to sleep when we're not here, admit it.* It was closer to the truth than he cared to admit.

He settled his teacup in the saucer now, careful, careful, don't chip the landing; deep breath. Then he stood up from the table to wave over the Kraken. Hullulla Huntmoon, come to visit for the first time.

Hullulla pulled the LeFleur Kraken alongside the veranda and killed the engine. Finley caught the lead line, tied it off, and helped unload the groceries she'd brought. Dried apricots and shots of vitamin D. Like Finley had always promised himself, his life was now full of many of the conveniences their family could never afford when they were little. Happenstance was more than happy to oblige special orders considering the siblings had become Big Spenders.

Jubilation House and the trade post had fallen into an easy partnership over the last decade. Together their industries powered the territory's economy. Each June Happenstance hosted a regional auction to sell the best repaired fortes and scavenged parts. Finley and Milda typically had five or six offerings a season, depending on luck, and they were known for the craftsmanship of their repairs. *Museum grade.* Even the instruments without crests met their reserve, and then some, and most were then loaded directly onto the ferry for the ship ride south to the continent. From there they flew east to be installed under white LED lights in museums alongside aquariums of Arctic octopus pips and totem poles pulled, fully preserved, from the Kamikaze River.

Like all those left in the territory, the Spahr family's farm still produced a substantial portion of their diet. The octopus herd they tended was smaller now than in the years when their whole family had worked together to salt and hang their wares from the kelp vines stretched over the old veranda, but it still produced enough for both Finley and Milda to be sick of pickled octopus arms by the end of winter. They'd expanded their crop range a bit too—the sunken *Victory* had proven a surprisingly fertile ground for a breed of savory urchin that Milda had learned to stuff with mushrooms and garlic and grill whole. Sea beans wound up the stilts still precariously balancing the house aloft and in the earth beds on the veranda they grew mint, beets, squash, and femur-size stalks of verdant boreal chard. They kept a goat for milk, as they had since they were kids, and a coop of birds on the west side of the veranda next to the cedar lean-to that Finley had built for Abraham Lincoln and his family.

Hullulla untied the last box of groceries from the back of the Kraken and handed it up. Then she shouldered a backpack and stepped over the railing onto the veranda, tanned thighs flashing through slits in her long tunic. When she preached she wore sailor-collared shirts buttoned to the chin and homemade wool trousers tucked into wading boots, her hair scrupulously oiled out of her face; no room for distraction. But now it wafted around her head, a wild halo with a bluish cast under the veranda lights. Hullulla had eyes, she had a dimple in the shape of a plum pit. Was this love? Finley thought it might be.

"You made it," he said, reaching for her backpack. He couldn't gauge from the size how much she'd packed; would she stay a few days? A week? The whole winter? RiverCamp had only recently disbanded and Hullulla's family expected her to move into the parsonage when it snowed. The possibility that Milda would be gone for months on the Bluefin tour, if not forever, while Hullulla spent the winter snowed in at the New Chapel spooning mush into Mrs. Huntmoon's bowl—he pushed the thought from his mind as she dropped her pack on the deck.

Grinning up at him, Hullulla cupped his face in her hands and kissed first one cheek, then the other. "I didn't know all of this was out here," she said. "You have a lovely home." Though Finley couldn't have put words to it, he sensed this was how his father, Fry, must have felt seeing Viola with her puffin-beak gloves whipping octopus limbs into the crowd. He could not look away. Nearly every Sunday morning that summer he'd convinced Milda to fly him north so he could sit on the sand while Hullulla preached atop the Custer&Sons. She was a marvel, the way she stitched her own life's stories into universal lessons of neighborly love, how she patiently fashioned dried porcupine ribs into dolls for the camp's children after Sunday school.

The final box of groceries contained a six-pack of Huckle Ale. Hullulla took out a bottle and cuffed the cap against the edge of the table. The cap flew off. She passed the bottle to Finley then popped off the cap of another for herself. Side by side they leaned against the veranda railing and looked out over the fjord; one of Abraham Lincoln's pups floated belly-up in the surf, batting at a float of seaweed. "I heard there's a party on the reef tonight," she said. "Last of the season. There's a flyer up at the trade post."

Typically Finley's sisters had to drag him from the veranda for social engagements. But only a few sips of ale and look how bubbly he already felt behind the ears; he surprised himself by asking, "You want to go?"

"Could be fun," Hullulla said, and slid her arm closer until their elbows touched. "We could make a night of it."

Finley'd planned to take her hunting. They couldn't range far on the Kraken, but he'd built a small trailer that pulled behind the machine to hold camping supplies. Before the weather snapped, sending them both scuttling to their winter dens, they'd camp the outskirts of the fjords where Finley was eager to show Hullulla the treasures of his own backyard: *look, tuning forks,* he'd say at sunset as a colony of puffins arced over their tent, beaks clamped around ancient Elinvar tuning forks. They'd wrap his sleeping bag around their shoulders, light a fire, and roast the highland beef kebabs packed under ice in the bottom of one of the grocery crates. He took a long swig of his ale then put his arm around Hullulla; she nestled against him and he thought of Temperance chiding him each week when they got back from RiverCamp: *It's okay to like someone other than just your family, you know.* Perhaps it was even okay to change plans for such a person. What could it possibly matter if they delayed their trip a day. "Sounds good to me," he said.

Reef parties attracted community members from all across the fjords, and beyond. On the appointed day young adults territory-wide rode Krakens or flew planes south to sing, dive, and zoom over the largest living reef in the Northern Hemisphere. The community Finley had grown up in had slowly re-created itself as others in his generation had laid claim to their own deeds, pilot licenses, and charter companies. Some of the girls from Temperance's ship *Victory* had taken over family businesses, though most found their niches in new industries. Plum Happenstance's older sister Bergot, for example, advertised a house-to-boat conversion service; her crew chainsawed fjord homes off their stilts and pontooned them on new fiberglass floats. And Meriweather Starr lured packs of tourists to the territory each summer for the health benefits of black sand facials under open-air tents staked along the bay. The territory had been transformed by their forays into early adulthood, though at heart they were all still young enough to appreciate a great party on the open water over the Arctic Reef.

There was always drink at these parties, of course. Jellyfish sours were a regional staple. Finley sometimes brought his own secret-recipe home brew, but his batches were unpredictable and it often ended up too strong for casual consumption. The first party of that summer was when Milda had reconnected with Jude LeFleur. Though she'd known him since she was a kid, they hadn't seen each other in years. By the end of the night Milda was tipping shots while riding behind Jude on the boardinghouse's Kraken, her head on his shoulder, and Finley thought, *Oh*. How fast allegiances slipped, how fast the world pivoted.

It was never Finley's intention to live a life of celibacy, though that was primarily what had happened. He had never pursued dating with urgency because it did not come easily. Most of the young women he met—Plum Happenstance, Hattie Pope—had no ambition to remain in the territory long-term. They visited for the summer season, like Temperance, and at the end of August they flew south to finish school and rekindle relationships with former boyfriends. Finley knew he always had the choice to flock with them, but he'd already invested so much life up here, it felt impossible to leave. His closet was full of wet suits of varying thickness. He didn't own a tie. He had no debts and some money in the bank, but he knew it would quickly run dry paying continental prices. He couldn't fathom what he'd do for work and feared he'd end up dependent on his father's family charity, no property to call his own, no purpose to his days other than the endless monotony of sorting enough stegosaurus bones to buy dinner. And none of that took into account Abraham Lincoln, who in his old age had become quite domesticated. When Milda and Jude had first begun kicking up a ruckus in his parents' old bedroom, Finley took up the habit of sleeping in a tent on the platform over the breeding tanks, where they staged their repairs. The sea lion soon joined him.

All summer with Milda and Jude, Temperance and Goldie, Jubilation House had felt like an oddball co-op, though Finley could hardly say this was unusual. Many of the families remaining in the territory seemed to live in unusual combinations like the Spahrs—uncles and uncles, siblings. Two dozen friends ran a co-op near the sea cove where they'd found the Bluefin a decade ago. The catch that launched a thousand ships. He could've done without the fuss around the catch, as it had set in motion Milda's eventual departure, but the fame had certainly helped them achieve a high bid at the Bluefin's auction.

So far that season Finley had found only three relics—including the Psalmist—a personal low. Milda had already traded off the Ravenwood and neither of the remaining fortes looked like they would fetch much of a price. He didn't want to acknowledge it to himself yet, but only three wrecks that summer was a foreboding statistic. There would come a day, soon, when even the best hunters were left without game to track. The ivory trade coming off the Kamikaze was a temporary substitute, but there were only so many lost piano keys for trout to swallow. Either way, he couldn't easily hunt by himself and wasn't sure what he would do if Milda didn't return when the ice broke that spring. He'd managed to secure a provisional flight license for emergencies, but he still didn't trust himself to pilot long distances. The Kraken was a useful machine, but it limited him to travel a couple hours in any direction.

A flock of doves whooshed across the sky. Evening. The fall had opened clean and crisp and Finley was glad he'd rescued a claw-foot bathtub from the fjord's floor to serve as a makeshift hot tub that winter. The bathtub had been down there as long as he could remember. When he brought it up to the veranda he'd pushed the eating table out of the way so it could face the mouth of the fjords. Every evening he filled the tub with hot water and whistled for Abraham Lincoln, who liked to curl alongside the cast iron as he bathed.

Before Finley had time to gather his own party supplies, Hullulla was back over the veranda railing, sitting on Jubilation House's Kraken. The engine revved. Hullulla slid back and patted the seat, beckoning Finley to sit in front of her to steer.

It took thirty minutes to reach the reef; Finley sensed the fireworks before they saw them—jubilant, tectonic flowers raining sparks across the water. Three planes had already landed. Music juiced through speakers mounted atop their hoods. A dozen kayaks were moored to each plane's floats and people lounged everywhere.

The hatch to one of the planes had been sprung open and inside was a massive aquarium filled with a frothy, light blue liquid. Jellyfish sours. By the end of the night everyone's tongues would be sparkling blue. The music was hippy. Several young men climbed onto the hood of one of the planes, then leapt off into the dark water.

At high tide the reef was easily twenty feet underwater, but at low tide it rose like the spine of a fossil. The reef spanned the length of the entire territory and over time breaks had been cut to create strategic shipping routes. It was otherwise a marvelous natural formation. Finley was a frequenter of the reef and he wasn't the only hunter. There was no better place to snuffle for loose parts. He made a mental note to return later to see if their party had shaken anything new loose.

It was still warm enough to swim in wet suits, but not for long. As they pulled up, Finley spotted Hattie Pope and Meriweather Starr sloshing drinks into cups and passing them out to the group sitting on their plane's floats. Hattie whooped. She leapt from the hatch into the water and swam toward another plane.

Finley clicked a button and lowered the spray dome. With Hullulla's arms around his waist, he didn't want to get off the Kraken. Too many parties he'd gotten sucked into elaborate obstacle races, paddling anchor in a borrowed kayak that cramped his knees. He thought briefly about heading them back home, but he didn't want to disappoint her. There'd never been anyone like Hullulla in Finley's life.

All summer he'd crafted excuses for Milda to fly him north to visit Hullulla, though his sister was no fool. Each Saturday morning she'd pack the Crusher with a crate of canned pips that she handed out at RiverCamp, then spend the weekend apprenticing under Auntie V. No one was more expert in shaping ivory beads, and Milda embroidered those she crafted to her maps, marking treasure. Meanwhile, Hullulla would take Finley down the river to the trader with loads of ivory keys pulled off the Kamikaze River and she bargained with confidence. The money she made went to Huntmoon congregants in rough straits, or would be tucked in Gussie's panniers for the New Chapel's reserves—her parents depended upon both her hauls and the money her brother Ezra had sent back from his telecom gigs.

Now Finley searched for a place to rope off the Kraken—ideally near a plane where they could relax in the hatch. He steered toward an empty, sleek flying coffin. A low-altitude glider with disco balls dangling from each wing. They tied off the Kraken and climbed inside. The seats had been removed to make room for a mattress. There was a stack of blankets. Candles. A bottle. Hullulla thumbed the cork and passed him a cup. "To the night."

"To the night," he said.

He pulled the door to the plane closed behind them.

"Hey." Hullulla put her hand on his hip. Out the window, up went a ThunderCrack. Fat gold coins sprayed down on the water as her finger traced his collarbone. Finley kissed her. Her fingers slid up into his hair, knuckles twisting his locks, as his lips brushed against her temple. Hullulla breathed into his neck. Then her mouth was on his and his head went ballooning out the plane. Windows blown free so it was just stars and water. Finley's chest hitched. Hullulla's lips tasted of salt and fish piss and their noses aligned along a meridian both somehow knew. *Click-clock,* bolts of cartilage locked into place.

It wasn't until that summer, as the frequency of his visits to Hullulla had increased, that he'd actually begun to fathom a life beyond his hunting partnership with Milda. While he had no desire to leave Jubilation House, he wouldn't mind having Hullulla for company, now and always, heating a samovar each morning for tea.

Hullulla had a thick white scar on her shoulder above the medieval cross tattoo. Finley traced the line, said, *Tell me.* Her stories were always parabolic. She told him of a long-ago trout, a great fawn-size trout, how violently the fish had fought. It was a great challenge. When the rainbow was finally hauled ashore she slit the belly and found inside a radius-length ivory key, full weight. Auntie V had used the ivory to carve a dozen new teeth and three went to Hullulla's brother, Ezra, to replace the ones he'd lost building broadcast towers.

Finley had his own scars. He still had his wet suit on, it was his standard uniform, but unzipped it now, pulling free his arms. Down one bicep snaked a crooked needle stitch from the winter when Abraham Lincoln's new mate nipped him. When he'd come inside, bleeding, Milda had pulled one of her reference books from the high living room shelf and opened to a page on epidermal repair. The first aid kit under the bathroom sink contained antibiotic cream and silk line for sutures; she gave him a stick to bite while she stitched the muscle.

Now Hullulla stroked a hand across the tattoo on his shoulder blade, asked, "What's that?"

"A map," he said.

"Doesn't look—"

"It's what the territory used to be."

He leaned forward, traced his thumb on her lower lip. He kissed her temple again. Kissed her neck. She made a noise.

"Is this okay?"

"Yes," she said.

Finley knew they would spend the rest of the night on the water, as he always did at these kinds of parties. They'd wake in the morning to the gray dawn rising over the reef and toss thermoses of coffee from one kayak to another. On the ride home Hullulla would press her cheek against his back as he drove the Kraken thinking how odd it was, how miraculous, that you could go your whole life with one definition of who you were, who you loved, only to wake up one morning with the sudden understanding that there was more than one way to form a partnership.

He closed his eyes. His world recalibrated.

THE MINUTE YOU stopped looking for something, wasn't that the moment you were supposed to find it? Love. A piano. A fish with an ivory key in its belly. After Hullulla fell asleep Finley pulled on his coat and climbed out of the plane and into the Kraken. Moments later he was skiing along the reef, alone. Dome down, spray like a cape. He'd barebacked nearly every inch of the fjords, but there was only so much he could see from above. As he went shooting along he whistled for Abraham Lincoln's companionship. The lion had tracked them; he surfaced and butterflied after the Kraken. They zoomed away from the party.

If there was a place in the world worthy of human prayer, it had to be the reef—coral enrapturing wooden sleds, hoopskirts pinwheeling in the current. The great underwater wall sieved the debris of their lives from the rest of the world. Tonight when he killed the Kraken's engine, he was the lone bird on the water. High tide. With the Kraken's dome sealed he could drop over one hundred feet without a single pop to the ears, but any deeper and he risked contracting the spins. His mother used to bring him and Milda out to the reef in the days before the family could afford scuba gear and they'd bob all afternoon. He'd never been able to hold his breath longer than thirty seconds, a minute. Now he could stay down much longer. The Kraken's bubble held forty-five minutes of oxygen, roughly the same as a whale lung. Finley was no fool but he'd always taken chances. You wouldn't catch him wasting his life tabulating accounts. So after midnight, on the last Sunday in September, a five-foot-eight-inch-tall fellow with his mother's temerity clicked a Kraken into DIVE and dropped in a burst of spray.

The curl had the backing of the moon and it dragged the Kraken away from the reef. Finley ground into second gear and powered back around. He flicked on the headlights. The reef was a shackle of heartbreak in every sense of the word. You could find what you could find out there, but you had to look for it. The headlights played across a sweep of anemones sucking face and his leg startled against the dash. Music blared from the speakers, the singer's voice high-keyed. The Kraken was at seventy feet and he began to feel the pressure of depth. It'd take time to acclimate and rise, but in the meantime, he steered along to see what he could make out.

On the other side of the reef, the shelf broke hard—it was a steep drop to the ocean floor. There wasn't a chance anyone would find something out there, not in those fathoms. Undiscoverable, all those subterranean colonies that stowed pirate secrets and reverent prayers and nothing breathed because there was no air, no air.

Finley had stars in the brain: ninety-nine feet and he knew he shouldn't drop any lower, but just a little more couldn't hurt. Third gear. The engine ground. His thoughts came too fast, bright sparks that flashed away before he could register them; *hypoxic memories,* his mother said of the way dizzy euphoria surged through their brains on deep dives. Not just deep—long; he'd been down too long. He knew he needed to get back to hydrate and sleep through the night. Up the Kraken puttered.

It was too dark to see much, but when the headlights played across a piece of bare wood he took notice. A turned leg jutted out from the reef and when he got closer he could see it was attached to the body of a piano shoved half angled into the coral. It stuck out just enough for Finley to spot a *B* lettered on the lid—the Napoleon. The usual swarm of barnacles crusted the leg, but the boards on the body looked almost polished in the glare of the Kraken's headlights. A full set of smirking ivory keys. Finley suspected it'd crashed into the reef only recently; snapped-off fronds of pumpkin-colored coral framed the instrument.

Briefly he wondered about lack of oxygen, if what he was seeing could actually be real. Had the piano somehow followed him here? No, ridiculous. He needed to get out of this dome. But he'd been hunting the Napoleon for fifteen years and wasn't going to let it escape again—fool him once, and all that. So he pulled a lever and two flat pieces of metal shot out the front of the Kraken. The lifting gate.

It took a couple of tries, but he rammed the coral until the water around him powdered in calcinated chalk and he had a good wedge under the Napoleon. If he could reverse and lift at the same time, he was sure he could pop the instrument from its place—easy as scooping out Abraham Lincoln's eye when the lion had been bitten by a sea snake. Finley gave the throttle some steam. One hundred and eight feet and he still had seven minutes of air, acres of time.

Nothing moved.

The Kraken stalled and he snapped back to second gear. Maybe instead of pulling the Napoleon loose he could push the instrument all the way through the reef to pop out on the far side. He cranked the levers. *Whip-pop* went the engine as first the piano, then the Kraken, broke through the reef and into the ocean at large.

But immediately they were sinking. The Napoleon was on the lift, but the dials whirled into the red. The Kraken dropped. Pressure deafened Finley's ears. The load was too heavy and if it came down to the piano or himself, he still had some sense.

He tried to shake the Napoleon off the lifting gate, but the forte was well wedged. He pushed the button marked ESCAPE HATCH, but the dome wouldn't retract. He doubted there was a bottom to this sea and with the piano loaded, he'd sink until he fainted from all the carbon dioxide fogging the windows.

His father liked to say that if you found the bones of something, they'd tell you the whole story—but that wasn't true, not even a little. If you wanted the full story you had to go further back. To the ways fate and injury orchestrated the moment.

The cemeteries in the territory were full of rule-abiding homebodies, grandparents taken by memory rot, but if you wanted to know about the true adventurers, you had to go hunting for the remains. Their ocular bones washed onto beaches, bodies deconstructed into electrons that hailed down on fields of sugar beets. At one hundred and eighty feet, Finley realized that anything could be a coffin. He never could lift the weight of the Napoleon, of all that it meant to their lives, all by himself; he didn't know why he'd ever thought he could. Without either of his sisters there to temper him, without Hullulla, there was no one to rescue him from miscalculating the Napoleon's weight other than himself. For not running the math on solid gold hammers.

If he considered himself rich before, that would be nothing compared to the sale of the Napoleon, but what he wanted to know was why this was the fate he'd made for himself. No one person could answer that question, least of all him. Before he blacked out he wondered who would find him one day and project, *Finley Spahr was this or that kind of person, he loved this or that kind of thing.* You could find the bones of a Big Catch and think they told the whole story, but they didn't. That was the lesson he'd been learning. That was the lesson he'd been learning his whole life.

Part IV

Midnight Fever

Maple

Huntmoon New Chapel
Eight and a half months after Finley's disappearance

Sunday afternoons Maple stitched up human beings in the New Chapel. Clinic day. They squeezed into pews, wheezed and groaned. She knotted interrupted sutures along bloodied lips. Set broken noses, her thumbs flinching cartilage. She defrosted bricks of immunizations and popped children in the bicep while they sucked molasses pops. *All done, little one,* she'd say, prying sticky claws off her stethoscope. Maple's father-in-law, Reverend Huntmoon, had no spine for this type of corporeal work. From the pulpit he balmed the maladies of the soul, and did it well, salting soup for widows and laying hands on the afflicted. But if you wanted somebody on Mount Resurrection to mend your fishhooked eyebrow, the entire congregation knew you wanted Maple.

"Feel that, Mapes?" Hullulla asked. She picked up Maple's hand and pressed it to her belly. Her skin undulated. *We finally got our baby*. Hullulla was pregnant with the baby of Finley Spahr, a piano hunter who'd disappeared off the Arctic Reef last fall. He'd gone hunting one night and never returned. Now Hullulla lay stretched on the table behind the pulpit, shirt raised. "What do you hear?" she asked.

Though Maple and Hullulla had grown up like sisters, they were now on separate trajectories, living divergent lives. As soon as the ice broke that spring Hullulla had left the New Chapel's parsonage for her bed atop the Custer&Sons at RiverCamp, where she spent her days fishing rainbows off the Kamikaze River. It was her seventh summer catching trout for the family's winter supply and she'd calculated every fish: forget weight—over the years Hullulla had hooked 19,304 trout. Once a week she'd loaded Gussie's panniers with rainbow steaks and money made from selling ivory keys to the trader, and trekked up to the chapel for prenatal care.

"Hold still," Maple said, sliding her Pinard horn across Hullulla's belly. Her friend was birthmarked with a trio of dainty, star-shaped speckles under her belly button and Maple wondered if she'd pass that down to the child. Already Hullulla smelled of milk. She had storm gray eyes and horse-spindled legs; she hiked across the plateau in high, gallumping steps. Maple had to jog to keep up.

The Pinard horn followed a longitude of veins before locating the baby's heartbeat. *Whompa-whompa.* "Galloping horses," Maple said. "Sounds good."

On the other side of the curtain that cordoned off the exam area behind the pulpit, a child cried, "Mommy, Mommy, Mommy." Maple yanked back the cloth. Three years old, ear like a roasted beet, clawing at the neck of a woolen sweater. "You have to be quiet," Maple said. "Or I can't hear anything." The mother, Mercy Pope, picked up the child and clutched him to her chest. "He's sick," she said. "He doesn't feel well." Maple was usually a contented person, but she heard herself say, "We all have problems."

Letting the curtain fall back in place, she chewed over this interaction. Maple knew there was a point in everyone's life where you looked around and realized that the world did not deal everyone the same flourishing hand. She was mild-mannered and reliable, an irony considering that every baby she'd ever carried herself had slipped from her womb as nonchalantly as a chicken loosing an egg. Three, four, a dozen malformations of anatomy and plasma over several years; not so much as a single tentacle to hold fast. Nothing reliable about that. If you didn't know the rest of the story, she could provide the abridgment: first came the blood. So fresh it was nearly bright orange. Clots. Then skin flakes sheer as gauze.

Maple had always wanted a family of her own; she'd lost hers so young. But the troubles of her failed biology were not secret in the community. During Sunday service it felt like everyone's eyes followed her. *When? When?* their pupils said. *Now? Soon?* The most recent of her longed-for children had dripped out of her womb at the same time that Hullulla had sprouted the one she was currently carrying. Hullulla had just returned from Disillusionment Bay, following the night when Finley had gone out hunting and presumably drowned in his Kraken. Or at least that's what Hullulla and Milda suspected had happened. One minute there, the next gone.

"All finished?" Hullulla asked, struggling to sit. Maple put a hand on her back and levered her up. Hullulla swung her legs off the edge of the table and pulled three ivory keys from a holster strapped to her thigh. She lined them up on the exam table. "Light week," she said.

Maple rinsed her hands in a basin of water and dried them on the towel tied around her waist. "It's still early in the season," she said, and picked up her clipboard to find the name of her next patient. Over a dozen parishioners waited in the New Chapel's pews.

"Half the fish don't have anything in their guts. I've never seen it like this," Hullulla said, hopping down from the table. She loaded the keys back into her holster to take to the broker. The New Chapel's yearly tithes were heavily subsidized by the ivory that Hullulla pulled from the river; they could not sustain their ministry if the resource dwindled. After dinner with the Reverend and Mrs. Huntmoon, Hullulla would ride Gussie back down the trail to RiverCamp to take her shift at the gutting table. Eight months pregnant and she couldn't be convinced to sleep in the parsonage. "Take it easy, Mapes," she said now, ducking out from behind the curtain.

After the clinic closed Maple made her way to the parsonage, where Ezra had left her a slice of rabbit-and-kidney pie. She ate by candlelight, the only sound in the house a tweeting cuckoo clock given to the Huntmoons by a former parishioner: one of several families—more than several, really—who'd decided against moving up to the plateau. Even some of the congregation that had originally followed them last summer had since migrated south. As she ate she reviewed one of her old nursing textbooks, wanting to brush up on the anatomy of the pelvic girdle in preparation for Hullulla's delivery. Cervical dilation. Prolapse.

She had delivered seven babies. One stillborn. With Mrs. Huntmoon's memory out of commission, Maple was the only midwife in the region, though even she could admit her practice was half prayer, half endurance. Washcloths on sweated temples. Encouraging words. *More, more, you're almost there.* In the end she'd stitch what needed stitching and go home.

Once she was done, Maple washed her dishes, blew out the candle, and padded down the hall to her bedroom. She'd been married to Ezra Huntmoon for three years, but she still didn't sleep well in his childhood bed. The feathers in the mattress poked the back of her neck as she tossed. "Quiet, love," her husband said as she climbed into bed, rolling over to rest a hand on her belly.

WHEN SHE WOKE the next morning, she found the New Chapel fluttering with the news that while most of them slept, three young boys from their congregation had floated the Kamikaze. Only two had returned. Balin Huckle, twelve years old, was missing. The boys had snuck out and created a makeshift skiff from a Roosevelt they'd found abandoned along the river. Though they'd done their best to chink the soundboard, almost immediately the piano began taking on water. "'Cause it wasn't a boat," Ezra whispered in Maple's ear. Maple took his hand, squeezed.

For a river, the Kamikaze had ire. During spring melt it became a gruesome mud-and-tumble current strong enough to cut Paleolithic shale. The banks a boneyard of loss. Everything overgrown with fireweed. The river wended southwest for nearly eleven hundred miles, cutting through the flooded Singing Spruce Forest, and every year there was a story of some kid like Balin drowning while trying to float the ice breakup. Each spring the water became all bergs and hypothermia, beavers working with fervor on chapel-size tapestries of willow and trout ribs. Up and down the river signs were posted:

FORD AT YOUR OWN LIABILITY. The current could take the legs out from under a grizzly.

As search parties organized, Balin's mother hung a rosemary wreath on the pulpit. Maple sat beside her and listened to the story of Balin's first day of school. He came out of his room in red shorts, a radish pinned to his lapel. *What's that?* his mother asked. He twisted the vegetable so that the leaves faced up. *My snack,* he said proudly. "We'll find him," Maple said, though she knew it unlikely. Hypothermia snatched its victims quick. Still, that was no message to send a worried mother. She squeezed the woman's hand, said, "Have faith."

As the rest of the congregation traipsed down the trail to look for Balin, Maple stayed behind to care for the elderly. Her mother-in-law had a sunsetting mind and hair like cotton candy; she couldn't be left alone. For years she had midwifed the territory, spanking newborns, and aside from Maple, she had the best stitches in the region. But in the past several months, she'd developed the dull-eyed look of a goldfish, her memory a match that flickered briefly before snuffing cold. Her hands shook so hard, she couldn't button her coat. While Maple scrubbed her exam table and set out fresh supplies in case Balin returned injured, Mrs. Huntmoon told her a story about when she'd first married the Reverend. She used to go down to the river every morning to beseech God for a child. "I was so young," she said. "I didn't know the difference between faith and conception."

Every day she dropped a small offering into the water. Folded cranes or toasted almonds, cockle shells and pinecones. One day as she knelt beside the river, a huge white peach came floating past. She spread her arms to show the size of the fruit: mythic, larger than a grizzly skull. "I took it home," she said, "and when I split open the pit, do you know what I found inside?" She brought her hands together, cupping an imaginary pit the size of an apple. Her violet irises were lost behind glaucoma clouds and with the crook of a finger she beckoned Maple closer. Hot breath in her ear, Mrs. Huntmoon whispered, "I found my baby."

"I don't know if that'll work for me," Maple said, continuing to set the loom for their morning craft project. She'd fallen pregnant for the very first time two months after her wedding. People had always told her that procreation was an easy feat, but for some it was really all disappointment and a spouse cocking his eye across the dinner table. Maple was medically adept and felt she had some authority when she said that human bodies were the strangest of creations. For reasons no one understood they expelled the things you wanted to keep and held fast to parts that could fester gangrene across your intestines.

Mrs. Huntmoon sat on the stool in front of the loom. She was determined to make enough lace for Hullulla's future wedding dress; she'd been working on the project in secret for months. Ten feet of floss undersewn with tulle, embroideries of bright yellow canaries.

Maple knew that Hullulla had no plans to get married—perhaps she'd have married Finley, but there wasn't anyone else. Mrs. Huntmoon's hands shook and she couldn't remember what she'd eaten for breakfast, but the weaving and embroidery gave her a purpose. Maple had hoped that the New Chapel would be a fresh start for all of them, that the clean air on the plateau would refresh her mother-in-law's neurons, but that hope had proven foolish—a skinned apple shriveling into an ugly, inedible thing.

The Reverend himself rarely preached anymore. Hullulla and Ezra had traded off Sundays until Auntie V established RiverCamp that spring; now, with Hullulla once again sleeping atop the Custer&Sons, the chapel's responsibilities had fallen to Ezra. He delivered short, tense sermons and chafed under the burden, Maple could see it—it was hard on him to watch their congregation thin month after month. Without the people who made up the New Chapel's community, they wouldn't have anyone to serve, and thus no real reason to stay. Each week she counted attendance, then bundled the ivory keys they received as tithes for delivery to the trader. They depended upon the generosity of their congregants.

WHEN THE SEARCH PARTY returned at the end of the day—bearing fillets from RiverCamp but no Balin—Maple spread her own wedding veil on the table beside the newly loomed lace for Hullulla. She got a pair of scissors and began cutting up the veil to make fishing nets. The ivory beads glinted in the evening light. "Don't you think you should save that?" Ezra said, walking into the kitchen. He placed his muddy boots by the door and came up behind her, putting his hands on her shoulders. "You might want it for the future. We might want it for—" He cleared his throat.

Maple put down the scissors. "For what? Our imaginary child?" She was snappish, she could hear it. But the veil now reminded her of a promise unfulfilled; she could keep it in the closet as a shroud, or give it a new purpose. If Hullulla wasn't having much luck finding ivory in the trout running that spring, they'd need to catch extra fish. Maple was no fisher, but even she knew how to dip a net.

As she sewed, Ezra told her about tramping the riverbanks in search of Balin. They did everything they could to teach kids how to float—summer swimming lessons, drydock classes after Sunday school—but it was never enough.

Maple threaded ivory beads onto a needle as Ezra casually mentioned that perhaps they should move away from such a dangerous river. The Kamikaze would only continue gobbling up the remaining buildings in Arctic City and any people still loitering foolishly nearby. Some of the families who'd already left had hitched rides south to the relatively more temperate waters of the Wild Beard Fjords, where they bought up small houseboats. Floating homes didn't care if the water continued to rise, so many people saw them as the housing of the future. And because they didn't require foundations, or stilts, they were relatively inexpensive. Fuel, motor, cistern, plumbing, and insulation. "I think we could do it, Mapes," he said, painting a picture of sea-salted mutton chops, a jigging line off the front porch. "What's holding us here?" he said. "I mean, really?"

Maple couldn't figure out how to distill their life into a succinct reply. *Family,* she wanted to say. *History. Faith*. "What about the chapel?" she said. "What about Hullulla and your parents?"

"They're all set up here. Cozy, cozy, cozy. Plus we'll visit! Isn't it time we chart our own course, just the two of us?" Ezra asked. "We wouldn't have to answer to anybody. Think of the freedom of running our own floating farm, just drifting around eating whatever we catch in the nets." But Maple was raised along the Kamikaze and she had trepidations. "Tell me what you're worried about," Ezra said. "We can work it out together."

Here it was: Maple understood rivers, the logic of water flowing south, but an ocean was an entirely different story. Everything dragged out to sea, coughed back to shore, dragged and coughed, an endless tug-of-war with the moon. She wasn't sure how to live in a place where everything she'd ever lost, dropped, or thrown away had the option of one day coming back to haunt her. "Trepidations like that," she said.

THE REVEREND WOKE UP the next day with a monstrous, banana-sick bruise on his shoulder. He'd thrown it out lifting driftwood in the search for Balin Huckle. Stiff-backed in a kitchen chair, he unhooked a makeshift sling. Maple put her hands on either side of his shoulder and pressed lightly. He made a low noise. "I have to set it," she said. "It's not going to heal like this." Here's what her father-in-law looked like in that moment: white hair pomaded into a swirl, plaid shirt and tie made of the same material. Without looking up, he put his hand atop hers and squeezed.

Her right hand braced the blade. She moved the Reverend's arm into position. "For thine is the glory," he said, as Maple lined up her other hand as a battering ram. A single thrust at the right angle would snap the ball back up into the socket.

"Ready?" she said.

He closed his eyes. "Forever and ever."

The shoulder took all the muscle Maple had, then more. She held him by the elbow and he wasn't wailing, but he wasn't far away either. Nothing seemed to fit. She readjusted her position so she could better leverage the arm forward, then snap it back. The Reverend muttered something from Psalms and she said, "Almost there."

"Oh God, oh God," he said.

Inexplicably, the Reverend's shoulder didn't set and instead they went freewheeling together to the ground in a force of torn tissue and windmilling limbs. Maple landed on her tailbone, right arm bent back to cushion the blow. Somehow her father-in-law flipped over her and landed on his side. Groaned. His mouth was bleeding and she'd have to stitch that later too. She struggled to sit up. Something hurt—the thumb on her right hand was articulated all wrong. Half severed, the tendons were exposed in a way that brought to mind violin strings. Her fingernail aimed down toward her elbow. A terrible sound hurt her ears. It wasn't until she felt the Reverend's hand on her shoulder that she realized she was the one screaming.

Ezra carried her to the exam table behind the pulpit, but for Maple it was all disorientation. Several people talked over her, though all she could see were eyebrows. There was a fracas of noise. Periodically an ear floated into view and she realized someone was leaning over her, trying to hear what she was saying. What she was saying was *I need a needle and thread*. Then suddenly she felt Hullulla's hand on her leg, warm, her voice saying, "Just lie still, it's going to be okay."

Maple and Hullulla shared a connection not easily explained by the ties of friendship. There was a separate ventricle in Maple's heart built entirely for her friend. When Maple awoke next, in her own bed, hand wrapped in gauze, Hullulla was asleep next to her. She put her good hand on her sister-in-law's belly and the baby kicked: one, two, staccato. Hullulla was wearing her pajamas and Maple must have been given something for pain because she was flashing out—her hand hurt and she must have been saying that aloud because Hullulla whispered, "I know, I know, love."

Maple didn't know how long she slept. She couldn't remember walking to the bathroom, either, but here she was. The parsonage had an ancient claw-foot bathtub reclaimed from an old soaking house. Big enough to bathe a horse. Maple heard a splash and realized she was already in the water. Her bandaged hand had been strapped high against her collarbone. Awkward angle, but it kept the wound dry. Something was gliding up and down her back and when she looked she could see Hullulla squatting by the side of the tub, swabbing her clean.

"There you are," Hullulla said.

Over the next few days Maple recovered. Not all at once and not completely, but enough to grip a fork. Enough to bring a spoonful of peas to her mouth. One day she caught a dragonfly, pinned it to a cutting board, and sliced off the wings. She threaded a needle and tried to hold it like usual but the damaged thumb had no strength. When she tried to stitch, the needle shook so badly the wing shredded. She had been told that Mrs. Huntmoon stitched her up. It was a rush job and looked it. Maple traced the puckering scar line. Even with her left hand she could have done better than this.

HULLULLA STAYED the night at the parsonage and woke up in the dark in labor. Ezra rustled Maple from bed—"Maple, Maple," his hand on her neck. Then he was at the door, pulling on boots. There was a noise outside and Maple was surprised to see the Reverend in the doorway. He was already dressed, a prayer book tucked under his arm. "Let's go," he said, and she realized that he must have been the one who came to wake them. She grabbed her kit and sprinted through the parsonage into the chapel.

Hullulla was buck naked in the prayer nook, shielded from view by the pulpit. On her hands and knees. Maple slid closed the curtains around the altar and approached with whispers. She took out her stethoscope. Clamps. The baby's heart pattered. Hullulla was breathing low and hard and Maple said as softly as she could, "I need to check." Hullulla nodded but did not open her eyes. Between them her belly hung low, moonish and magnificent. Maple got her bearings and navigated to the birth canal. Up went her left hand. At first she felt a dangling limb: a leg, she thought. But no. There was no foot. She poked deeper, hunting for the heart-cleaving of breached buttocks, but instead her fingers tangled up in what felt like fishing line. A contraction hit and Hullulla pressed her palms to the floor.

She was sonorous, moaning in the key of deepwater whales. Maple's arm was squished up inside her sister-in-law and when the uterus relaxed she pulled free to find her arm slicked to the elbow in fluorescent blood.

It was a case of placenta previa and everything was prolapsing. The umbilical cord—thick as a thumb and robin's-egg blue—fell loose, coiling on the floor between Hullulla's feet. Maple roved her stethoscope across Hullulla's abdomen searching for the baby's heartbeat. There, no. There, no. Another contraction. "Can you push?" she said. "Can you push right now?" Contraction, contraction. Hullulla grunted and more of the cord dropped, this time with a glob of pulpy, placental strings, and Maple knew they were in trouble.

There was a reason everything was supposed to happen in a particular order. Birth, childhood, death. You didn't want to end up like this, all jumbled together, if you could help it. The cord was trying to drag the baby earthward while the baby's head worked as a battering ram against the web of placenta. The baby couldn't come out unless it tore a hole, but that would cut off the organic motor that had been operating its internal organs for the last nine months. You could run the numbers however you wanted, but this was how you lost, every time: *six seconds, seven, eight*—no heartbeat, no air—*nine, ten, eleven*—too long, much too long—*twelve, thirteen, fourteen.*

Take it from Maple, your whole world could go to hell just that fast.

She wanted to call for Mrs. Huntmoon, but it was the middle of the night and the old woman's mind orbited away while she slept. Auntie V at RiverCamp was much too far off to fetch in time. Maple crouched and roved the stethoscope. There, finally. Heartbeat, heartbeat. Mild and thready, it wouldn't last long. Hullulla was spread-eagled on the floor, hiccupping. Blood watercolored her thighs. Maple emptied her entire bag. Bandages and splints. Ether. Thread. Whiskey. A leather sheath, unzip, lay it flat. Three scalpels in graduating sizes. Surgical scissors.

Mentally Maple backtracked through her notes, trying to remember pelvic geography. She heard herself calling for Ezra, calling for the

Reverend. "Hold her legs," she said. "Don't let her move an inch," she said. "Not one centimeter."

Smooth and firm, Maple opened Hullulla from hip to hip. The skin peeled away and up burst a layer of tallow-colored fat. Tract cutting, rough, then she was into the fascia. Fibrous. Her shoulder worked hard to drive the blade. She pulled the abdominal muscles aside and she knew she was almost there: the peritoneum like overexposed film, clouded and delicate. "Scissors," she said, and Ezra put them in her hand. Bladder, bladder, watch out. Another layer like film and she could see it: a frightening new planet. Exposed like this, the uterus looked so vulnerable—a loom of muscle. One nick and she was in. The baby came out looking half melted: waxed and slick. Ezra scooped it up, snipped the cord, and they were gone.

Maple rocked forward in concentration. If she had a prayer of saving Hullulla's life, the moment was now. The placenta had gotten stuck in a half-life, a bath stopper, and she had to cut it free in pieces. Thick hunks, cow tongues, slapped onto the stone floor. The needle fumbled. Her right thumb could barely pinch the eye. *Five, six, pick up sticks, seven, eight.* Too slow, too slow. She switched to the other hand and bit deep into the uterine wall. Her left wrist had no nuance and the needle wobbled like crazy: a metronome set to a frantic tempo. She did her best to stuff everything back inside, pulled the fascia tight, and ham-fistedly made her way through the rest of the repair.

Hullulla had a pulse, but barely. Her feet were cold. Maple smeared the hair off her own face and smelled iron. There was too much blood. Just way too much. Seeping up from somewhere she couldn't stanch—a dark, disturbed place. Maple felt something shift in the air, a beak cracking the first chip of shell. She grabbed another needle and now she was double-fisting, blurring through fiber—*nine, ten, a big fat hen, eleven, twelve*—dig and delve, cross-stitched fascia, patterns of pearls.

"I hear bells ringing," she called. "What's that? Do you hear that?"

The last layer was all skin. An uneven river snaked at the bottom of Hullulla's belly.

"Those are the bells of heaven," the Reverend said, shakily slumping down onto the nearest pew.

The scar, the one they could see, was a patchwork. Ugly.

More bells, so loud Maple's hands shook.

"Maple," said the Reverend, trying to rise; his legs wouldn't hold him up; when had he gotten so old? "Maple, stop."

Maple heard the baby crying on the other side of the curtain. Hullulla's lips turned the blue of a violet, and then she was gone. Maple knew this as clearly as if she'd seen a frost settle across her friend, ear to ear, a quinzee melting and two girls who never made it out. Not everybody got to see the faces of their children when they steamrolled into the world, but someone almost always witnessed the dying. The way a pall swept, a bright purpling, strange lights. She cut the threads and put her head on her knees. Maple wept.

MAPLE LOVED EZRA with a warm, peaceful endurance, but her love for Hullulla had always run a bit deeper—a dangerous, scalding spring that built and built pressure. She'd loved each of the babies she'd conceived and the chapel pews, wood scarred with epitaphs. *M.B. + M.M.*, soundboards lashed in place of armrests. Ezra talked about framing their new houseboat with this same sort of holy precision: "It's all possibility," he said. But nothing felt possible to Maple after Hullulla's death; she couldn't imagine staying and she couldn't imagine leaving. A new home where Hullulla had never sweated, teased, or sang; or the chapel where she'd died. What kind of choice was that?

The Reverend and Mrs. Huntmoon believed their congregation would one day return, though Maple didn't share their optimism. Their community couldn't even track down Balin, a single lost boy; it was unrealistic to imagine they'd have better luck finding dozens. Even if they did, they'd have to convince them to return and it was not a simple sell. The old line of historic homes along the river below had either flooded or washed away and many families balked at spending their free time leading yaks laden with groceries up the trail to the plateau. The ivory that Hullulla had brought off the river had been a mitigating factor—it had funded a community pantry and flour, rice, and sugar rations for those struggling. Without it, the Reverend and Mrs. Huntmoon could retire on a pension that'd cover their own food and heat, but little else. There wasn't even enough in the coffers to afford the supplies they'd need to get four adults through the winter. Practically, they'd all have to find another way to go on.

They weren't the only ones. RiverCamp had lost Hullulla both as a preacher and as one of their best fishers. Auntie V and Saura rode yaks up to the New Chapel as soon as they heard about Hullulla's death, panniers stuffed with salted trout; they left these beside the chapel's door and quietly slipped away. Inside, Maple was busy cleaning up Hullulla, swabbing dried blood from her thighs. She'd then dressed her friend in a crisp linen dress picked out by Mrs. Huntmoon, and together they wove lilacs through her braids. Once they were finished, Maple headed to the parsonage, where the Reverend sat in his favorite chair, facing the fire, absently fiddling with the buckle on Auntie V's pannier. "Are you hungry? I'm not." He gestured to the satellite phone on the table. "Someone has to tell the Spahrs," he said, voice raspy.

Maple dialed Milda, then Temperance. Both said they'd fly up the next day in time for the memorial. Hullulla had often said that she didn't want to be buried in the New Chapel's graveyard—she wanted to float down the river in a shroud. "But the fish'll eat you!" Maple had said when Hullulla first mentioned this, alarmed at the thought. "That's the point, Mapes," Hullulla replied. They'd host the service at RiverCamp, followed by a community feast.

"Maybe she'll float off and find Finley," Milda said over the staticky line.

"Maybe," Maple said. Just before hanging up she cleared her throat and brightened her voice. "Don't forget you're an aunt now. I think it's okay to be happy about that."

. . .

FOR THE SERVICE they laid Hullulla atop the Custer&Sons, and Maple draped the shroud with the wedding lace loomed by Mrs. Huntmoon. Sunshine canaries, half finished. All of the residents of RiverCamp came down the beach to join, many bearing gifts for the new baby. Rabbit fur booties, knit vests, and canisters of yak milk lotion piled up under the Custer&Sons, along with a set of blocks carved to look like Jubilation House's old stilts from Temperance, and an antique set of tuning forks that Milda had once found with Finley. The Reverend stood next to the Custer&Sons to read a passage from *Old Testament Tykes;* then he and Ezra carried Hullulla's body down to the water line, where they'd prepared a makeshift raft. It would break apart somewhere downriver.

Afterward Ezra set up an eating table so they could feast and share memories. The table quickly filled with platters of salmon berries and smoked cod. Everyone wanted a peek at the baby, born with a thick ruff of Hullulla's blue-black hair, and they passed her around the table while she slept. "She's got Finley's cowlick," Milda teased, thumb gently rubbing the baby's hairline. "Poor girl." When the baby finally got to Auntie V she pushed back her plate theatrically and swept her into her arms. "There she is," she said, tucking an extra blanket around the newborn. "Now come with me, little one, I've been waiting all day to show you Hullulla's lucky spot on the river."

Hullulla's lucky spot would in all likelihood wash away in the next year or two. And RiverCamp would migrate downriver again, leaving behind the Custer&Sons, the ivory traders, and easy access to the trail up to the New Chapel. Maple watched Auntie V walking the baby toward the bank, wistful that a newborn would never remember this place or the people Hullulla had loved. None of them could preserve it for her. The baby opened her eyes and wailed. Auntie V pressed her cheek to the newborn's to whisper in her ear. A furled, pink fern. "There there, you're all right," she said. "Auntie's got you."

. . .

BEFORE SHE AND Ezra left for the Wild Beard Fjords, Maple sewed a last round of bloomers for what students remained, preparing to creep into the chapel in a few weeks to begin the school year. Ezra expected it would take them a couple of years of houseboating before they'd break even. "We'll farm the holy shit out of the fjords, Mapes."

"Language," she said.

For now the Reverend and Mrs. Huntmoon planned to stay in the parsonage and the neighbors that remained promised to check up on them. But Maple expected that within the year they'd be living with them again, floating through the fjords on a new boat. Maple kept an old crank-prop sewing machine in the back of the chapel and she spent their last night at the New Chapel feeding linen to the needle. At dawn Ezra appeared at the door with the baby swaddled. Maple fed her, strapped up, and headed down the bluff to walk the river. "Look, fish," she pointed out. "Look, birds."

Pretty much everyone in Arctic City had been schooled under the tutelage of Mrs. Huntmoon. Maple's mother-in-law believed children learned best by tromping the woods. Every day, come rain or sleet, come fog or chill. At random times Mrs. Huntmoon would rattle a handful of seedpods onto a tree stump and say, "How many?" These were what passed for math lessons. Now when Maple looked around at the New Chapel, the river, her family, all she saw were the natural world's numbers: 19,304 trout. Twenty-two hours of daylight. One, two, ten, a dozen keys. Fifty-five bucks per key, or half a pint of whiskey and a case of creamed corn.

Maple stacked the sewn bloomers on the pulpit and when she got home Ezra was frying rooster for dinner. The Reverend had fallen asleep on the couch. "My girls, my girls," her husband said. Ezra took the baby and flew her into the air. "Are you ready for an adventure? Because we've got big plans for you, little Umi." He lowered her until their noses touched. Gently, he nuzzled his new daughter and she cackled, drool dripping down her chin. They danced over to Maple. The chicken was burning, but instead of tending to it they kissed the baby's cheeks. They kissed her fat thighs. They said, *We'll always take care of you*. They said, *I'm so glad you're ours*. Mrs. Huntmoon had bundled Hullulla's wedding lace on the table—she wanted them to save it for Umi. Maple held an edge of the fabric over her eyes and Ezra said, *Where'd she go? Peekaboo,* Maple said, then covered her eyes again and waited for her husband to say, *Where'd she go? Where's Mommy?*

"Here I am," Maple said.

Moose

Arctic City
Early September, first homestead expedition

On they rode, through what passed for starlight, scraping the bottoms of the flour barrels, breath skunked from raw espresso beans, straight through a narrow pass in the Resurrection Mountains and into Arctic City. Several miles north they'd cross the Kamikaze River, and from there it was ten days to the homesteads. Rocket broke the train down early in the day so they'd have time to head to town and bargain over local supplies. Arctic City had never been a bastion of civilization, and it was still no more than five skeletal buildings on a dirt street. Lumber mill. Boardinghouse heated by a lean-to smoke hut. Their train brought a hell of a commotion into town, and the owner of the post dragged tables and chairs into the street. Anyone with any coin left was in a generous mood—*shots for the gentlemen, shots for the ladies*—and those who'd incurred debt borrowing tools or supplies from neighbors now tried to make these right. The owner of the trade post watched everyone with eyes like fruit flies as they streamed into his shop.

Later that night, a group formed to discuss the possibility of staying in Arctic City. They could open clam shacks, dental practices, a chapel, an official port of trade. The idea took up heat as it became clear that the train had simply, irrevocably, lost too much time to get their new properties set up for winter on the permafrost—not on purpose, not with any sort of decisive finality, but in the manner of an aging clock that loses first a second, then a whole minute, then an evening. Before you know it you're glancing at the mantel and noticing it has been 2:17 for three days. Snow could fly any day.

By the time they left for the Kamikaze River crossing a few days later, most of the train had decided to stay behind. One hundred and forty-three out of 157 families. Some had given up on the idea of homesteading entirely, seeing instead opportunity in the swelling territory capital. The group had whittled itself down to a small troupe of what Arthur called "The Faithful." The Mayflowers, the Huntmoons, Grandpa Happenstance, Mr. and Mrs. Crockett, and the family of piano prodigy Billie Starr. "We don't need a whole cast to set up a decent society," Arthur said. "All we need are some community cornerstones."

Despite the train's meager numbers, they managed to argue for hours about where to ford the river. Rocket insisted that the standard crossing was impassable—he thought they ought to head for the second crossing, a full five days north. "I know all you want to do is cross, but the river's too high," he said. Everyone was ringed around Rocket's sled, listening, save for Moose, who was still embalmed in blankets a few feet away. His buttocks itched where they rubbed against the sled's slats.

"Five days is too high a cost," Arthur said. "We need to cross tomorrow."

Rocket looked at Papa Mayflower when he said, "It'll cost you more than time if you drown."

"The dogs know how to swim," Papa Mayflower said, gesturing at his team curled in the sun. "If the current takes us, they'll fight for the shore same as the rest of us."

Rocket thumped his fist on his sled's helm. Moose had never seen him so animated. "What I'm trying to tell you is that there's one chance at this—if the sleds lose the surface, there's no team in existence that'd be able to pull them out."

"Well, I don't see how we have any other option," Arthur said, fiddling with the sun goggles looped around his neck. They'd be of no use on the water.

"Not doing it, that's the option."

"Be serious," said Arthur. "Look what we've gone through just to get here."

After dinner they sledded to the bank to survey the crossing. Summer storms had swelled the river beyond what Moose had ever seen—white water; swift. As he watched, a carcass of an indeterminable animal bubbled to the surface and went spinning downriver. He had no idea how deep the water was, but it didn't really matter—the biggest problem would be trying to cut across the current. They'd put in a couple miles upstream, Rocket said, and float the sleds downriver while slowly paddling to the far bank. "If we just wait a few days, the water'll go down and it'll be so much simpler. Or we could go farther to the second crossing—"

"What if it rains again and delays us even longer?" said Papa Mayflower. Behind him stood his ambush of sons: matching gray linen shirts, craggy hair. They didn't have the traditional cast of violent men, but taken together they rendered an unsettling effect—you could see in the way the Mayflowers held themselves that they had no intention of stalling. If Moose knew anything about Arthur—the man who'd single-handedly back-carried the Napoleon off the ship—he knew there was no way his stepfather was going to concede, either. Una stood beside him, fiddling with her ring, and Moose wondered if it had occurred to her that someday she might cross-stitch this very moment into their family history.

He tried to think of something to say that would cheer her up, but nothing came to mind. Truth be told, it was growing hard to put his attention toward anything but his own discomfort. The brace's buckles pinched, and on the rare occasions that he managed to drift to sleep he was awoken by the tectonic plates of his bones grinding against one another. What he wanted more than anything was to get off this sled. On the other side of the river, the permafrost stretched wide and flat as far as he could see—as with any journey like this, they were now closer than they'd ever been, but between his condition and his mother waddling around, sucking her teeth as though her hips burned, it no longer seemed certain that their family would reach their plot with all the same parts they'd had at the outset.

"At least it's a clean shot once we get across," said Arthur. "Ten days and we're home."

That night, no one slept. To make the crossing easier, they removed the runners from the sleds and loaded them atop the trunks—these protruded like the tusks of sea beasts. They felled spruce to nail under the slats for extra buoyancy. Moose caulked for hours. Rocket made rounds to survey preparations, pulling ropes to make sure the loads were cinched in place. Their guide didn't say much, and after he left, Una wandered off and returned with a handful of prairie tomatoes—tiny, sour fruits. At this time of year, they were usually setting gradient pyramids in their market stall: Beefsteaks and Cherokees. If they sold enough, their coffers would be full all winter. Moose didn't exactly want to return to that life, but he felt a prick of nostalgia remembering who he and his mother had been before all this, and how swiftly Arthur's intrusion in their lives had changed this dynamic. Una ruffled his hair. There was tomato skin in her teeth when she said, "Almost there." Their journey might be nearly over, but Moose knew another lay just beyond: building a cabin, hunting caribou for winter meat. And another after that. Somewhere in there his new sibling would arrive, disrupting their ecosystem as Moose learned to read new maps spelling out the laws of brotherly affection. Not every journey required a sled; some occurred purely in the mind, or the heart—and the next came hot on the heels of the last, nary a break in between.

Ezra

Jubilation Houseboat
Fourteen years after Umi's birth

Just shy of midnight. Stars overhead as Ezra Huntmoon shifted the engine to low and plowed the newly renamed Jubilation Houseboat over Minion Huckle's seabeds. Plowed right across the property line of his former telecom foreman, plowed deep into private property so that their family could plunder kelp by starlight. It was a chill night and the water had no color.

Descended from Abel Huckle, baron of the Grand Boreal Railroad Company, Minion had inherited twenty thousand acres of seabed along the lower Resurrection Mountains. Farming and easy silverback whale poaching if you were into that line of sport, which Ezra wasn't, though he'd caught his share of trout; he'd often visited Hullulla at RiverCamp when he was younger, watched the knives flash at the gutting table. Auntie V called count as the communal bowl filled with fisheyes. *One, two, chop, chop, save the head for soup*. She'd insisted on inspecting the ivory teeth that she'd whittled for him whenever he came by. "Show me that old handiwork," she'd say, pulling down his lip.

He hadn't seen Auntie V or anyone else at camp for years. After Hullulla died he couldn't bring himself to go back—everyone had a story about her there. Then after the Reverend and Mrs. Huntmoon had passed away, there was little reason to return to the New Chapel either. Instead he'd thrown himself into houseboating and finding crops where they could. They migrated with the seasons, dragged fishnets behind the boat, set traps for wild hares on uninhabited islands, and foraged plateaus for salmonberries and wild yams. A proprietary, peppery strain of kelp grew on the western border of Huckle's acreage, and he monopolized it—he wouldn't sell it or give it away, certainly not to Ezra, so once a month they sped the houseboat out there in the dark and took all that they could.

"Wouldn't it be great to settle somewhere again?" Maple said as they pulled on neoprene balaclavas. "Build a house on solid ground, grow our own strawberries." She clipped dive weights to her belt. "Stop all of this, you know, transience."

"I'm not sure that's realistic," Ezra said. "Remember how we don't have any money? And a child to care about?"

His wife stepped into her flippers. "I remember," she said quietly.

There was a click, then a slide, and suddenly the veranda was puddled in light. Umi lurched in the kitchen doorway nursing a bowl of cereal. "What's going on out here, parents?" she said. Like a photographic negative, Ezra saw himself through his fourteen-year-old daughter's eyes: though he once had the trapezius muscles of a railroader, he was now all white chest hair and propeller scars. He had lived a life. In the sudden light, their veranda was an embarrassing litter of his empty home-brewed kelp ale bottles. He sized all of this up, looked at his daughter, and said, "We're not up to anything, what's up with you?"

"You two think you're so stealthy but you're not."

"It's just a night swim," Maple said. "See, dive lights."

"Night swim!" Ezra said.

Umi eyed her parents. "You know that I know what you're actually doing, right? I know where we are. I could help."

"We'll be back in a couple hours," Maple said. "Try to get some sleep."

Umi spooned up the last of her cereal. "Where do you want me to move the boat if you're not back by sunrise?"

"Don't move the boat," Ezra said.

"Just if. Just in case of emergency."

"Don't move the boat under any circumstances."

"I won't, God. But if I had to—"

Ezra helped his wife climb onto the railing. They flicked on their oxygen tanks. "Don't move the boat," he called as he and his bride fell backwards into the sea.

WHEN THEY RESURFACED hours later, the boat was gone. "Well fuck it all and damn it," Ezra said. He'd choked down half a lung of seawater and had a hangover to rival Zeus. He kicked around, splashing uproariously. They'd hit a good score—a couple spools of organic vines to brew into ale—but now in the daylight their bright yellow jackets were cankers on the water. They pulled the tabs and the vests inflated. "We're getting too old for this," Maple said. "I'm getting too old for this. What are we still doing out here? I mean, really?"

"We're stealing from the rich to feed the poor," Ezra said. "And who's poorer than us? Who needs a basket of manna more than us?"

"I think you're getting lost in your own oratory."

"Just be on my side, that's all I'm asking."

Treading water, Maple sighed. "I'm really trying."

Before they had a chance to orient themselves, a skipper came buzzing across the surface of the water. Farm patrol. Ezra and Maple, they were the only living things in sight for miles—even the otters knew to give the nearby sea caves a wide berth. A young man chewing a corncob pipe steered the boat's helm. Helix Huckle, Minion's nephew up from the continent for the summer, stiff-nosed, in fern-patterned shorts. He pulled alongside them and killed the motor. "Hello, Huntmoons," he said. "Whatcha doing out here on our private property?"

"You don't own the water," Ezra said.

"We sure as shit do. This is Huckle territory."

"I'm allowed to swim. We're all allowed to swim."

"Swim, yes, but not pinch our crops. Get in the boat so I can see what you took."

"Can't you just pretend you didn't see us?" Maple said.

"If you don't get in the boat I'm going to have to hook you."

Ezra's wife looked at him. "We don't know where Umi is," she said. "We could be out here all day." Maple swam to the boat and Helix helped her clamber aboard. Her teeth were chattering so hard Helix handed her a wool blanket stamped PROPERTY OF HUCKLE FARMS; Minion was never one to miss a chance for corporate exploitation. Ezra started swimming—if Helix wanted to bring him in, he'd have to catch him first—but the boat was on him before he could even deflate his vest enough to dive. Helix reeled out a shark hook, leaned over, and clipped Ezra's dive belt. "It doesn't have to be this way," he said. "You can still get in the boat."

"I've made my choice," Ezra said.

The skipper clicked into high gear and Maple was thrown backwards. Prow tilted up. With Helix distracted, Ezra stuffed the kelp pods inside his wet suit. Rope unspooled and unspooled, slack on the water. Ezra fumbled with the hook and then everything went tense all at once—the rope, the hook, his body skipping across a wake of foam. Ass down, sky the color of a puffin egg, his daughter nowhere, his legs tangled in kelp, and bills to pay—always bills to pay. *Whap, whap, whap,* life bruised Ezra Huntmoon from tailbone to nape.

HUCKLE MARINA WAS located in the lower stretch of the Resurrection Mountains, not far from what remained of the New Chapel. The chapel had been falling apart Umi's whole life. Part of the roof had caved in and hauling supplies up to the plateau to repair a structure that no one lived in was not in the family's budget. It was an impossible location to support, both financially and spiritually. The congregation that Ezra had known as a child, the families he'd preached to as a young man—they were all gone. They'd either died off like his parents or moved south to gentler weather and unspent soil.

The Kamikaze River had continued to expand, first soaking up Arctic City, then swallowing more and more of the bank headed south. Soon anyone left would have to decamp to rafts, or boats, though no one could predict if "soon" meant in ten years or one hundred. But the time had already come for Jubilation House. Within a year of Umi's birth, a storm washed through the first floor and settled, unwilling to recede. By then Milda had decided to stay down south full-time with Jude. She told them that the house was a gift for Umi, if they wanted it. They did. Ezra hacked the foundation off its stilts, mounted it onto floats, and installed the best motor he could afford.

Ezra's daughter also held property rights to the fjord itself. The deed was safely secured in a deposit box at Disillusionment Trade Post. Milda had been adamant Finley would've wanted to leave this inheritance to his only child, a daughter he'd never known existed. Both Milda and Temperance did their best to kindle a relationship with Umi from the continent; they wrote letters and called when the solar-powered phone on the houseboat came within range of a broadcast tower. Once a year they visited the territory, rented a plane, and zipped through the fjords, Umi riding copilot as a proud navigator. Viewing sinking structures from the air, it was clear that while homes could be repaired, demolished, or moved, as Finley had known, land held an independent value. Belief in that power of deeded land to transform lives had begun the great migration to the territory in the first place.

When they pulled up to Huckle Marina, Ezra could see Umi on the dock, trying to force open their boat's padlock. He climbed out of the water and lay next to her, panting, his legs harnessed in a cat's cradle of kelp flowers. Umi overshadowed him. "Maybe next time you should trust me," she said. "None of this would have happened if I'd just moved the boat when I wanted to move the boat."

"You were supposed to be sleeping."

"The last I heard this was a family business. I live here too."

"It's not a business when it's stealing something somebody else owns," Helix said. He crouched and unzipped Ezra's pockets. Out fell a strip of raw pearls, a knife, a dive compass, and a sea cucumber. Maple took the oysters they'd pinched for breakfast from her dive bag and set them on the dock. Helix was comical gathering all of this into his arms. "Well, I hope you've learned your lesson," he said.

"You really nailed us big-time. Good job." Ezra tried to stand, but with the kelp in his pants, his balance was troubled. "Now where are the boat keys?"

"My uncle wants to see you before you go. You've got to come up to the house."

"Minion? Not today—we can break bread next time."

"He said you're supposed to come."

"The last time I saw him he threw a fucking fish plate at my head."

"Language," said Maple.

Ezra whispered: "He threw a fucking plate at my head."

"That was over twenty years ago," his wife said.

The sea cucumber writhed out of Helix's arms and splatted on the deck. Meat, no bones, slice it any way you wanted. Helix picked it up and said, "Anyway, he's got your keys."

"Oh, just come on, let's get this over with," Umi said. She started walking and they followed. The dock led to a stone staircase cut into the bluff. Helix whistled and out of the surf rose the heads of a pair of sea lions. They waddled past the group and started climbing the shale steps wending from sea level all the way up to Huckle Manor—four stories of brick lit with an eerie white light.

When Ezra was young and still had decent spryness in his step, he'd apprenticed under Minion Huckle on crew #237 of the Grand Boreal Telecom Company—Minion the foreman, Anker Starr in charge of wires and demolitions, Ezra constructing towers. The three of them, they tore the territory apart. Ezra was a crew-cutted reverend's son with a prayer on his tongue and a work ethic in his heart, and he took to hammering up broadcast towers as though he'd been built for no other work on earth.

Joining the crew had been Ezra's first adventure away from the Old Chapel. Hullulla and Maple had run away once, as girls. While they were gone a great storm had swept over Arctic City and after a few days, people began to assume they'd frozen to death. Two girls who'd made an unfortunate and seemingly fatal mistake. While the Reverend prayed, and snow piled, it was Ezra who'd climb up to make sure the light remained on in the Old Chapel's steeple. When the girls came trudging home up the frozen river, he'd been the first to spot them. He was in the steeple and he reached over to clank the old bell. It was a moment he never forgot, watching Hullulla and Maple return as though from three days entombed, fresh and alive, holding hands, oblivious to the worry they'd caused, or how abandoned he'd felt envisioning the rest of his life as an only child. He'd have gone with them if they'd asked, but as usual they hadn't included him in their plans. He didn't climb down right away and they walked under him and into the chapel without even noticing he was there.

MINION'S HOUSE WAS an industrial monstrosity—if you could imagine spires, the house had them. The surrounding air was gone to static and bats. The crude that used to come off Huckle Sound once powered most of the territory. For every successful investment that Minion had made since their telecom days, Ezra felt he'd somehow managed to make an equally disastrous one. Moving his father's beloved chapel up Mount Resurrection, high ground both moral and otherwise—that's how the Reverend saw it—had cost him most of his telecom severance. When the glacier finally melted, fresh water had to be piped up from the Kamikaze below, and more money was needed to bolt pipes and spigots up the side of the mountain. Whatever remained, paltry sum that it was, had been spent fixing up the houseboat.

Since then, for the last fourteen years, the Huntmoons had been stalwarts of local boating culture. They floated free, no curfew, and they weren't the only ones. Property was a luxury most average people couldn't afford, so a whole community had sprung up devoted to Huck-Finning a new existence. The Huntmoons were luckier than most in that regard. They frequently anchored in the fjord where Jubilation House had once stood to scavenge the surrounding area. The farm's seabeds were no longer fertile enough to grow crops, but they caught enough to eat. And it gave them some sense of home, especially in the summers, when Milda and Jude, and Temperance and Goldie, returned, and they all slept under the sea lion fossil hanging from the attic rafters once more. It felt to them all like Finley was painted across every wall of the house, much like the giant map still tacked to the living room's ceiling. The first years the memories felt so oppressive that Milda had refused even to go up the ladder to the attic, but now when the aunts were in residence, retelling childhood stories, the house felt as full and jubilant as it had when they were kids.

For the most part, the Huntmoons lived off the land. The houseboat's hull colonized crustaceans for market and they took slack jobs when they could get them—Ezra shingling roofs, Maple sewing sleeping bags and running ad hoc medical clinics. They chartered groceries, slaughtered meat, took bribes. When Ezra could get his hands on decent kelp he brewed ale that always sold well at Disillusionment Trade Post. That used to be enough to get by, but as more and more public land sunk, it was becoming increasingly difficult to find any land crops to pick.

Property owners across the territory had gotten busy demarcating the new borders of land and seafloor they claimed had always belonged to them. This left everyone else to fish the skinned outskirts. Ezra wanted to tell Minion that he had taxes to pay too, he had his own necessities. Umi wanted to visit her aunt Milda on the continent and it wasn't free. Maple was tired of pissing over a hole into the sea and the houseboat was showing its full age, telephone wires he'd strung in the walls buzzing like a herd of cicadas. *A bathtub wouldn't hurt,* his wife said. *And I'd probably take a refrigerator if someone was offering.*

Ezra wheezed as they climbed the steps to Huckle Manor. When they reached the top he didn't even have a chance to knock before the door opened and Minion said, "Huntmoon." Gouty and a decade older than Ezra, his former foreman was chewing ginger to lower his blood pressure. "Hard to believe you're still out here doing this—getting a bit ridiculous for a man your age."

"Like you'd even miss what we take."

"This is my land," Minion said. "I don't have to have a reason for wanting you off it."

Ezra dripped like a black rain cloud on the porch. "I don't live my whole life just to piss you off," he said. He knew that in Minion's version of their history, Ezra was a bandit, a former employee with no respect for the law.

Minion stepped back from the door. "Come in, we can hash this out like grown-ups," he said.

All five of them tromped inside. If the outside of the manor was forbidding, the inside only reminded Ezra that he'd forever be his father's prodigal, a reverend's son still struggling to make more than a reverend's salary. He and Maple had never lived in a house as opulent as Minion's, and probably never would. It was a showcase of extravagances: percolators, self-washing windows, a floor made of reclaimed sled slats.

They followed Minion down one hallway, then another. The adults left Umi and Helix in the kitchen and went into an adjacent, velvet-wallpapered study. A giant mariner's desk faced a window overlooking the sea. Down below, the houseboat eddied against the dock, roof shingles peeling like cancered skin. Ezra and Maple sat in chairs facing the desk, and Minion took his place, saying, "I already called the ranger. She says if you come back here she'll impound the boat. I thought I'd do the decent thing and give you an official warning first."

"What the hell, man."

"I have a family too," Minion said, adjusting a picture on his desk of a gaggle of kids that included young Helix. "And honestly, you're way too old to be living this way."

Ezra started to cross his arms, but the kelp pods in his suit crunched. Not wanting Minion to notice, he casually gripped the armrests on his chair. "It's called a lifestyle."

"What if we just promise that we won't come back?" Maple said. "Can't we just do that and go?"

"You can't promise something I haven't agreed to," Ezra snapped.

Maple put her hand on his arm. "Just listen to what the man's saying."

"I lost three teeth," he said, waving at Minion. "Are you forgetting that this man knocked three teeth out of my head?"

Minion leaned back in his chair and looked between them. "You know there were justifications," he said.

"Fine," Ezra said. "Is that all you want? We won't be back. We'll be Good Samaritans. What's yours is yours, amen. Can we go now?"

For a moment Minion regarded him. Then he slid open a drawer and a ring of keys rattled onto the desk. "Make better choices," he said, unclipping the Huntmoons' boat key.

After, as they descended to the beach, Ezra could feel the weight of Huckle Manor watching them, making sure they didn't deviate. Ezra was clammy and Maple silent. The stairs were steep, and what they had to show for their efforts tonight was nothing except for the kelp pods hidden in Ezra's jock. They boarded the boat and Maple whizzed the motor. Of the two of them, she was the superior navigator.

"I want to hear the story of how you lost your teeth," Umi said, sitting next to her father. "What happened?"

"Another time."

"*Dad*. You've been saying that since forever."

"You're still a kid."

"Nobody can be a kid their whole life," Umi said.

The story was: Minion and Ezra had worked together for years. During that time they'd developed a natural team spirit. The Reverend's church had only ever held a mediocre claim on Ezra's soul and after he'd gotten a taste of the world, he couldn't imagine returning to spend his life handwriting sermons in a dank study, delivering salvation with the sweep of a hand. Minion had introduced Ezra to liquors he'd never tasted, bathhouses where their hairy knees rose above steaming water. And before he'd known Maple as the bone of his bone, he hadn't always upheld the vows of chastity he took at his first communion. Years on the road wore down even the bravest of souls, and like all men, Ezra had some weaknesses. That's how everything fell apart.

Skinny-dipped and high on the fat of the day, the broadcasters had gone tomahawking through the old sled ruts. This was ritual, racing off steam—Ezra against Anker, both of them against Minion. The girl he'd known before Maple, hair like straw, had chased Ezra until they were tackled together in a heap. Ezra was high on hormones and she was laughing, had her hands on his belt, nails those dirty little half-moons, and there was a pulse between them. She rocked her hips and a galaxy away, perched on clouds, heaven's angels startled awake—

"Wait," Umi said. "Is this the story of how you fell in love with Minion's sister? Because I already know that one."

"It's more complicated than that."

"Because Minion found out," she said.

"So your mother told you? I don't know why I even bother pretending I'm the one telling you about my life."

Minion had discovered Ezra and the girl together in the sleeping bag, and upon doing so, had grabbed the nearest hammer, winged back, and let the force fly. The instant before Ezra'd had the nonsense struck out of him, he'd sensed how everything might have turned out different—better timing; Minion for a brother-in-law; a pack of little straw-haired children. But the next second he was unconscious, kicked off the crew. One fell swoop. Death, resurrection, an auroral bruise from chin to ear, three missing molars. He moved home to recuperate, and that's when he really got to know Maple. She'd tended his injury, swabbed his forehead with ice. Read favorite passages of scripture; braided the whole family faith bracelets. After that, there was no real question of their intimacy—he'd asked, "Do you?" And she'd said, "I do."

NOW MAPLE SET coordinates for the Wild Beard Fjords, and Ezra steered the boat away from Huckle land. They needed to recuperate and replenish supplies. All told, Ezra figured they only had enough cash for a couple days of supplies and more fuel.

The water had a chop and he gave the wheel a firm hand. Once they were out of view of the manor he unzipped his suit and out fell the pods he'd managed to filch.

"Gross, Dad, those were down your pants," Umi said.

"Like I had a choice."

"You had plenty of choices, that was just so clearly the wrong one."

It had been a long night and they were all exhausted. The sun began to tinge the clouds and Umi said, "I can hold the wheel for a while if you want to get some sleep."

"Are you sure I can trust you to keep us on course?" Ezra said.

"Oh my ever-loving God, Father."

When Ezra woke up six hours later they were idling into the Wild Beard Fjords. There were several inlets before the Spahrs' fjord, and their houseboat floated past a cinnamon-colored Victorian with a rainbow of kayaks tied to the dock. In the next fjord over, long-term resident Paris Starr was in her glass-block veranda shower; she whistled as the Huntmoons passed, raised an arm, scrubbed her armpit. At the next fjord Sylvester Pope stood shirtless at his grill. There was an aquarium mounted to the railing and he fished an arm in the water, pulled out a sea star the pink of electrified helium. Tossed it into the fire. Ezra could smell the waft of the meat from the boat.

Their own fjord stood empty, save for the stilts barely poking out of the water. They roped the boat to the Sea Lion stilt. Maple was still asleep on their bed, hair tatted with sea weeds. Ezra closed the bedroom door behind him and went out onto the veranda, where Umi was struggling into one of her mother's old scuba suits. Everything was too big and it gapped. There was a giant blue hose coiled on the deck, the waterline, and Umi prepared to dive under the boat and hook it up to the freshwater cistern they kept bolted to one of the house's old stilts. At sea they mostly drank desalinated water, which tasted like fish piss, but at the fjord the water was fresh. Ezra could already taste it: snow melt, piped from inland muskegs, one hundred percent glacial melt, iced and delicious. "You got this?" Ezra said as Umi shouldered the hose. She climbed onto the railing and spread her arms as though she were about to take flight. "Pretty sure I was born for this," his daughter said.

Umi came up spluttering not long after and Ezra helped her out of the water. They pulled their chairs into the sun, he cracked an ale, and together father and daughter took their leisure. Inside, he heard the shower spit water; Maple must be awake. After a night in the water his gums ached along the line where his molars—ivory chiseled from a key that his sister, Hullulla, had pulled from the belly of a trout—were sewn into place. He ran his tongue along the puckered stitch line. Spit. There was blood in the sputum, so he headed to the bathroom and peeled down his lip. He'd healed as well as anyone could expect. A quick swish and the blood was cleared from his mouth. He was still looking in the mirror when his wife poked her head from the shower and they locked expressions. "Hot water's out," she said. "I only got two minutes."

This blasted boat. They were always low on fuel. Ezra went into the bedroom, opened a cabinet, and cranked the handle on the generator. It flickered blue, light green, blue. Out. He kept a spare canister of fuel jury-rigged under the kitchen sink and when he went to get it, Umi was there. Sitting at the table reading aloud from a flight school brochure. "If you're not going to let me learn what you do, I should just go to flight school now," she said. "I'm your daughter, but I want a profession."

"You're too young," he said. "We'd miss you." The can under the sink was empty and the fuel tank read a flat red E. Out came the jar behind the flour, their bank of mothballed money. One, two. He counted bills. Three, four.

"You could always try caring about me less," Umi said.

Five, six. "You know I can't do that."

"You haven't even tried."

Maple came into the kitchen then, fresh-washed, and now it was all hands on deck, find the money where you can. They pulled out everything they had: a crate of tinned mussels, several liters of ale, pickled sea cucumbers—usually they got a fair price in Disillusionment, at least enough to buy fuel for their next run, so Ezra added them to the stack. He had an intuition for judging price and when everything was on the counter he could tell there wasn't enough. His head fell in his hands and Maple rubbed his back, saying, "It's all right, we're going to be fine. We haven't starved yet, have we?"

"What's wrong with Dad?" Umi said.

"We're adults," Maple said. "That's what's wrong."

Ezra didn't have a lazy man's tendencies. Like Hullulla, he was raised to lead a congregation, although his sister had gotten the natural ear for their father's brimstone. Ezra had managed to lead the New Chapel for a few months, but the gift had not come to him naturally. He'd always been more of a light sport when it came to matters of holiness—he had a romantic's temper; give him his health and the sunlight of the Lord and he'd gladly toil the land for a living.

During his years on Minion's crew, Ezra grew to become the fastest tower builder on the line. When he'd first met Minion's sister, he'd been full of cock-swagger, molded into a true Huckle man—and then in the blink of an eye, there was Minion looking down at the pair of them leg-wrapped in the bottom of a sled rut. The disdain he'd felt for himself then at realizing that he'd turned into exactly who Minion had preached him up to be.

There was a *bawk* and the sound of seagulls taking wing. The boat was at anchor but it tipped sideways and the money jar went rolling across the counter, spilling coins before hitting the floor in a shatter of glass. Through the window Ezra spotted a sea lion trying to hoist itself over the railing onto the veranda. The lion brayed and the boat rocked. The animal was not full-grown, but it had heft, and the chickens penned outside the bathroom window beat their wings against the wire in fear. *Protest, protest,* they squalled. The lion belly flopped onto the deck and the boat shifted back to neutral. Ezra ran over, slid the door to the house closed, flicked the lock. Tawny and sprawl-balled, the lion pressed its face to the glass—eyes like space stars, whiskers stiff enough to sweep a room.

All at once Umi was at the door tapping the glass. "Heel," she said. "Be good."

"Honey, he's a wild animal," Ezra said.

"He's not wild, Dad."

"What are you talking about?"

"He's got a collar," his daughter said.

The lion rolled over, basking in the sun, and Ezra could see the glint of metal at his throat: PROPERTY OF HUCKLE FARMS. "You stole one of Minion's lions," he said.

"You were stealing stuff."

"Yeah, but I have a good reason. I have a family, you're just a kid."

"Kids have families too," Umi said.

Before Ezra could stop her, his daughter had unlatched the door and held out her fists for the lion to sniff. The animal licked her knuckles, rose on hind legs, batted his flippers. "He really wanted to come with us," she said. "He made this totally sad face."

"Minion's going to put two and two together and hit the roof," Maple said. "We have to take him back."

"Nobody saw me—even you guys didn't see me."

Ezra squatted and rubbed the lion's ears. "I bet he can do all kinds of cool shit," he said.

"Ezra," Maple warned.

"I'm not saying we keep him—I'm just saying, maybe we don't give him back."

"You know a sea lion can swim, right? If he wants to go home he can always get there himself," Umi said. "This isn't our problem."

"It's a problem if it gets us into trouble," Maple said. "I'm telling you now—as a family, we're not making good decisions. We should be reevaluating all of these choices."

"Anybody want to go for a swim?" Ezra asked.

"Can you stay focused, please."

"It's a beautiful night."

Maple pushed off the counter and opened a cupboard. She took out a knife, a net, a mini-harpoon, and handed them over. "If you're going out, at least bring back dinner," she said.

. . .

IN THE WATER the lion cut a figure—Ezra was in flippers but the lion easily triple-lapped him. This stretch of coast was a barnacled wasteland, one fjord after another, each skinnier and more infertile than the last. There were a few luxury houses built into the sides of cliffs, but most of their hydraulics were so rusted, they were one strong gust from calving into the sea. Ezra had always imagined Minion's sister in a house like this, her life delicately perched above so much salt—she and Minion had come from high money. Ezra meanwhile became literate in the chapel at the age of two by watching his mother's eyes scroll hymns. Their church preached a spirit of kindness and his family was always lending itself out to those in need—they smoked fish for the elderly and kept bread bowls on the communion table stocked: *Come unto us all who are weary and take what you need.*

Every coin that passed through the chapel's coffers was blessed and accounted for. The Huntmoons gave frugality a new name—his mother cut his hair until his wedding night and his sister sewed his traditional plaid work pants. But while Maple could always stitch fine lines, Hullulla had never been able to contain the vibrancy of her spirit—her seams were wonked, his cuffs fraying. She showed endearment to her older brother by concerning herself with his spiritual health. "Pray with me," she'd say as she tipped her chest to the sun.

Now when Umi asked for her birth story, Ezra told her everything, how they were handmaided in their journey of becoming her parents. He liked to think her life would not have been so different if Hullulla had lived, if Finley hadn't drowned. Either on this boat or at River-Camp, his daughter was probably destined to grow up unanchored, a child who of course fantasized about the day when she would fly.

Ezra's mask smelled like ale and there was murk in the water. Visibility: moderate. The lion was clearly pacing himself because anytime he got a lead he swept back underneath, bringing up the tail of their partnership. Ezra turned his scope underwater, scanning for edibles. All at once the lion dove. Deep into the dark and then he was gone. The water's depth varied all over the territory, the shelf rising, then dropping hundreds of feet. Ezra had half a tank of portable oxygen strapped to his thigh and he hooked up. Flicked on the searchlight. He swam down until he couldn't see any farther—at the twenty-foot mark, no light cut the shadows, and he had only a mini-harpoon for ammunition. Nothing good would come of him going any deeper. While he waited for the lion to resurface, he chiseled abalone off a nearby shoal. There were only a few, and he could tell by their weight that they weren't meaty, but Maple would boil a sipping broth to last through the weekend.

He was working the knife, dropping shells into the net, when a shadow passed behind him. He turned around and there was the lion, nose to nose with him, a gigantic octopus clamped in its mouth. The creature was the color of sand. Alive. Native breeds like these were famously hard to capture—they thrived in deep water and were barely perceptible to the human eye. Ezra could see spray across the lion's eyes and down his flank; he'd gotten inked. He pushed the creature against Ezra's mask and at first Ezra had no idea what to do. A cephalopod that size could drown a human. The arms were a writhe of anger and even the lion was having trouble managing control. The animal shook his head and Ezra could see teeth, so he kicked up to the surface. In the air he released his oxygen and the lion followed him up, presenting the octopus to him, again. This was when Ezra realized that the lion must have been a trained receiver—he'd made the capture, and the rest was up to Ezra.

What came next was gruesome; Ezra had never done it before. Lift folds of skin to find the eyes—and that must have given the lion some confidence because its jaws softened, slightly, but Ezra could see it—and soon the whole catch was released into his hands. The weight took him by surprise and under they went, but he had the upper hand, and there was no way he was getting the force strangled out of him today. The lion back-floated away, leaving Ezra to the battle. To prepare the meat properly for cooking he needed to give it a beating; this was the fun part. Ezra had knuckles. He punched the octopus, stunning it, then felt around for the vulnerable patch of skin behind the octopus's eyes. The next part wasn't his favorite chore, but it was paramount to dispatch the creature as quickly and humanely as possible, and when it came to building a home for your family, you had to do what you had to do. Bubbles out the nose, he leaned in and bit the brain out of the octopus.

BACK IN THE FJORD, Ranger Starr's boat was pulled up alongside Jubilation Houseboat, orange lights spinning. The lion had gone off hunting so Ezra swam back alone. It wasn't until he threw the net onto the deck of their boat and climbed out of the sea that Ezra noticed Maple was already on their veranda and Minion was on the ranger's boat. The foreman was wearing mirrored sunglasses and a grimace. "This is exactly what I didn't want to happen," Minion said. "I want my lion back. And don't you dare say, 'What lion?' "

"If I'm supposed to have some idea as to what you're talking about, I don't," Ezra said.

"He's missing. I know you took him."

Ezra gave the ranger his most baleful gaze. "I would never steal someone's pet."

"He's not a pet, he's a business investment," Minion said. "And if you don't have him, how'd you capture that giant octopus all by yourself?"

"I have talents."

"Bullshit."

"Just because you think I don't know how to do something doesn't mean you're right."

"He's worth more than your whole boat put together. Watch this." Minion took a whistle from his pocket and hit a pitch. They all waited for the lion to appear. He didn't. "I know one of you is responsible for this," Minion said, glaring at each of them in turn. "I warned you. I'm lodging a formal complaint now—write him up," he said to Ranger Starr.

"Did you actually see him take the lion?" she asked. Ankina Starr was the daughter of Ezra's former broadcast companion, Anker, and was now a young woman in a green half-sleeve wet suit. She had a high school diploma and eight months on the job. "I can't exactly write him up for stealing something he doesn't have," she said.

“Of course I didn’t see him, this is his profession. He’s goddamned stealthy.”

Ezra grinned impishly when he said, “Thank you.”

This comment shifted Minion to high throttle. He pushed his sunglasses onto his forehead and placed both hands on the railing. “Let me search his boat,” he said. “I can prove what’s mine is mine. What’s that Bible story, Huntmoon, about coveting what you don’t have? Seems like not everyone around here has actually learned that lesson.”

“That’s enough, Minion,” Maple said. “We told you, the lion’s not here.”

Ezra’s wife knew what she knew about his past—how worried he was that if he didn’t fall in with the broadcast crew he’d end up living the second generation of his father’s formalistic life. Now she was married to him and his heathenish past, mother to a child she didn’t carry. Poor as she’d ever been. Ezra picked up the octopus. In his hands it became a braying whip and thank goodness his shoulders still had their power. He rounded back. Smacked the head into the railing. Everyone flinched at the show of violence. Again. And again. It wasn’t until he felt Maple’s hand on his elbow that he realized he was two dozen strokes to the wind and the skin had split. Flushed, he stopped and said, “Maybe your lion just ran away. Ever think of that?”

“He’d never do that. I trained him myself,” Minion said. “What are you even going to do with the level of meat he can haul? It’s not like the two of you can use everything he catches.”

“There are three of us,” Maple said.

“Same difference.”

“No,” Ezra’s wife said. “It isn’t.”

Religious born or not, Ezra had observed that most families adhered to their own similarly invisible borders—the unknowable longitude at which an uncle becomes a father, a foreman a brother, a childhood friend the wife you nestle alongside at night. Boundaries that force you to make choices—where to rest, how to fight, what to eat, who to love. The only family Ezra had in this world floated this dilapidated boat with him, and if they could score enough game before the ice set, they might be able to anchor somewhere warm for the winter. What guilt he bore from not automatically turning over the lion to Minion was appeased by remembering his foreman's own law of enterprise: take what there is and make what you can. Ezra followed this example, and his daughter was now following his—thieving for the family a potential future, all of which weighed heavily against whatever lingering respect Minion might still have harbored for their partnership gone past.

"There're an awful lot of lions in the ocean," Ezra said. "Pretty tough to identify just one."

THE LION TURNED UP hours later, a second live octopus in his mouth. By then the ranger's boat was long gone. Ezra immediately unbuckled the lion's collar and tossed it into the fjord. "So, that's that?" Maple said. "We've made our decision?" She was standing in the kitchen clipping octopus limbs to a rigged-up drying line. The house smelled like oatmeal and vinegar and Umi was at the table studying aeronautical charts of the territory, a pair of flight goggles pushed into her hair. Ezra's daughter was of a certain temperament—serious even as a little girl, she saw the world with an aviator's scope. Unlimited. Promising.

"You know a plane doesn't have to be expensive," she said. "We could get a used one. I can find us a good deal. When I get my pilot's license I can fly you guys all around."

"I'm more focused on the here and now," Ezra told her.

"This is my here and now," said Umi.

"Well, do you want a hot shower in the current here and now, or not?"

"Do."

"Then get your coat, we've got to make a fuel run," he said.

Ezra didn't want to take the boat out of the fjord, so they walked around the veranda to the side where they kept their kayaks roped up. Umi picked a green double-hatch and squeezed into the back spray skirt. They paddled to Disillusionment Bay, floating past a few more finger-length fjords along the way, the water in each a calming, foamy teal. Something red, a crop, bloomed on the seafloor and Ezra could see divers threading among the vines and defoliating them as they picked a crop of ripe sea grapes. Coming up on the bay like this reminded him of the years he'd spent riding his favorite yak, the Holy Ghost, up and down Mount Resurrection—from afar both Arctic City and Disillusionment appeared imperial in their own rights. Tiny mountain communities backed by heirloom spruce.

Up close both cities had muddy streets and DON'T FEED THE BEARS signs shot through the neck. And now the Happenstance family was laying waste to a major corner of beachfront real estate in order to expand the trade post; many of those who'd left the Resurrection Mountains had settled near Disillusionment and the summer tourism trade still thrived. The expansion would allow the trade post to filter territory mail, broker livestock, immunize the children. The bay also now boasted a rustic sauna where tourists sweated like cooped chickens. And in the old graveyard Paris Starr had taken over the campsites for tourists who enjoyed sleeping atop the territory's dead. *Minnie Mayflower. Finley Spahr. Unamelia Price-Bloomer.* Most were just headstones; few of the graves had actual bodies.

Together Ezra and Umi roped the kayak to the town's dock and walked down the beach. While the trade post's expansion was being built, the Happenstance family was selling supplies in the free air. Spread across the sand: cast iron, flour, salt-and-sour strips of caribou. Fuel prices had gone up since they were last here five months ago and Ezra had to barter what was left of his last batch of ale to cover the difference on the three canisters they needed. The sea cucumbers were traded for their weight in salt. The mussels for a sack of lemons.

As they turned to leave, Umi pointed at the water and said, "Look." Floating toward them in the surf was a blue, back-dented HawkHatch: a one-seater, low-altitude training plane. The words FOR SALE BY OWNER were spray-painted across the side.

"Really?" Ezra said. "Is a plane all you can talk about these days?"

"You won't talk to me about the things I actually want to talk about."

"If I could buy a plane, don't you think I'd already have done it?"

The money they had left would pay for a couple more days of food, then they'd be back to the open sea. Already they'd zipped through most of the lucrative seasons—next week in the Archipelago of Lost Saints they'd clean up on sea beans, as they did every year—but the days of drawing a drachma, any drachma, from the intestines of a trout were long gone.

He and Umi were halfway back to the dock, lugging their groceries on their shoulders, when a woman walked past with a bouquet of octopus arms on sticks. Charred octopus, suckers seeped. They set down their bags and followed her back to a Happenstance kid who traded her five canisters of fuel—more than they'd made in months—for the bundle of limbs. Ezra tried to appear casual when he leered into the kid's face, said, "How much? How much was that?"

"That's private business."

"Let's say I'm an investor. Let's say I'm a go-getter."

The kid bit off the tip of one of the arms, grease dribbling down his chin. "Whole? Alive? What are we talking about?"

"I can get what you need."

The kid quoted a price. "I can get you more if you bring them in alive," he said.

"Seriously?"

"There's a market, yeah. Breeders. Tourists. Let me be the salesman."

"How am I supposed to get it to you without drowning first?"

"There's a reason most people don't take that option," the kid said.

"Well, do you have anything that could, like, at least hold one? Something it couldn't escape from?"

"We've got that old butter churn."

Ezra pulled out the last of the coin.

"I'll take it," he said.

By the time they got back to the boat, Maple had already spiked the second octopus through the brain. The body hung on the wall drying beside the family's old bearskin. Maple was sitting at the table weaving. Back-forth went the needle as she rounded limbs into rosettes. *Viola Bloomer's Octopus Rosettes.* "Old recipe," she said, "very old." As Ezra watched Maple's handiwork, her once-broken thumb half a lag behind the other, he thought about what it must have been like all those years ago when she and Hullulla had worked the river together. Hooks in the water, cedar in the smokers. *Head, tail, belly,* clapped knives at the gutting table. How lucrative fishing used to be and how jealously every living creature was bogarted today—everything levied, everything taxed. If Minion's kelp grounds weren't six hours away, Ezra would be tempted to get drunk right now and try another round of stealth diving. Helix couldn't possibly catch every marauder with the heart of a night owl and innate tidal intuition.

When the ocean was about to turn, that was the moment you couldn't teach—the tide hauling skirts, the magnetism of first loves. Ezra had wept his way through many a riptide, trying to decide whether to float south as far as his free spirit would take him. Or beat the waves bloody knuckled as he butterflied back to shore—propelled by nothing so much as an unknowable combination of conviction, latent strength, and the desire to snuggle beside his wife. His daughter meanwhile was relaxed, oblivious on the roof above, tracking the planes zooming east into her future.

IN THE MORNING they all woke up late. No sign of the lion. Ezra fried abalone for breakfast and the three sat in a line on the veranda sucking coffee. After breakfast they pulled on their wet suits, grabbed gear, and climbed down into the green kayak. Ezra was at anchor; Maple, fore; Umi straddled the middle deck between them, hugging the butter churn. As a family they'd been pickled like this before—brinked on bankruptcy; it was a familiar trope.

After clearing the mouth of the fjord they broke west, away from population. Umi's feet dragged through the water but she didn't seem to mind. Ezra didn't know where to go, only that to pay for more groceries, more fuel, they needed to find either the lion or a crop they could sell. From the pocket of her jacket, Maple removed a pair of octopus rosettes and handed them out. They snacked. Afterward Ezra whistled, hoping the lion would hear the pitch, until Umi said, "Please stop. You're so off-key you don't even know how off-key you are."

"Here, boy!" he called.

"He's not stupid," Umi said. "He knows how to come back to us."

"Or Minion picked him up."

"Then I'll just have to steal him again," said Umi.

"No," Ezra said. "You're done with that."

"I don't know what your philosophical objection is to me helping out, but I'm getting sick of it," Umi said. "Now's your chance to train me. My mind's superimpressionable right now, right? What if I'm the secret to our family's success? And all this time you didn't know, and thought I was just ordinary, when I could have been helping?"

"I'll be the adult," Ezra said. "You just be the kid."

"It's kinda hard to be a kid when you might have to hock the boat on which you live."

"Nobody's selling the boat."

"I have eyes," Umi said. "I have ears."

There was an inlet up ahead with a sandbank big enough to beach the kayak. They pulled in. Maple rolled up her pants and waded into the shallows, calling for the lion, while Ezra and Umi struggled into scuba gear. You never knew what was down there unless you looked, and they'd had good luck at plenty of random stops like this: baskets of puffin eggs, halibut with lazy eyes, even the square fishing crate they dragged into the living room once a week to use as a bathtub. From the sandbank, the floor of the inlet sloped deep—their dive lights could barely cut to the seafloor. Below Ezra the sand rose and fell in hilly embankments overgrown with scraggle grass; at two cents a pound, the crop wasn't even worth the trouble.

Umi was swimming under him when all of a sudden she stopped and raised her fist to signal. Ezra swam down to her level. There was an ancient submarine half eroded into the side of one of the underwater hills; he could see it, several of the portholes busted clean. He swam through one of the jagged openings. The territory was full of strange dioramas like this—abandoned sites where all you could do was wonder how they came to be. He checked the engine room for mechanical parts, but they'd already been raided. He was kicking back out of the porthole when Umi gestured for them to surface. Up they went. In the air he pulled off his mask and said, "What? Did you see something?" And she said, "It's Mom."

They were a couple hundred yards away, but when he looked back at the spit of sand he could see Maple using the butter churn like a shield, jousting away the lion, who was holding the largest octopus Ezra had ever seen by the scruff. Limbs were everywhere, one wrapped around the lion's neck, another tiptoeing across the sand toward Maple's foot. The creature was spitting ink in all directions. Maple had an indigo sunburst on her shoulder, spray across her neck. The octopus's eyes orbited to take in the whole scene. Even from a distance Ezra knew his wife's inclinations—she was bouncing her feet carefully, trying to figure out how to take the creature alive. Without a moment's hesitation, he and Umi hit the water. Break, breathe, kick go the legs. The octopus continued to advance on Maple—half walking across the sand, half propelled by the lion's pride in his own hunting abilities—and Ezra went under. Up. Breathe. The butter churn looked laughably small as Maple parried and all at once Ezra was dragging himself onto the sand. He kicked off his flippers. Ran.

The octopus was an Arctic Giant, so brilliantly white it was almost indistinguishable from a small calved iceberg. On land the body flickered like a manifestation of the northern lights: purple, streaks of green. Ezra was on the cusp of the situation and without thinking he launched himself into the fray, arms wrapping this strange amoeba of glow. They lifted off the sand. Maple yelled his name as they went free-twirling. Crashed. The octopus jelly-caked under him like the world's strangest shock absorber. No bones, and this was why—it could take the beating of a 180-pound man and still muster the energy to jet ink in his eyes. He couldn't see anything. Blinked. He tried to wipe his eyes on the sleeves of his scuba suit, but he couldn't get them clear and then the world was overcast in a gauzy indigo wash.

Eight arms was too many. Ezra grabbed blindly for anything to hold, but even in the sand the skin slicked out of his hands. He didn't know what he was gripping when he heard Umi say, "Hold it, Dad." Heat crept down his neck. They were making a full-family effort: Maple trying to stuff the octopus into the butter churn limbs first, Umi whipping the body with the kayak paddle. Ezra didn't know what a giant of this size would bring, but if they got it alive he was prepared to barter for a great deal of worth. He rolled up into a half sit and tried to get his bearings. From a distance, the lion barked commands and there was sand in everyone's ears. Maple got out her elbows and with a one-two punch they managed to get half of the octopus into the churn. It was easier now that the momentum had been broken. Ezra kicked. More jousting, then the lid slotted into place. Maple clamped it closed. They all breathed free. Looked at one another.

"That was awesome," Umi said.

There were times when Ezra caught sight of his daughter from a certain angle and up rose a sticky, old-fashioned feeling—it happened now, the nostalgia of Hullulla's genes glimmering through layer upon layer of nurturing. When his sister was fourteen, the same age Umi was now, Ezra was already gone working for Minion. He sometimes wondered what might have happened if he'd stayed home—would Hullulla have ever taken up residence at RiverCamp? Would she ever have met Finley? Or would she and Ezra have grown so close that they'd have naturally found a way to co-helm the pulpit?

The thing nobody had told him about being the prodigal of the family was that it was a lifelong affliction. The relapses just kept coming. Ezra had his own guilt for the life he'd led, but none so profound as seeing the look of pride in Umi's eyes and realizing exactly what sort of life he'd been indoctrinating her into all this time—they ate hand to mouth, they were on the ranger's radar, they spent what they made and made more. A few more years and Umi would be all trained up—*prime,* as she said—shaped into a full-time prodigal. Ezra knew from experience that by then it would be too late. Only the most extraordinary of circumstances could change the established trajectory of your life.

"Come on," he said. "Let's go sell this beast."

"Dad. You're bleeding," Umi said.

Ezra put a hand to his face. Something warm dribbled from the corner of his mouth and it was blood. He wiped it away, but this only served to highlight what must have been a bruise to the jaw. He fished a finger into his mouth and found that one of his ivory molars was loose. His tongue lifted the tooth and he felt underneath the web of exposed tissue. Several of the stitches had ripped out. Ezra didn't know what softened his gums—days and days in the water, age, desperation. His tongue worried the tooth back and forth until it broke free. He spit it into his hand. Even after all of these years, the molar was full weight, in remarkably decent shape. He held it out.

"Someone's going to have to resew me," he said.

"That's a lot of ivory, Dad," said Umi. "You've had that this whole time?"

"It's my tooth."

"A tooth you can sell isn't really, like, a *tooth-tooth.*"

How to explain to his daughter his attachment to this piece of half bone—or, how to explain it in a way that flattered his character. When he got smacked with Minion's hammer his natural teeth had shattered on impact. Auntie V had repaired the gums, tucked them around these new molars, and Ezra had been biting with them ever since. His daughter had only ever known him with this smile. He tucked the tooth into his pocket and aimed their kayak back toward the bay. The butter churn could float, but octopuses were notorious for escaping the inescapable, so when they loaded back up he held the barrel in his own lap. The lion came frolicking after them as they rowed back toward Disillusionment Bay to sell their bounty and settle their debts.

AFTER EZRA TRADED the octopus to the Happenstance kid, they got dinner from the food truck parked outside Paris's cemetery. He and Maple held hands as they wove among the graves of the territory's ancestors. They discussed his tooth and what they might get if they sold it. It was all but impossible to pull ivory from fish anymore—the keys were scarcer and the fish much warier. In the years that had come since, no single enterprise had risen up to breach the economic loss as the piano-hunting industry went bust, and this had left many people, like the Huntmoons, to spend their lives in migration.

The ranger's office backed up to the cemetery and in the window there was a bulletin advertising the conversion rate for the going bounty on ivory. Ezra blanched seeing that it had spiked to an all-time high. It seemed that southern outfitters were begging for anything that the territory had left. He took his tooth from his pocket now and held it up to the sun. The ivory was chiseled into an angled, shallow-root molar cut. He closed his eyes to guess the weight.

"Let me see it," Maple said. Her fist closed around the tooth. She concentrated. When she opened her eyes she said, "How're you feeling?"

"Raw," he said.

"We'll get you another one."

Up ahead Umi stood hip-jacked against a picnic table, conversing with a family of tourists all wearing SPAWN WHILE YOU CAN T-shirts. His daughter had blue-black braids just like Hullulla and her aunt's spark of intelligence. "I don't have many friends," she was saying. "We live on a boat, so we're always moving." Her face tightened—she had no siblings and spent long hours reading flight logs and writing letters to her aunts Milda and Temperance. Umi's whole life had been painfully realistic—Ezra wondered what she'd think of this time in her life when she became an adult herself, how she'd see her parents once she was old enough to leave and choose her own family.

"The thing is," he said, "I actually have two more molars."

"What?"

"You could pull them. We could pull them all, move Jubilation House to the top of the bluff. Fix it up. We could live there."

"Are you listening to what you're saying? Pulling out your own teeth is barbaric," Maple said.

"You know it's the right thing to do. Let me make the right decision for once."

"It's going to hurt."

"You're fast. The teeth don't even have roots. Easy. You've done this before."

"For cause. When there's an infection. I don't go around pulling perfectly normal—"

Umi wandered up and said, "What's the haps, parents? Seems like there's some serious discussion happening over here."

"You want to be part of the family business?" Ezra said. "Is that what you really want?"

"Don't," said Maple.

"You got a job for me?" said Umi.

Ezra put a hand on his daughter's shoulder. "Actually, I've got two."

Though most of the world was content to live two by two, Ezra had learned that some relationships only found their natural rhythm in threes—that ancient symmetry of triangles. When the tourists headed back to their campsite he lay across their picnic table. Trees, dusk, he had a nice view. Maple threaded a needle while Umi said, "Open up, Pops." She held down his tongue with a stick, said, "They're already loose. This'll be a piece of cake."

What happened next smacked him at high velocity. Suddenly there were fingers in his mouth and the taste of high-fructose sweat. He grunted. His teeth didn't have roots so there wasn't anything to break from the maxillary arch. Probably he should have thought of pulling them a long time ago. But he'd been raw with emotion the day that they'd been sewn into place—he'd been rampaging hard for years—and giving up even more of himself didn't seem possible.

Something snipped and his mouth filled with blood.

When the first tooth came out Maple moved in to stitch the gum. Crosshatch, tie the knot. Was it painful? God, yes. His daughter got after the second tooth with speed. Once it was out, an emotion swelled up in him that he didn't immediately recognize. Tears sparkled. His tongue found the torn tissue. There was something cathartic about the new gap—room for possibility: love, what it begged of him, what he gave over, willingly or not. The absolute relief of all those memories, the misspent years of his youth, finally bleeding out of him.

A MONTH LATER, Jubilation House had been lifted out of the waves and fitted with a new roof and solar panels, situated on a plateau overlooking the fjord that Umi had inherited. Ezra still hadn't replaced his teeth. He wasn't sure if he ever would. His tongue preferred to worry the scar. They had traded all they had to rehabilitate the house. New cistern. Insulation. Umi had the entire attic to herself. She thundered back and forth while Ezra and Maple drank tea downstairs. Somehow their new lion, which Umi had named George Washington, managed to find his way to the top of the plateau each evening, more often than not dragging an octopus that the family killed, dried, and salted.

About Ezra's life, he would tell you that the paths that had led him, they twisted. How impossible it was to determine which decision led to the next as it was happening—what choices he made and what choices were taken from him—how the trajectory had only ever been clear looking back: from life as a reverend's son unwilling to preach his own witness, to a horned-up broadcaster rutting in full view of the moon, to himself as he stood now: no other way it could have gone. He stood on Jubilation House's veranda with wind in his chops, wrapped in the Bloomer family's grizzly bearskin. It technically belonged to Umi now, it all did—the house, the fjord, Moose's homesteader journals, Viola's sheaf of recipes. It'd be enough, it had to be enough. He spooned cereal as a tune whistled in his head. He surveyed his family's final kingdom.

Moose

Kamikaze River Crossing
Early September, first homestead expedition

They ate nothing for breakfast the morning of the river crossing. Rocket warned that the Kamikaze current would make even a hardened sailor puke up his liver. As they readied their sleds, families made one last effort to lighten the loads. Moose's mother placed her wedding dress, crystal decanter, and empty pickling jars in a shallow rut a hundred yards back from the bank and Moose helped Arthur cover it over with river rocks. "That should keep the wolves at bay," Arthur said, brushing dirty hands on his pants. They'd dig it up next summer on their supply run to Arctic City. After hitching the teams, the few remaining families sledded through a field of wheat-colored reed grass to the bank of the river.

The Mayflowers hit the Kamikaze first. The brothers had stripped to their undershorts. As sunrise broke in a glorious, coppery dial, they drove their sled into the water. The current took them faster than anybody expected. They disappeared from view just as Arthur *hupped* his family's dogs after them. When the slats hit the water, spray kicked up on all sides. Moose was reclined on the front of the sled, the bearskin he'd appropriated serving as a spray skirt. The dogs yipped at the cold. Arthur cracked a whip overhead and they heaved forward in two synchronized lines.

Behind them Moose could hear first one sled, then another, hitting the water, but there was no time to look back before they all went jackknifing through the first run of rapids. The far bank swept past at a frightening speed. Arthur enjoined the dogs to pull their own weight, damn it, and Moose twisted around to see his stepfather gripping the helm one-handed, using a giant paddle to steer them away from boulders that would have shredded the slats. The sled, and Moose with it, heaved over the largest rapid. They smacked down. Moose was blinded by a fit of foam and nausea. With his paddle, Arthur tried to dodge them away from the rocks, but as they skimmed out of the rapids they went speeding straight for the Mayflowers' sled.

Hamstrung on a boulder, the Mayflowers' sled had tipped sideways. The brothers monkeyed over the trunks, trying to cut loose enough ballast to drop them level. The Bluefin's lid had snapped open and water gurgled through the strings. There was Mama Mayflower leaned over the side of the instrument, bailing water with her hands. As Moose watched she pulled a knife from her boot and began sawing the ropes holding the forte in place. Before she could cut the piano free, the Bloomers' sled hit them broadside. One of the runners punctured straight through the Bluefin's bench, which sent Mama wheeling backwards into the water. In a flash, a blur, the combined force broke both sleds free from the boulder and they all went cruising downriver.

Moose had no view whatsoever of the world ahead. He struggled out of the bearskin. Gripped one of the runners for a handhold and with some difficulty managed to pull himself upright. The back end of the sled was now almost fully sunk, his mother trying to stay out of the water by crawling atop the Napoleon. She looked like a ship figurehead come to life. Behind her Moose could see the helm, but no Arthur. Then all of a sudden his stepfather was by his side, cutting loose the top trunks and pushing them off into the water. Arthur worked with precision, sending their possessions bobbing to drop weight. Moose shoved against the Mayflowers' sled, trying to dislodge them, but they were thoroughly interlocked. He unholstered his rifle and pounded the hilt against the crush of the Bluefin's bench until somehow, miraculously, the sled hinged open. When it swung to the side he could see that someone had already chopped the Bluefin free. The brothers dove into the water after it.

With what felt like no warning, the front end of the Bloomer sled hit an underwater boulder and spiked vertical. Rising, rising. His mother was scooped into the body of the Napoleon. Kicking boots. She'd sewn them from leather Moose had gifted her last winter, the soles made of buffalo tongue. That was the last he saw of her before he himself went flying backwards off the sled with nothing but his leg brace and his rifle loaded with a single shot. He hit the water with a wallop. Flipped upside down, somersaulting as his arms freewheeled, before the wood in his leg brace buoyed him to the surface. Just in time to dodge out of the way of the Huntmoons' sled. Auntie Huntmoon straddled the front, punting her oar and hollering at Uncle: "Heave faster, Seltzer, for God's sake." Pumpkin was strapped to her back, fists waving, shouting down the sky. Then Seltzer Huntmoon. Gripping the helm, running on the water as if it were land.

With some difficulty Moose managed to flip around and see upriver: nothing but rapids and trees; crusty mountains along the horizon. No one else riding to help. He was closer to the far bank than the starting side, and in that moment he didn't have the constitution to keep searching for his family, so he made for the near shore. Although the Kamikaze had been a bitch to manage with the sled, if you didn't fight the current too much it did a decent job of floating you where you wanted to go. Moose got knocked under once or twice, but the flotation of his leg brace saved him. Again and again it bobbed him to the surface. When he got near the bank he grabbed for reeds and clawed himself out of the water. Retched into the sand. Twisted around to get a view of where in the hellfire he'd landed.

Far downriver the Bloomer sled bobbed. Bluffs rose straight from the banks on both sides, framing it as it headed toward a run of rapids. Did anyone even know Moose had fallen off? He felt his pockets for a whistle to catch attention. No luck. As he levered himself up, he saw Arthur raise an ax, and *thwunk thwunk,* into the river went the rest of the Bloomers' trunks. A bare sled—nothing but the Napoleon. Moose could see only half the dogs. Buckled together, the whole team would drown if the sled went down. The sled whipped around to face downriver. No one had control of the dog team; reins trailed in the water by one of the sled runners. Moose's mother roosted atop the Napoleon like a bedraggled sea bird. Una gazed upstream: Did she know he'd fallen off? A boy could hope.

And then, in a moment no longer than a heartbeat—that's how fast these things happened—the river forked and his parents forked with it, leaving him cold and alone in the world. In that way not entirely different from how he'd made his entrance twelve and one quarter years ago, undergoing that dreadful labor passage, the doctor hauling him into the light. Smacking his bottom, pronouncing, "He's got the hide of a moose calf, Miss Price." His mother, depleted of all strength, struggled forth from her bedclothes. Gently suckling him in the crook of her arm, wiping the vernal smears from his face, saying, "Welcome to the world, my little moose."

~

As a young man, Moses "Moose" Bloomer built a homesteader cabin of wood and bone along the Glacial Front. Unlike much of his train, he had survived. He eventually achieved all that his family, Arthur Bloomer in particular, had once desired: a belly warm with yak milk and a flourishing garden—but his winter nights were haunted by the natural opera of the permafrost, and he had no instrument with which to duet.

Just as Thornton had predicted, the land between homesteads stretched so far that Moose could not see his neighbors. He knew they were out there. He'd eaten fruit loaves in their parlors and slept in their haylofts—often tracking their progress with greater attention than his own. A regional sheriff, he eventually became what passed for a lawman in the territory and swore an oath to uphold the covenants agreed on by the surviving homesteaders.

As a young man Moose made his early money as a railroader under the supervision of Abel Huckle. The decade he worked the rails he was steadily stripped of various parts of himself—three fingers and an earlobe to frostbite, proof that he did not follow the birds south each winter—but none were wrenched from him with the violence of the field medic holed up at Arctic City, who was waiting to take his leg below the hip when he first rolled into town at twelve years old. Fate must have spared some pity for him as he remembered little of the procedure—hazed memories of Rocket finding him gasping for life on the riverbank. Beached for two days, he was sun-rashed and hallucinating, his leg a fester of pus. Rocket loaded him onto his sled and they went jostling downriver until he found a gentler crossing, and from there they rode all the way back to Arctic City. Moose remembered the sky flipping whitewashed overhead, and a canteen of whiskey. The medic wiping the grease of dinner off his hands, selecting a saw and saying to a quartet of men, "Hold him steady." That he had recovered any semblance of mobility and went on to have a career after losing a leg was testament to the way he'd adapted to life in the territory. Moose fashioned a narrow, custom sled pulled by a trio of dogs; onto this sled he loaded railroad ties and fish plates for the teams laying rail across the territory. He didn't roam far anymore, but for years he'd spent much of his time on the road delivering correspondence and stamping deeds. Moose with his bedroll, lantern, and book—*Old Testament Tykes* borrowed from the Huntmoon chapel. He collected letters and stories; he listened to little kids prattle recitals on instruments brought north in later years.

Though Moose was not old by the world's standards, at fifty-one he felt he'd lived a ripe life. He had his regrets and had learned that a man could not easily shake the haunting dissonance of abandoned hopes. He'd spent years trying to isolate the off-kilter trait that caused their train to haul too many pianos too far into harsh environs, hoping to create some sense out of that summer. But what he'd learned was that homesteaders were not apt to favor logic over fancy—they were glittery idealists, philosophers, dreamers. If they paused to consider the folly of their dreams they would probably never have left home.

On Moose's mantel you could find a strange contraption of nature to which he had allotted great personal meaning. Some years ago, when he'd made camp at the hot springs, he'd noticed a strange flute of bone and filament floating in the center of the main pool. He swam out and pulled the object to shore. A five-foot-tall creation of rib loops and spinal knobs, everything woven through with piano wire. All those years ago, in what was the last truly pleasurable memory of his childhood, the bear that attacked the train must have fallen in such a way that the caribou's antlers were driven through the Lockwood's strings before forcing themselves into the meat of the animal's sternum. The result, which anyone could admire, was a striking contortion of nature; disparate pieces welded together so thoroughly that there was no way to achieve a dismantlement without destroying everything. Similar objects no doubt littered the rest of the countryside, their history crushed against the history of other hapless souls, everything muddled together so that it would take a true historian to puzzle out the disparate strains.

As Moose recounted these memories to his son it occurred to him that too many of his queries remained unanswered. Thornton was never found. While Moose had recovered in Arctic City, he'd expected that at any moment his friend might rap on the door. Cheekily enter the room bearing a handful of wild yams. If he had a brother in this life it was surely Thornton, and the loss of his companionship, especially now—when they might have rocked on the porch, watching the stars wink up in the sky—filled him with a rank sort of sentiment.

Over the years Moose had sledded nearly every mile of the territory, but he had yet to see a single mark of Arthur's sled. Nothing had ever washed up. And yet still he'd held on to a hope that his mother had found her way to shore and was living the high life in an abandoned trapper's cabin. That one day a young boy might seek him out, extend a hand, and say, "Good to meet you, Brother."

Moose wasn't the only child who lost a family to the river crossing. A young girl named Posie Starr had been picked up along the river's shore. A prospector with gold eyeteeth and a knapsack full of rabbit bones found her using the heel of her boot to trowel beetroots. Blue-lipped, pneumonia rattling her lungs, she had been lost for ten days. As far as anyone knew, her parents and brothers had gone down with their sled. Now in the winters, people claimed that you could sometimes spot a gentle-looking lad staring up at you through the ice when you were skating the river. Green-eyed, wild and afraid. Moose had never seen one of Posie's brothers himself, but the image haunted him—later, after they'd married and become parents to a son, nothing pierced Moose quite so keenly as the realization that the territory would always find a way to tax what it wanted. They'd begun their journey with nothing but the family's sled, and somehow it had taken both that and a great deal more. But his son had a different perspective on the place than either of his parents; he was born on the land and, though he didn't have a generations-long claim to it as the tribes did, he hadn't had to spend his youth laying tracks or claiming deeds either.

Once a year Moose and Posie traveled to the site of their train's failed crossing. They walked the Kamikaze looking for anything that had drifted up onto its banks. Arrowheads. A trunk of stained glass. Journals bloated and illegible. At one point Posie wandered into the woods to relieve herself, and when she returned, she took his hand: "Come." He crutched alongside her. Set back a dozen feet from the riverbank they found Mippy Fromm's RosePlayer—a sweet-colored upright. Knowledge of nature's cycles told Moose that the piano must have been deposited on land during spring's runoff, when water flooded the banks in every direction. Every available surface of the forte was carved in rosettes. They traced their fingers over the boards, marveling that they hadn't warped in all that time. In fact, there was no sign at all that the RosePlayer had spent nearly forty years at the bottom of the river. Moose ceaselessly mulled the topic over in his mind, and the only conclusion he was left to draw was that the chill of the river had acted as a preservative—holding everything to the state it had been in when it sunk.

Moose believed that he might still have a linger of midnight fever insomnia, or else the appearance of the RosePlayer would not have affected him so deeply. Instead, it had kindled in him the ridiculous hope that his mother had also been hibernating on the floor of the river, perfectly preserved in the body of the Napoleon, just as his brother was preserved in her belly. Both of them waiting for the day someone might discover them and breathe life into their lungs anew. He couldn't convince himself that this was a logical hope, for he was well aged and knew that in a few years he'd be gone too, and his stories with him. He only hoped that someone would remember his testament as the first Bloomer to settle the territory, his joys and losses.

Every origin story had to start somewhere—Moose fell asleep to the sound of his son chopping wood, hoping he'd imparted to him temerity and verve. Enough that one day he might strike off into the wild to reclaim all that the Bloomers had lost.

Part V

Festival of Old Souls

Umi

Jubilation House
Late February, six months after moving the house atop the fjord

All day I, Umi Huntmoon, beheaded the chrysanthemums my family would sprinkle on the ice when the territory's ancestors rose from the dead the next morning. The Festival of Old Souls was new and venerative. Over the centuries every family with a history in the territory had lost homesteaders, railroaders, hunters—everyone had kin pickling under the ice. My own natural parents were both gone in this way: my mother, Hullulla, her body drifted down the Kamikaze River; my father, Finley, was once presumed missing at sea.

Now found.

The Napoleon and the Kraken that Finley had disappeared in had both bubbled up under the ice along the reef a few months earlier; a murky skeleton trapped forever in a glass dome, the whole installation barnacled to the side of the reef. Given the status of the Napoleon—the last of the great beasts from the first expedition—the territory designated the site an official historic landmark. The forte would not be resurrected. Instead, those who'd never hunted before could now dive the reef or skate the ice and thrill at the discovery anew. This tangible embodiment of history in the territory—of the fortes and those who'd hunted them—drew great attention, and advertisements for expedition tours filled the community corkboard in the trade post. And now the territory's community would soon gather over the site.

Of my birth parents, I had only a few photographs and the memories that had been shared with me. In one picture Hullulla stood atop the blackened Custer&Sons, face in profile, wind whipping pages of the book she held open—what a sight. Oily black braids and roses under the skin of her cheeks. In another photo, Finley sat cross-legged atop the hood of the ChickenCrusher. He looked relaxed and young, flight goggles pushed high into his hair. They had loved each other, the family told me; this was well, this was good. The parents who raised me, Ezra and Maple, had taken me to visit the New Chapel every summer, but I'd only visited RiverCamp where Finley and Hullulla met twice. Once as a baby for Hullulla's funeral, and once again last summer after moving the houseboat to the plateau when our family went back to rescue the Custer&Sons where Hullulla had preached. Now the piano was the centerpiece of our living room.

The Custer&Sons faced our veranda, which now stretched over the edge of the fjord and was held up with steel struts braced into the cliff wall. From our vantage on top of the plateau, you could almost see all the way to the Arctic Reef. During the festival everyone in the territory would fly down to the reef to search for their own lost family members. For several hours some would sing. Some would pop tents and pay their homage in private. People were already flying up from all over the world. Popes and Starrs and LeFleurs, charismatic and dogmatic and native, the festival belonged equally to everyone. All this merriment was scheduled to begin soon, the third week in February, as the northern lights were in spectacular array.

The week before, chrysanthemums had arrived by the bucketload at Disillusionment Trade Post. It was common practice to sprinkle the flowers over the graves of the dead. Ranger Starr had roped my aunt Milda into flying round-the-clock shifts to deliver flowers to their neighbors. Milda typically visited in the summers, but she'd flown up special for the festival. Her old ChickenCrusher had been scrapped years before so now my aunt flew a six-seater SeaBird that she'd picked up on the bay. I rode along on a few of these flights, studying her at the pilot's wheel. Though it was February and the air was cold, the sky was clean and free of chop. We never returned home empty-handed. To thank us for delivering the flowers, our neighbors gave us candles and ale, hand brewed. They fed us suppers of fried oysters. The community in the fjords had morphed into a combination of plateau homes, like ours, and houseboats with no fixed anchor. We cared for each other year-round and rather than exchanging money relied on an elaborate, long-term barter system.

We were best known for our octopus rosettes, a recipe passed down from my grandmother Viola. I knew my grandmother only by reputation, particularly the story of how she'd rescued Finley from drowning when he'd first discovered the Napoleon. Viola Bloomer's heroism was the reason I'd eventually been born, and as the last of those with the Bloomer surname she'd forever be renowned in the territory. As her descendant, I knew that I'd inherited more than just the fjord she'd bought and passed down—she'd also left behind our family's ironclad will to live off-grid, in a place where we could fashion our own luck.

Late last summer, after we'd relocated Jubilation House to the top of the fjord, Aunt Temperance and Goldie Mayflower had moved up from the continent and bought their own houseboat. It now floated in the fjord attached to the sea lion piling. My aunts lived on the boat throughout the fall and joined my parents and me in building additional houseboat docks. New decking fanned out from the rest of the decayed stilts that had once perched Jubilation House above the tide. During tourist season the upcoming summer we planned to rent dock space to traveling houseboaters and tourists and split the profits. It would take all of us to run this new business.

For houseboaters we needed to provide fresh water, food delivery, and electricity, generated from a raft of solar panels that now floated over the sunken *Victory*. For tourists, my aunts would provide historical experiences. A houseboat tour north to the New Chapel and Huckle Farms. Kayak camping in the Wild Beard Fjords. Whale spotting in the lower Resurrections. Goldie was scuba-certified and had already booked several dive tours to explore the sunken *Victory*.

KAMIKAZE FARMS: HOMESTEADER TOURS, read the new logos on our family's T-shirts. These hung in the bathroom, waiting for us to don them for the festival.

I'd kept our chrysanthemum buds chilling in the bathtub until right before cutting, a practice adored by our new goat. The nanny clopped in several times a day to nibble loose petals off the water. I let her because, for now, the goat and I were alone with the baby and since the flowers had arrived I'd noticed that the goat's milk tasted sweeter. Tonight I gave a bottle to my cousin Finn, who drank it straight, cream dripping down his chin. Finn and I had been alone in Jubilation House for the last few hours while the adults ran errands on Disillusionment Bay. He was Milda and Jude's late-in-life baby, the child that doctors had told Aunt Milda she would never have. Finn T. LeFleur.

After Finn was born, I'd lobbied my parents for a trip south to visit my aunt. Milda and Jude lived in a duplex close to the university campus. I had a surprisingly difficult time trying to adapt to life in a house attached to another house. Semidetached. It was a far cry from the expanse surrounding the houseboat where I'd grown up. All night I listened to the neighbors whisper-arguing through the wall: *Didn't I say?* and *Why do you have to?* They said their city was not a big one, but still it amazed me how everywhere there were people. People shoving flyers into my hands, people snapping gum, people jostling me without excusing themselves. There was grime and oil on all surfaces, or at least that's how it seemed: tarred highways, peeling paint. Germs.

I wasn't often sick growing up, almost no one in the territory was. We weren't exposed to much, at least not anything serious, and because we could go for weeks without seeing anyone outside of our own families, we rarely even contracted colds. But I was ill most of the time I was visiting the continent. The food rumbled my stomach. It was no perfect society the way I'd envisaged it, and it seemed to me that the people toiled just as hard as my parents and I had our whole lives, only in different ways. On the continent they bought their lettuce off a grocery cart, their meat frozen, and these expenses added up, compared to either my parents or, more recently, our sea lion pup, George Washington, bringing home dinner. I was also used to wearing a simple jumpsuit day in and day out, my hair done in a long seahorse braid. At fifteen years old it had never occurred to me to buy a pair of heels, or earrings, or to have someone other than my mother trim my hair. It had never occurred to me that these things would be the price of admission into life on the continent, or how disorienting it might feel not to have access to a boat.

The skies down south were broad and highly regulated, the only planes I saw beefed-up commercial liners designed to hold a couple hundred passengers. The closest ocean was hundreds of miles away from Milda and Jude's house. Instead I walked everywhere, an ease of mobility that was new to me. My aunt and uncle's city was flat and laid out in a functional grid. Young people waved from bikes. Drivers of solar cars honked. I was told I had a strange air about me, especially at first, being the niece imported from the territory. Aunt Milda took me out to get my hair set in curls, she bought me a second pair of shoes, then a third. She took me to an opera, where the soprano sang an aria about the efficacy of vaccines. Other days we wandered the local art museum, Finn strapped to Milda's chest, to see portraits of former business leaders—*so-and-so built the largest factory; so-and-so employed fifteen percent of the population.* Oil barons, railroaders, brothel keepers, miners.

In one museum gift shop I purchased for Finn a Make-Me-Better doll similar to the one that Milda had sent me when I was a baby. I still had mine. It was now tucked into the rib cage of the sea lion fossil that hung over my hammock in the attic of Jubilation House, eyes peering down to watch me as I slept. The doll zipped open across the stomach so that all of its organs could be removed and it came packaged with a mask and gown for the owner. It had sat on my dresser in Milda's house for days before I gave it to the baby. A daily reminder of how unpredictable life could be, and how little immunity I seemed to have for any existence outside the territory.

It had been a relief to go home. In the time I was away my parents had built an extension atop Jubilation House's roof. Now when I opened the hatch that had previously led to the roof's solar panels, I stood inside a glass dome. A Kraken-inspired bubble atop our house, atop the fjord, from which I could see for leagues. Before winter set in, my father had built another small addition, this time to the main floor—a second bedroom with a great bay window facing north. This was my mother's favorite spot in the whole house. She would sit at the window, winding octopus arms according to the Bloomers' old family recipe, and tell me that on a clear day she could almost see the New Chapel's spire. All those miles north.

I put Finn down for a nap and collected the compost buckets. Steps had been cut into the side of the fjord leading all the way down to the old octopus breeding tanks. Restoring the submarines had been relatively easy and the sea lion pup I'd named George Washington in remembrance of Finley's childhood pet Abraham Lincoln had brought back new, live hens until the tanks were stocked. The herd we kept these days was smaller than what the farm had previously produced, but they were loyal. The hens who'd chosen to make the submarine their home for the winter had each selected her own nook, hidden caverns between rocks, in which to nest. Outside, they piled up the remains of their previous meals: shells and bones. It was much too dangerous to scuba down under the ice to sweep the debris away, so all winter the middens would grow. I expected that by spring there would be some formidable stalagmites. The hens tended them carefully and it was obvious that they took great delight in adding pieces. The reverence of this practice was new to me.

When I was growing up on a houseboat, hoarding trinkets had been discouraged. There wasn't much storage space, first of all, and we were constantly on the move. Adding weight to the boat made it drag, which reduced fuel efficiency, and fuel cost money. The only pets I'd been permitted as a child were light and contained. A jellyfish named Margaret who'd lasted twenty-six days. A sea cucumber being fatted for a holiday meal until I grew too attached to it and hid all the kitchen knives so my new friend wouldn't be sliced. Charming the Cucumber then lived in an aquarium by my hammock for over two and a half years. But animals that had bones, muscles, and hooves were too heavy to waste weight on. We needed to travel light when poaching crops—even George the sea lion pup had to swim alongside the boat. But now that we were stationary, and I saw that not all families lived so slight on the land, I realized that there was freedom in fixing my family's location to a point around which the rest of the world spun.

I dumped the compost buckets into the octopus tanks and climbed the steps on the side of the fjord to the house. A light fur of snow had piled up on the veranda and my boots left tracks. I'd been gone for only a few minutes. As I slid the door closed I could see that Finn was still asleep. Soon, when the adults returned, the SeaBird would ski to a stop alongside the veranda and Aunt Milda would throw down a rope as she descended. She'd been away since lunch delivering flowers. Uncle Jude had gone with her to photograph territory families preparing for the festival.

It was the middle of the afternoon and the sky was dark and shiny. For a babysitter I had no real experience. I'd never had a sibling. But I imagined I would have felt no less love for one than I felt for Finn. And to me it seemed that Jubilation House was nothing but a hazard for him, only nine months old and inclined to put everything in his mouth, everything including a spool of piano wire that cut up his gums and a two-inch tin prospector figurine that came from nowhere and had no home I knew of. When Finn went down for his naps I combed the floor for things we'd dropped during the afternoon, trying to ease the worry of him finding a marble, an ivory nub, any little thing that sticky fingers could push into his throat and lodge there, choking him. I had tried before to admonish him with my tone. I looked sincere, said, *No, no, no,* but he only smiled up at me, giggling, clutching his prizes to his chest.

It wasn't just dangers inside Jubilation House. Outside, hazards in the territory were rampant. Bad oysters, a tipped kayak, plane crashes, weather, drowned pianos. These were just a few of the things that could kill kids, that did kill kids every year. My own family tree was testament to that. After Finley disappeared, Aunt Milda had given up hunting. Her heart for the industry was gone, she said.

She'd come out of retirement only once—to help us retrieve the Custer&Sons.

The forte had Bible verses carved up the legs. It had spent the last decade, at least, belly-deep in the Kamikaze. If we'd waited another year or two it would have washed downriver, same as all the other drowned pianos. The Custer&Sons showed considerable wear but none of us had a gift for restoration—not even Temperance, though she'd restrung the hammers. But to me there was a comforting familiarity to the natural spirit of the piece. I liked to rub the worn spot on the lid where I knew Hullulla had once stood to preach.

Clearing out the instrument had been one of the first things that Aunt Milda had done when she arrived last week, and now it served as Finn's crib. There was a padded mattress in there so that he wouldn't cut himself on the hammers, which also had the effect of dampening sound when his feet overhung the lip and banged on the keys. Above his head a laundry line wound around the living room, and from this hung drying diapers, my underwear, Finn's first wet suit: impossibly small. Aunt Milda had mail-ordered it from a catalog. Together, these things soothed him to sleep.

When Finn woke up, I lifted him out of the Custer&Sons and watched him scoot across the floor. Pause. Pinch up and examine in the light the things he found. Eat them. I rushed over to finger the bits out of his mouth. "No, no, no," I said gently, but my eyes were serious. He crawled toward the glass door leading to the veranda and pulled himself up. Pressed his face to the window. He was wearing corduroy shorts, no shirt. "You can't go swimming right now," I said. "It's the middle of winter."

Now there was dinner to make and dishes to wash and Finn's bath and someone had to feed the chickens that were pecking at the bathroom wall as though they could burrow a secret tunnel inside. There were hours and hours of this, I didn't know how many. Because I had no siblings and was used to spending all my time around adults—I didn't often think about the hope my parents had pinned on me as the only "child" in the family. But now it wasn't just me anymore; I was no longer the sole representative of the future, nor the family's only hope to pass along deeds, traits, and dreams to the next generation. Though Finn was just a baby, I felt a great sense of relief that he and I shared this job, and as he got older, we could help each other figure out what came next. The family's new operation was too big for any one person to run alone. We needed each other, Finn and I.

FOR BREAKFAST THE MORNING of the festival, Aunt Milda pressed pancakes. We'd be on the ice all day and needed to stock up on calories. When I came down the attic ladder, everyone was already at the table. Goldie held Finn against her chest with one arm and with the other diced a pancake into tiny squares. Temperance poured two glasses of pear juice bought at the trade post yesterday and set one by Goldie's plate. Finn squirmed. He yawned. Goldie tickled his chin with a finger. He smiled dreamily, eyes closed, and relaxed against her. He'd had his morning porridge already, I could see; white curds had dried at the corners of his mouth. Goldie carried him over to the Custer&Sons and laid him on his back inside.

"I can't believe you let him sleep in there," Temperance teased Milda as she held out her plate for a pancake. Milda flipped one on.

"He likes it," she said. "Look at him."

I looked around the living room. "Where's Dad?"

"He went with Jude to load up the Kraken," Milda said, spooning new dollops of batter onto the skillet. She waved away a sizzle of smoke and pointed. "More pancakes on the table."

My mother came out of the bathroom then, her hair braided and pinned to her head in a tight crown. She had tea-colored hair streaked white, a bony nose, and wore long underwear patterned with embroidered jellyfish under her Kamikaze Farms T-shirt. She'd sewn everyone in the family a matching set for the festival, including hoods to tuck under our hats.

My mother held a basket of chrysanthemums on her hip, which she set in the middle of the table. Aunt Milda sat down across from her and they each reached for a bud. Popped it off the stem. The goat came trotting out of the bathroom and nipped the stems on the floor.

After breakfast we washed the dishes and got ready. We laced up our skates. The territory's reef had been leaking debris for decades. Bright clouds of JupiterMoon jellyfish juiced through the cracks. Over the last few years they'd bred in historic numbers and the reef had quickly become their cornucopia. They podded by the millions under the ice, eating flaked skin and bacteria.

Along the reef the ice had been cordoned off with orange lanterns in both directions. When we arrived I immediately recognized faces. Old man Happenstance with his longtime girlfriend. Sylvester Pope. The Starrs. My own family immediately began sprinkling blooms. The buds I'd painstakingly cut for hours flew out of our gloves and drifted across the ice in a dark mist.

The ceremony of this moment, such as it was, was whatever we wanted to make of it. Fifteen years ago, Finley had gone down with his Kraken at this reef. The transmitter was never recovered but it was his last known location. Even without the transmitter, Aunt Milda knew him well enough to know where he'd gone when his head was high with drink. And she knew that with compromised inhibitions he could easily push himself too far. It surprised no one when the Kraken first had reappeared: Finley's skeleton trapped inside, the lifting gate holding the Bloomer Napoleon pianoforte. Now I watched my aunt skate off alone between the lanterns. Down the spine of the reef to where the ice was opaque and there was nothing to see.

The plan was to pitch our tent and wait for the sky to light up around midnight. *Ghost fishing*, my mother called the aurora borealis. Spectral juleps and dinosaur greens, our ancestors dipping fishing lines down to earth. Inside the tent, we ate food from tins to pass the time. Aunt Temperance took out a packet of hand warmers and we cracked the Day-Glo sticks. The Bloomer family bearskin was taken out and spread across the floor of the tent.

After eating we lay down, top-to-tail, tail-to-top, and dozed while wind slacked against the tent walls. It was surprisingly warm inside. When the tent door finally unzipped, the outside world was lit with an aurora cutting bleeding red arcs across the sky. Uncle Jude stood with his eye pressed to his camera lens, having a field day.

I wrapped myself in the grizzly fur. I was the best on skates of all of us, so I slid Finn into a carrier harnessed to my shoulders. He delighted in grabbing hold of the bear's ears. Slowly I skated out after Aunt Milda into the night, the ice now refracting color from below as clouds of JupiterMoons scuttled up to claim their heritage. The jellyfish were so numerous it took a while for me to realize that I was also skating over bones. Scalped skulls. Ribs woven with seaweed. At first it was just fragments of humanity, but gradually the aurora whoophollered and when I looked down, I was staring into the souls of local ghosts: an entire generation of bluebloods, preserved, floating under my skates.

Never had the territory seen our past so clearly. The JupiterMoons lit up the skeletons from within. There were so many of them, so close, and their ranks appeared to stretch for leagues. Some were wool-clad, some had knotted silk ties. Hair slicked into topknots or snarling in the current. One in a gauzy dress moonshot and see-through, one with totems tattooed wrist to bicep. Their faces, those that still existed, looked like wax replicas. Skin preserved as if with an artificial agent, caverns for eyes. A canoe floated under my feet, filled with squid.

I took Finn down and together we knelt on the ice. We ran our gloves over the frost as we looked and looked—the Napoleon was too far down to see from the surface but I knew it was there. What would Finley even look like after all this time? Frozen like a diorama subject inside the dome of the Kraken. If Hullulla appeared I wondered if she'd still have a scar across her belly. I knew that I'd been cut free from her during birth, to save me from drowning in my own amniotic fluid.

My aunts wanted to search for their mother, though they didn't expect to find her. But the point of the festival wasn't really to find what we hoped to find—it was the search itself.

In all directions the sky stretched high and wide, a dome of blood vessels, and Uncle Jude skated on ahead of the rest of the family. He wanted to get shots from all angles. Pictures of little Finn trussed in layers of fur, a face mask, my father pulling the sled with our survival trunk. Under the ice as far as we could see, up rose the Arctic's dead.

Few in this procession spent their time hunting anymore. Not even my own family. That boom had fizzled. Yet still so many people stayed in the territory, still relatives and tourists continued to visit. "Somebody has to take care of things when I'm not here," Aunt Milda liked to say. Ever since my visit to the continent, I had realized that it took muscle to make a life you were proud of, no matter where you lived. It took choices. With Jubilation House now safe atop the fjord, next summer I could take flying lessons in the SeaBird and get my provisional pilot license. A lot had been passed down in my family, that was clear, though our legacy in the territory was what would outlast all. Not the piano my father Finley had tried for a decade to rescue, but this: a half-ruined planet, relatives disinterred, an orange tent planted on a moonscape hinterland, and all of our family ghosts perpetually caught somewhere between now and an unsettled tomorrow.

One day Finn would be old enough to hear the family stories for himself. Like how Aunt Temperance bore the scars of her encounter with Queenie the octopus for the rest of her life. How she'd taught herself to scuba-dive so she could excavate her sleeping cabin in the sunken *Victory*. The trick with family stories was figuring out where to start, how far to go back. *My father, Finley, drowned for the first time.* That always seemed like a natural beginning. But the more I learned, the more it was clear that to understand the full story of my heritage I'd eventually have to go back much further still. To Moose Bloomer and the sentiments that brought a generation of our ancestors to this territory in the first place. To all the twisted ambitions that turned the territory into a place so many still called home.

Tonight after our family skated home and put baby Finn to bed, we'd sit around the table playing cards. Pinochle in honor of my grandmother Viola. My aunts would slap aces. The adults would pour whiskey into one another's teacups. I would forfeit the bid, counting cards, until at last I drew a winning hand. A king, a marriage, nearly every heart in the deck. I would add up the points in my head. A fortune. Until Aunt Temperance said, *Time to tell us what you got, Umi.*

Okay, here was one.

I laid down my cards.

Once upon a time, there lived a family.

Acknowledgments

This book would not exist without the unwavering support of Johnathan Shaw. I wish for everyone such a partner. Our adventurous daughters, Freya and Violet, remain a constant source of inspiration and whimsy. Thanks to my parents and siblings, especially my sisters, Tressa Langford and Jazlyn Chambers—early and faithful readers. Peter Ho Davies, Michael Byers, and Eileen Pollack provided early guidance at the University of Michigan. Brenda and Sarah Campen both hosted me during a research trip to Alaska, and thanks to the Murphy family for a quiet place to write. Janet Silver, agent extraordinaire, swooped me up when *Pillagers'* was ready for outside eyes. Fellowships and grants from Yaddo, the Vermont Studio Center, Willapa Bay AiR, the Ucross Foundation, the Sustainable Arts Foundation, the Hambidge Center, and MacDowell—which miraculously welcomed me three times—transformed this book. Finally, I cannot imagine a better editor than Naomi Gibbs; I'm beyond grateful for her insight and editing prowess.

A NOTE ABOUT THE AUTHOR

Kendra Langford Shaw holds an MFA from the University of Michigan and has had fellowships at MacDowell, Yaddo, and the Vermont Studio Center. Her stories have appeared in *The Antioch Review*, *StoryQuarterly*, and the *Mid-American Review*. Born in Alaska, she is now a city councilwoman in Billings, Montana, where she lives with her husband and two young children.

A NOTE ON THE TYPE

The text of this book was set in Sabon, a typeface designed by Jan Tschichold (1902–1974), the well-known German typographer. Based loosely on the original designs by Claude Garamond (ca. 1480–1561), Sabon is unique in that it was explicitly designed for hot-metal composition on both the Monotype and Linotype machines as well as for filmsetting. Designed in 1966 in Frankfurt, Sabon was named for the famous Lyons punch cutter Jacques Sabon, who is thought to have brought some of Garamond's matrices to Frankfurt.

Composed by North Market Street Graphics,
Lancaster, Pennsylvania

Designed by Cassandra J. Pappas